The Hidden He♥rt

This Large Print Book carries the Seal of Approval of N.A.V.H.

The Hidden He♥rt

Jane Orcutt

Thorndike Press • Waterville, Maine

Published in 2004 by arrangement with WaterBrook Press, a division of Random House, Inc.

Thorndike Press® Large Print Christian Romance.

The tree indicium is a trademark of Thorndike Press.

The text of this Large Print edition is unabridged. Other aspects of the book may vary from the original edition.

Set in 16 pt. Plantin by Al Chase.

Printed in the United States on permanent paper.

Library of Congress Cataloging-in-Publication Data

Orcutt, Jane.
 The hidden heart / Jane Orcutt.
  p. cm.
 ISBN 0-7862-6748-8 (lg. print : hc : alk. paper)
 1. Women pioneers — Fiction. 2. Indian children — Fiction. 3. Large type books. I. Title.
PS3565.R37H53 2004

           2004051621

To my parents —
Ben and Doris Hooks —
and all our Central Texas ancestors

As the Founder/CEO of NAVH, the only national health agency solely devoted to those who, although not totally blind, have an eye disease which could lead to serious visual impairment, I am pleased to recognize Thorndike Press★ as one of the leading publishers in the large print field.

Founded in 1954 in San Francisco to prepare large print textbooks for partially seeing children, NAVH became the pioneer and standard setting agency in the preparation of large type.

Today, those publishers who meet our standards carry the prestigious "Seal of Approval" indicating high quality large print. We are delighted that Thorndike Press is one of the publishers whose titles meet these standards. We are also pleased to recognize the significant contribution Thorndike Press is making in this important and growing field.

Lorraine H. Marchi, L.H.D.
Founder/CEO
NAVH

★ Thorndike Press encompasses the following imprints: Thorndike, Wheeler, Walker and Large Print Press.

Prologue

West Texas
Spring 1868

Laughing, twelve-year-old Elizabeth Cameron chased a butterfly all the way up the gentle hill behind her family's home. The sun was too warm and the grass too green for her to remember Mama's warning about straying while Papa was off on his preaching circuit. Besides, she'd soon be too old to sneak away from the chores Mama and seventeen-year-old May now did. Since Noah had run away, Papa said he relied more than ever on his two remaining children, even if they were girls.

Yee-yee-yees! ripped through the air. Shocked, Elizabeth stopped. Below her, heavily painted Indian braves swarmed from the house, their arms loaded with possessions: Mama's multicolored shawl, a shiny metal pot, Papa's pearl-handled letter opener. One brave chased and caught the old sow, then slit its throat. Another set the log cabin ablaze.

Two fierce warriors dragged Mama and May, screaming, toward waiting horses.

7

Panic pumping like a spring flood, Elizabeth turned and ran down the far side of the hill. She'd overheard hushed stories about Comanches, stories too terrifying to mention.

Clawing at an abandoned animal burrow, she ducked her head to squeeze inside when someone grabbed her by the braids, jerked her up, then pushed her down in front of him. Frozen with fear, scalp burning, she stared up at his face. Dark eyes — evil — stared back. His lips thinned under an aquiline nose, and his skin glistened like bright copper. Under a buffalo-horn headdress, his pitch-black hair billowed over bare shoulders. Except for scary slashes of red paint, he wore only a breechcloth and moccasins, with a small leather bag around his neck.

The warrior touched Elizabeth's wooden cross necklace and laughed when she flinched. Then he threw back his head and yelled, and dozens of other warriors appeared on horses loaded with blankets, clothes, and trinkets. Sobbing, Mama and May were tied facedown over separate horses.

Mama! Elizabeth tried to scream, but no sound came out.

The Indian jerked her off her feet and

swung her upright onto a horse. She barely had time to grab the mane for support before he tied her feet together under the horse's barrel. With another loud cry, the Indian leaped behind her and spurred the horse into a gallop. Terrified, she tried not to lean back, for the Indian smelled of grease and sweat.

What were the Bible verses Papa had drilled into her and May? All she could think of was the picture above her bed, now burning with the house. Jesus. *Jesus!*

Hours later, when it began to turn dark, they finally stopped. Indian women, old people, and children poured out of tepees, chattering and yelling in a strange language that hurt Elizabeth's head. Barking dogs jumped and snapped at her legs.

Someone cut her free and hauled her down from the horse. Two women pulled her braids and poked her skin, but Elizabeth jerked away. "Mama!" May screamed in a high-pitched voice.

The Comanches seemed attracted to her and Mama's blond hair. Yanking the yellow strands, the black-haired women babbled feverishly.

Something evil filled the night air, vibrating to the deep sound of drums and a snapping bonfire. At its edge an elderly woman staked a tall pole, and several women dragged Elizabeth forward and lashed her to it.

The brave with the buffalo horns stroked May's hair. "Mama, help me!" Eyes wide with terror, she screamed as he threw her to the ground.

Another warrior claimed Mama.

Terrified, agonized, Elizabeth squeezed her eyes shut against their torturous cries. Where was Jesus? *Love your enemies. Pray for those who persecute you,* he'd said, but wasn't he supposed to protect his children?

Mama and May went silent, and Elizabeth cautiously opened her eyes.

The buffalo warrior was striding toward her, grinning. Elizabeth trembled, praying silently. *Love your enemies. Love your enemies. Love . . .*

He grasped her by the chin, his dark eyes burning. When she didn't say anything, he yanked her mouth open and thrust two fingers inside to poke and prod. Elizabeth coughed and gagged, especially when she realized with a wave of dizziness that she'd tasted blood. Oh, May. Oh, Mama!

He laughed at her inability to speak, and someone handed him a long lance covered with red paint and matching ribbons. He grinned at her then paced away from the fire. The crowd cheered as he readied the lance.

Elizabeth's knees weakened with fear, but the tight leather bands held her upright. *Oh, Jesus. I don't want to die!*

Yelling, the brave ran toward her with the point aimed at her breast.

An inexplicable warmth flowed from Elizabeth's heart and spread to her limbs. Then the leather ropes binding her loosened and fell. As if on fire, her tongue also loosened. Raising her freed arms, she heard her own voice speaking. *"Tah Ahpoor perkune tome ovat . . . Uh honny mooach sooahkut . . . Umah sooahahihk beetahroa . . . Tah sokovah, tome ovat hiameewite . . ."*

The words spilled out of her mouth, and the crowd stared, mute. The brave's cry died in his throat as he stopped midstride. His proud face grew perplexed, and the lance quivered in his hand.

The words stopped. Elizabeth slowly lowered her arms, and the strange sensation ebbed away, leaving her weak. *Let me die now, Lord.*

In the silence, an older man moved forward from the crowd. Many bowed their heads as he passed. He stopped in front of Elizabeth and studied her face, his curious eyes searching deeply into hers. Then he lifted her cross and, with the other hand, pointed down at the broken bonds, back at Elizabeth, then at himself. Smiling, he took her hand and led her from the carnage at the campfire and toward a tepee.

Elizabeth was terrified that she had been claimed for some sort of pagan marriage, when a woman and a girl about May's age entered after them. Staring, the woman thrust a buckskin blouse, skirt, and moccasins into Elizabeth's hands, then stripped away her shoes and torn clothes. She threw them outside the tepee, leaving Elizabeth no choice but to wear the clothes she'd been given. Suddenly the woman brandished a knife, and Elizabeth backed up in terror. The girl touched Elizabeth's shoulder from behind and began loosening her braids. After she'd freed all of Elizabeth's hair, the woman chopped it chin-length like theirs.

Grunting, they offered her a foul-smelling stew. Elizabeth shook her head. They shrugged and handed her a buffalo robe, pointing at the edge of the tepee. She obediently curled up on the hide, covered her head, and wept.

Why did you let Mama and May die? They were so good! They always did what was right, while I always skipped my chores or got repri-manded for mentioning Noah's name. Why did you spare me? *What were all those strange words I spoke?*

She wanted to roll into the fire. She wanted to die. She wanted to run out of the frightening, smelly tepee and away from her savage captors, but she shook with fear. Where could she go anyway? They were somewhere on the barren Staked Plains, away from any towns, away from anyone who could help her.

Oh, Papa, please find me! she sobbed silently until she fell asleep.

Sunflower, the girl who had been in the tepee that first night, took Elizabeth under her wing. When it was apparent Elizabeth could no longer speak their language, as she had that first night, Sunflower insisted she learn quickly. Her father, Walks Far, was what was called a shaman — a medicine man. He had claimed Elizabeth as a daughter, to learn the source of her *puha,* the medicine that had empowered her to speak the tribe's tongue. When she could finally speak the proper Comanche words, she haltingly told him, his wife — Gray Dove — and Sunflower the stories she'd always heard about Jesus, the Son of God.

From that first night the tribe named her Speaks of Her God.

Although he did not fully believe her stories, Walks Far seemed to trust her and shared his healing practices with her. She marveled at the power of God and his plants, trees, and grasses to break fevers and set bones. Acknowledging Walks Far's gifts, she humbly served alongside the medicine man and offered up prayers for the sick among them.

The tribe's initial suspicion shifted to grudging respect as they saw her prayers frequently answered. More admirable was her genuine concern for each patient. She laid her hands on gnarled, arthritic limbs and cooed to crying newborns while praying or singing softly.

Every night she prayed that she would be able to forgive them — for their murder of Mama and May. And little by little, her anger dwindled, replaced by mercy, and she found it easier to talk to Walks Far and his family about the Lord.

Yet Sunflower remained perplexed. She worried over Elizabeth's words while they collected water at the river. "There's only one Sure Enough Father," she said. "The Great Spirit. Yet you talk about this God, this Jesus, and this Spirit. That makes three!"

Eyeing the rapidly setting sun, Elizabeth dipped her water pot in the river. "The three are one, Sunflower."

"I know, but —" Sunflower broke off and pointed at the cottonwood trees, her voice dropping to an excited whisper. "There's Eyes Like the Sun."

Elizabeth shivered at the sight of the brave who had captured her. Despite the respect she had gained from the tribe, Eyes Like the Sun always stood aloof from her, his stare and scowl condemning. One day Sunflower let it slip that he hadn't forgiven Elizabeth for her stronger medicine — how she had humiliated him. No young Comanche woman had ever made medicine on her own, much less a white woman.

Elizabeth fearfully studied her older friend, knowing Comanche men frequently did their courting when the women went for water. Sunflower pretended she hadn't seen the warrior, but coyly straightened her shift.

"I'll go back by myself," Elizabeth said, rising. Sunflower didn't protest.

Elizabeth scurried up the path. Head down, she ran straight into Eyes Like the Sun. His strong hands grabbed and steadied her.

"You should watch where you are going, Speaks of Her God." His eyes gleamed dark as night, and his hands tightened.

She bit back her fear.

He laughed and held her fast with one hand while the other lifted the cross she still wore. "Perhaps one day we will see that your god is not so powerful after all. One day when you are not a little girl." When he lowered the cross, he deliberately brushed her shift with his hand. He laughed again and released her, then trod softly down the path to Sunflower.

Elizabeth squeezed her eyes shut, trembling. "Papa, please find me! Do you cry for me the way you did when Noah left home?" Gripping the water pots, she knelt in the path. "Mama always said you know best, Lord, but I want to go home!"

A year after Elizabeth's capture, Eyes Like the Sun took Sunflower as his wife. To the tribe it was a perfect match — the beautiful young woman wed to the courageous warrior many believed would be the next chief. To Elizabeth, the union was as frightening as the rumbling of the earth beneath a buffalo stampede — her best friend married to that man who still wore Mama and May's blond scalps on his lance.

One day Sunflower shyly presented her with an unblemished doeskin shift she'd secretly made — Eyes Like the Sun would never have let her waste her time on such a lavish gift for her friend. Elizabeth knew the immeasurable time and love that had created the precious offering. Touched by her kindness, she accepted with tears brimming in her eyes at her love for the young woman. Yet even more precious was the day Sunflower knelt beside Elizabeth at the river and said that she, too, believed Jesus was the only way to the Great Spirit.

A year stretched to two, and the doeskin and moccasins felt more natural to Elizabeth than the restricting dresses and shoes of her girlhood. She embraced the Comanche life but not their beliefs. She cringed whenever the warriors returned with stolen horses or fresh scalps, but she sought after God as Mama had said she should do, and she felt a sense of peace that he was with her, watching out for her.

One evening Elizabeth went as usual to the river to collect water along with the other women. As she dipped her pots, she closed her eyes and hummed a prayer of thanks. Mama's and May's deaths hurt less now that Sunflower was her sister in Christ. Perhaps others from the tribe would follow. The Comanches loved their children, and she prayed they would see their Sure

Enough Father loved them enough to sacrifice his only son.

Oh, Lord, make me an instrument of your peace. Use me as you see fit, even when I don't understand.

Suddenly the hair on her arms prickled. She hastily opened her eyes and saw that all the other women had left. Unnerved, she rose and found herself face to face with Eyes Like the Sun.

He studied her, cocking his head. "You are not a scrawny girl anymore, Speaks of Her God. Perhaps I will take you for my second wife."

"Sunflower would not like that. It is not the way of believers."

Eyes Like the Sun grabbed her by the arms, and the full pots fell and cracked. "I know what you have been telling her. You have turned her against all that the People believe!"

Elizabeth trembled. "I have only told her about Jesus. He died and lives again for everyone."

"Liar!" He slapped her across the face, and she stumbled. "He is the white man's god. Not the People's!"

She straightened, rubbing her cheek. Tears filled her eyes. "He loves everyone, Eyes Like the Sun. Even you."

18

He shoved her to the ground and grabbed her cross. "I am tired of hearing about your god."

"Let me go!"

He clamped a hand over her mouth, and his eyes shone bright and cold like a blue flame. "If Sunflower would not like me to have a second wife, then we will not tell her. She would be hurt to learn you came to me."

Panicked, Elizabeth tried to claw his hand from her mouth. She tried to rise, but Eyes Like the Sun pinned her fast, and the bag around his neck dangled in her face. "Who will she believe? Her warrior husband or a traitorous friend?" Releasing her mouth, he twisted her own leather necklace against her throat until she gasped for air. She struggled against him, but he yanked at the treasured doeskin shift. Unable to scream, Elizabeth felt the darkness press in around her until it seemed to crush her very soul.

After he was finished with her, Eyes Like the Sun spat on her and laughed. "Now who has more power — your worthless god or me?"

In the days that followed, Elizabeth couldn't eat because of the sickness inside her as she went through the motions of

19

living. She tried to tell an eager Sunflower more about Jesus, but the words felt wooden on her tongue. Despite her efforts to avoid him, Eyes Like the Sun found her alone again one day. And again another day. Then another, until the days ran together.

Weeks passed when Sunflower joyfully announced that she was with child. She chattered incessantly about babies and couldn't spend enough time playing with the tribe's little ones. Elizabeth's soul sickness intensified.

When the time came for Sunflower to give birth, Elizabeth tended Sunflower as she had many others. Assisting the midwife, she burned sage to purify the tepee and helped knead Sunflower's abdomen to hasten the birth.

At last the long labor was over, and Sunflower's grandfather stood just outside the birthing tepee as tradition dictated and asked the sex of the child.

"It's your close friend," the midwife called, signifying a boy. She frowned down at Sunflower, who hugged her rabbit skin–swaddled baby. "Put the child in the cradleboard now."

"Oh, just a moment longer, please!" Sunflower's sweat-stained face radiated joy as she studied her son.

The midwife clucked her tongue at the new mother's foolishness. "I must get rid of the umbilical cord and afterbirth, Sunflower. Speaks of Her God will make you see reason."

Sunflower held out the child, but when he wailed indignantly, she cradled him close again. "He will be strong like his father. He's beautiful, isn't he?" she said over his cries.

"Yes." Elizabeth thrust out her arms, struggling to conceal her revulsion. The last time she saw Eyes Like the Sun, he'd walked by as she prepared the birthing tepee. He silently touched the pouch at his chest then pointed at her cross, mocking her faith, mocking her loyalty to Sunflower. He knew the silence Elizabeth would keep to spare her friend, and he leveled that knowledge against her as he once had the lance.

Sunflower placed the crying baby in Elizabeth's arms. Instantly he quieted, and Sunflower smiled. "You must marry, Speaks of Her God. Wouldn't you like a child?"

Elizabeth stared at the baby's face, the embodiment of both her tormentor and her dear friend. Raising a tiny, quivering arm, he yawned, his smooth, dark skin glistening with newness of life as he nestled in her arms.

He was beautiful — perfect and innocent, knit together by God. Everything about him was preordained, from each dark hair on his head to the length of his days.

Yet Elizabeth's stomach churned with recurrent nausea and fear. What would her own child look like? The child she now carried in her belly.

Gunfire rang out, and the midwife pushed open the door flap. "Bluecoats!"

Frantic, Sunflower pushed herself up. "Give me my son!"

Elizabeth handed him over and helped a trembling Sunflower into her clothes. Outside, screaming women scurried to gather children. Dogs barked at the sound of approaching horses and bugles, some yipping as they were silenced.

Eyes Like the Sun rushed inside. "Sunflower! You and the child must go with the others. The warriors are covering the escape."

She smiled weakly and pushed back the rabbit skin to reveal their child. His eyes lit with fierce pride, then he pushed Sunflower outside. Elizabeth tried to follow, but he grabbed her arm, his face mottled with rage.

"I know the truth you tell no one," he said through clenched teeth. "The child you give me will be a son too. Do not think to run to your soldiers now, Speaks of Her God."

"I will never leave Sunflower!"

He leaned closer. "And I will never leave you either. I will watch while you cry with birth pains, and I will watch while you raise my son."

He unsheathed his knife and pressed the tip to her shift. "Then when you feel safe, when the time is right, I will rip him from your side as easily as I can cut out your heart now! He will fight with the People to defeat you and the white man. He will never speak of your god!" He touched his leather pouch. "I have seen it. I know."

"No!" Elizabeth jerked free and drew back. Eyes Like the Sun reached for her, but a flash of light cracked between them, booming. Eyes Like the Sun's blood splashed across her face. Howling, he clutched his head in his hands and staggered away.

A field of blue sliced through the scattering Comanches. Elizabeth ran in the direction she'd seen Sunflower go as warriors fought and died around her.

"Sunflower!" Elizabeth screamed when she caught sight of her friend. The frightened new mother stumbled over sagebrush and fell, the baby screaming in her arms. A blue-uniformed soldier leaped from his horse and took aim.

"No-o-o!" Elizabeth cried, desperately trying to reach Sunflower in time. *Crack*, the shot rang.

She grabbed the soldier's arm just as he fired a second shot. "No! She was my friend!"

Whirling on her, the soldier raised the butt of his rifle. When his eyes met hers, he blinked. His mouth dropped open, and he lowered the rifle.

The English words sounded strange to her own ears. "She was my friend!" Sobbing, Elizabeth fell to her knees beside an unmoving Sunflower and her now silent baby.

She'd thought they were still in Texas, but at the nearest fort, they told her it was Indian territory. The captured Comanches — old people, women, children, and mortally wounded braves — were herded onto a holding ground until the government could decide their fate. The soldiers tried to coax Elizabeth into joining the officers' wives, but she refused. Her place was with Sunflower's grieving parents.

Gray Dove wailed her sorrow and, in honorable Comanche fashion, never mentioned her dead daughter or grandson's names.

Elizabeth lay shivering on the scratchy, ragged government-issued blanket for days, sick at heart and sick in body. She told no one about the child in her womb.

Gray Dove tried to tend her. "You must eat, daughter," she said, kneeling beside her to offer a bowl of the choicest rationed meat. "Your mourning is enough."

Elizabeth turned her face away. How could she tell Gray Dove the truth about the child she carried? She had become like family to them over the years, and taking a tribal woman by force was unthinkable in their culture. No one would believe she had not willingly gone to Eyes Like the Sun. They would laugh at Sunflower, even though she was dead, for never suspecting the treachery of a friend.

"You are young," Walks Far said, hoping to cheer her. "You should go back to your people and find a husband."

Never. What white man would want a tainted woman with a half-breed child? She was ruined.

Walks Far and Gray Dove looked so sad that Elizabeth finally forced herself out of bed only for their sakes. For two years they had cared for her, raising her as their own child. Now their only true daughter was dead. Elizabeth did not want to be the cause of further grief.

Several days later, two privates flanked a captain's wife as she marched into the compound, demanding that Elizabeth come with them. After an unsuccessful round of cajoling, they carried Elizabeth kicking and screaming to the officers' quarters.

The wives fussed over her, assuring her she was safe. They cleaned her up for what they called fit society and exchanged judgmental whispers when they saw the bulge of her stomach.

"Poor dear. She's in shock."

"Those savages!"

Immediately redoubling their assurances, they never mentioned the baby or asked Elizabeth to respond to their increased prattle.

She knew the fluttery-handed wives meant well, but she couldn't tell them she viewed their husbands as no less murderers than the warriors who killed Mama and May. Sunflower had been her friend, and they had shot her and her newborn baby. Walks Far and Gray Dove, along with the other Comanches, would be sent to live on a reservation like caged animals. She tried to go to them, but the soldiers wouldn't allow it.

She did not know what had happened to

Eyes Like the Sun. He had obviously taken a bad shot to the head. She remembered the sight of his bloody face. Surely he had died in the battle.

Her head ached, and her body betrayed her with constant exhaustion. The soldiers told her they had found Papa in Texas, and they would take her home. Elizabeth's weary spirits lifted. At last she would be free of violence, free to go home and weep for a time. Then she would birth and raise this baby, who was surely as innocent as Sunflower's had been.

Papa had rebuilt the little log cabin, and it looked different. The fresh wood seemed cold and unfamiliar, not at all what she remembered as home. Elizabeth swallowed hard, trying to forget the day she'd left.

Papa looked different too — older, his hair grayer. Tight-lipped, he listened as the soldiers related how they'd found her. Their eyes tactfully avoided her Comanche-short hair and her form, which now rounded against a gingham dress the officers' wives had given her.

Papa thanked them for their help and bid them good day. When they were well out of sight, Papa turned to Elizabeth. He had never been particularly loving with her or

May, but she longed for him to take her in his arms to reassure her everything would be okay. She would give anything to just cry.

"You're as wicked as your brother, Noah," he said in a low voice. "You couldn't die with your mother and May. You had to live and shame me."

"I didn't do anything wrong."

"Liar! You watched them die! Why didn't those pagans kill you, Elizabeth?"

She trembled.

"Answer me!"

"I couldn't do anything, Papa. I couldn't even talk! Not until God gave me the words."

"Those words came straight from the devil to protect you."

"No!"

"They spared your life because you consorted with them! You look like them, you smell like them, you even . . . even . . ." He drew a deep, angry breath.

Elizabeth stepped forward, weak and dizzy. "Papa —"

"I am no longer your Papa. I will feed you and clothe you and do my best to correct your spiritual faults, but I will be protected from your shame." He grabbed her shoulders. "I'll raise your half-breed brat, Elizabeth, but know this: If you ever have anything to do with the child, if you show one ounce of affection, I will turn it out. *Do you understand?*"

Stunned, she nodded quickly.

He pressed his lips together. "I'll make certain you do."

Taking up his whip, the one he used for herding oxen, Reverend Obadiah Cameron dragged his daughter to the barn.

One

Elizabeth sat ramrod straight on the hard bench outside the general store and stared at the dusty main street. The frontier town squatted at the edge of Texas civilization like a naughty child excluded from play. Farther west lay the vast and arid Staked Plains, where only the cocky or foolish dared venture.

Fort Griffin owed its very existence to such desperation. Even though it was only midmorning, a burly saloon keeper tossed a drunken soldier out into the street. Two laughing buffalo hunters just in from the kill stepped over the man without a moment's thought.

Cursing, the sergeant shoved himself to his feet. An early-to-work harlot rushed forward to help, but the soldier pushed her aside and staggered toward the fort on the bluff. Rebuffed, the girl shrugged and touched the greasy buckskin-covered arm of one of the hunters. She whispered something into his stringy hair, and leering, he followed her swaying hips through a dark doorway.

Elizabeth shivered, anxious to put Fort Griffin far behind her. The fallen and unrepentant didn't frighten her nearly as much as the decent people of Reverend Obadiah Cameron's congregation. Or the memory of her father himself. Keeping to her end of their bargain, she'd dutifully played the organ every Sunday and fixed her gaze on her father as he beat the pulpit.

Four months after her return to Texas, Elizabeth had given birth to Eyes Like the Sun's child, a dark-haired boy she named Joseph even as her new stepmother, Helga, whisked him from her body. Soon they all moved to Fort Griffin, with the lie that Joseph had been abandoned on their doorstep. Helga had brusquely tended to the child until her death just a few months ago. Then Father had died too.

Now after five years, Elizabeth and Joseph were alone.

Behind her lowered black bonnet, she hid a smile. She wanted to shout, to sing, to dance, anything to express the lightness inside, the ease of her soul. She was free! *Free!*

Sudden guilt raced through her. Honor

31

thy father and mother, the Bible said. A daughter shouldn't rejoice at her father's death.

She fingered the leather strip around her neck.

"Elizabeth?" A small brown hand eased between hers and the necklace.

Elizabeth's heart caught in her throat. "Yes, Joseph?"

"I'm afraid," he whispered.

"God will take care of us. Before he died, didn't Reverend Cameron ask the Lord to do just so?"

"Yes'm, but —"

"Then it will be so. Remember what the Bible says: 'In God have I put my trust . . .' "

" 'I will not be afraid what man can do unto me.' Psalm 56:11."

Joseph drew his hand back to his lap. He sat as straight as Elizabeth did, his feet perfectly still under the bench. Helga had demanded strict obedience, and he had learned well.

A passing army wagon churned up dirt from the street, and the soldiers nodded at Elizabeth as they passed, pointedly ignoring Joseph.

Weighted by doubt, her heart sank. She'd lived with this precious child since his birth, but she'd never been allowed to know him — how could she protect him? Would people in Belton slight him as they had here? Fort Griffin was the only home Joseph had known, but the townspeople never completely accepted his presence. She'd overheard their whispers.

"Don't know why the preacher insists on keeping that savage kid."

"He'll just grow up to be a murderer like all the rest."

"Ought to be on a reservation."

"Or dead. The only good Injun is —"

Elizabeth scanned the street for her brother, Noah. Four years ago — not long after they'd all moved to Fort Griffin — he'd sent a fat letter that somehow found its way to their home. Father ripped up the unopened envelope, but not before Elizabeth read the return address. Last month when the doctor said Father's heart was giving out, she'd sent a brief note. Noah made it to Fort Griffin in a hurry, but not in time to see Father alive.

Elizabeth told him about Mama and May, but she left out her own part in the story, exactly the way Father had trained her. Sad-eyed, Noah said he had wanted to apologize to Father and Mama in person, to ask for their forgiveness. He was a true believer now.

Over late-night coffee, he asked about Joseph.

Elizabeth began the practiced lie, but the words twisted on her tongue. Her brother's probing eyes burned into hers, and she finally, haltingly, whispered the whole story.

Noah's reaction startled her. Her strong, tall brother — a U.S. marshal — actually wept. He choked out promises that he would take care of her and Joseph, but she turned a deaf ear. For the first time, she had her own plans for their future, and they didn't include any man.

Now her brother came toward them carrying a small paper bag. Relieved, she rose. She smoothed her black calico skirt and checked Joseph's posture as he took his place beside her.

Noah squatted in front of the boy and held out the bag. "I got you something for the trip."

Joseph's brown eyes widened. "Stick candy!"

"What do you say, Joseph?"

"One, two, three . . . four pieces! Thank you!" Joseph held the bag up to his nose and smelled the candy with delight.

"You're welcome," Noah said, grinning. Rising, he met Elizabeth's look, and his ex-

34

pression sobered. "Are you sure this is what you want?"

She clasped her hands together. "It was always Father's idea to live in Fort Griffin. Not mine. Now that he's dead, I see no reason to stay."

"My farm in Colorado is perfect for the three of us, and I have wonderful neighbors. The Jordans are strong Christians and even have three children around Joseph's age."

"You have your marshal work to keep you busy."

"I only have one more obligation to fulfill, then I can quit. The farm's enough to support us. And I'll buy some cattle."

She softened at his concern. "You haven't seen me for nearly thirteen years, Noah. You don't really know me. Besides, the Sanctificationists are dedicated Christian women. Their founder said she had room for me and Joseph to live with her family."

"But Father's only been dead a few days. I nearly missed his funeral, and now you're leaving before we can talk things over."

"There's nothing more to talk about. Can't you just be happy for us?"

Noah's face darkened. "Happy? When everybody at Father's funeral wept over the *sainted* Reverend Cameron?"

Elizabeth glanced at Joseph, who was still absorbed with the precious paper bag. He looked like a miniature adult in his best wool trousers and jacket.

"Father is dead," she said softly. "And now Joseph is my responsibility. I will raise him to serve the Lord, and we will be safe." *From men.*

Noah's gray eyes gentled. "You have a lot of love buried inside you, Elizabeth. I remember the little girl who used to throw herself at me for a hug every day. Do you remember when the missionary stayed at our house and told us how the Chinese were starving for food *and* God?"

She nodded slowly.

He tucked a wisp of hair behind her ear. "You cried, Elizabeth. Then you got the three shiny Christmas pennies you'd saved and dropped each one in the missionary's hand. There wasn't a dry eye in the room." He clasped her hands. "I know you need time to heal, but please don't shut yourself away from love in this women's group. Listen to your heart."

She laughed softly. "Remember Jeremiah? 'The heart is deceitful above all things, and desperately wicked: who can know it?' "

"And what did God promise in Ezekiel?

36

To give us a new heart and a new spirit. He said we would be his people, and he would be our God. *He* is the key, Elizabeth. You can't run from love or him!"

She sighed. "All this talk about hearts and love doesn't mean anything. It's giving myself over to God's will and doing his work that matter. That's what the Sanctificationists practice."

"Obedience is better than sacrifice —"

"I know that!"

"But obedience must come from the heart. An obedience of faith, not works . . . an obedience of *love*."

A bugle blared in the distance, and the street bustled to life. Shopkeepers, patrons, and idlers spilled out into the morning heat, jostling each other to see the stage's arrival. Elizabeth moved even closer to Joseph to protect him from the crowd.

With a sad smile, Noah hefted their carpetbag and basket. "If you won't listen to reason, then I guess this is good-bye."

Elizabeth nodded, not trusting her voice.

The stage rolled up. Noah looped Elizabeth's arm through his and extended his free hand to Joseph. The little boy's eyes glowed at the sight of the horses.

Noah tossed the bag and basket up to the driver then bent down. "Have a safe trip,

Joseph. Maybe you and Elizabeth can come visit me sometime in Colorado. Would you like that?"

"Yes sir. And thank you again for the candy."

Noah straightened and touched the boy's head. Catching himself, he extended his hand, offering the child a grown-up handshake. Elizabeth struggled with a myriad of confusing emotions. She tried to smile, but her lips trembled.

Immediately Noah drew her into his arms. Despite his tenderness, Elizabeth froze. Her stomach twisted, and she forced herself to breathe deeply.

"Come on, folks, we've got a schedule to keep!"

His arms loosened, and she stepped back quickly. Noah bent and kissed her cheek. He looked so serious, so sad. "Don't let go of God's love, Elizabeth. Don't ever let go, no matter what happens," he said hoarsely, then turned to lift Joseph into the coach. When he helped Elizabeth up, his hand lingered on hers. She stared down at him, wanting to say something but unable to find the right words.

Noah squeezed her hand then slowly released it. He nodded once for reassurance, then shut the door.

The coach was nearly full. Elizabeth held Joseph's small hand and steered him to the middle bench's inside seat while she took the window. Joseph folded his hands over his sack and gravely gazed outside.

"Gee haw!" the driver shouted to the horses as they pulled away.

Elizabeth caught a last glimpse of her older brother before the stage pulled away. Noah raised his hand in farewell, his face grim. Then he was gone from sight.

The stage lurched and rocked, and her knees bumped those of the sole passenger sitting on the rear-facing bench. She gasped when she realized it was a man. "I'm sorry!"

He smiled wryly and tipped his hat. "I wasn't seriously injured."

"Yes, but —" The words stalled on her tongue. The stranger's smile hadn't faded, but hardness shadowed his mouth and cold blue eyes. He crossed his arms and stretched back, a lean, virile panther studying its prey. Elizabeth quickly dropped her gaze and saw a well-oiled gun belt, its row of shiny, deadly cartridges, and the ivory handle of an equally shiny, deadly gun.

"Indians!" On Joseph's far side, a drummer gestured wildly at a string of tepees camped along the Brazos River. Beneath his oily hair, the man's face turned white. "Blow the bugle! Get your guns! Get the —"

The man with the gun laughed. "These Indians are friendly, Tenderfoot. They've camped below the fort as long as it's been here."

The color rushed back to the drummer's face, and he hunched his shoulders in embarrassment, glancing suspiciously at Joseph.

Following his gaze, the man with the gun studied Joseph for a moment, then Elizabeth. Unnerved, she fumbled in her skirt pocket for her small black Bible. She opened it at random, hoping her voice didn't sound as quavery as her insides felt. "It's time for our lesson, Joseph."

The boy immediately straightened. "Yes, Elizabeth."

"John 3:16."

"For God so loved the world, that he gave his only begotten Son, that whosoever believeth in him should not perish, but have everlasting life."

The practice relaxed Elizabeth. "Matthew 5:5."

"Blessed are the meek: for they shall inherit the earth."

"Psalm 23:1."

"The Lord is my shepherd; I shall not want."

The other passengers had gone silent. The drummer leaned forward and smiled, revealing large yellow teeth. "How about John 11:35, boy?"

Joseph wrinkled his small nose in concentration. "Jesus wept!"

"Very good." The drummer winked at Elizabeth. "You've certainly trained the little heathen well, miss."

The man with the gun clamped a hand on the drummer's arm. "Keep your opinions to yourself, friend."

The surprised drummer shrank back. "J-just making an observation."

"You made it." The gunman released his arm with a hard shake. "Now leave the lady and the boy alone."

The drummer turned away.

Trembling, Elizabeth clenched her hands over the Bible. Joseph sat straight as ever. His dark eyes met the stranger's and warmed. Smiling, he tilted his paper bag forward. "Would you like a piece of candy?"

"Won't your ma mind?" he drawled.

"She's not my mother."

"Your sister then."

"She's not my sister either. She's just Elizabeth."

She flushed. "Joseph, please don't bore this man with our business."

The man caught her eye. She glanced away but could feel his grin. She could also feel his gaze as he studied her, but she knew her face was hidden by her mourning bonnet. Her shapeless black dress would allow his lecherous eyes only a guess at the figure underneath. And if that didn't discourage him, her wooden stick cross certainly would.

He wouldn't look long. She dressed so that none ever did.

She heard him turn to Joseph. "You don't look old enough to already know all those verses."

"I'm five." Joseph pushed the bag forward. "Please, mister. Have some candy."

The man reached into the bag. "Perhaps your . . . Elizabeth . . . will share with me?" He snapped a peppermint stick in two and held out half to her.

Did he think she was some sort of mare she hoped to appease with a lump of sugar?

He smiled knowingly. "It's just candy. Not a marriage proposal."

"It wouldn't be proper for me to accept something from a stranger."

He shrugged and lazily pulled his hand back. "Suit yourself. I'm just trying to be pleasant."

Elizabeth pressed her lips together and opened the Bible to shut him out. She turned to Joseph for a new verse when she felt the stage jerk back hard, then rock forward.

"Whoa!" the driver called. A horse whinnied.

Flung from the bench, Elizabeth felt her heart jump to her throat. Joseph! She threw out a protecting arm but only paddled the air then hit something solid that momentarily knocked her breath out. The coach halted, and slowly the world stopped spinning. Stunned, she found herself sprawled across the stranger's lap, trapped close in his arms.

Her heart quickened, blood pounding in her ears. He narrowed his eyes but didn't release her. "Are you all right?"

"Please let me go!" she choked out.

He relaxed his arms a fraction, and she scrambled away.

A loud wail sounded over the other passengers' moans. Sprawled on the floor, Joseph dragged a hand against his nose. "The c-candy broke!"

Elizabeth's shoulders sagged with relief, and she helped him back up on the bench. Praise God, he wasn't hurt! "Oh, Joseph, they're only peppermints. Please don't cry!

What would Reverend Cameron say?"

Joseph sniffled one last time then carefully set down the bag. "H-he'd tell me to act like a little man."

Elizabeth nodded. "Life is full of hardships much worse than broken candy."

"Why, you cold-hearted little prig," the stranger muttered.

Before she could reply, the driver poked his weathered face through the window. "Sorry the horses got spooked. We'll stop here for lunch if you folks are all right."

The other passengers grumbled, but the stranger glared at them. "We're all fine. Nothing bruised but a few feelings."

Still mumbling their displeasure, the passengers accepted the driver's help to disembark. "— speak to the stage line about their employees —" Elizabeth heard one man say. The drummer glanced at the gunman then jumped from the stage.

The driver held out his arms. "You next, sonny."

With a tear lingering on his face, Joseph looked back for reassurance. Elizabeth nodded, moving behind him.

The stranger slung the forgotten paper bag over her arm. "It's not all broken. You can probably salvage some for him."

Without turning, she jerked her head in

acknowledgment. "I'll see what I can do," she said stiffly, then followed Joseph down from the stage and away from the man with the gun.

Pulling out fried chicken from their basket, Elizabeth and Joseph stood on the banks of the Brazos River and studied the enigmatic man upstream. Leaning against a cottonwood, he idly skipped a stone across the river, the cartridges in his gun belt gleaming with his movements.

Joseph carefully swallowed a bite of his drumstick, then turned with a serious expression. "Do you think Reverend Cameron is really in heaven?"

Elizabeth nearly reeled backward. Joseph's innocent question touched on her own recent doubts, compounding her guilt. She often wondered if her father was anywhere near the throne of God. "The Bible tells us that if we believe in Jesus, we'll go to heaven."

Joseph pondered that for a moment. "Do you think Reverend Cameron believed in him?"

"He was a preacher long before I was even born," she hedged.

"Does Jesus love us like Reverend Cameron did?"

The picnic basket in Elizabeth's hands felt weighted. "The Bible says Jesus loves us."

"But did Reverend Cameron love us?"

She tried to swallow the hard lump in her throat, but it refused to budge. "Joseph, I —"

The stranger down the bank flipped a stone, and it skipped across calm water several times before sinking. "He's really good!" Joseph said with awe, forgetting his question. "He's probably hungry. Can we give him some of our food?"

"A man like that can fend for himself."

Joseph chomped down on his drumstick, chewed thoughtfully, then swallowed. "Why don't you like him, Elizabeth?"

"I never said I didn't like him. I just don't think it's wise for us to be too friendly with a stranger."

"But remember when you told me the story about the good Samaritan? The man he helped was a stranger."

Elizabeth sighed heavily, shutting her eyes. "Joseph, that was different."

"How?"

She opened her eyes and looked down. Her son's brown eyes pleaded wistfully, and her defenses crumbled. "You're right. Good Christians should share their food. You may take him a drumstick."

All smiles, Joseph snatched a leg and headed across the bank.

Caleb Martin tossed another stone into the river, keeping a wary eye on the woman and boy eating downstream. He'd seen the kid sneak envious glances his way, as though he'd like to trade the food for a few moments of fun.

Noah Cameron hadn't said anything about a boy, much less an Indian.

Caleb flipped another stone, smoother this time, and watched it skip three times before sinking in the currents. His boyhood friend Nathan Hamilton still held the all-time record of eight skips. Caleb grinned, then instantly sobered.

Those carefree days were long behind them both. Now Nathan was serving time in Wyoming for grand larceny. By all rights, Caleb should be in the penitentiary, too, but Marshal Noah Cameron had intervened on his behalf.

"You'll get your pardon," Noah had said back in Fort Griffin. "You've been a model deputy for me the past three years, since I vouched for you. You've always been one step from prison, but now you're only one step from freedom. When this last assignment's over, I'll meet you in Cheyenne, and the governor will personally hand you that piece of paper you've worked for."

"So when do we start?"

"*You* start." Noah leaned forward. "But I'm trusting you with something a lot more important this time than arresting outlaws. You're going to be watching over my sister."

"Hold on, Cameron."

"She'll be on the stage to Belton. You'll travel with her and —"

"I said *hold on*. I'm not a nursemaid."

"You'll do for a bodyguard. She's nineteen years old, Martin, and pretty, though she doesn't know it." Noah's eyes steeled. "I'm going to trust you despite your reputation with women."

"Watch out for her yourself if you don't trust me."

"I offered, but she was emphatic about going alone. I wish she'd never heard of this place, but she's dead-set."

"What's in Belton?"

"Some sort of crazy women's group has started there. They call themselves the Sanctificationists. They claim they've been set apart by God. Some have even left their husbands. They believe in economic freedom for women. And celibacy."

"That ought to please you." Caleb grinned.

"As long as she's not married, but I hope she's not using this group to shut herself away from men. I'd like to see her get married one day."

Caleb crossed his arms. "This is blackmail, Cameron, but if it means my pardon, I'll get your sister to this group. When she finds out you sent me —"

"Don't tell her. She'd never forgive me. I've fixed up a real job for you in Belton. You watch her for one year, and you'll be a free man. You just keep your distance — I'm not sending you there to matchmake. I just want to be sure she's safe."

Caleb chunked a rock into the water. It was blackmail, all right. Even if he wanted to tell Elizabeth Cameron the truth, he couldn't. Until Noah secured his pardon, Caleb could still go back to jail.

Imagine Cameron worrying about Caleb and his pious sister! She was so swathed in black clothing, he hadn't even gotten a good look at her face or hair. The fact that Noah had said she was pretty was extra incentive for Caleb to get on the stage. If he was supposed to guard her, she might as well be worth watching. He'd willed her to look like his ideal woman — blond, full lips, and deep, inviting blue irises.

He'd been severely disappointed when

she finally glanced up. She had brown eyes — *mud* brown eyes — and a face he could only charitably describe as plain, with its too-wide nose and thin lips. Dark brown hair poked out from under the ridiculous black bonnet's brim. The ugly wooden cross looked like two twigs lashed together with old leather and was the sorriest excuse for a religious necklace he'd ever seen.

Her attire and demeanor did more to suppress his desire than enflame it. Noah Cameron's little sister would definitely be safe in Caleb's care.

"Excuse me. I'm supposed to give this to you."

Surprised, Caleb glanced down. The boy was holding out a drumstick, his smiling face hopeful.

Caleb accepted the drumstick. "This isn't *your* lunch, is it?"

The boy shook his head. "Elizabeth says good Christians always share their food."

Caleb caught his breath. "Is that a fact? Well you can tell Miss Elizabeth . . ." He frowned. "Never mind. I'll tell her myself."

Eyes shining, Joseph danced alongside as Caleb marched across the bank. Noah thought his sister was pretty? This black-garbed, self-righteous creature looked and acted more like a grackle than a woman. She'd picked at the boy all morning, and now, just to ease her pious conscience, she tossed Caleb her leftover crumbs.

Standing toe to toe with her, he scowled. "I don't think I should accept food from a woman I haven't been properly introduced to."

Her cheeks reddened. "I didn't think of that. I suppose we could prevail upon the driver or one of the passengers."

"I'd rather have the boy."

"Joseph?"

Caleb hunkered down. The kid was the only sane person he'd met since Fort Griffin. "He can handle it, right?"

Joseph nodded with enthusiasm.

"Good." Caleb cupped his hand around the boy's ear and whispered his name. "Got it?"

Joseph nodded, beaming.

Caleb rose, and Joseph cleared his throat. "Miss Elizabeth Cameron, may I present Mr. Caleb Martin?"

Caleb nodded gravely. He could go along with the game. It seemed to mean a lot to the boy.

"And, Mr. Caleb Martin, may I present Miss Elizabeth Cameron?"

The black bonnet bobbed once.

Silence. The boy looked on anxiously.

Caleb cleared his throat. "Who's your young traveling companion?"

Elizabeth looked flustered. "This is Joseph."

"Joseph what?"

The boy's expression faded from cheerfulness to shame, and he dropped his extended hand. "Just Joseph," Elizabeth said. "He's never had a last name."

Caleb solemnly held out a hand. "Pleased to meet you, Just Joseph."

The boy giggled and accepted the handshake. His small hand felt warm in Caleb's. "How do you do, Mr. Martin? Are you headed for Belton like us?"

"Call me Caleb, and as a matter of fact, I am."

Elizabeth shot Joseph a silencing glance, but he persisted. "Why are you going there?"

"I've got a job as a railroad surveyor. That's somebody who studies the land and figures out the best way to lay tracks. They'd like to build a rail line through Belton."

"Bo-o-a-a-rd! Time to board, folks!"

Joseph charged up the bank. "I'm going to look at the horses before we have to go!"

"Be careful!" Elizabeth hastily gathered

the remnants of the lunch, flushing as Caleb bent to help. "You never said anything about going to Belton, Mr. Martin."

"You didn't ask." Caleb shoved a napkin into the basket. "Why were you two standing up to eat?"

"We didn't want to get grass stains."

Caleb laughed. "I doubt that Joseph cares."

"Why, of course he does! He knows better than to get his clothes dirty."

"He's a *boy*. When does he run and play?"

"Joseph doesn't do those things."

Caleb grabbed Joseph's paper bag and rifled through the basket, retrieving a bundle of sugar cookies. Elizabeth tried to snatch them back. "I need to finish packing! They're about to leave!"

Brushing her hands away, Caleb crushed, then sprinkled the peppermints on the cookies. "This is for the boy."

"Bo-o-a-a-rd!"

He snatched up the basket with its bulging contents and bounded up the bank, Elizabeth following closely at his heels. Joseph pointed at the stage. "Look at the horses!"

Caleb held out a cookie. "Here, Joseph. Just because something's broken, doesn't mean it can't be useful."

"You put the candy on top!" Joseph chomped down, sending crumbs and peppermint flying. "Mmmmff." Mouth full, he smiled with worshipful eyes at Caleb.

Caleb shoved the basket at Elizabeth, then turned. He could feel the smolder from her glare all the way back to the stage.

"Elizabeth, look!"

Elizabeth glanced up from her knitting needles. Joseph sat knee-to-knee with Caleb Martin, hanging on the man's every scant word since lunch.

Joseph beamed. "Mr. Martin showed me how to make a rabbit shadow with my hands. See?"

"That's very clever." She smiled, then quickly ducked her head. She didn't want to chance meeting Caleb's gaze.

"Elizabeth!"

"Shh, Joseph. Remember Joshua's admonition: 'Ye shall not shout, nor make any noise with your voice.' "

Joseph bowed his head. "Yes ma'am."

Elizabeth smiled at his obedience then intercepted Caleb's scowl. Self-conscious, she bent over her work.

The morning's joyous freedom had fallen into an afternoon of doubt. Surely she was right in going to Belton . . . wasn't she?

Father might be dead, but the lie he'd enforced lived on. If he had died years ago, she would have immediately spoken up and lovingly claimed Joseph as her own. But over the years, she'd seen how cruelly people treated illegitimate children. Much less half-breeds. It was for his own good that she kept him at arm's length.

Joseph must never learn about Eyes Like the Sun. Never. She would shield him from his heritage of violence for the sake of his life, for the sake of his soul. She could never acknowledge him as her child, but it was a small price to pay to keep him safe. Hidden from the world, they would learn the Scriptures and serve others. It would be a simple, happy life.

A dirt clod flew into her lap. She tossed it back out the window and started to unroll the leather curtain, then stopped, her stomach tightening. Mesquites and post oaks dotted the gently rolling plain like lonely sentinels guarding the horizon. The old feeling momentarily overwhelmed her, the fear that she was still a captive in that desolate land.

Elizabeth looked away and met Caleb's studious gaze. Something in his expression held her attention. She could see the curiosity in his eyes, in his handsome face, in the way he sat — relaxed — as though it were only a matter of time before she poured out her heart to him.

She straightened her spine. He would have a long wait.

He grinned lazily as if reading her thoughts. "We cross the Brazos again before we get to Fort Worth, Miss Cameron. I'd like your permission to take Joseph fishing."

"Fishing?" She let out a pent-up breath.

"Doesn't the boy like it?"

"My father was a preacher, Mr. Martin. We didn't have time for fishing."

"Isn't that what that book you're carrying is all about? Jesus fishing for the souls of men."

The drummer cleared his throat and leaned around Joseph. "I wonder if I might be so bold as to ask where you're headed, miss? You and the boy, that is."

Caleb turned slowly. "I thought I told you to leave the lady and the boy alone. Strangers shouldn't stick their noses in other people's business."

"It appears to me the lady doesn't much care for your attention, either, *stranger*."

Caleb leaned forward, his cold eyes close to the drummer's. "Leave them alone."

The drummer glared back, and Elizabeth

instinctively threw an arm around Joseph. "Mr. Martin wasn't bothering me, sir," she said, hoping to diffuse the situation. "But thank you for your concern."

"Does that mean I can go fishing with Caleb?"

Caleb glanced sharply at Joseph, then grinned when he saw the adoring expression on the boy's face. He leaned back, chuckling. The drummer flushed under his collar and stared out the window.

Elizabeth's face burned, and she loosened her arm from around Joseph. "You may call him Mr. Martin, not Caleb. And no, you may not go fishing."

"But —"

"No."

"Why not?" Caleb hadn't lost his grin.

Elizabeth clasped her hands for composure. "Because I don't know you. It wouldn't be proper for you to take him out alone."

"You could come with us."

"That wouldn't be proper either."

"You two ate lunch with me — alone."

Why was this man so persistent? He seemed bent on insinuating himself into her life, even to the point of violence. "That was charity."

His eyes hardened. "Lady, I don't take

charity from anybody. Especially not from a prudish miss who's dressed up like a grackle."

"A . . . a what?"

"A grackle. One of those huge, black birds that —"

What a horrible, hateful man! "I know what they are, Mr. Martin. And I hardly see that my attire is any of your concern. Any gentleman would know the reason and never question it. But since you seem to require an explanation, I'm wearing black because I'm in mourning. My father is recently deceased!"

Caleb grinned. "Then that explains why you're so excitable."

"*Excitable?* I'm not —" She clamped her mouth shut.

Silence filled the coach. Elizabeth hunched her shoulders against the others' stares. How had she gotten herself into such a spectacle?

Joseph stared with open admiration at Caleb Martin. "Can I hold your gun?"

"Joseph!"

Caleb turned. "Don't worry, Miss Cameron. I've had this Colt revolver since the war. The last time I let someone touch it was when I had it converted to fire .44 rimfire metallic cartridges."

"Was it broken?" Joseph said.

"No. I wanted it to fire better."

"Really? How many men have you shot?"

Appalled, Elizabeth found her voice. "Young man, you know that guns are wrong. Fighting's never the answer!"

"Sometimes fighting is the only answer." Martin smiled sardonically. "Sometimes it's the only way to obtain freedom."

"Would you fight for me?" Joseph said. "Some boys —"

"That's enough, Joseph," Elizabeth said. "That's in the past back in Fort Griffin. You will not talk about those boys, do you understand?"

He bowed his head. "Yes ma'am."

"Mr. Martin would no doubt recommend you fight such bullies in the future. And you know what the Bible teaches about violence."

"Yes ma'am."

Caleb crossed his arms. "I wouldn't recommend anything until I heard the entire story. But it's plain you don't want the boy to speak the truth."

"I don't want him to dwell on an unpleasant situation that's now behind us."

"Sometimes unpleasant situations need to be aired, Miss Cameron, or they fester."

59

Elizabeth raised her chin a notch. "You sound like a man who speaks from experience."

"And you sound like a woman who has none."

The others' tense stares pressed against her. She thought her father's harsh words had made her accustomed to criticism, but Martin's barb hurt deeply. She drew a deep, steadying breath. "Perhaps I do speak without proper knowledge, Mr. Martin. I apologize for my shortcomings."

Martin stared skeptically. Abashed, she turned her head, hoping all he could see was the side of her bonnet.

Oh, Lord, why was this man here? To wreck her confidence? Before, Father or Helga had always told Joseph what to do, while she awaited her own instructions. But the boy was her responsibility now, her *duty* to train up in the way he should go.

She would smooth matters with Joseph in a moment, but right now she needed to collect the scattered pieces of her hard-earned composure before it fell apart at Caleb Martin's feet.

Several hours later, the stage stopped for a break. Leaning against the coach, Caleb gritted his teeth as he watched Elizabeth and Joseph take in the shade under a cottonwood. She pointed up at a raucous blue jay and glanced hopefully at Joseph, but the boy turned his head and scuffed the ground.

Caleb wondered what she'd said to discourage the boy this time. The grackle had a real knack for it.

At least she'd bought his story about going to Belton to survey. It was true he'd be working for the railroad, but what little he knew about measurements and grades came from Noah Cameron's hurried instructions about the assignment.

"Bo-o-a-a-rd!"

Caleb straightened and watched Joseph and Elizabeth make their way toward the stage. The boy kept his eyes fixed on the horses pulling at the braked, empty stage. Caleb swung Joseph up into the coach then grabbed Elizabeth by the waist and swung her up too. "Mr. Martin, really! I —"

He was just trying to be helpful — the prudish snob couldn't even let him be a gentleman. Caleb clenched his teeth and forced himself to touch the brim of his hat. "I'll ride above for a while, Miss Cameron."

Joseph's face fell. "Do you have to?"

As much as he liked the kid, Caleb didn't want to incur the grackle's squawking. He didn't even want to look at her prim face and church-mouse dress. "Sorry, Joe."

"His name is *Joseph*."

Mad enough to spit, Caleb spun and climbed up top. "Well!" he heard Elizabeth say. "I've never met anyone so rude!"

"I like the name Joe," he heard the kid say sadly. Caleb gritted his teeth and found a seat. She had a real way with the boy, all right.

Hours of pounding hooves and flying dirt did little to alleviate his anger. Cursing Elizabeth Cameron, he grimly pulled his bandanna up over his mouth and nose. It was her fault he was riding up here.

He yanked his hat down and braced himself to keep his precarious seat. He just might forget about his assignment, his pardon, and especially Noah's little sister. What sounded best right now was a hot bath, a stiff drink, and some female company — not necessarily in that order.

"Whoa, there!"

The driver pulled on the reins, and Caleb straightened. They had reached the bridge crossing the Brazos. The road from Fort Griffin had followed the river, but now they would leave it behind until another crossing downstream between Fort Worth and Belton.

The horses clopped across the narrow,

weather-beaten boards over the river rushing below. Caleb crossed his arms and tipped his hat over his eyes.

Suddenly the horses nickered with alarm and strained against their harness. The driver raised up, shouting, "Water moccasin!"

Caleb clutched the seat. "What — ?"

The horses reared back, dancing with fright. The driver struggled to gain control, but the horses jerked the reins from his hands. Lunging, he missed the reins and fell screaming from the coach.

Crashing through the flimsy wooden rail, the coach teetered. The frightened passengers screamed. Caleb scrambled to grab the reins, but they were beyond his reach.

The side wheels rumbled over the edge, and the coach listed. Shrieking, the horses struggled against the weight, but the coach seesawed up and down in a slow-motion tilt. As the animals struggled, the coach twisted until it finally plunged like a toy tossed to the raging waters below.

Caleb hurled through the air, his stomach lurching. He had a vague impression of the river below just before he hit the water with a sickening blow to the gut and head.

Two

Caleb coughed, sputtering water, gasping for air. His arms flailed against the sinking pull of the river's current. His forearms hit hard wood, and he grabbed the lifeline and held tightly. Near exploding, his fire-stoked head pounded. He forced his eyes to focus but saw only black.

"It's all right. Let me help you." Something loosened his grip, and he dipped below the water's surface.

Panicked, he fought whatever held him. "Let go! I —" he gurgled when he once again surfaced.

"It's all right. I'm here." The voice closed around him, soothing, easing him to his back, atop the water. He struggled, thrashing painfully until he lost strength and surrendered, spent. Prepared to drown, he was surprised instead to find himself supported in the water while the voice murmured encouraging words. Caleb relaxed and let the water enfold him.

Somehow he was back in Kansas, a kid again. He and Nathan were running to the river, whooping, excited to be free on a Sunday afternoon. Racing to be first to touch the big cottonwood, Caleb turned to see how far behind Nathan lagged.

Something solid hit him square in the forehead, knocking him flat on his back. The countryside around him crumpled like a piece of paper. "Nathan!" He tried to sit up, but pain overwhelmed, and he lay paralyzed. "Nathan, what happened?"

"Shh." A soft hand rested against his forehead. "Lie back, Mr. Martin."

He tried to see the form connected with the voice but could only discern the hand as feminine. It must be his sister. That was it. "Samantha? Where's Nathan?"

"Please, be still. You'll be all right, but you must be still."

He tried again to sit up but could barely move his head and arms. Something crunched when he moved. "I . . . I'm going home now. Gotta lie down."

"You're already lying down. But you must be still or you'll disturb the leaves. They're all we have to keep you warm."

Leaves? He shifted and heard crunching again. This time he could feel his hands moving. A stab of pain shot through his

65

head, and he groaned.

"You *can* move. Good." The soft hand returned to his forehead. "I have to go, but I'll be —"

Fearful, Caleb cried out. He didn't want to be left alone, helpless, with the pain.

The hand curved against his cheek. "I won't leave you. I promise."

Moaning, he shivered, leaves rustling around him.

"Mr. Martin, please open your mouth."

"But —"

Something bitter dribbled onto his tongue. He gagged, thinking he might get sick, but the bitterness dissolved into a warm peace that lightened his head, and he drifted away on a cloud free of pain.

He awoke to the morning sun warming his face. Judging from the brightness, it was close to noon. Stirring, he groaned. He must have had one wild night to have such a head pounding.

Shifting against the hard ground, he realized he was surprisingly weak and sore. And he was covered with leaves. Hundreds of them. Somebody had practically buried him. He gingerly lifted an arm and saw his faded undershirt. Somebody had removed his clothes.

"You're awake!"

A small form popped up beside him. Caleb grinned. The sight of the boy brought everything back into place, including the stagecoach wreck. "Are you all right, Joseph?"

The boy nodded with enthusiasm, pointing. "Elizabeth —"

Caleb tried to sit up but found movement painful. He followed the direction of Joseph's finger and saw Elizabeth straighten over a campfire. Her hair was loose around her shoulders, and her dress was ridiculously wrinkled. "Good morning. Joseph, please go wash up at the river."

"Yes ma'am!" Joseph scrambled up, shooting leaves everywhere.

Caleb relaxed. Elizabeth looked so calm, he decided everything must be fine. From his experience, women usually got hysterical at the least sign of danger.

Elizabeth laced her fingers together. "I'm glad you're awake. God spared me and Joseph from certain death, Mr. Martin. And now, thankfully, he's spared you too."

"How are the others?"

Elizabeth bowed her head. "No one else survived. They were swept downriver."

If he didn't dislike her so much, Caleb would have felt sorry for the bedraggled grackle. She'd probably endured a terrifying experience. He couldn't remember, but he must have pulled her from the wreckage before he collapsed himself.

She gathered up what looked like weeds and a hollowed-out rock filled with liquid and knelt at his side. When she stretched out a hand to his head, he jerked away. "What do you think you're doing?"

She smiled patiently, as though he were a child. "I'm going to check that wound. You got a nasty cut when you hit your head, though you probably would have drowned if the log hadn't kept you afloat."

"What?" He stared as she pulled back something leafy from his forehead. "What is *that?*"

"Dandelion leaves." She tossed them to the side and plucked a handful from the new pile. "I put yarrow on the wound to keep it clean and to numb the pain. Then I applied some slippery elm bark for healing and covered it all with the dandelion leaves. And the willow-bark tea brought your fever down."

He eyed the liquid concoction in the rock. "I suppose you want to give me more."

"It'll keep your head from hurting."

Caleb groaned and raised a hand to his temple. "It's already throbbing. I don't think you can do much about it."

"Drink this. I've had it many times before, myself."

He shrugged. What choice did a man have with a splitting headache? He tried to raise his head but groaned at the pain and fell back.

"Let me help you," she said softly, slowly elevating his head. The touch of her hand was soothing, yet strong. She pressed the cup against his lips, urging him to drink. His eyes met hers over the rim, and he downed every drop. Leaning back with a grimace, he worked his tongue over his teeth and lips. "Ugh. Bitter."

Elizabeth laughed. "Men make terrible patients, Mr. Martin."

"Is that right?" Despite the throbbing of his head, Caleb couldn't resist smiling. Her laughter sounded almost musical.

She smiled back shyly. "Men hate to be helpless." Her hand rested cool and smooth against his brow.

Caleb closed his eyes, deciding he liked her touch. Since she was in an apparently good mood, maybe she'd help fill in the gaps of his memory. "How did I get here?"

"I pulled you off the log to shore."

"All by yourself?"

"I helped Joseph out first. He can't swim." She eased her hand away. "It wasn't anything dramatic."

He never would have suspected the preacher's daughter had such spunk. Or strength. And where'd she learn so much about medicine?

Caleb looked with grudging respect at the black-garbed woman. "It was much more dramatic than you seem to realize. You saved my life. I don't take that lightly."

She dipped her fingers in a paste spread on a large leaf. "You're right, of course. Life should never be trivialized. But my role means nothing. The real work was in the Lord's hand. You and Joseph and I are safe."

She gentled the paste into his wound, and Caleb gritted his teeth against the pain. "We're safe as long as I have my gun."

"But you don't. It must have fallen in the river."

Exploding with a curse, Caleb pushed her hands away. "Do you know how long I've had that gun, how long it took me to get it in prime condition?"

Elizabeth rose. "You should get some sleep now. Maybe you'll feel like eating when you wake up again."

"How do you know I'm not — ?" Caleb stopped. The thought of food did turn his stomach. What could she have found to eat, anyway, stranded as they were?

He watched as she bustled back to the fire and laid something over a bed of rocks. He wanted to ask what she was doing, but his eyes wouldn't stay open long enough for him to even form the question on his lips.

" 'O God, thou knowest my . . . my . . .' "

" 'Foolishness,' " Elizabeth prompted.

Joseph grinned with relief. " 'Foolishness; and my sins are not . . . not . . .' "

" 'Hid.' "

" 'Hid from . . . from . . .' "

Elizabeth sighed. " 'From thee.' Listen, Joseph: 'O God, thou knowest my foolishness; and my sins are not hid from thee. Let not them that wait on thee, O Lord God of hosts, be ashamed for my sake: let not those that seek thee be confounded for my sake, O God of Israel.' "

Night had fallen, balmy, and Caleb listened while Elizabeth recited the rest of the psalm. She and Joseph huddled together on a log close to the fire.

The crackling punctuated the sudden silence. "You remember words so good, Elizabeth," Joseph said in hushed awe. "Do you think I'll ever be as good?"

"With enough practice you'll learn many verses too. Remember how many

71

Reverend Cameron knew?"

"He must have known the whole Bible."

"He taught me how important it was to memorize verses for times like this. We lost the Bible in the river, Joseph, but we can recite the words we know." She rose. "I'd better check on Mr. Martin."

Caleb cleared his throat. "No need. I'm awake."

"So you are." She stood beside him. "How do you feel?"

Caleb considered, taking stock. "Better. My head doesn't hurt nearly as much."

"The willow bark is amazing. God has provided much healing in nature."

Caleb sat up slowly, grateful that only his head hurt. "I don't know about God's healing, Miss Cameron, but you're certainly an angel of mercy."

Rock cup in hand, Elizabeth knelt before him. Her eyes met his, and for a moment he saw pain in their brown depths. She blinked, and it disappeared. "I'm no angel, Mr. Martin. Just an instrument of the Lord. As all believers are."

He studied her face. She reminded him of his sister. Samantha was blond and blue-eyed, but she had the same peaceful demeanor when she talked about God. Or at least she had three years ago, the last time

Caleb had seen her.

"Drink this." Elizabeth handed him the cup.

Caleb held his palms out. "I've had enough of your potions."

"You haven't had nearly enough. You're still weak. This is a tonic."

"And it'll probably turn me into a frog." He pushed the cup away. "No."

"If you don't drink it, I won't give you your clothes back."

He grinned and crossed his arms. "That won't bother me if it won't bother you. It certainly wouldn't be very *proper*, now would it, Miss Bess?"

"It wouldn't." She raised her chin. "But Joseph and I can travel alone, Mr. Martin. Surely even you wouldn't dream of hiking out of here without your clothes."

Caleb gritted his teeth. She meant it! The stubborn prig would actually leave him stranded. "Fine," he bit out. "Give me your concoction."

Elizabeth smiled in triumph. She raised the cup to his lips, but he snatched it from her hands and downed the contents. It didn't taste as bitter as he'd remembered. He stared suspiciously at the remaining drops. "What was it?"

"Juniper berry tea. It's good for thickening the blood and as an all-around invigorator."

"The best invigorator I can think of right now would be a good shot of whiskey."

Elizabeth frowned. "Don't you know that strong drink is raging and whosoever is deceived thereby is not wise?"

"I never claimed to be wise. Just thirsty."

"And Jesus said that anyone who drinks of the water he gives shall never thirst, for his is a well of water springing up into everlasting life."

Suddenly his head throbbed harder. Sighing with exasperation, he eased back to the leaves. It was too much to hope that she'd just go away and let him die in peace.

"One more day of rest, then perhaps you'll be ready to travel." Elizabeth leaned back and clasped her arms around her knees. She yawned, then immediately looked abashed. "Oh, I'm so sorry! That was exceedingly rude."

By the firelight, she looked more like a girl and less like a starched puritan. "You're allowed to be tired," he said grudgingly. "You've done the work of several men for two days now."

She turned away, clearly embarrassed by his praise. "If you feel well enough, sit by the fire. There's food and coffee."

"*Coffee?*"

"It's only chicory, but it makes a decent substitute. You roast the roots, then grind and boil them like coffee beans."

Elizabeth Cameron continued to mystify him. She'd saved his life and kept herself and Joseph comfortable and fed while he'd been unconscious. Now she offered him coffee as though they were all sitting in her parlor!

"What's wrong? You're smiling."

"Is smiling against your religion?" Caleb's grin deepened. "Why, no, it must not be. You smiled when you got me to drink your witch's brew."

"It was hardly an evil potion, Mr. Martin."

"You'd better call me Caleb. You did remove my clothes."

Mortification crossed her face. "J-Joseph helped me. And I . . . *we* did it to keep you warm."

Caleb laughed. She was certainly easy to tease. Despite her proficiency for survival, she was still a woman. A most enigmatic, curious woman.

Still looking unnerved, she turned. "Joseph! Come to bed. And please bring Mr. Martin's clothes."

Joseph retreated out of sight.

Caleb lightly rested his hand on Elizabeth's. "I was serious about calling me Caleb."

He felt her shudder, then she jerked her hand away. "I refuse to ignore certain civilities just because we're temporarily removed from civilization. As a gentleman, you owe me that much."

"I never said I was a gentleman, Elizabeth."

Her lips parted, but no sound came out. The flickering firelight danced like a halo behind her head, bringing out gentle red highlights. Easing himself up, Caleb let his gaze follow the length of her hair and was surprised to see the stick cross still hanging around her neck. He absently reached out to touch it.

Elizabeth gasped and scrambled to her feet. "How dare you?"

"I didn't mean —"

"I'm not some cheap woman for your amusement!"

Caleb felt his chest expand with anger. Why did she always assume the worst about him? He wouldn't grab a woman like a barbarian conqueror! "I didn't mean anything," he ground out.

Her face blanched, and she strode to the fire.

Joseph ran up, panting, nearly knocking Elizabeth down. She gripped his shoulder. "Please be careful!"

He stepped back. "Y-yes ma'am."

Her face softened, and she awkwardly patted his arm. "Please give Mr. Martin his clothes while I fix him something to eat. Then it's time for bed."

"Can't I stay up to talk to him?"

"No. We're heading out tomorrow, and we need a good night's sleep." She turned away.

Joseph dutifully deposited the shirt and trousers in Caleb's hands. "Do you really feel better, Mr. Martin?"

Caleb ruffled the boy's hair. "Whenever you're around, I always feel better." He rose on unsteady legs, thrusting out his hands for balance. Joseph instinctively stepped closer, and Caleb braced a gentle hand on the small shoulder as he stepped into his trousers. Holding on a moment longer than necessary, he said, "Thanks, Joe. If it weren't for you, I'd have fallen on my face."

Joseph's face lit up, then he glanced over his shoulder. With her back to them, Elizabeth knelt at the fire and poured fresh liquid into the rock cup.

The boy's cheerful expression fell. "I wish I knew why she's always so unhappy. I guess it's my fault."

Caleb jammed his arms into his shirt sleeves. He'd like to wring Elizabeth Cameron's stiff neck. Couldn't she see how she crushed the boy's spirit by denying him her love? Caleb had half a mind to grab Joseph and run far away. Even he'd make a better substitute mother!

Elizabeth glanced up. "There's a cup of coffee brewing on the fire. There's also some boiled wild onions, cattails, dandelion roots, and henbit. It may not be gourmet fare, but it will do."

"Fine. Thank you." Surprised by her continuing resourcefulness, he wouldn't dream of complaining. Not about the food anyway.

Elizabeth urged Joseph to the bed of leaves, then spread the remainder over him. "Good night, Mr. Martin," he called.

"Good night, kid."

The faint strains of childish prayer drifted toward him, and Caleb grinned when he heard his name mentioned. Elizabeth probably hated to hear Joseph hold him up to God.

Using a stick, Caleb pushed the rock cup away from the fire, cradled the cup with the front tail of his shirt, then hesitantly swallowed Elizabeth's chicory. It was surprisingly good, certainly much better than the makeshift coffee he drank in the army.

The woman was a mystery. How could she reveal so much of her warm, merciful nature one minute, then freeze like a winter mountain lake the next?

And how *had* that flimsy cross survived the wreck in the river?

Eyes Like the Sun stood poised on the south slope of the cone-shaped sacred hills the white man called Medicine Mounds. With his one good eye, he scanned the horizon east and west, waiting intently.

His first vision quest had been here as a youth yet untested in battle, when he was still known as Little Step. Eager to prove his bravery, he had gathered a pipe, tobacco, buffalo robe, and material to create a light, then set out for the sacred hills. As tradition prescribed, he stopped four times to smoke and pray, finally climbing the flattest hill to achieve his personal vision and medicine.

Facing south, he waited patiently, fasting, smoking, and praying near darkness. At night he covered himself from head to toe with the buffalo robe, then rose at dawn to face and receive the power from the sun.

On the fourth night, he lay down to sleep, the vision unfulfilled. There was no moon, and clouds covered the stars. Weak with hunger, he despaired of success and begged the spirits for power. When at last he stood and faced the morning sky, he raised his eyes and met the sun, whose blazing glory showed him the truth of the future.

He saw that Sunflower, still but a young girl, would stand by his side. He saw a son follow his warrior father into battle to reclaim land that had been won and lost. He saw a human sacrifice enable the warrior to count coup on all his enemies.

He saw so much that when he came down from the ancient hills, the truth glowed from his eyes for all to see. Even Walks Far, the wisest man in the tribe, acknowledged it, renaming him Eyes Like the Sun.

Soon after, the young man with the new name rode into his first battle, a raid on a Kiowa camp. There he committed the three noblest acts of a warrior: counting coup on an enemy, helping a dismounted comrade in battle, and standing his ground while outnumbered in the face of certain death by the enemy.

Frightened by his bravery, the Kiowas scattered and ran. Later the People sang of Eyes Like the Sun's heroics while they shamed the Kiowa captives. Sunflower stared at him with awe across the blazing fire, and once again he glimpsed the future.

Now Sunflower and their newborn son were gone, killed in the raid that claimed one of his eyes. He had taken several wives, but none had yet produced a boy to fulfill the vision.

He had thought last year would bring the People's resurrection. He joined with the great Eeshatai, who had powerful medicine. It was said he brought people back from the dead and could not be harmed by bullets. Under his leadership, many warriors gathered north of the river to hold a sacred sun dance with the Kiowa, Cheyenne, and Arapaho. It was a spiritual gathering, making Quanah, the great half-white warrior their new war chief.

But later the bluecoats raided and killed over one thousand of the People's horses and burned their supplies to prevent them from hunting or moving across the prairie. Buffalo were no longer plentiful, and in defeat many of the People went to the reservation. Those who had not were slowly starving.

Lately even Quanah himself talked of surrendering.

Eyes Like the Sun touched the medicine bag that hung at his chest and contained the objects that gave him power. A ball from a buffalo's stomach for invincibility in battle.

A bird's claw for courage. Herbs for healing.

The vision still beat in his breast. He would lead any who joined, but he needed a son. He would take yet another wife, as many as necessary. Surely at least one would be fruitful. If not, he had a son elsewhere, even if he was half-white.

From the west approached a horse and rider, pack mule trailing behind. The rider should have waited at the bottom of the hills, respecting the power of the spirit there. Instead, he rode boldly up the face of the hills, his greasy mane flapping behind him.

Eyes Like the Sun's empty socket ached beneath the hide patch, but he remained stoic despite his revulsion for the white hunter. Perhaps this time he had brought better guns.

At the top of the flat hill, the man halted. He dismounted, grinning. "Howdy there, ol' Eyes. Gotcha any good squaws lately?"

The sound of the white man's garbled language made Eyes Like the Sun frown.

The man grinned broader. "Greetings," he said in Comanche. "I've brought some meat and a couple of Henry rifles." He jerked his head back at the mule. "You can get it yourself once you give me some wampum. You savvy? Good old Yew-nited

States greenbacks. Not some of them Indian gee-gaws."

Eyes Like the Sun didn't move. "Did you find my son?"

"Weren't too difficult. Not many little Injun boys running around these parts. Not this far south of the reservation in Fort Sill anyway."

"Where is he?"

"I saw him in Fort Griffin, but he's headed to Belton. That's a little town down near where the Lampasas and Leon Rivers meet. Down where your people used to hunt and raid but can't get at no more. Too many white folks now."

Eyes Like the Sun raised his chin. "Let me see one of the rifles."

Still grinning, the man plucked a Henry rifle from the mule's pack and handed it over. "There's five more just like it." He held out his hand for payment.

Eyes Like the Sun studied the dry, cracked stock and the barrel that had rusted inside and out. He had been cheated yet again.

"Now how about that wam—"

Eyes Like the Sun raised the inferior rifle and squeezed the trigger. It was a dishonorable, white man's way to defeat an enemy, but he was in a hurry.

Three

Elizabeth bit back a cry as she stumbled over a rock. All day they'd walked the stage road, but she refused to complain about her aching feet. She carried a makeshift petticoat bag of herbs she'd collected. Determined to press on, she hiked the bag a little higher on her shoulder.

Caleb turned, his eyes narrowing under the petticoat bandage she'd wound around his forehead. "You all right?"

She nodded.

"You sure?"

"I'm fine. Really."

"A wagon's coming!" Breathless, Joseph raced up the path to join them. "It's a . . . big wagon . . . covered . . . with lots of fur and bones sticking out. One man's driving. I heard it 'way off and climbed a tree to see."

"Joseph!"

"Relax, Bess," Caleb said. "He's a good trail scout."

Joseph pointed. "There he is! Look!"

Before Elizabeth could turn, she heard the creaking of wheels and a man's loud admonitions. The recipients of his guidance were two oxen hitched to a canvas-covered wagon. The beasts plodded patiently, oblivious to the man's command to pick up the pace.

Joseph raced toward the team.

"Joseph! Be careful!" Elizabeth rushed forward, but Caleb pulled her back.

"Let him be. And for once, don't question what I tell this man."

"But —"

"Hush!"

"Whoa, Merlin! Whoa, Arthur!" The driver reined in the oxen. He set the brake, then rested his elbows against his knees and studied the threesome. "What are you folks doing way out here?" He glanced at Caleb's bandaged head, then at Elizabeth.

"Mornin'," Caleb said pleasantly. "Our stage wrecked several days ago at the Brazos, and we've been on foot since. Can you give us a ride to Fort Worth?"

The man pushed his dilapidated bowler aside and scratched his head. "Well, sir, I suppose I could. I'm heading to Fort Worth myself."

Joseph clambered up a spoke and peeked under the canvas. "Elizabeth! Look at the bones! Hundreds of 'em. And hides too!"

"Get down from there!" Elizabeth yanked his hand back from the canvas. "I'm sorry, sir. Please forgive us."

The man chuckled, a smile crossing his weathered face. "That's all right, missus. Your boy's like all the rest . . . naturally curious." His face fell as he glanced down at Joseph, then at Elizabeth and Caleb. "But he ain't your boy, is he? He's an Injun."

Caleb put an arm around Joseph. "He's ours, all right. Now . . . about the ride."

The man stepped down from the wagon. "The boy'll have to ride in the back, but the two of you will fit on the seat with me." He doffed his hat, revealing wisps of graying brown hair on a nearly bald head. "My name's Phineas Grimes."

Caleb extended a hand. "I'm Caleb Martin. And this is Elizabeth, and the boy is Joseph."

Phineas nodded, smiling broadly. "Mrs. Martin."

Mrs.! "Why, I'm —"

Caleb wrapped an arm around her. "No need to thank the man, dear." He smiled down at her as though he were the most attentive, loving husband in Texas.

Elizabeth narrowed her eyes. What kind of trick was he trying to pull?

"Here you go, Mrs. Martin," Phineas said, holding out a callous hand to help her up to the seat. Elizabeth reeled from the strong acrid smell that clung to him, reminding her of the hunters who'd wandered through Fort Griffin. They had the same pungent aroma that never disappeared no matter how vigorously they said they scrubbed. She scooted to the edge of the seat and caught another strong whiff, this time from the sun-broiled hides in the back.

Joseph poked head and shoulders through the canvas opening and held out a bone. "Look! It's from a real buffalo. Imagine, Elizabeth!"

Phineas climbed aboard and picked up the reins. "I thought the boy was yours. Why does he call his ma by her Christian name?"

Elizabeth clasped her hands. "My father was a preacher who believed in not only visiting orphans in their affliction but in sheltering them too."

"Ah." Phineas slapped the reins against the oxen's backs as though Elizabeth had explained everything. Caleb stared at her curiously, then turned to Phineas for small talk.

The wagon lurched forward, and Elizabeth glanced back at Joseph. He apparently didn't have a care in the world, playing happily in the piles of sun-bleached bones and putrefying hides.

"Yes, buffalo hunting's good right now," Phineas said in response to Caleb's question. "And it'll get even better when the train tracks they're laying come through Fort Worth. There's a big demand for hides and buffalo tallow. Folks back east are buying up the bones for china, buttons, combs . . . you name it. I'm hoping to fetch a good price in Fort Worth."

"Hunting must be fairly dangerous, what with all the Indians still lurking around," Caleb said.

Phineas played the lines between his hands and shifted in his seat. "The army's convinced most of the Comanches to head up to the reservation at Fort Sill. About the only ones left are renegades . . . the worst of the worst. Quanah Parker and his bunch, among others."

Elizabeth paled. "Others? Who?"

Phineas shrugged. "Can't rightly say that I've heard. All I know is that there's still hostile Indians who don't have the good sense to know they're defeated. Maybe we shouldn't have driven them off their land, but I figure it's too late to speculate. They can either go to the reservation or die on the plains. The buffalo won't last forever, and if there's a market back east, you can be certain men will hunt."

"You mean men will do anything for a dollar, no matter who it hurts," she said.

Caleb frowned, curious at Elizabeth's statement. Surely back at Fort Griffin she'd heard stories of the depredations committed against white women and children. So why was she defending them? "What do you know about those savages?"

"I know what I've seen."

Caleb remembered the string of tepees downriver from Fort Griffin. She and her father had probably visited their charity upon that group and falsely decided all red men were as peaceable and friendly.

He clenched his jaw. What did he care what she thought? Pious little mouse. Now that she'd saved his life, she'd probably try to save his soul.

The sun gradually lowered behind them, and Caleb wondered if Elizabeth realized they'd have to make camp. Since their conversation, she'd stared listlessly at the passing scenery. Only recently had Joseph quieted down, a sure sign he was tiring.

Phineas pointed to the right, his smelly

ragged coat sleeve nearly brushing Caleb's nose. "Over that ridge is the Trinity River. That'd be a grand place to make camp. Tomorrow we'll cross, then lose the river until we get to Fort Worth."

"I thought we'd be there tonight." Elizabeth's face puckered with worry. "Although I lost all my money in the stage wreck."

Caleb draped his arm across her shoulders. "I know you were hoarding your butter-and-egg money, but we'll make do, dear. You forget I have money."

Her eyes blazed, but Caleb shot her a look that stemmed any protest. He smiled inwardly with satisfaction; the little bird wasn't so hard to tame after all.

Over the ridge and just shy of a cottonwood grove, Phineas set the brake. The Trinity River rushed below, its sound punctuated by the plaintive drone of cicadas. The sound reminded Caleb of Elizabeth's harping.

Yawning, Joseph stuck a tousled head through the canvas opening. "Are we in Fort Worth?"

"We'll have to spend another night in the open," Elizabeth said.

Joseph gave a tired cheer.

By the time Caleb reached Elizabeth's side of the wagon, she was already trying to climb down. She brushed away his attempt to assist her. Exasperated, he grabbed her by the waist anyway and set her on the ground.

"What about me?" Joseph trembled at the distance to the ground.

Caleb smiled and stretched his arms up. "Come on, jump!"

"I c-can't!"

"Sure you can. I'll catch you."

Joseph drew a deep breath. He closed his eyes, thrust his arms out behind him, and pushed off. Caleb braced his feet and caught the small body against his chest. Giggling, Joseph squirmed with delight, and Caleb pulled him closer. He laughed from the sheer pleasure of hearing Joseph's uninhibited enthusiasm and whirled the boy in a circle.

Joseph threw his head back and spread his arms out wide. "Whee! Keep going! Keep going!"

Breathless, Caleb slowed to a stop. "Let me catch my —"

He caught a glimpse of joy in Elizabeth's eyes before she frowned and gave them a stern look. Caleb eased Joseph down until the boy's feet touched ground. "We have to make camp."

"Aw —"

"Joseph, please keep a wholesome tongue," Elizabeth said. "Mr. Martin is right. We have a lot to do before we can eat. You and I will gather firewood."

"Can't I go with you, Caleb? Please?"

"Joseph . . ."

"But I want to go with —"

"Come with me, Joseph. *Now.*"

Caleb gritted his teeth. He could see Phineas leading the team to the river. "Go help Mr. Grimes, Joseph. Elizabeth and I need to talk."

"No, Joseph. Come with me to gather firewood."

Caleb turned, mad enough to throttle her. "Joseph, go help Mr. Grimes," he repeated evenly. "You can gather firewood while you do."

Elizabeth's eyebrows raised. "But —"

Caleb's expression hardened.

Elizabeth blinked. "Joseph, do as Mr. Martin says. He and I *do* need to talk."

Grinning at the promise of adventure, Joseph skipped down the path to the river. Caleb watched until the boy had caught up with Phineas, then turned. "You're not a fit guardian for that child. You spoil his every opportunity for fun."

"Fun?" Her face flushed. "If you have your way, Joseph will turn into a slacker who's never interested in an honest day's work! I'm preparing him for a lifetime of obedience and servitude."

"Obedience and servitude to who? You? Or maybe you mean the God of that cross you wear around your neck. I've been wondering how that hideous thing made it through the wreck, but now I know. Like Joseph, it was probably too scared to fall apart!"

She covered the cross with her hand. "It did fall apart," she whispered. "I salvaged the leather and found new sticks to make another one."

"Why bother? The stage wreck was probably God's way of getting rid of that ugly thing. All those people probably died just so God could tear those cheap sticks from around your neck!"

Her eyes misted. "God wouldn't do such a thing."

Caleb groaned inwardly, feeling guilty. After all, the grackle *had* saved his life. He closed his hands around her upper arms and softened his voice. "Look, I —"

Flinching, she drew back. He dropped his hands, annoyed at her skittishness. "Just let up on Joseph. He's a good kid and deserves to have some fun."

Elizabeth squared her shoulders. "The

Bible says that by correcting a child, you save his soul from hell."

"But doesn't the Bible also say the Lord has compassion on those who fear him, just as a father has compassion on his children? I've never seen you even give Joseph a hug or a kiss!"

She hesitated. "Love was often in short supply around my home. My father believed in discipline and obedience."

"What do you want from Joseph — fear?"

"The fear of the Lord is the beginning of wisdom."

The Bible quoting was exasperating. "Do you want Joseph to fear *you?*"

Elizabeth looked surprised. "Do you think he's scared of me?"

"Sometimes. There's a difference between the fear of God the Bible talks about and fright."

"I never figured you for a Bible quoter, Mr. Martin."

"There's quite a few things about me you haven't figured." He crossed his arms. "Not that you're entitled to know, even if you are supposed to be my wife."

She blushed. "Why did you tell Mr. Grimes that lie?"

"You must have seen the buffalo hunters in Fort Griffin. They're not usually honorable men. If Grimes believes we're married, he's less likely to bother you. Besides, what do you suppose he'd think about an unmarried woman traveling with a man?"

A rare smile curved her lips. "You're actually concerned about my reputation."

"I'm concerned about the reputation of any lady." He paused, more curious than he was willing to admit. "Was it true, what you told Phineas about your father sheltering Joseph?"

She raised her chin and clasped her hands. "Yes. He was taken in as a newborn. His parents died, and he was left on my father's doorstep."

"You don't act like you know him very well. Didn't you help care for him?"

"My father and Helga . . . my stepmother . . . never thought I was capable."

"*Capable?* How old were you?"

"Fourteen," she said softly.

Caleb remembered how flighty his sister, Samantha, had been at that age. His parents might not have trusted her with an adopted baby either. "What happened to your ma?"

"She died several years before Joseph came." Elizabeth drew in a deep breath. "Father married Helga to care for Joseph. She had recently lost her husband and child. She died a few months before Father, so now there's only Joseph and me."

"I guess you don't have any brothers or sisters," he said casually.

She smiled. "I have one brother, Noah. He's ten years older and lives in Colorado." The smile faded. "I . . . I had an older sister, May, but she died with my mother."

Caleb glanced at Elizabeth's profile, wondering what memories she held. Had she liked her stepmother, or had she resented the intrusion of a new woman in her father's life? And what about Joseph? Maybe she'd resented his unexpected presence too.

Noah Cameron hadn't told Caleb nearly enough about his sister. "Why are you and Joseph going to Belton?" he said, pressing.

"We're joining the Sanctificationists. They're a group of women committed to economic independence from men. The leader, Mrs. McWhirter, doesn't see any sense in obeying a drunken husband or any other male."

Caleb only half-succeeded in smothering a laugh. "These women have a pretty fancy name for such a stern belief."

"They're sanctified — set apart for God's use."

"And that's how you want to live? How you want Joseph to live?"

"Yes."

At that, any compassion Caleb had felt fell away. She might be satisfied to live with a group of man-hating biddies who disguised their beliefs as religious piety, but Joseph wouldn't. Especially as he grew older. The boy already had enough strikes against him. Did she want him to be ashamed of his Indian heritage *and* his masculinity?

"This lie we told Phineas is for your own good," he said brusquely. "So try to show a little love for the kid, like he's really ours. If not for Joseph's sake, then your own."

He turned and stalked off before he had to listen to one more Bible verse.

After a dinner of possums Phineas had hunted, Elizabeth took the dirty plates and Joseph down to the river for washing. Later when she laid out Joseph's blanket for sleep, Caleb spread his alongside. Joseph chattered away, and Elizabeth frowned. Caleb Martin had somehow worked his way into their lives — at least until Fort Worth — like a cocklebur under a saddle.

"Ouch!" She stepped on a rock and sank to the ground.

Caleb hunkered down beside her. "Your foot all right, Bess?"

Elizabeth glanced at Phineas, fast asleep

on the other side of the fire. "Fine, Mr. Martin. And why on earth do you persist in calling me by that awful name?"

"It makes you seem more human."

Joseph giggled. Elizabeth tried to silence him with a look but knew he was unable to see her face in the darkness. "Joseph, lie down on your blanket now."

His laughter died. "Yes ma'am."

Elizabeth rose to spread her own blanket, but found her way blocked by Caleb. She tried to brush past him, but he stepped in front of her. She tried the other direction, but he blocked it also. Frustrated, she sighed loudly. "What do you want from me, Mr. Martin?"

He folded his arms across his chest. "An honest answer. You don't take teasing. You don't take compliments. What *do* you take well?"

"I take my time getting to know strangers. Now may I please go to sleep?"

He grinned, then stepped aside. "Certainly."

Elizabeth snapped open her blanket and spread it beside Joseph's. Caleb returned to his bedroll, removed his boots, and lay down, hands over his stomach.

"Do you want to say prayers with us, Mr. Martin?" Joseph asked hopefully.

Elizabeth gritted her teeth and pretended not to hear. Caleb sat up. "I'd be honored. If Elizabeth doesn't mind."

"Prayer is open to everyone," she said.

"You go first, Elizabeth. You know the biggest words," Joseph said.

"Very well." She closed her eyes. "Father —"

"Can we hold hands?" Joseph whispered.

Elizabeth's mouth went dry. "I . . ."

"That's what my family always did," Caleb said, extending a hand. Joseph grabbed it and Elizabeth's, then bowed his head.

"Elizabeth?"

She stared at Caleb's outstretched hand. His palm looked strong and secure, and he curved his fingers, beckoning.

If not for Joseph's sake, then your own, his words returned to her.

She hesitantly placed her hand in his, then squeezed her eyes tightly shut. "Father, thank you for guiding us safely through another day. You truly are the protector of your children, and he that walks in a perfect way shall serve you."

"Bless Mr. Grimes — and thank you for sending him to give us a ride!" Joseph chimed in. "Bless Elizabeth, an' Mr. Martin, an' me, God. Bless the oxen, and the poor possums we ate for dinner tonight. If they're in heaven, tell them we're sorry, but we were awful hungry!"

Elizabeth started to conclude the prayer, but Joseph whispered loudly, "Mr. Martin, don't you want to talk to God?"

"Uh, no, Joseph. Not tonight."

After she finished the prayer, Joseph yawned and flopped down on his blanket. "G'night, Mr. Martin. G'night, Elizabeth."

"Good night, Joseph." She smoothed his hair, then lay down beside him. She surreptitiously watched as Caleb lay back and closed his eyes. His face softened, losing the serious expression he normally wore. She could see the gentle rise and fall of his chest, and she remembered how he'd held her against him when the stagecoach horses got spooked.

She squeezed her eyes shut tight, fear washing over her in a wave. Why was she allowing such thoughts to contaminate her mind? She certainly didn't have any room in her life for a man — much less one as irritating as Caleb Martin! She shivered and involuntarily scooted to the farthest edge of her blanket.

"Elizabeth!" Joseph moaned, rolling over.

"Go to sleep."

"I'm c-cold."

Startled, she opened her eyes. Joseph had managed to tangle himself in his blanket and now lay with his arms wrapped around his body for warmth.

"Poor Joseph," she murmured, gently disengaging the shivering child. She pulled him onto her blanket and covered him with the other. Instantly, he pressed up against her, molding his back against her front.

Elizabeth instinctively curled around him, shielding him with her warmth. He sighed, burrowing closer, and soon relaxed.

She watched him sleep, listening to his childish snoring. He hardly seemed like the child of Eyes Like the Sun. He was all trust and innocence. Would he eventually inherit his father's hatred and violence?

Swallowing hard, Elizabeth tentatively laid an arm across Joseph's waist. Eyes Like the Sun probably wasn't even still alive, she reminded herself. She would keep him from his father's heritage of hatred. She and Joseph would be safe in Belton, hidden along with the terrible truth they shared.

She glanced over at Caleb, who slept soundly, and gently rubbed her chin across Joseph's thick hair. Relishing the feel of its silkiness against her throat, she tucked him closer against her heart.

Four

Elizabeth stood in front of the mirror and held the ready-made dress against her body. Sighing, she refolded it to its original creases. Blue was unsuitable, and the collar was too low. She knew better than to hope for a dress that met her needs.

Once they'd reached Fort Worth and said good-bye to Phineas, Caleb Martin steered her to the hotel selling stage tickets and immediately announced to the clerk that he needed three to Belton.

She drew him aside, her patience with his overprotectiveness wearing thin. "We'll go to a church. They'll take care of Joseph and me. It wouldn't be proper for us to continue to depend on you. Romans 13:8 clearly says to owe nothing to anyone."

His face darkened. "I'm the one owing. You saved my life —"

"Anyone would have."

"— and took care of me. I insist on buying your tickets."

Elizabeth snapped her mouth shut. She was tired of arguing with this disagreeable man. "Very well. Thank you. We shall pay you back in Belton."

"And I insist on buying you and Joseph new clothes."

"Now *really*, Mr. Martin."

"Look at yourself. That black outfit was ugly to begin with, but it's torn and muddy now."

Elizabeth's face flushed. "Please, Mr. Martin, lower your voice."

"And would you stop calling me Mr. Martin? It's either Caleb or Martin. No *mister*. You'd think a woman who'd undressed a man would have the gumption to call him by his first name."

"*Please* lower your voice!"

Caleb folded his arms across his chest. "Only if you'll head over to that dry goods store and see if they have something you can wear."

Humoring him seemed the lesser of two evils. "Very well, Mr. — Caleb," she said, turning on her heel.

She rifled through the few other dresses the store had for sale. Yellow, another blue, pink . . . didn't they sell black? Ah! Brown. That would suffice until she got to Belton. She eagerly unfolded the dress and held it up. The collar even stood high enough to nearly brush her chin.

The shopkeeper's wife ambled over, studying the dress with a critical eye. "Your man said you all are leaving on the next stage. That's about fifteen minutes from now."

Elizabeth cringed at the idea of being linked to Caleb. "Do you have a changing room?"

"Through that curtain to the office back there." The woman laid several yards of white material in Elizabeth's arms. "Your man said you'd probably need these too."

Elizabeth scurried through the curtain. Her man, indeed!

She undressed and slipped the new petticoats over her head. They swirled past her hips, and she blushed again to think that Caleb had chosen them for her.

The bell on the front door tinkled. "Elizabeth Cameron!" Caleb boomed.

"Elizabeth!" Joseph echoed happily.

She hastily fastened the last dress button, then adjusted the cross on its leather string.

"Elizabeth!"

She sighed. She'd hoped to pin up her hair, but the ribbon she'd chosen earlier would have to do. Perhaps that would do something to improve her bedraggled hair.

Her cheeks warmed. Who was she trying to impress?

"E-liz-a-beth!"

She shoved the curtain aside. "I just had to change clothes."

Caleb leaned against the counter. Standing beside him, Joseph cheerfully licked a lollipop.

Caleb frowned. "Why'd you get a brown dress? I was hoping you'd get a color more —" he broke off and turned. "Throw in that brush and comb there too."

"Yes sir!" The shopkeeper retrieved a silver-backed set from its shelf display and proudly presented the pair to Elizabeth. "Do you like them?"

Awestruck, Elizabeth accepted the shiny brush and comb. "They're beautiful. I never had anything but wood." She raised her eyes to meet Caleb's. He was studying her so intently, she could barely find her voice. "Thank you."

He shifted uneasily. "It's not as nice as you think. My sister had a set like that — the silver tarnishes if you don't clean it."

She smoothed her fingers down the scrolled back of the brush, then across the stiff bristles. "It doesn't matter. The set is lovely."

The woman held up a carpetbag. "How

do you like this, dearie?"

Elizabeth ran her fingers over the brilliant multihued tapestry. Father had always disdained color as frivolity. "It's lovely too," she murmured.

The woman pushed it across the counter. "Open it. It's yours."

Elizabeth glanced up with shock. "This beautiful bag?"

Joseph danced beside her. "Open it, Elizabeth! See what's inside!"

She glanced at Caleb, who nodded. "Go on, Bess. We have to hurry or we'll miss the stage."

Flustered, she fumbled with the leather strap. Inside the bag were replacements for everything she'd lost in the Brazos River, from a soft white nightgown to a toothbrush and hairpins. Everything was new and clean, including the black Bible with gilt-edged pages.

Her eyes misted, and she stared up at Caleb. He cleared his throat. "Joseph insisted on the Bible."

Joseph tugged at her sleeve and pointed at himself. "Caleb bought my clothes too."

She stepped back to examine him. "Why, new trousers, shirt . . ." She was humbled by Caleb's benevolence, yet mindful of what she'd always been taught. "It's very generous of you, but we can't accept all these things. A dress is one thing, but this is too much, Caleb."

"You and Joseph can't go wearing ragged clothes to your new home." His smile deepened under his sparkling blue eyes.

Elizabeth's breathing quickened. "I don't know. I —"

Joseph laid his wet lollipop on the counter and reached into the bag. Before Elizabeth could reprimand him, he pulled out a corset she'd missed. He spread it in front of him like an accordion. "Hey! What's this?"

Elizabeth dropped her gaze to the floor, wishing she could sink beneath the planks. Even Caleb glanced away, suddenly finding interest in the far end of the counter. The shop woman grinned.

"Well? What is it?"

The woman laughed. "It's a corset."

"A *what?* What's it for?"

Elizabeth turned to shush him, but the grinning shopkeeper tucked the garment back in the bag. "All proper ladies wear one, son."

Joseph made a face. "But it's so stiff! Do they wear it around their head when they have a headache?"

The woman laughed until her face turned red.

"I thought you might need a new one," Caleb mumbled to Elizabeth.

"I . . . I don't . . ." She closed her mouth to prevent any further humiliation. She'd never worn a corset in her life. When she'd turned old enough, her father forbade her to wear what he called the trappings of Jezebel.

"I'll not have you displaying your form like a harlot," he thundered, pacing heavily.

"But, Papa . . ."

His face darkened. "To you, my name is *Father*."

She lowered her eyes and clasped her hands. "All the girls my age wear one. And they're allowed to attend dances and . . ."

His heavy steps halted in front of her. The air grew warm — deadly calm like the quiet before a twister. Flexing his bony fingers, he clasped his hands behind his back. Without looking up, Elizabeth knew his cold blue eyes had pinned her, judged her, and once again found her guilty. An icy shiver of dread coursed down her spine. Forcing herself not to quiver, she waited in silent terror like a condemned man before execution.

"Have you forgotten that I can forever remove that child from your presence?"

His words struck fear in her soul, and she forced herself to cover any expression of emotion by biting the inside of her lip. "No,

Father, I haven't forgotten. I'm sorry for my disobedience."

But apologies had never been enough.

Caleb nudged her. "Elizabeth, what's wrong? You look pale."

She drew a shaky breath. Caleb might not be attracted to her, but he thought she was a lady. Her father had always shown her what a sinner he thought she was. "Your gifts are more than generous," she said. "I'll accept them on condition you let me pay you back."

He scowled. "You're not in debt to me."

"Then I can't —"

"All right, all right." He held up his hands in surrender. "When we get to Belton, you have to do something for me."

"S-something?" Her heart pounded. What kind of payment would a man like Caleb Martin expect?

He grinned. "You and Joseph have to take me on a picnic."

"Oh, boy! Can we sit on the ground and everything?" Joseph said.

Caleb laughed. "Of course, Joe. After we eat, we'll toss a ball, hunt for frogs . . . whatever you want to do. That is, if Elizabeth agrees."

Flustered, she lowered her gaze and saw his holstered new gun, its walnut grip gleaming. His blue eyes locked with hers, and he smiled lazily. He seemed so certain she'd say yes. Was his generosity really a calculated manipulation?

Elizabeth studied him dubiously. She would pay the debt she owed, but she would be careful. Very careful. She raised her chin. "We'll go on the picnic."

"Hooray!" Joseph nearly upset a display of apples, but the cheerful shop woman merely handed him one to eat.

Caleb smiled at Elizabeth, then reached into his pocket. She watched as he handed over the coins, and her stomach sank with fear that she was acquiring a debt with unspecified terms.

They were the only passengers on the stage trip to Belton. The limitless plain of North Texas changed to gentle grassy hills carpeted with young bluebonnets and red-tipped Indian paintbrush. Elizabeth took no joy in their color, preferring to keep her eyes on Caleb and Joseph. Her mind was preoccupied.

The boy laughed with childish glee. "Tell me another story!"

Elizabeth chewed on her lower lip, eyes darting between the spellbound boy and the smiling man. Could she relate as well with

Joseph as Caleb did? Could she be her son's spiritual leader? The prospect of a misstep was frightening. Suppose she was too lenient or didn't talk about God enough. Or talked about him *too* much and drove Joseph away.

She loved the perfect shape of his small mouth and how his brown eyes widened with suspense or lit up with excitement. His face was so expressive, so translucent. How could anyone reveal so much with just a curve of the mouth and a flash of the eyes? Joseph's innocence stirred the embers of a maternal fire she didn't know she possessed. She wanted to pull him onto her lap and smother him with hugs and kisses — five years of affection Father had forbidden her to give.

She forced a deep breath. She was growing to care too deeply for this child who symbolized the fear she'd endured well before his conception. Sometimes when she looked into his eyes, she could see the reflection of her own terror. Other times she could see the features of Eyes Like the Sun in Joseph's small face.

Leaving Joseph occupied with a wooden soldier purchased in Fort Worth, Caleb scooted over beside her. She sucked in her breath at his nearness. The coach suddenly seemed warm and confining.

He studied her a moment, then leaned closer. His blue eyes held her spellbound, and blood rushed in her ears. Caleb's face, so close to hers, looked somber. "What are you thinking about when you're so quiet, Elizabeth Cameron?"

Fear swept through her like prairie wildfire. Those hypnotic eyes were so lulling, so alluring. The serpent in the Garden of Eden must have looked at Eve exactly the same way.

She wanted to call Joseph, to draw attention away from herself, but she was frozen with panic. With great effort, she drew a deep breath and inched away. "I'm quiet because I strive for peace and silence. Saint Peter admonishes women that God admires a meek and quiet spirit."

Caleb laughed. "Your Sanctifi-what's-it ladies don't sound like they share your goal. I've yet to meet a man-hater who was meek and quiet."

"Man-haters?" Indignation unseated sorrow and terror. "Do you think the Sanctificationists are a bunch of rolling-pin-thumping wives and pinched-face spinsters?"

"Those are your words, Bess. Not mine."

"Well, I —" She folded her arms in front

of her breasts. What in the world possessed her to even dream of unburdening her heart to such a cad? To him, she was obviously just another shriveled old maid.

"Ah, come on, Bess. Don't sit there like a puffed-up toad."

She struggled to retain her composure. "You've already compared me to a grackle — now a toad? Thank heavens we're going our separate ways soon. I only hope Belton is large enough so that I don't even have to pass you on the street!"

"That's more like it." He grinned. "You're much more interesting when you show some spunk instead of that saintly reserve. And no matter how large the streets of Belton, I intend to claim my promise from you, Miss Bess."

"Do you want a picnic or just another opportunity to aggravate me?"

"Both."

Joseph plopped down between them. "I want a picnic! Can we go today?"

Caleb grinned. "I wish we could, but we have to get you and Elizabeth settled in your new home. Then I'll come calling."

Elizabeth's stomach knotted. *Come calling?* He made it sound as if he planned to be her beau!

"Aren't you gonna stay with us?"

"I'll be close by, Joe. You can count on that."

The driver blew the bugle to announce the stage's arrival. Nervousness crept into Elizabeth's stomach, and the doubts she'd carefully squelched in Fort Griffin rose full force. She wanted to be accepted, to leave the past behind her. But she didn't know the Sanctificationists — they were strangers, after all. Suppose these godly women sized her and Joseph up for who they really were? Suppose they placed the same judgment on her that she'd always seemed to face, the judgment her father placed on her? The Sanctificationists were her last hope, her refuge from the world. Her refuge from men.

"The husband is the head of the wife, Elizabeth," her father had said. "She must be his servant and obey his commands. And it is his responsibility to answer to God for her. You'll never have a husband, but I want you to understand what marriage means."

Elizabeth clutched her bag tighter, but it slipped through her fingers. She bent to retrieve it and almost bumped heads with Caleb. "Here." He handed her the bag then studied her. "You're white as a sheet. Don't tell me you're nervous about meeting your Sancti-fanatics."

"I'm not nervous. It's just been a long trip."

Caleb's expression sobered. "Yes, it has. When you say your prayers tonight, be sure to thank God for me that the three of us made it."

"You should thank him yourself."

The coach rocked to a halt before he could answer. Someone opened the door, and Caleb got out first. He held up his arms for Joseph, who jumped without hesitation. Caleb set him in the dusty street, then reached up for Elizabeth, swung her down, and turned to claim their bag.

Unsettled, she straightened the sleeves of her dress. The stage had stopped in the middle of a busy main street. Bold signs announced a pharmacy and bookstore with a law office upstairs. Saddles and harnesses, buggies, surreys, phaetons, and a carriage repository were housed in buildings painted with the name A. D. Potts. Several wagons and horses stood outside a large hardware store, a printing office, and a post office.

Elizabeth drew a deep breath, satisfied. The town seemed respectable enough. "Well, Joseph. We're finally here."

"Yes ma'am." He edged closer, fumbling frantically for her hand.

"Why, whatever is the —"

Two older boys on the boardwalk laughed loudly. "Look at the Injun who thinks he's like us! Where's your moccasins, kid? Where's your bow and arrows?"

Heavenly Father, so soon? "Just ignore them, Joseph."

He pressed against her, trying to hide behind her skirt. "All right," he whispered.

"Whoo, whoo, whoo! Look at us make a rain dance!"

A small crowd had gathered and watched, bemused. Elizabeth cringed. She bowed her head. "Father, forgive them," she whispered. "They only know what they've been taught."

She raised her head and saw one boy pull back on a loaded slingshot. She quickly knelt to cover Joseph and held out a hand in a gesture of peace. "If you'll just —"

The rock grazed the back of her hand, and blood trickled down her wrist. She stared at the wound, stunned. The boys couldn't be much older than ten. She and Joseph had encountered taunting before, but never physical violence.

"Leave her alone!" Joseph clutched her around the waist, sobbing.

"Hey!" Caleb bounded toward the boardwalk, and the boys started running. "Stop right there!"

The crowd clustered closer, swelling in size, and the boys panted to a halt. The younger ducked his head, but the older put on a brave face as Caleb reached them. "W-we didn't mean nothin', mister."

Caleb grabbed them each by an ear. Ignoring their yelps of pain, he led the boys from the boardwalk and all but dumped them at Elizabeth's feet. "Now apologize to the lady!"

The boys rose from the dirt, clutching reddened ears. The younger's freckled face was streaked with tears, and a torn overall strap hung off his bare, bony shoulder. The older looked as though his hair hadn't seen a comb in days, and a skinned knee peeked through a threadbare patch on his trousers. He sniffled loudly.

Elizabeth's heart went out to them both. "They're only boys."

"They're still responsible for their actions." Caleb grabbed the slingshot out of the older boy's hands and poked him in the back. "You were the shooter, son. You go first."

"Ow!" The boy rubbed his back. He glared at Caleb, but one hard look made him turn to Elizabeth. "Sorry, lady," he mumbled.

Caleb prodded him again, more gently

this time. "Apologize to the boy too. His name is Joseph, and he'll be living in this town, so you might as well make friends. Joseph, come out here."

Joseph peered around the protection of Elizabeth.

The older boy scuffed a bare foot in the dirt road. "I'm sorry I tried to hit you," he muttered.

The younger glanced at Caleb, then Elizabeth and Joseph. He gulped. "I'm sorry too."

"That was fine, boys," Caleb said. "Now let's go find your fathers so you can tell them what you did."

The boys glanced at each other, then down at the dirt. The crowd, which had been silent before, suddenly buzzed with speculation.

"Ain't it enough they apologized?"

"He *is* only an Indian kid. And the lady ain't hurt bad."

Caleb's face hardened, and he circled the crowd. "Whose kids are these?"

No one stepped forward. Most people either shuffled their feet or looked away.

"I asked who these kids belong to."

More feet shuffling. Finally a thin man with a bushy mustache stepped out hesitantly. "The oldest one's Hez Taylor's. The younger belongs to Matthew Quimby."

"Where can I find Mr. Taylor and Mr. Quimby?"

"Most likely at the Big Nan Za saloon."

Elizabeth fought rising dread. "These boys will get into a lot of trouble. Please let it go."

Caleb shook his head. "They could have seriously hurt someone. Their fathers need to know so they can be disciplined."

The older boy bit his lip as if to keep from crying, and silent tears poured down the younger one's face. Elizabeth knew that look of fear. "*Please* let them go. I'm all right. Joseph's all right."

Caleb set his jaw. "Come on, boys, which way to the saloon?"

The Taylor boy pointed down the street. "Th-that way. But please, sir. Don't bother my pa. He'll probably be playing cards."

Caleb steered the boys down the street. "I'm sure he can take time from his busy day to have a talk with his son."

Elizabeth grabbed her carpetbag. Wide-eyed, Joseph slipped his hand into hers.

Outside the saloon, Caleb set the boys to the side of the swinging doors. "You boys wait here, and I'll bring your fathers out."

"*Please*, mister!" The Quimby boy's blue eyes teared again.

"Sorry, son. You should have thought of the punishment before you committed the crime." Caleb disappeared into the smoky haze of the saloon.

Elizabeth heard laughter and the clink of glasses, then silence. She heard low voices, followed by a loud curse and the scraping of chairs. The swinging doors pushed outward, and a large, unkempt man in torn trousers and a ragged Confederate shirt staggered out.

"Edward Taylor!" he thundered, reeling. "What d'ya mean by interruptin' my mornin'?"

The older boy pulled back, eyes wide. "I didn't mean anything, Pa. It . . . it was an accident."

Elizabeth inched forward, shadowed by Joseph. "It was a misunderstanding, sir. Your boy —"

The man wheeled on her, and his rheumy eyes narrowed in a gaze that raked her up and down. He grinned. "Well, now. Whadda we have here? The new schoolmarm?"

Elizabeth froze. Caleb ambled across the porch, but she could sense his wariness. "Leave her be, Taylor. You deal with your boy. When Quimby sobers up, he can deal with his."

Hez Taylor turned. "Unless she's your wife, mister, I can look all I want. And even then, I reckon it don't matter. A woman's only good for cookin' and —"

Elizabeth closed her eyes against the degrading words.

The Quimby boy glanced around nervously, then took off in a run. Edward Taylor moved closer to Elizabeth, trembling. She stretched out an arm, and he moved under her protection without shifting his eyes from his father.

Deadly calm, Caleb straightened. He slowly flexed his fingers, his eyes a hard blue. Elizabeth had never seen anger displayed so silently.

"Apologize to the lady."

Taylor drunkenly ignored the warning in Caleb's voice and merely grinned like a boy in a schoolyard fight. "I ain't apologizin' to no stuck-up, tight-laced schoolmarm type."

"Apologize, Taylor."

The grin slid from the drunken man's face, and his eyes hardened. "Fine, mister." He feinted toward Elizabeth, then dropped low, fumbling for a knife in his boot.

Instantly Caleb stomped his boot heel on Taylor's instep and grabbed his wrist, twisting. Yelping, Taylor dropped the knife.

He lunged for Caleb, and they crashed to the porch.

Taylor hooked Caleb around the throat. He stretched for the knife, but Caleb elbowed him in the gut and kneed him under the chin. Taylor howled with pain. Caleb kicked the knife, and it clattered across the porch and into the grass.

Face red with rage, Taylor rammed a fist into Caleb's stomach. Caleb reeled backward.

Taylor spied Elizabeth cowering and lunged toward her. In one liquid motion, Caleb drew his gun and pressed it against Taylor's head. The hammer clicked back.

Taylor's eyes widened. "Please, mister!" he choked out.

"Apologize."

Aghast, Elizabeth pressed a sobbing Edward and Joseph against her. She trembled, her knees so weak she could barely stand. Her stomach rolled in heated waves, and she thought she might be sick right there on the porch.

Taylor gasped for air. "I . . . I'm sorry!"

Caleb uncocked his gun and shoved Taylor away. The wheezing man reeled to the edge of the porch and retched over the side.

"Pa!" Edward rushed to his father.

Taylor rose unsteadily, wiping his mouth with the back of his shaking hand. When he saw Edward, he whipped off his belt. Edward cowered, glancing wildly for an escape.

"Don't *ever* bring such trouble on me again, boy. Now git home!" He flicked the belt against the boy's legs, and Edward cried out in pain, then scrambled off the porch. With a murderous glance at Caleb, Taylor followed his son in close pursuit.

Trembling, Elizabeth raced down the porch steps and shouted, "Don't hurt that boy!"

Caleb grabbed her in a hard embrace. "It's none of your business. Edward's his son."

She struggled against him. She felt with all certainty that Hez Taylor was going to beat his boy as her own father had beaten her — she knew that look in Hez's eyes all too well. "Let go!"

"Don't interfere, Bess." Caleb tightened his arms, and Elizabeth shivered at the tone of his voice.

Her stomach lurched, and panic rose, overwhelming and strangling. She pushed against him. "Please, let me go!" she whispered hoarsely.

"Calm down, Elizabeth. He's gone."

"Let go!" Fear fired a path to her

pounding head, and without thinking, she sank her heel into his shin. Cursing, Caleb released her so suddenly she tumbled to the dirt.

Elizabeth scrambled away, then collapsed in a heap. Feeling dizzy, she doubled over, shaking.

"Elizabeth!" Joseph flew off the porch and wrapped his thin arms around her.

"J-Joseph!" She weakly opened her arms and gathered him against her. The feel of his soft, wet cheek calmed her panic, and she buried her face in his hair. Oh, Joseph. Precious, sweet Joseph.

They rocked back and forth, silently sharing their mutual fear. She wanted to reassure him over and over that she'd never leave him. That she'd never let anyone like Hez Taylor, Caleb Martin, or Eyes Like the Sun touch a hair on his head.

"It's all right now. He's gone." Caleb knelt beside them.

She shrank back, clutching Joseph. "G-go away!"

"I was just protecting you, Bess," Caleb said in a low voice. "He was going after you with that knife."

She saw that Caleb had already replaced the deadly revolver at his hip, and a shiver of fear ran through her. "Leave us alone.

Joseph and I will find our way to the Sanctificationists."

"I'll hire a buggy and give you a ride."

"No! Just . . . *go!*"

Caleb looked from her to a silent Joseph. He rose, sighing. "If that's the way you want it."

Elizabeth watched as he strode down the street. She held Joseph tightly against her, savoring the contact. For five years she'd waited to touch him like this. She wanted to hold him close all day, but they had to find their home. They had to find safety.

Five

Joseph insisted on holding her hand all the way to Martha McWhirter's house, pressing against her whenever they passed someone on the street. Fortunately, no one did more than smile politely or tip a hat. Perhaps the saloon incident had preceded their presence.

Joseph tugged on her hand. "How much farther, Elizabeth?"

"Two streets over."

His small brown face screwed up with worry. "Are you sure we can live there?"

"Mrs. McWhirter said she'd take us in if I would keep house for her."

"Will she take me?" Joseph lowered his head.

"Why, of course she will!"

Joseph fell silent again as they continued down the dusty street. "What about Caleb? We'll see him again, won't we?"

She halted abruptly. "We most certainly will not. You don't have to worry about that."

"But he looked so sad. Almost as sad as you. He really looked sorry, Elizabeth."

"Sorry or not doesn't change what happened."

"But maybe if we —"

"No. I should have trusted my first instincts."

She had been right all along; he was a violent man. Had she saved his life from the Brazos only to turn him loose with that gun on the rest of the world? What a difference between the gentle patience he'd shown with Joseph and his brutal manhandling of Hez Taylor.

She shivered. Caleb's blue eyes were just as deceptive as she'd suspected when she first saw him on the stagecoach.

They turned into the yard of a white limestone house. Elizabeth halfheartedly smoothed her hair, wishing it were pinned up so she didn't look so young. Joseph straightened at her side and even spit on his hand to slick down his hair.

They knocked on the door and waited a few minutes until a girl in a work dress and apron peeked out the door. "Yes?"

"I'm Elizabeth Cameron, and this is Joseph. Mrs. McWhirter is expecting us."

"Mrs. McWhirter didn't say anything about anyone calling today."

Elizabeth shifted the bag in her hands. "I wrote her several months ago. She said that I could work for her in exchange for room and board. We've come to join the Sanctificationists."

"Who is it, Molly?" An older woman appeared at the door.

The girl stepped back. "This is Elizabeth Cameron, ma'am. She says you're expecting her. She says she's here to work for you." The girl's face inexplicably clouded.

"Miss Cameron!" Mrs. McWhirter held out a hand. "I remember your letter. Something about your father dying?"

"Yes ma'am. I've wanted to come here for a long time, but it wasn't until he passed away that I had not only the freedom but the necessity of finding a new home."

Mrs. McWhirter smiled warmly. "Here I have you standing outside. Please come in. It's a pleasure to meet you. And who might this young man be?"

"This is Joseph. He was an orphan left in my father's care."

"And now he's in yours," Martha finished. "Both of you, please step this way. Molly, take the young woman's bag and fetch some water please. They look like they've had a long travel."

As she followed Martha inside, Elizabeth

studied the spiritual leader of the Sanctificationists. Martha wore a plain gray dress and apron with several pages of what appeared to be scripture tucked in the bib. She had a serious but kind face and looked more like a housewife than a preacher. Her only imposing feature was her red hair.

Martha settled herself in a ladder-back chair. "I believe in being direct, Miss Cameron. I usually have several boarders, and I had an empty bedroom when I received your letter. However, I took in Molly three weeks ago when her parents died of the grippe. Unfortunately, that means I no longer have any room for you and Joseph."

Elizabeth's heart sank. Had they come all this way for nothing? She didn't have a nickel to her name. Everything she owned was a gift from Caleb, the man she'd promised Joseph they'd never have to see again. What would she do now?

Mrs. McWhirter laughed gently. "Don't look so downcast. I have another place for you. Anna Mannheim's been blind from birth, and her husband died several years ago. She was fine for a time by herself, but now she's nearly completely bedridden from advanced arthritis. She's a cheerful woman who truly loves the Lord." She paused. "Can you care for an ailing woman?"

"Elizabeth is like a doctor," Joseph said proudly. "She saved Caleb's life!"

"Joseph," Elizabeth murmured.

"Who is Caleb?" Martha asked blandly.

"He's the man we met. He bought our clothes!"

"We were in an unfortunate stage accident, and he was kind enough to replace our ruined clothing," Elizabeth said hastily.

Martha raised her eyebrows. "I hope you're not planning to continue a relationship with this man."

"Oh, no ma'am!"

"Good. We believe we must abandon everything to do with the flesh and live for the church. That is why we have chosen to separate ourselves, as far as possible, from the world." She lowered her voice. "And since you're not married, our celibate practices will not interrupt your life."

Elizabeth flushed under her collar. "No, of course not."

Molly bustled into the room, water glasses in hand. "Here you are, miss. Little boy."

While they drank, Martha braced her hands against her thighs in a gesture of finality. "So. What you must do is go to Anna's farm. Tell her I sent you to help out.

I've prayed for someone to come, and here you are."

Doubts poked through Elizabeth's relief. What was this Anna like? Would she be stern and cruel? What would a feeble, blind woman think about an Indian boy living under her roof? Elizabeth hastily concealed the worry from her face. "I'm grateful Joseph and I are needed. We enjoy helping other people, and we'd be delighted to help Mrs. Mannheim."

"You'll join us for prayer meetings, of course. If you truly want to be part of our group, Elizabeth, you must pray for sanctification. I once dreamed of the Bible as a clock with a key. A voice said to take the key and wind it up. I've studied the Bible fervently since then."

Elizabeth felt shivers run down her arms. Here was someone who truly had the attention of God!

Martha smiled. "But we'll talk more about this later. Right now I have to get back to my biscuit making. Molly will show you the way out."

She retreated into the kitchen, leaving Elizabeth somewhat bewildered at the abrupt dismissal. "Thank you," Elizabeth called. "It was a pleasure to meet you."

She watched as Martha sank one hand

into biscuit dough. With the other hand, she pulled out the leaf of scripture tucked in her apron, studied it, then set it aside. Plunging both hands into the flour, she squeezed her eyes shut in deep concentration. She pressed a floury arm against her head as though to stem a terrible ache and swayed back and forth.

Elizabeth looked on, awestruck. Somehow the ordinary kitchen had become holy ground, a sacred place of worship. She felt that if she but stepped into the room, she would be blessed beyond measure. At last she had reached the place God intended her to be, under the power of a truly godly person. A woman. Not a man who wanted to control her like a horse with a bit in its mouth.

After sundown, Elizabeth and Joseph trudged beyond the giant oak Molly said was the final landmark to Anna Mannheim's farm. Blistered feet aching with each step, Elizabeth felt exhausted. She had carried a weary Joseph for the past hour, and he had long since fallen asleep.

With a prayer of thankfulness, she staggered down a narrow lane that had to be the Mannheim farm. A lamp glowed softly in the window. Gratefully grasping the handrail, Elizabeth pulled herself up the porch stairs of the two-story limestone house. Her knees buckled as she adjusted Joseph's weight and raised a weary hand to knock.

She heard the heavy clump of boots — a man's gait — and her heart beat faster. She'd thought Anna lived alone. Had she reached the wrong house? Frightened, she turned, but the door opened slowly. A short, middle-aged Mexican man with a thick mustache held a lantern high. He smiled at her and Joseph. "Sí?" he said in a soft voice.

Elizabeth cleared her throat. "I . . . I'm Elizabeth Cameron, and this is Joseph. Mrs. McWhirter sent us to . . . to Anna. Anna Mannheim." She sighed. "We must have taken a wrong road somewhere."

His smile widened. "No, no! This is Señora Anna's home. She's been expecting you." He gestured with the lantern, stepping back from the door. "Please. Come in, señora."

"Thank you, and it's señorita. I'm not married." Elizabeth stooped to lift the bag, but the man reached it first.

"I'll get that. You need to put the boy down; you look tired. Go up the stairs. The left room at the top is ready for you." He smiled proudly. "My wife, Marisa, washed the sheets just this morning. Señora Anna will be happy to meet you."

"May I meet her now?"

"She has already gone to sleep for the night, señorita. I think maybe you and the boy need to do the same."

Elizabeth hobbled up the flight of stairs carpeted in faded red. The man followed closely behind, his lantern casting a giant, wavering shadow of her and Joseph. She shivered and turned into the doorway on the left.

He followed her into the room, and she felt a moment's panic. She wasn't totally convinced she was in the right house; she still hadn't seen the mysterious Anna. She clutched Joseph like a shield, and the man's eyes met hers as he straightened from placing her bag on the bed. "Forgive me." He set the lamp down. "I will wait outside while you settle the boy."

Relieved, Elizabeth laid Joseph on the double bed. The head and footboard were a rich maple wood. Underneath a crazy quilt and crisp sheets, she felt a plump feather mattress.

She undressed Joseph down to his underwear, closing her eyes in appreciation for the soft mattress. She wished she could get ready for bed and curl up next to Joseph without another word, but sleep could come later. She tucked Joseph under the covers then picked up the lamp.

The man waited in the dark by the stairs. "I must ask your forgiveness for not introducing myself," he said. "I am Gustavo Orozco, a good friend of the señora. My family and I live up the road, and Marisa and I look in on her now that she can no longer get around so well."

Elizabeth relaxed. "That's very kind of you, Mr. Orozco. I look forward to meeting your wife and children. May I see where Mrs. Mannheim is in case she needs me during the night?"

Gustavo seemed pleased. "Follow me, *por favor*. She has been sleeping downstairs in a small room off the kitchen ever since the arthritis. First, she couldn't manage the stairs, then she couldn't even walk. She lies in bed all the time now. Marisa or I come to fire the stove and prepare her breakfast."

"How long has Mrs. Mannheim been like this?"

"Almost a year now," he said. "She has always been blind, but you would never have known by her enthusiasm for life. Her husband — the señor — strung a clothesline from the house to the barn so she could even do chores. Losing the use of her legs was bad enough, but now the doctor says her heart is weak." He bowed his head. "She is ready to be with the Lord, but Marisa and I are too selfish. We want her with us."

Elizabeth swallowed. She'd probably want to be with the Lord, too, if her physical condition were so poor. "Please take me to her. I'd like to check on her before I go to sleep." She stopped short at the bottom of the stairs. "Maybe she would prefer someone else to care for her."

Gustavo looked at her stick cross. "You're a believer, no?"

"I believe Jesus is Lord."

"Then you are the one the Father has sent. Why do you doubt? The señora said God told her someone was coming."

"Mrs. Mannheim must be a very old woman, Mr. Orozco. Sometimes older people think they hear from God when they're really hearing the longings of their own hearts."

Gustavo shook his head, the smile never disappearing. "No, señorita," he said gently. "Señora Anna is not like that. But you will see for yourself when you know her. For now, I will show you where she is, then I must go." He turned toward the kitchen.

Elizabeth shook her head, sighing. She was definitely going to have her hands full.

If she had anywhere else to go, she would probably grab Joseph and head back into the night. But the promise of the feather bed upstairs encouraged her. Surely she could humor an old woman and ease what might be her last days on earth. If Anna Mannheim wanted to believe God talked to people like a real father, Elizabeth could play along.

Passing through the kitchen, Elizabeth noticed an old cookstove and a handsome sideboard. She held the lamp high to avoid stumbling over a trestle table with four chairs. Gustavo gestured toward a small room off the kitchen.

Elizabeth entered cautiously, not quite certain what she would find. At first she didn't see anything at all, except a double bed and a hard chair on the far side. Only when she held the lamp closer did she see a small form huddled under a blanket, a long gray braid spilling over the edge.

She blinked. The woman was no bigger than a child. *This* was Gustavo's señora? Elizabeth moved to the side of the bed and held the light closer. Deep wrinkles lined the woman's forehead and sunken cheeks, yet her expression was calm and trusting, and her lips curved slightly upward. She had an old woman's wizened face combined with a child's carefree expression. Elizabeth had never seen anyone look so relaxed. "She must have great relief from the arthritis while she sleeps," she murmured.

"You mean her smile? Señora Anna always looks like that." Gustavo laughed softly and moved toward the doorway. "I will leave you now, señorita. Marisa and I will come in the morning to show you around."

"Good night, Mr. Orozco," she called, but the front door had already closed. Sighing, she looked at Mrs. Mannheim one more time. The old woman might appear happy, but she was still a person with a need.

Elizabeth knelt beside the bed. She carefully set the lamp on the floor and bowed her head. "Father, thank you for bringing Joseph and me here safely. Help me to help this woman."

Sleepy, she nodded, then jerked her head up. She was so tired, she could lay her cheek against the bed and fall asleep sitting on the floor.

Elizabeth lifted the lamp and trudged upstairs. She barely had the strength to undress for bed, but at last she slipped into the warm confines of the feather mattress and soft covers. Enveloped by the security of the bed and the warmth of Joseph sleeping beside her, she wondered if for the first time in her life she had truly come home.

"Women!"

Caleb slammed his empty whiskey glass upside down on the doily then raked a hand through his hair. He'd paid a month in advance for a boardinghouse room and drunk his way through half a bottle. And he still couldn't get Elizabeth Cameron out of his mind. The image of her huddled in the dirt, hugging Joseph, burned in his brain. Too bad he hadn't had a better shot at Hez Taylor, just one punch to lay him out. Seeing that drunken maniac pull that knife, Caleb had lost all sense of reason and let instinct kick in.

But instead of being grateful for his help, Elizabeth had flailed like a trapped animal and told him to get out of her sight. Imagine her wanting to run after Taylor and his kid. There was no telling what would have happened to her!

"It's not just women," he muttered. "It's one *particular* woman."

He turned the glass over again and poured. He'd thought about looking for a woman, to redirect his energy, but he kept picturing the sad look on Joseph's face.

Blast. The kid was working his way under Caleb's skin, all right. Just like Noah Cameron's sister.

Where had *that* come from? It was true she had a plain sort of attractiveness. She was no simpering, lily-handed girl either. Elizabeth Cameron could probably cook a man a fine meal and keep him in line at the same time.

He caught sight of himself in the mirror and set down the drink. The wound on his forehead stood out under a shock of blond hair, and he examined it closely. Elizabeth had certainly done a good job of keeping him alive.

His expression darkened. He wasn't about to let her off the hook. He'd give her a few days to cool off, then he'd track her and Joseph down and get that blasted picnic over with. She'd be satisfied, and he'd spend the next year watching her from afar. Then at last he could head back to Wyoming.

Frowning, he reached for a piece of paper and a pen. This one-horse town didn't even have a telegraph office, and he had to let Noah Cameron know they'd arrived safely.

The sooner he had his pardon, the sooner he'd be free.

Six

Elizabeth awoke to the sound of a rooster, sunlight already spilling from behind the delicate lace curtains. Feeling a huddled mass of warmth against her, she discovered Joseph had breached her side of the bed during the night and staked a claim on her pillow.

Yawning languidly, she rose and tested muscles relaxed by the first full night's sleep she'd had since Fort Griffin. Then, feeling guilty for reveling in carnal pleasure before morning prayer, she dropped to her knees.

"Father, thank you for sheltering Joseph and me in this home. May we be worthy for the task you've set before us, and may we strengthen Mrs. Mannheim's body and spirit through our humble obedience to your calling."

She rose, feeling even more guilty. She should have been downstairs long ago to light the fire and prepare breakfast. She dressed quickly and pinned up her hair.

Glancing at Joseph, she debated whether

to awaken him or allow him to sleep. A childish snore emanated from under the covers, and she smiled. She would let him sleep.

Elizabeth raised the window sash higher, letting in a rush of springtime air. From the second story, she could see what darkness had covered the night before. Besides marigold beds, the front yard was speckled with oak saplings. Beyond the yard and across the road were gently rolling, uncultivated fields dotted with mesquite and cottonwoods. The land was optimistically green now, but she knew once the spring rains ceased, the fields would eventually wither and brown under the hot Texas sun.

Leaning out the window, she took a good look at the road. A dusty narrow ribbon, it dipped out of sight just beyond the magnificent live oak. She leaned her elbows on the sill, imagining picnics under the spreading shade of the tree's mighty arms.

Suddenly remembering Anna Mannheim, she rose and hurried down the stairs. Gathering her courage, she peeked in on the elderly woman. She hadn't shifted positions since last night, and Elizabeth feared she was dead until she saw the slow, steady rise of the blanket. Grateful that the woman was not only alive but also still asleep, she turned to the cookstove.

"Now I'll really have to hurry," she chided herself as she checked the ashpit. Finding it empty, she murmured a prayer of thanks for Gustavo's thoughtfulness. She opened all the dampers and draft regulators wide, then built a fast fire by stoking the firebox with dry wood. She chose whole logs for a long, steady fire, knowing she would most likely spend the morning baking.

She stood back to watch the flames and spied an apron hanging on the pantry door. Slipping the white material over her head, she tied a bow at her waist. "I guess I've officially made myself at home."

She frowned. Gustavo hadn't said how long Mrs. Mannheim usually slept in the morning, nor had he said whether she should be awakened. With a heart full of sympathy for the ailing woman, Elizabeth tiptoed into the connecting room and paused beside the bed.

A hand suddenly pushed back the blanket to reveal sightless blue eyes in a smiling face. "There's no need for such quiet," Anna Mannheim said, her voice thick with a German accent. "I was only praying."

Elizabeth covered her mouth. "Oh, I'm sorry!"

Mrs. Mannheim laughed and pushed herself upright. She reached for her pillow, but Elizabeth grabbed it first, plumped it, and wedged it behind the woman's back, anxious to please. "Is that better, ma'am?"

"Yes, my dear." She patted Elizabeth's hand and directed her gaze at Elizabeth as if she could see. The smile never left her face. "You are very kind to help. I've been waiting for you with much impatience."

"You have?" Elizabeth skirted the foot of the bed, moving to the chair on the far side.

"Though my God is more company than I could ever ask, I get lonely for human companionship. Gustavo and Marisa are dear friends, but they have so much work to do. They have little time to sit and talk."

Elizabeth drew a deep breath for courage; if she didn't tell Mrs. Mannheim the truth right now, she might never find the strength. Though sightless, those blue eyes seemed to pin a person. "I'm Elizabeth Cameron," she heard herself say. "And before we go any further, there's something you should know. I brought a little boy with me . . . Joseph . . . a boy my father took in. My father was a preacher, but he's dead now. Joseph and I have come all the way from Fort Griffin, which is —"

Mrs. Mannheim chuckled. "I know where it is, child. Please don't be nervous. A boy in the house will be a wonderful thing. He will bring frogs and track mud and —"

"Joseph isn't like that."

Mrs. Mannheim's face fell. "He isn't?"

"No. He's quite obedient for a five-year-old. And he can recite Bible verses and fetch whatever you need."

"What a shame. I would enjoy a little boy much better."

Puzzled, Elizabeth wondered if there was something wrong with the woman's hearing. "He *is* a little boy."

"Really? He sounds more like a servant."

Wincing, Elizabeth bowed her head, waiting for further criticism. When Mrs. Mannheim didn't respond, Elizabeth hesitantly looked up. Instead of a frown or a scowl, a radiant smile filled the woman's face, and the whole room seemed to light up.

"No calling me 'ma'am,' " she said. "I will call you Elizabeth and you will call me Anna. *Ja?*"

"Y-yes." Elizabeth perched on the edge of the chair. She folded and unfolded her hands, wishing she could get back to the kitchen. So far she hadn't done anything useful.

The wrinkles around Anna's eyes deepened as she leaned toward Elizabeth. "You should also know that you're sitting in Jesus' chair."

Elizabeth went cold. "What do you mean?"

"That's Jesus' chair," Anna said cheerfully. "I invite him to sit down and we talk. This way I always know he's beside me."

Elizabeth jerked to her feet, flustered. "I'm so sorry! I didn't know." She glanced at the chair, half-expecting to see Jesus with a disapproving expression.

"Elizabeth!" Joseph flung himself into the room, dressed and exuberant for adventure. He smiled when he saw her. "I couldn't find you, and I'm hungry! When's breakfast?"

"Joseph, where are your manners? This is Mrs. Mannheim."

Anna turned. "So this is the boy I've been wanting to meet. Come and tell me about yourself."

Joseph bounded forward, pulling the chair closer. "My name's —"

"*Joseph!*" Elizabeth yanked him up by the elbow and stood him on his feet. "That's where Jesus sits."

"Jesus?" Joseph turned to Anna, his eyes shining. "Oh, good! Can I sit in his lap?"

Anna threw her head back and laughed, then patted the chair. "*Ja,* Joseph. You most certainly may. That's where he wants us, don't you think? If I could manage, I would sit in that chair all the time. But since I can't, you must sit there for me."

"Thank you!" Joseph planted himself firmly in the chair. He drew his feet underneath himself and leaned forward. "I never met anyone who was blind before. Do you close your eyes when you sleep?"

Anna made a serious face, as if she were pondering the question with utmost concentration. "I'm not certain."

"Maybe I can watch you sleep sometime, then I'll let you know."

The small woman's laugh was generous, and the sound filled every corner of the room, not with volume but intensity. She leaned forward to pat Joseph's cheek. "You and I are going to get along just fine, young man." Her hand strayed to his head. "You are . . . you are . . ."

She rubbed a thatch of hair between her gnarled fingers. "Your hair feels much like the Orozco children's, but you aren't Mexican, are you?" she said softly. A cloud passed over her face, and she paused. "You must be Indian."

Elizabeth's heart beat faster. She wrapped an arm around Joseph, trying to draw him back. "Yes, Mrs. Mannheim. If that is displeasing, we will leave now."

Anna dropped her hand. She leaned back against the pillow, looking weary for the first time. "No, Elizabeth, it does not bother me," she said softly. "Jesus loves all of his little children."

"¡Hóla! Hello, Señora Anna!" Childish voices rang out above the sound of a wagon pulling into the front yard.

Anna brightened again. "The Orozcos!"

Mortified, Elizabeth released Joseph. "I haven't prepared anything for breakfast. I haven't even looked in the pantry!"

"Time for that later," Anna said. "If I know the Orozcos, they've brought enough food for everyone."

"Señora Anna! Señora Anna!"

Five children rushed pell-mell into the room. The youngest just barely toddled, but she followed her older brothers and sisters without question. Braking just short of the bed, they wrapped their brown arms around Anna's neck in a tangle of kisses to her wrinkled cheeks.

"Hello, children!" Anna eagerly returned their affection, twisting this way and that to kiss one smooth cheek after another.

Joseph hung back, shy. Elizabeth also felt overwhelmed. A slim, brown woman entered, her hands full of covered platters. She caught Elizabeth's eye and smiled. "Hello!"

She spoke up over the children's chatter. "You must be Señorita Cameron. I am Marisa Orozco."

The joviality of the room was contagious, and Elizabeth smiled back and stepped away from the commotion. "It's a pleasure to meet you, señora."

"The pleasure is mine. And you must call me Marisa." She nodded at the bed. "That is Joseph?"

"Yes." Elizabeth glanced over her shoulder. Joseph had been drawn into the crowd by Marisa's eldest boy. The four older Orozco children avidly vied for Anna's attention, while the littlest one leaned against the bed and pounded happily on the blanket. Elizabeth smiled. "Your children are lovely, Marisa. What are their names?"

"Rafael is nine, Teresa is eight, Santiago is six, Pedro is three, and Juanita is one." She smiled approvingly as Joseph patted Juanita gently on the head. "Your Joseph fits right in."

Elizabeth glanced at her son. In more ways than one, Marisa was right. Joseph's warm copper skin was more similar to the Orozcos' than the white children of Fort Griffin. She strongly suspected that even if Joseph were green, the Orozco children would have accepted him.

"The children are fine. Will you help me with breakfast?" Marisa said.

Elizabeth followed Marisa into the kitchen. "You were very kind to bring it."

Marisa smiled as she unwrapped the plates, revealing an array of flour tortillas and boiled potatoes. "Gustavo said you arrived late last night and that you and the boy looked weary. I thought I would bring a meal, then show you where everything is."

She smiled at Elizabeth, then on impulse, threw her arms around her. Embarrassed, Elizabeth felt herself stiffen and awkwardly patted the woman's back, amazed to hear soft sobs.

Marisa sniffled and pulled away. Wiping her eyes with her knuckles, she laughed. "I always cry when I'm happy! We have prayed for you for a long time, Elizabeth. Now you are here, and the señora will help you."

Elizabeth smiled gently. "I'm glad to be here to help Anna. You and Gustavo have done more than even good neighbors should."

"It has been no burden. We will be here to help you as well." She turned away to call Rafael to collect eggs from the henhouse.

Elizabeth frowned. What did Marisa mean about Anna helping *her?* She wasn't the one blind and crippled with arthritis!

Suppressing a sigh, she followed Marisa's instructions on wrapping the tortillas in a wet towel to heat. What a strange place she'd landed in.

From the head of the room in the Union Church, Martha McWhirter gazed in turn at each of the gathered women. "The *Bible* is our authority!"

"Amen," Molly murmured, eyes shining.

The other women stirred excitedly. Martha stepped closer and held out her hands. "Before I was sanctified, I didn't know whether God had ever answered any of my prayers. I felt he was a cruel leader — I lost three children and a brother. I looked for God's guidance."

Several women nodded their heads in agreement.

"Then one morning as I made breakfast, I felt as though someone had poured water over and through me. An inward baptism!"

"Yes!" Iola Bigelow, a prune-faced spinster, swayed in her chair, moaning.

Martha raised her hands. "This, my dear sisters, was the Spirit of God! And this convinced me that all outward ritual was dead. Those who live good lives will be with God after death. But you have to submit to

151

God's will and do his work. Inactivity is a sin, and practical work, no matter how lowly, is virtuous."

Elizabeth felt a shiver run up her spine. Martha seemed to speak right to her own tortured soul. More work! That's what she needed to ease the ache she felt, the fear. She squirmed in her chair, trying to generate the enthusiasm she felt in the room.

Martha's voice rose to a fevered pitch. "*Pray* for sanctification! We must leave our families and separate from the world. Otherwise, we cannot be the Christians the Bible speaks of!"

"Yes, yes!" Applauding, Iola Bigelow leaped up. The other women were on their feet in an instant, whooping with near delirium.

Elizabeth was the last to stand. She glanced around nervously, hoping no one noticed how manufactured her clapping felt, how feeble her voice of agreement.

Why didn't she feel what they did? Martha said work was virtuous; that must be the answer. She would go home and hit her knees — not in prayer but in work — for the sanctification that the other women seemed to have so easily obtained. She would throw herself into caring for Anna and Joseph — and the Orozcos, too, if nec-

152

essary — until she pleased God.

The group dispersed into buzzing pockets of conversation. Despite her resolve, Elizabeth felt more heavyhearted than when the prayer meeting began. She picked her way through the women to find Joseph, who had been sent with the other children to another room. Someone tugged at her sleeve, and she turned.

Tears streamed down Iola's bony cheeks, and she blew her hawklike nose into a handkerchief. "Wasn't Sister Martha wonderful? Didn't you feel the Spirit move in the room?"

"Oh yes," Elizabeth said hastily. "As if, as if —"

Joseph trudged into the room. His face lit up when he saw Elizabeth, and he threw his arms around her legs. "Elizabeth! Can we go home now?"

Iola screeched. "Whose child is *that?*"

With a surge of protectiveness, Elizabeth wrapped her arms around Joseph. "He's God's child, Miss Bigelow."

Joseph glanced up in surprise, then offered her a smile. She smiled back and gave him a quick squeeze.

Iola snorted. "No child of God is a heathen *Indian,* Miss Cameron. They're savages! All of them! We ran them out of this county years ago — they haven't been back since."

"Joseph is just a boy," Elizabeth said calmly. "He may be of Indian blood, but I can promise you he knows nothing of war parties or scalping or whatever else you think Indians do."

Martha hurried over. "What's wrong, sisters?"

"It's him!" Iola pointed a bony finger. Joseph shrank back against Elizabeth.

Martha looked puzzled. "Why? What's he done?"

"Done? Does he have to *do* anything? He's an Indian! You know what they're like!"

Martha laughed gently and slipped an arm around the disgruntled woman's shoulders. "I'm sure Joseph is a fine lad, Iola."

Iola sniffed. "Miss Cameron would do well to heed your words about abandoning family ties, Martha. She seems entirely too fond of that pagan child if you ask me."

Elizabeth trembled under Iola and Martha's scrutiny and glanced down at Joseph. What would they do if they realized the truth?

"I'm quite sure Elizabeth is well aware of the need to dedicate oneself to God alone," Martha said mildly. "She has heard me speak of giving up any flesh that interferes with spiritual commitment. Since she is merely Joseph's custodian, I'm sure she is eager to dedicate herself to our church. Aren't you, dear?"

Elizabeth looked into Joseph's solemn, dark eyes, then back at Martha. Her heart pounded, and her palms felt sweaty. "I . . . I . . . don't know," she whispered.

Joseph bowed his head. Martha patted Elizabeth on the shoulder. "You need more prayer and contemplation. You'll find the way." Then she moved to talk to others gathered in clusters.

Feeling miserable, Elizabeth lowered her gaze. "Yes, Martha."

Iola snorted in triumph, then flounced off. Elizabeth unwrapped her arms from Joseph and opened the door, leading the way from the Sunday school room.

Caleb leaned against the rented buggy, mentally recounting the cracks in the Union Church's door. He'd learned where the Sanctificationists met but had no idea what time they'd finish.

He checked his pocket watch once again, careful not to crush the handful of wildflowers he'd picked. He didn't know their name, but he'd seen them frequently while surveying and decided the small red sunflowers with yellow tips would look nice in Elizabeth's hands.

He grinned down at the bouquet. He was acting downright dotty by bringing her such a peace offering.

The front door opened, and Caleb straightened. Heads bent low, Elizabeth and Joseph trudged hand in hand down the steps. Caleb fixed a smile on his face and stepped directly in their path. "Hello."

"Caleb!" Joseph threw his arms around him.

Caleb thrust the bouquet at a startled Elizabeth. "I picked these for you. I don't know what they're called, but I thought you might like them."

"Indian blankets," she said, looking stunned. "Some people call them firewheels."

"Oh. Well, they reminded me of you."

Joseph tugged on Caleb's trouser leg. "Can I have a hug?"

Caleb laughed and swooped down on the boy. "Sure, Joe."

He growled playfully, bear-hugging him. Joseph squealed with delight. Elizabeth watched, silent and solemn.

Caleb gave Joseph a final squeeze. "I missed you, kid," he whispered against the boy's ear.

Joseph cupped his hand around Caleb's ear and loudly whispered, "Me too."

Caleb laughed and set him down. He gestured at the buggy. "It's a beautiful afternoon. May I take you two for a drive?"

"Thank you very much, but we have to go home. Anna will be expecting us."

"Anna? I thought you lived with Martha McWhirter."

"She didn't have room for us, so she sent us to live with Anna Mannheim."

"She lives on a farm," Joseph put in happily. "And she has chickens and goats and cows! Rafael showed me how to collect the eggs. The hens pecked me, but I got their eggs!"

Caleb laughed. "Good for you, Joseph." He turned to Elizabeth. "May I see you both home?"

The other Sanctificationists strolled out of the church, chattering loudly. When they saw Caleb with Elizabeth, they stopped abruptly. Iola smirked and whispered behind her hand to a companion.

Elizabeth blushed. "Please go away, Caleb."

"You *did* promise to go on a picnic with me," he said loudly. He smiled impishly at Elizabeth's shock, relishing the speculative buzz from the church steps. Old hens. He'd heard talk from dismayed husbands about the Sancties who refused to share the marriage bed.

"Can we talk about this later?" Elizabeth whispered urgently.

"Later?" Caleb made no effort to keep his voice low. "Why, sweetheart, you know how fleeting life can be. Remember those nights we spent on the riverbank? Remember how —"

Elizabeth clapped a hand over his mouth. "All right! You may take us home. But please! Not another word!"

She lowered her hand, and he grinned. The buzz had escalated into full-blown outrage.

"Did you hear what he — ?"

"And she —"

"But what about — ?"

One woman raised her hands for silence. "Sisters! We will not judge!"

Caleb assumed it was Martha McWhirter, their self-appointed ringleader, for everyone fell abruptly silent. He tipped his hat at them, lifted Joseph into the buggy, then with a smile for the stone-faced Elizabeth, gave her a hand up.

Joseph bounced on the leather upholstery. "A buggy ride! Look at the horse, Elizabeth! Look at this seat! It's beautiful!"

On the far side of the buggy, Elizabeth maintained her silence. Caleb took up the reins and gave her a questioning look. She stared straight ahead, clutching the bouquet against her brown dress. Caleb made a mental note to buy her a new one, something with a little color this time. And no more overly modest high-necked collars either.

Caleb suppressed a smile at her stubbornness. She'd pout all afternoon if he'd let her. "You're going to have to tell me how to get there, Bess," he said.

She gave him curt directions, her eyes leveled straight ahead. Caleb called to the horse, nodding cheerfully as they passed the disapproving women on the church steps.

Elizabeth kept her eyes fixed somewhere between the horse's ears until they were well out of town. "You didn't have to embarrass Joseph and me," she finally said.

Caleb turned. "Joe, were you embarrassed to see me?"

"Not a bit!" Joseph bounced on the seat a few times for good measure then turned his head so Elizabeth couldn't see his smile. Caleb winked at him.

"Well, *I* was embarrassed," Elizabeth said in a low voice. "What will those women think?"

"They're probably green with envy, Bess. I didn't see any of them with offers of buggy rides home."

She pressed her lips together, and Caleb chuckled inwardly. She took herself so seriously, it was comical. Did she really want to seclude herself from men forever, or had she been so hurt in the past that she was really just crying out for a man to love her?

"Turn in just beyond that giant live oak," Elizabeth said.

Joseph's eyes shone with anticipation. "I can't wait till you see the chickens!"

Caleb smiled. "I can't wait to see 'em either. I want you to show me all around the farm."

Elizabeth shot him a black look then turned away. Caleb dug an elbow in Joseph's side. The boy grinned back, squirming in his seat.

They pulled into the front yard, and Caleb slowed the horse. The porch was sagging, and the chinked limestone could stand repair. Several oak saplings also needed to be staked for survival against spring storms.

"Mrs. Mannheim is a widow?" Caleb helped Elizabeth up the front porch steps.

"Yes." She eased the door open, then turned, her expression stiff. "Thank you for the ride. Joseph, come inside."

"Whoa." Caleb braced the door open with his hand. Joseph grinned up at him, then slipped under his outstretched arm. "We need to decide on a date for our picnic."

Elizabeth sighed audibly. "Very well. Come inside if you must, but wait here. I want to make sure Anna is all right."

Joseph ran toward the back of the house. "Anna! Anna! Caleb's here! He brought us home from church!"

Caleb chuckled. He could tell by the way Elizabeth straightened her spine that she was none too pleased with Joseph's announcement. Apparently she was hoping she could slip Caleb in and out of the house without having to introduce him.

Suppressing a grin, he followed her to the kitchen. He could hear Joseph's voice in the next room. "And he's gonna see the chickens!"

Caleb heard a soft chuckle. "I imagine the man's seen chickens before, child, but you're right. These will be special because they're *your* chickens."

Elizabeth's voice broke in. "Anna, please drink the willow-bark tea. You know it makes your legs feel better. I knew we shouldn't have left you."

Caleb entered the bedroom. Perched on a

161

chair, Joseph leaned over a frail old woman delicately propped up in bed. Elizabeth stood with her back to the door, raising a cup to the woman's lips. The woman shook her head, and Caleb could see she was blind.

"You know it makes me sleepy. And besides" — smiling, she nodded at the doorway — "you have company."

Elizabeth turned, frowning. Joseph leaped from the chair. "It's him, Anna! It's Caleb!"

Elizabeth set the cup aside. "You might as well come in so I can properly introduce you."

Joseph grabbed Caleb's hand and pulled him around the bed. "Sit here. This is Jesus' chair!"

Anna smiled broadly. Caleb cast a puzzled glance at Elizabeth, who merely shrugged. "Anna, this is Caleb Martin."

He took the woman's wrinkled hand between both of his. "How do you do, ma'am?"

"I'm Anna Mannheim," she said, then leaned forward. "I've been hoping Elizabeth's young man wouldn't stay hidden."

"Anna! He's not my . . . young man. I haven't even said a word about him!"

"Joseph did. That's all he can talk about.

Caleb said this, Caleb did that." She squeezed his hand, and he could have sworn she winked.

Caleb cleared his throat. "It's nice to meet you, ma'am."

"You must call me Anna." She sat up straighter. "You two young people go sit in the parlor. Joseph and I will talk."

Elizabeth looked downright nervous. "But don't you want to hear about church? Don't you want some dinner?"

"You can fix the food in a little while. And as for church, I have a good idea what those *dummkopf* women talked about."

Caleb grinned. He already liked this woman. "Anna," he said, "I was noticing that your porch could use some repairs, and a few other things . . . I'd be glad to help out."

"Why, thank you." Anna's face brightened. "My neighbor Gustavo has had his hands full just keeping up with his own farm. If there's any work to be done, Elizabeth will repay you with dinners. She's a wonderful cook."

"I know." Caleb leaned forward. "Have you ever tasted what she does with cattails and wild onions?"

Anna chuckled, then patted his hand. "You'd better hurry and marry her. A girl that takes care of people as well as she does, and is as pretty as she is, won't be alone long."

Elizabeth cleared her throat. "That's very kind, Anna, but you should know that I'm not pretty. Not at all."

"Yes, you are!" Joseph planted his fists against his hips. "You're the prettiest woman I know. Isn't she, Caleb?"

Caleb caught Elizabeth's gaze. She blushed furiously and looked away.

"The world's idea of attractiveness is vanity," Anna said softly. "The beauty lies in whether or not a woman fears the Lord. Elizabeth serves him daily, every minute and every hour."

"I . . . I'll go start something to eat," Elizabeth murmured. "Joseph, please come help me."

He winked at Caleb, then followed as she fled the room.

Anna patted Caleb's hand. "Joseph told me everything that's happened since he met you. His child's eyes have picked up what his mind does not yet understand." She paused. "Do *you* understand?"

Caleb frowned, bewildered. "I don't know what you mean."

Anna laughed gently. "You will."

"I'm heating some soup, Anna," Elizabeth said from the doorway. "May I bring you some?"

"Perhaps later, *liebchen*." She yawned. "If you two will excuse me, I'd like to take a nap. I am sleepy even without your willow-bark tea." She fumbled for Caleb's hand as she eased down on the bed. "I enjoyed talking with you, young man. We must speak again."

Caleb rose. "Yes, Anna. I promise we will."

"*Gut.*" She smiled, then rolled slowly to face the window. Her shoulders relaxed, and within moments she was asleep.

Elizabeth waited for him in the doorway, then walked him to the kitchen table. She served Joseph, then set two more steaming bowls on the table. Elizabeth gestured Caleb to a chair, then sat on Joseph's far side.

"Thank you." Caleb took up a spoon, hesitating. "Do you want to ask a blessing?"

Elizabeth nodded and they bowed their heads. Caleb remembered to say amen when she'd finished.

"Amen!" Joseph picked up his spoon and began slurping.

Caleb sipped slowly and soon realized that Anna had spoken the truth about Eliza-beth's cooking. He hadn't tasted such wonderful chicken soup since his mother's. "I'm sorry if I embarrassed you back in town," he said gruffly.

Startled, Elizabeth glanced up, then lowered her gaze again. "No, I'm the one who's sorry. Every time you show Joseph and me a favor, I seem to overreact."

Joseph's spoon clattered into his empty bowl. "Can I go out to play?"

"*May* I."

"Well sure, Elizabeth. You can come too."

"No, I mean . . ." She glanced helplessly at Caleb, who offered her a smile. She blinked, then nodded at Joseph. "Go ahead."

"Hooray!" Joseph let the back door slam behind him.

While he ate, Caleb surreptitiously watched Elizabeth. She glanced up then quickly away. They continued to eat in a silence punctuated only by spoons clinking against bowls, and Caleb tried very hard not to slurp his soup.

When he was down to the last spoonful, Elizabeth cleared her throat. "Meet us here next Saturday, and we'll picnic down by the creek."

Caleb set his spoon by the empty bowl. For some odd reason, he wanted to stay longer, but she had effectively dismissed him. "That sounds good. Say good-bye to Anna and Joseph for me."

Elizabeth nodded, rising.

"Don't bother seeing me out," he said, setting his hat on his head. "You probably want to make sure Anna eats."

Elizabeth smiled softly. Raised to meet his, her warm brown eyes beckoned innocently, tempting him to kiss her. Inwardly chiding himself for an overactive imagination, Caleb smiled and touched the brim of his hat. "Till next Saturday, Bess."

Elizabeth lifted Anna's tray and scowled at the nearly full bowl. "Are you sure you can't eat more?"

"I'm afraid I just don't have much of an appetite," Anna said. "I find myself relying more on God and less on food."

Elizabeth headed for the kitchen. "I hardly think God wants you to starve yourself."

She heard a low chuckle from the bedroom, and when she returned, Anna was smiling mischievously. "I'm sure your gentleman friend won't starve. I have a feeling he'll be coming around here quite regularly."

Grateful that Anna couldn't see her

blush, Elizabeth sat on the bed. "He's not exactly what I'd call a friend."

"That's what I said about my Rudy until I walked down the aisle with him."

At Anna's words, Elizabeth's heart skipped a beat, but she managed to maintain her composure. "Marriage isn't for me."

"Nonsense! I meant what I said to your Caleb. You'd make a lovely wife. You should be joined to a husband, making a home and family for yourselves. Not tending an old woman."

"I enjoy living with you, Anna. This is the happiest home I've known."

Anna's hand strayed to Elizabeth's cheek. "Didn't your mama and papa make you happy?"

"After my mother died, my father was never the same." She paused. "He remarried so Joseph would have a woman to raise him, but he never loved me anymore. He threw himself into preaching."

"If Papa was preaching and this stepmother was taking care of Joseph, what did you do?" Anna said softly.

"I did what I was told and tried to stay out of the way. My father wouldn't even allow me to have friends."

"Or beaus?"

"No."

"So now your papa has died, and you have come to Martha McWhirter to learn how to live without men."

Elizabeth clasped her hands together. "The Sanctificationists are a godsend. I don't want to depend on a man for love or for support. I don't want a husband to rule over me."

Anna laughed softly and caressed Elizabeth's cheek. "My poor little *liebchen*. Is that what you think marriage is? A man ruling over a woman?"

"Of course! The husband is the head of the wife just as Christ is the head of the church."

"Yes, but —"

"So the husband must answer to God for the wife. She has no say. She's thrown under a yoke of slavery to the man."

"Elizabeth, Elizabeth. Who has filled your head with such garbage? You must go back and read those passages in the Bible carefully. Promise me you will."

"I know what the Bible says. Wives must be subject in all ways to their husbands."

Anna opened her mouth to reply, then abruptly closed it. She smiled and squeezed Elizabeth's hand. "We will talk of it later. Now tell me about the meeting."

Elizabeth's stomach knotted. "Martha is

a very good speaker."

"Too good, perhaps. What did she say?"

Elizabeth tried to remember her specific words but could only recall that she'd been the only one apparently unmoved by them. "She said we must be sanctified and do God's work."

Anna sighed. "Yes, I've heard her say that before. What else?"

Elizabeth thought hard. In her mind she saw the women leaping to their feet, applauding, and the tears streaming down Iola Bigelow's cheeks. "She said that to be good Christians, we must separate ourselves from the world."

Anna's sightless eyes seemed fixed on Elizabeth's face. "And do you do this, *liebchen?*"

"That's why I came to Belton."

Anna thought for a moment. "You know verses very well. What did Jesus pray about his followers and the world in John 17?"

Elizabeth racked her brain but drew a blank. Father would have criticized her severely for not knowing her Scripture. "I don't know it, Anna," she said bleakly.

"John 17:15. 'I pray not that thou shouldest take them out of the world, but that thou shouldest keep them from the evil.' "

Relieved, Elizabeth picked up the words. " 'They are not of the world, even as I am not of the world.' Yes! Now I remember!"

"And what did Jesus then ask of God?"

Elizabeth's smile fell. "Why, he, he —"

"He said, 'Sanctify them through thy truth: thy word is truth.' " Anna leaned forward. "Sanctification, Elizabeth. Being set apart for God. Holy. Do you know what that means?"

Elizabeth cleared her throat, trying to push down a lump. "Of course," she whispered. "Certain believers are reserved for God's use."

"Just *certain* ones?"

"Yes." A chill raised goose flesh on her arms. "People he selects. People he thinks are worthy."

"What makes a person worthy in God's eyes?" Anna paused. "Are *you* worthy?"

Elizabeth wrapped her arms around herself, shivering. Anna stared at her with those enormous cloudy eyes, waiting for an answer. Elizabeth tried to speak, but a sob broke in her throat.

Anna held out her arms, her face soft and luminous. "It's all right, *liebchen*," she murmured. "Come to me."

Elizabeth didn't know how she moved forward — for Anna was surely too weak to

171

have moved toward her — but she found herself enfolded in Anna's embrace. The small arms didn't feel as bony and thin as they looked, but strong and warm. They were a mother's arms, they were a father's arms. Far more than flesh and bone, they were love personified, love unquestioning and whole.

With a gnarled hand, Anna pressed Elizabeth's head to her breast. "Whatever happened does not matter, Elizabeth. The Lord knows the plans he has for you. Not for evil, but to give you a future. And a hope."

The words rang against Elizabeth's heart, cracking open a tiny crevice like chisel against stone. She smothered a sob. "Where is this future? Where *is* my hope?"

Anna rocked her gently. "The answer is the same, dear one. It is in your heart . . . the Christ who is in you, your hope of glory. And hope does not disappoint." She paused. "You do believe that Jesus is the Christ, the son of the living God?"

"Y-yes! Ever since I was little."

"Then you must believe that he will be faithful to complete the good work he began in you," Anna said softly. "Run the race he set, Elizabeth, and fix your eyes on him. *Only* on him."

Elizabeth drew a deep breath and pulled

away. Embarrassed at her outburst, she hastily wiped her eyes with the back of her hand. Crying would do no good. "I'll try, Anna."

Anna patted her shoulder. "That's *gut*, my dear. You are too young to be so sad."

The chill disappeared, but a suffocating tightness lingered. Elizabeth rose from the bed. "I'm going to check on Joseph," she said, not waiting for a reply.

Outside the back door, she leaned against the house and drew in great gulps of calming air. She willed her hands to stop shaking and forced down the threatening emotions.

Anna meant well. She probably saw Elizabeth as just another child — like Joseph — to be comforted.

Fix her eyes on Jesus? How could she even look at him when she was such a filthy disgrace?

Seven

Caleb pretended to groan under the weight of the basket as he adjusted it in his hand. "What have you got in this thing? It must weigh a ton."

"Fried chicken, cornbread, chocolate cake, jars of lemonade — Oh!"

At Elizabeth's cry, Caleb glanced back. She'd stopped short. Her face was pale, and she clutched her side with a sharp intake of breath. Alarmed, he stepped toward her. "What's the matter?"

She waved him away, pressing a hand to her side. "I felt a little dizzy. That's all." She drew a quick breath. "It must be the sun." The color rushed back in her cheeks, and she seemed to breathe easier.

Relieved, Caleb stepped away. "We can always go back."

"I'll be fine."

Caleb resumed walking, slower this time. Frowning, he glanced at Elizabeth. Her elbows were close to her sides, and she smiled weakly. He shrugged and turned, deciding to concentrate on the path.

Nolan Creek flowed southeast to where it would pass south of Belton to empty into the Leon River. Bluebonnets, Indian blankets, Indian paintbrushes, Queen Anne's lace, and a smattering of evening primroses splashed the green banks like buckets of blue, red, white, and pink paint. Caleb set the basket down under a stand of cottonwoods. "This looks like a good spot."

Elizabeth shook out the quilt in his direction, and together they let it billow to the ground. She knelt on one side and began to empty the basket.

"Let's fish first!" Joseph jumped and held on to a low branch. He swung gleefully, bending his knees to perpetuate the motion. "Whee!"

"There'll be plenty of time to fish." Caleb chuckled, tickling the boy's armpits.

Joseph's giggles intensified. "Caleb! That ti-i-ck-les!" His hands slipped, and he lost his grip.

Laughing, Caleb caught the boy against his chest and held him close. Then he began spinning in a circle, growling playfully. "Do you know what I do with little boys I catch hanging from trees?"

Joseph threw his head back, laughing. "What?"

"I make them eat Elizabeth's wonderful cooking, then I take them fi-i-i-shing!" Caleb swung him down to land by the seat of his trousers on the quilt. Whooping with delight, Joseph rolled over and bounded up. "Do it again!"

Laughing, Caleb dropped to the quilt and leaned back on his elbows. "Maybe later, Joe. If we don't help Elizabeth spread out the food, she may not let us eat."

"Neither one of you will want to eat after that whirligig display," she said, then winced.

"Give me that." Caleb grabbed a platter of cake from her hands. "I think we'd better go back. I've never seen you look so pale, Elizabeth."

"I'm fine. Really."

He gave her a dubious once-over. "You look thinner. Have you been getting enough to eat?"

"Yes." She flushed under his gaze.

Joseph eyed the plate of fried chicken and smacked his lips. "Maybe we'd better eat first after all."

Caleb laughed.

Elizabeth poured three glasses of lemonade then filled a small plate for Joseph and another plate with larger servings for Caleb. But Caleb noticed her own plate held only a small chicken wing.

She bowed her head. "Caleb, would you please ask the blessing?"

Surprised at her request, he set down his plate. "If you want me to."

Joseph thrust out his hands, and Caleb accepted one. Elizabeth took the other and held out her free hand, Caleb covering it with his own. Her skin felt smooth and cool.

"Uh, God, thank you for this food and for, uh, this lovely day. Thank you that we have enough to eat and a place to lay our heads at night. Uh, amen."

"Amen!" Joseph broke the circle and snatched up his drumstick. "Mmmm," he said over a mouthful. "Chicken!"

Caleb sunk his teeth into his portion, the meat juicy and tender. "No offense, Elizabeth," he said between bites, "but this beats your cattails and onions any day."

He continued to dig into the meal, eating with gusto. He'd never tasted such crumbly sweet cornbread. Even Samantha wasn't this good a cook.

He reached unashamedly for second helpings all around, when he noticed Elizabeth had inched to the edge of the quilt. Her breathing was labored, and her face was white. Caleb set aside his plate. "All right, Miss Cameron, are you going to tell me what's hurting you or am I going to have to see for myself?"

She backed away. "I'm . . . fine!"

"No you're not. What's wrong?"

"N-nothing!" She scrambled to her feet.

Caleb leaped up and stormed closer. Foolish woman! "Did you bruise a rib? Break one? Let me see."

"No, Caleb!"

"Yes!"

Elizabeth clenched her hands. "It's the corset, you nosy man! I've never worn one before!" She clapped a hand over her mouth and flushed.

Caleb's mouth twitched with amusement. Who would have thought the prim, stiff woman he'd first met on the stagecoach was a newcomer to ladies' undergarments? The capable woman he'd known suddenly seemed like a little girl playing dress-up in her mama's clothes.

Elizabeth hiccuped, and Caleb chuckled. "I don't" — she struggled to draw a deep breath — "see what's so funny about this." She glared at Caleb and hiccuped again, loudly.

Caleb laughed outright. He tried to stop, but the more he looked at Elizabeth, red-faced and hiccuping, the more humorous the situation seemed. "You looked . . . fine the way you were," he managed to get out. "I never knew you didn't wear a . . . a . . . corset!"

Her shoulders shook, and Caleb instantly sobered. Blast her, now she was going to cry. "Ah, come on now."

She giggled. "It *is* pretty silly, isn't it? You buy me . . . the thing to be nice, and I . . . wear it to look nice."

Surprised, Caleb stared. "You wore the corset for me? I like you the way you are, Bess. A dress with some color in it would suit you better, but you . . . why, you're shaped just fine."

"Do you mean that?"

"Yes. I think blue would be more becoming."

"No," she whispered. "The last part."

Caleb resisted the urge to let his gaze sweep over her. Did she think he hadn't caught a glimpse of her figure? Hadn't guessed at the womanly curves her dress covered? She'd apparently never realized she was a desirable woman. He hadn't really either. "You look fine. Is it so wrong for me to think that?"

"Yes! . . . No!" She stepped back. "I mean, I don't know. It . . . it confuses me."

She drew a deep breath and winced with pain.

"Go take that thing off," he said, exasperated. "You don't have to go back to the house, just head over to those cottonwoods downstream. Joseph and I won't watch."

She eyed him suspiciously. "You promise?"

He made two quick slashes across his chest. "Cross my heart."

"We won't look!" Joseph bounded up to Caleb's side. "We're honest men, right, Caleb?"

"Right."

"All right. But only because I'm about to suffocate." She limped toward the thick grove of cottonwoods.

Caleb watched until she faded among the trees. He pictured her unfastening the white corset, and his imagination took a definitely improper turn.

"Caleb?"

"*What?!*" Caleb started.

Joseph blinked and stepped back. Caleb laid a hand on the boy's shoulder. "Sorry, Joe. You surprised me."

Joseph beamed. "Can we go fishing?"

Caleb glanced wistfully at the cottonwoods. What he really needed was a cold swim. "Fishing it is."

"Hooray! Do you have some string? Can I carry the poles? Do we have to dig for worms?"

Caleb laughed. "Yes, I brought some line. Yes, you can carry the poles, and no we don't have to dig for worms because I brought some bacon rind for bait. I thought we might also try to catch some crawfish."

Joseph stopped dancing. "What's that?"

Caleb ruffled Joseph's hair. "You'll see, Joe," he said. "Just wait." What a privilege to initiate this child into the joys of boyhood. Through the years, he'd forgotten the wonderful innocence of it all.

Elizabeth peeked around the trees three times to make sure she couldn't see Caleb or Joseph. She was so anxious to be free from the restricting garment, her fingers flew down the buttons of her dress.

The breeze brushed her bare arms, and she shivered, glancing around once again. The wind danced across her exposed back above the corset and chemise. She absent-mindedly rubbed bumpy skin.

What did the scars look like after all these years? She'd never once glanced at them in the mirror, afraid that reality might prove worse than imagination. Sometimes it was better not to know the truth. She'd long grown accustomed to high-collared dresses and nightgowns.

Closing her eyes, she rotated her neck and let the wind and sun caress the scarred flesh. What would it be like to be unblemished, like Solomon's bride in the Song?

Her fingers brushed the leather strip, and the stick cross suddenly seemed to weigh heavy. She wanted to rip it off, but instead used both hands to attack the corset.

The hooks popped, and she whipped the offending garment from around her body. Her breasts heaved under the chemise with the first full breaths she'd had all day. Holding the corset away from her body, she smiled, realizing how ludicrous she must look displaying it like a hunting trophy.

Laughing, she raised it with both hands and tossed it into the creek, watching with delight as it washed downstream.

Seated on the bank ten yards upstream from their picnic site, Caleb and Joseph were both barefoot, their trousers rolled up to their knees. Joseph's face was screwed up with rapt attention as Caleb showed him how to cast.

Smiling, Elizabeth gathered the remains of their lunch. She recognized Joseph's expression only too well; her father had demanded seriousness. From the day of Joseph's birth, it was understood that he was not like them, not a part of them. Father would provide shelter and food, a religious education, and occasionally a stiff hug, but Joseph was treated more like an unwanted houseguest than a child who needed nurturing.

Yet he flourished as if God himself filled the void in his life. One day Elizabeth was taking down laundry from the clothesline when she heard a whispered voice from behind Helga's prized rosebushes. Tiptoeing closer, she found three-year-old Joseph, unscathed by thorns, deep in one-sided conversation. Pressing against the side of the house, she listened with maternal love and fascination as he spoke to his heavenly Father. He told all about the people in his small life, what he liked to eat, how he loved to play outdoors, and how much he liked God's house where Reverend Cameron preached. He was such a treasure. She was glad he could grow and blossom without her father's domineering hand. He liked Caleb so well.

Caleb finished baiting the boy's line, and the top of Joseph's willow pole danced in the air. Just then Joseph caught sight of Elizabeth and waved. "Look, Elizabeth!

We're ready to fish!"

She felt a rush of pride and smiled. "Yes, I see. I hope you catch a big one!"

Caleb finished baiting his line, then straightened to full height. Elizabeth noticed how tall he stood and how his shirt moved with his broad shoulders. His hands looked tan and strong as he showed Joseph how to drop his line into the water, then cast his own beside it.

Elizabeth swallowed a hard lump. Caleb Martin was more patient with Joseph than any man had ever been. He had gone out of his way to make the boy happy. In return, Joseph chattered like a monkey to him, excited to be in his presence. They looked so natural together, so comfortable in each other's company. Caleb could teach her child what she had no knowledge of, lessons that only a man could pass on to a boy, a father to a son. Since Joseph became her responsibility, she'd assumed she could teach him everything. But she could see that wasn't true.

The Sanctificationists didn't believe their children needed the presence of a father. Many members had moved away with their children or demanded that husbands and fathers leave. There was even talk of the group buying a house for members and their children to all live together.

Martha said it was foolish for women to depend on drunk or abusive husbands. But surely they weren't all like that. Elizabeth had seen several of the Sanctificationists' husbands in Belton — they looked like the walking wounded. She'd even overheard one man, near tears, telling the general store owner how his wife and children had left him. He'd gone quiet when he saw Elizabeth, but the hurt hadn't disappeared from his face.

She glanced at Caleb. He and Joseph were as solemn as though in church. Caleb leaned over to whisper something, and she caught her breath at the sight of his blond hair against Joseph's black. The contrast was oddly pleasing.

Elizabeth smiled, drowsy from the sun's warmth. Anna was right; she had been working hard lately, searching desperately for the holiness that she hoped would come from her labors. Just for today, she would relax. Martha had even spoken that morning about the necessity of a day of rest.

She threw the cornbread crumbs out to the birds, then sat on the quilt. The chirping of sparrows overhead and the babble of the creek lulled her into contented peace, and she lay back. She smiled again at the light and dark heads, which melded into one as her eyes fluttered shut.

"Joseph! Your cork's sunk! You've got a bite!"

"I do!" Joseph scrambled to stand while pulling back on his pole. "I feel the fish!"

Caleb laughed. "Well, pull him in, boy! Let's get a look at him."

Joseph yanked his pole up and back, and a medium-sized catfish flopped onto the grass. "What a beauty!" Caleb held up the line so Joseph could see the twisting fish.

Joseph gingerly touched the slippery-smooth side, then the flipping tail. He gulped as Caleb carefully removed the hook from the fish's mouth.

"What's wrong, Joe? Aren't you happy?"

Joseph stared at the gasping fish. "I . . . I think I want to throw him back."

Caleb tossed the fish into the bucket of water and knelt down. "You feel sorry for him?"

Joseph nodded, near tears. "I thought I'd be excited when I caught one, but he looks so unhappy with his mouth and gills flapping."

Caleb wrapped an arm around the boy and drew him close. "You're what some people call sensitive, Joe. Do you know what that means?"

Solemn, Joseph shook his head.

"You're more aware of things than most people. You care about things others wouldn't even think about. Like fish."

"Or Elizabeth?"

Caleb smiled at Joseph's thought progression. "What do you mean?"

"I don't want her to get hurt."

"Nobody's going to hurt her. You either. And if you really want to let the fish go, we can. But can I tell you a story first?"

Joseph smiled. "I like your stories."

"Good." Caleb set Joseph on his lap. The boy settled in, his look of adoration obvious. Caleb cleared his throat. "Do you remember the story of Adam and Eve?"

"Sure!"

"Then you remember God told them they were in charge of all the animals. God doesn't want us to be mean to them, but I think he wants us to eat them when we need food. Any fish we catch will be for you and Elizabeth and Anna."

Joseph's face relaxed, and his gaze darted to the bucket. "Do you think it'll hurt when he dies?"

"I don't know. I hope not."

Joseph moved away. He sat down and

propped his face on his hands, elbows against his knees. Caleb waited patiently for his next question, hoping he'd have the right answer. He wanted Joseph to know he could always come to him for the truth.

"Reverend Cameron hurt a lot when he was sick," Joseph finally said. "Elizabeth sent me in to see him, and he cried so hard he couldn't talk to me." He paused. "That's the last time I saw him."

Caleb edged closer. "Do you think he was crying because he felt bad?"

"I don't know. Before he got sick, sometimes I . . . I wanted him to hurt."

"Why, Joe?"

His small lower lip quivered. "Because . . . because sometimes at night . . . when they thought I was asleep . . . I could hear him yelling at Elizabeth."

"What about?"

"I don't know. But the next day she'd look real sad, and she wouldn't even talk to me."

"What about Reverend Cameron?"

"He'd look real sad too."

"Like he was sorry?"

Joseph shook his head. "Like he was tired. I . . . I didn't want him to die! I just wanted him to stop making Elizabeth sad!" He buried his face in his arms.

Caleb lifted him and held him close. "Shh, Joe. You didn't make Reverend Cameron get sick. He was old. It was his time to die."

"But what if Elizabeth d-dies next? First m-my real parents left me, then Helga, then Reverend Cameron. Elizabeth's the only person left!"

Caleb tipped Joseph's small chin up. The smooth, copper face was streaked with tears, his brown eyes large and wet. "Elizabeth is young and not likely to die anytime soon. And she'd never leave you." He paused. "And neither would I."

Joseph threw his arms around Caleb, and his small body heaved with a sigh. "Don't ever go. I love you, Caleb."

Caleb rubbed his cheek against Joseph's hair. "I love you, too, Joe," he whispered hoarsely.

Joseph sighed, nestling in Caleb's arms. Closing his eyes, he relaxed. In a few minutes, he was asleep.

Caleb studied the boy's face. Who could ever abandon such a child? With his dark skin and eyes, he must have been a lovely baby. Why had his parents left him?

He'd definitely fallen for this sweet kid. He wasn't sure how he'd keep his promise, but keep it he would. "You're not going anywhere I can't keep an eye on you," he whispered.

Caleb carried him back to the quilt, surprised to find Elizabeth sleeping. He laid Joseph on the far side, then eased between them. With a sigh, he stretched out his legs and drank in the breeze under the shade. It was only early May, but the day promised to be a scorcher.

Lying on her side, Elizabeth burrowed her head further in the pillow of her arm. Caleb smiled. She looked more peaceful than he'd ever seen her. He studied the soft curve of her lips and wondered what it'd be like to kiss her.

As if she'd read his mind, she blinked. When her eyes focused on him, she gasped and scrambled up on her elbows. "H-how long have you been here?"

"Just a few minutes. You must have been awful tired to fall asleep."

She studied him warily. "It's warm today. The sun made me drowsy."

"Anna says you've been working too hard. You probably needed the rest."

"Nonsense. Where's Joseph?"

"Over here asleep." He could read the anxiety on her face and sought to put her at ease. "Let's take a walk."

"What if he wakes up?"

"We won't go far." Caleb rose and extended a hand. "Come on, Bess. We'll stay where we can see him."

"Well . . ."

He turned his hand palm up and beckoned with his fingers. "Come on," he whispered.

She stared at his hand. He saw her draw a deep breath, then let it out slowly. She rose and placed her hand in his.

Caleb felt a jolt at her touch. He gently curled his fingers around hers and led her down to the creek. Gesturing to the spot where he and Joseph had sat, he remembered she disapproved of grass stains. But to his surprise, she sat right down by the abandoned fishing poles.

Caleb sat beside her, the silence between them broken only by gurgling water and the hum of insects. He tossed a stone in the water, then another. "I didn't get a chance to show Joseph how to catch crawfish," he heard himself say.

"Did he get tired?"

"We-e-ll, yes. He cried himself to sleep."

She glanced back at Joseph. "Is he all right?"

"That depends." Caleb shifted uncomfortably. "Joseph seems to think he might have caused your father's death."

191

"Why on earth would he think that?"

The taut expression on her face made Caleb wish he'd never brought up the subject. "Apparently he used to wish your father would get hurt after yelling at you."

"That was so late at night," Elizabeth whispered. "Poor Joseph! I didn't know he'd heard."

Caleb idly palmed another rock. "What about you, Bess? How did you feel about being yelled at?"

She studied her hands. "It didn't matter how I felt. Father said I deserved it."

"That's ridiculous." Infuriated, Caleb hurled the rock, which sank with a loud splash. "You're the most stubborn woman I've ever known, but you're so good! You care about people; you're hard working and accomplished at everything you do; you love God . . ." Exasperated, he let out a long breath.

"Father's criticism was intended to improve my character and ensure my reputation," she said gently. "Please, Caleb. I'd rather not talk about him anymore."

Caleb saw by her sad expression that the subject was painful. He spied something moving in the water, and hoping to cheer her, grinned. "How are you at catching crawfish?"

Her brows arched over shocked eyes. "I've never caught them in my life!"

He yanked her up by her hand. "This is the perfect time to learn."

"But I don't . . . I've never . . ."

"Don't tell me you're *afraid!*"

Her eyes narrowed and darkened. "I'm not afraid."

He laughed. "That's the spirit. I don't believe you're afraid of anything, Bess."

Using a knife, he cut off several inches of string. "Tie this around the bacon rind like this, see? Now you do it."

She pinched off a piece of rind then wrapped it securely, leaving several inches of string for a tail. "Now what?"

"You won't like this part." Easing down to his stomach, Caleb dropped the bait in the shallow water along the creek bank. He grinned, waiting for her protest.

"You want me to get down like . . . like *that?*"

"I'd think that any woman who can keep herself, a man, and a boy alive for several days can stoop to such a level." He paused. "Unless she's not good at really *difficult* hunting."

She dropped to the grass. "Do you think gathering all those plants was easy? Do you think making those salves was easy?"

Caleb swished his bait in the water to attract his quarry. "Don't forget forcing me to drink your medicines."

"Yes! You weren't exactly the most cooperative patient I've ever had." She studied him critically. "Does that really work?"

He grinned at her, sprawled on her stomach with her black-stockinged legs kicked up behind her at the knees. "Try it and see, Bess."

She dipped the bacon in the water. "Here, crawfish," she crooned. "Come on."

Caleb expected her to continue the sweet talk, but suddenly she grew silent, her expression deadly serious. She stilled, poised for the hunt.

Caleb felt an intense rush of pride and awe. This, evidently, was the Elizabeth he hadn't seen when he was unconscious, the Elizabeth who had saved his life. Underneath the manners and ladylike posturing was a woman as determined as any warrior.

She levered herself to her elbows, eyes fixed on the string. "One's after my bait!" she whispered.

"Don't let him have it. Make him come up the bank."

She lured the hungry crawfish with the bacon, and Caleb leaned over slowly. When the crawfish had nearly cleared the water, Caleb grabbed him behind his claws and tossed him in the bucket of water with Joseph's fish. He wiped his hands on his thighs and grinned. "Congratulations, Miss Cameron. You've just caught your first crawfish."

She straightened, eyes glowing. "That wasn't difficult."

"The hardest part is patience."

"And cleaning your clothes later." Elizabeth glanced down at the grass and dirt on her dress front and grinned.

"If you really want to get into the spirit of fishing, you ought to take off your shoes and stockings. Then you can get your feet wet."

To his surprise, she nodded. "Why not?" She looked shy again for just a moment. "But you'll have to turn your head."

Caleb complied, grateful for Elizabeth's cheerfulness.

"You can look now." She stood in the shallow water, skirt modestly skimming the surface.

"You better hike up that dress or you're going to ruin it for sure," he said.

She flushed but raised it slightly. Caleb could see her toes wiggle, and a look of contentment came over her face.

He unbuckled his gun belt and laid it on

the bank, then waded in beside her. "Feels good, doesn't it?"

"Heavenly."

Caleb held up his bait. "Ready to catch some more?"

"Can we catch them standing up?"

"Just don't let 'em pinch your toes."

They bent over, searching for more crawfish. Dangling her bait with one hand, Elizabeth clutched her gathered skirt up with the other. Caleb tried to keep his eyes on the water, but he couldn't help catching an occasional glimpse of her shapely white calves and shins.

Six crawfish later, Elizabeth plopped down on the bank and dangled her feet in the water. "That's enough. I need to rest."

Caleb tossed the last crawfish in the teeming bucket and sat beside her. He stuck his feet next to hers, and the water swirled around his ankles. Basking in the afternoon's companionship, they sat in silence.

Elizabeth rearranged her hair on top of her head, then ran a finger between her neck and the high collar.

"I can't tell you how much I've enjoyed this day," she said, sighing.

Caleb eyed her openly. Swishing her feet in the water, she leaned her head back, eyes closed, to let the sun warm her face. A smile played at her lips, and he thought she had never looked more beautiful. She was simplicity and innocence.

He took up his gun belt and rose. "Do you always wear that thing?" she said.

He glanced down, surprised to find her studying him curiously. "Except when I sleep." He secured the belt in the buckle, then sat down again.

"Why do you wear it all the time?"

"*Why?* It's needed. Our run-in with Hez Taylor should have convinced you of that." He drew the gun and held it out for her inspection. "Look at it, Bess. It's a weapon, but it's meant to protect."

She stared at it skeptically. "It looks different from the gun you had before the stage wreck."

"It's one of the newer models," he said, "the Colt .45 Peacemaker. It's already equipped to fire metallic cartridges."

"I hardly see how anyone can call it a peacemaker," she said, shuddering.

Caleb reholstered the gun. "It's only as dangerous as the man who holds it. In my hands, it's a defensive weapon. I'm only going to use it if somebody threatens me first. Or you and Joseph."

She looked at the gun, then his eyes.

"I care about both of you," he said. "Now

that you've taken me on this picnic, you don't have to see me anymore. You've kept your end of the bargain. But the truth is that I want to keep seeing you." He didn't understand why he was attracted to Elizabeth Cameron, but it wasn't for a quick night of pleasure. His feelings for her ran deeper than that — he had never felt this way about any woman. "Will you let me call on you, Bess?"

"What would the Sanctificationists say?"

Hang the old biddies! "What do *you* say?"

"I say . . ." Her gaze darted to Joseph, then back to Caleb. "I say yes. You may call on me." Her eyes flashed a warning. "But Joseph must go everywhere with us."

Caleb nodded. He couldn't imagine Elizabeth without Joseph, or Joseph without Elizabeth. The boy and woman were like joined puzzle pieces — how they fit into his life he wasn't sure, but he wanted to find out. "I wouldn't have it any other way."

Elizabeth wordlessly lifted the supper tray from Anna's lap. Caleb had departed, Joseph long since tucked in bed, but Elizabeth felt crowded in Anna's presence. She had sensed those fathomless eyes on her all evening, as though Anna were assessing

Elizabeth's true condition, the depths of her soul.

Elizabeth had presented a calm front, but inside she was a turmoil of emotions. She'd wanted to hide here in Belton. She'd wanted to be left alone with her son to serve God. She'd wanted to put the past behind her and start anew.

Now she didn't know what she wanted. Caleb Martin had battered her hiding place at Anna's farm and the solid fortress of Elizabeth's heart.

She set the tray on the floor with more noise than necessary. One glance at Anna — waiting patiently with open arms — and Elizabeth curled up on the bed. She tentatively pressed her cheek against Anna's thin shoulder and shivered. "I'm so scared."

Anna stroked Elizabeth's hair, respecting her silence. "You are afraid of Caleb's attention," she finally said gently.

"He asked to call on me, Anna. No man has ever cared enough to seek me out like that."

"You forget Jesus. He is the perfect lover."

Elizabeth cringed. Jesus had seemed far away for so long. She could love him at a distance with worship and service, but Caleb was a man.

"You are not afraid of Caleb, you are afraid of your own feelings, *ja?* You are afraid to open your heart."

Elizabeth raised her head. "What makes you say that?"

"They that are after the Spirit, mind the things of the Spirit."

"I don't understand."

Anna tightened her arms around Elizabeth. "We as believers are given the Spirit, so God can speak to us with spiritual thoughts in spiritual words. God reveals everything to us by the Spirit, not by our eyes or ears. And it is not a spirit of fear," Anna said softly, "but a confidence that we can call on God as our father. His love is tender, *liebchen,* like a papa's."

"My father didn't love me very much. He said I wasn't good."

Anna clucked her tongue. "There is no *gut* or *schlecht* . . . bad . . . with God's children. Only love and forgiveness. Take your Caleb, for example. He is one of God's own, though he won't admit it. He thinks he is not *gut,* but in God's eyes he is. When he returns to his papa God, he will know true love. As will you."

"Love can be so powerful, Anna. It binds one person to another. I had a friend who couldn't see the evil in her own husband.

She loved him with all she had to offer, and he . . . he betrayed her."

Anna was silent for a long while. Elizabeth could hear the grandfather clock ticking in the front room.

"Tell me about this friend who has so influenced your opinion of love and men," Anna finally said.

Elizabeth let out a quiet breath. "Everyone loved Sunflower. But though she loved her husband blindly, he was not true to her. She became a believer, and he hurt her in ways she never knew."

Anna tenderly smoothed Elizabeth's hair. "You need to call on God to heal the hurts of your own life. He is always present for you."

"I wish I could believe that."

"All you have to do is ask Jesus. He will help your unbelief."

Elizabeth freed herself from Anna's embrace. *Fix your eyes on Jesus. Ask Jesus.* The words rang in Elizabeth's mind. Her heart felt heavier than ever. "Good night, Anna."

"Good night, dear one."

Elizabeth lifted the tray and blew out the lamp. In the sudden darkness, she nearly tripped over the chair.

That night Caleb sat at the table in his

room, pen furiously scratching against paper. He'd waited a few days to write his latest report to Noah, trying to decide exactly what to say about Elizabeth.

He leaned back in his chair and studied the letter. "Noah. Your sister and the boy are living with an elderly woman on a farm. They seem happy enough, and the woman is glad for the help. I'm keeping a close eye on them all. In fact, Elizabeth and Joseph and I went on a picnic today. I —"

He crumpled the paper and threw it across the room in disgust. What was wrong with him? The next thing he knew, he'd be telling Noah he loved Elizabeth! That would go over well. Caleb pictured Noah's reaction to that revelation. Caleb, an outlaw, in love with Noah's innocent sister. Elizabeth was from a decent family — they surely wouldn't have wanted the likes of him.

Caleb's own family had been decent and good, but he'd long since abandoned the lessons of his youth. He and Nathan had gone to war seeking revenge for their parents' deaths, but all they'd found was a bunch of dumb, scared kids like themselves.

Caleb stared out the window, watching twilight descend. He could still remember the first time he'd killed someone. He'd gotten separated from his regiment and was running alone down a Tennessee hill toward the battle ahead. He'd nearly tripped over a fallen Rebel hiding in a gully. The kid couldn't have been more than seventeen, and he'd been shot in the leg.

They'd stared at each other for half a second, then the kid had raised a trembling hand and leveled a revolver. Like a child's game, Caleb expected the boy to smile and say, "Gotcha!" But when he saw the pale trigger finger quiver, Caleb reacted on instinct. Without even steadying his rifle, he caught the kid in the forehead.

When the war was over, he and Nathan started stealing. After all the deaths they'd seen — all the deaths he'd caused — stealing didn't seem so wrong. He'd never killed anyone during any of the robberies, but he'd wounded a few. Somehow he'd acquired a reputation as a gunslinger.

Nathan had been sentenced to prison, while Caleb was assigned to work with Marshal Noah Cameron. After nearly a year, Caleb asked the marshal why he'd been given deputy duty instead of a prison cell like Nathan. Noah laughed, his gray eyes twinkling. "I guess that's just the luck of the draw, Caleb. Maybe the judge thought you'd feel more guilty if your buddy sat in prison while you were free. Who knows?" Then Noah sobered and said, "I asked for the deputy assignment because I figured you just needed a reminder of God's mercy and forgiveness."

Caleb narrowed his eyes. "I got baptized when I was twelve. That doesn't exactly make me what you call a believer."

"You're right about that. Baptism is just a symbol. But you're a believer, all right. Once you get that godly light in your eyes, it never goes out no matter how low you let the wick get. You've been running around in darkness for a long while, but God will shed his light again. All you have to do is ask for it."

Caleb drew out another sheet of paper. He copied the first letter word for word, leaving out the part about the picnic, then tersely signed his name.

Eight

Joseph skipped ahead of Elizabeth down the road, singing one of Anna's folk songs. He tried his best to imitate the German words. "Mustard den, mustard den soon start a henhouse, start a henhouse under mine shafts blabbers here . . ."

Elizabeth chuckled. "I think that's *Muss i denn, muss i denn zum Städtle hinaus, Städtle hinaus, und du mein Schatz, bleibst hier.*"

Joseph walked backward to face her. "Do you really like *das lied*, Elizabeth? Anna says I sing good."

"You sing very well, Joseph. Now we should practice our scriptures."

"Aww." He faced forward again, stopping to let her catch up.

Elizabeth put an arm around his shoulders. "Isn't it fun to walk to town for a change?"

"I wish Caleb would hurry and fix that wagon wheel."

"I wasn't going to tell you until later, but

Anna gave me a penny so you could buy a stick of candy."

"Candy? Hooray!"

"So let's do our Scripture memory lesson first."

Joseph grudgingly smiled. "All right."

"Let's see . . ." Elizabeth thought hard. Joseph was getting so good at their lessons that she had moved on to different verses. "Can you recite all of Psalm 23?"

Joseph easily remembered it, not missing a word.

"Now try John 14:27."

Joseph thought hard. " 'Peace I leave with you, my peace I give unto you: not as the world giveth, give I unto you. Let not your heart be troubled, neither let it be afraid.' "

Elizabeth hid her pleasure, not wanting Joseph to be prideful. "One more, then we'll stop. Try Philippians 4:4."

" 'Rejoice in the Lord always: and again I say, Rejoice.' "

"Good, Joseph." Elizabeth nodded. "You've done well."

He glanced up, and his expression almost took her breath away. For a moment, his brown eyes pierced her like Eyes Like the Sun's, searing her heart to its core. Then the corners of his lips turned up, and he was Joseph again, beaming and happy.

They walked on, silent, passing fields of fading wildflowers. May had rapidly turned into June, and the bluebonnets were giving way to primroses and black-eyed Susans.

Joseph dashed to the side to pluck several straggling, washed-out bluebonnets. He raced to catch up with Elizabeth then presented the bouquet with all the seriousness of a bashful suitor.

She pressed the flowers against her heart. "Thank you, Joseph. These are my favorites."

Beaming, Joseph shoved his hands into his trouser pockets and kicked at a rock. "Anna says she likes to sing German songs."

"Yes, I imagine she does."

He pulled back his foot to give the rock an extra hard kick. "She says it reminds her of when she was a little girl. Did you know she didn't even know English when she and her husband came to America?"

"I believe I've heard her say that."

He caught up to the rock and kicked it again, ran up to it and kicked it even harder. The rock skidded down the road and veered into the tall grass. Joseph ran ahead and pawed through the stems. A grasshopper jumped out, and he let the grass fall back in place with a loud sigh. Elizabeth caught up with him, and he fell in step beside her, shoulders hunched, exuberance spent.

She had begun considering what sort of dress material she would buy when Joseph tugged at her arm. "Do you think I'm a Comanche?"

Startled, she felt her heart beat faster. "Yes. By birth."

"Is that why people don't like me? I've heard the Comanches are very bad. But Anna said they couldn't all be like that. She said my real parents must have loved me very much to leave me with Reverend Cameron."

Elizabeth fingered the white tops of the drooping bluebonnets. "Do you wonder about your parents very much, Joseph?"

"Sometimes. Mostly I just wonder if they were nice people and why they didn't keep me."

"They probably couldn't take care of you, so they left you with someone who could," she said, then added, "Someone who would watch over you and love you."

He glanced up shyly. "I'm glad it's you, now, Elizabeth. You and Caleb."

"Caleb?"

"He said he'd never leave me."

Elizabeth tried to keep the surprise from her voice. "When did he say that?"

"The day of our picnic. When we were fishing."

Elizabeth's heart pounded against her ribs. Weeks had passed since that picnic. Caleb was too busy surveying to come out to the farm during the week, but at her invitation, he had spent every Sunday with her, Joseph, Anna, and the Orozcos.

She didn't know whether to be pleased or upset by Joseph's revelation. What did Caleb mean — he'd never leave him?

She quickened her pace. She'd considered stopping in to see Martha and Molly while in town, but decided she and Joseph would do well to transact their business and leave. The sooner they purchased their supplies, the sooner they could get back to the safety of Anna's farm.

Elizabeth ordered and set aside the staples first — flour, sugar, lard, kerosene — saving the decision of new material for last. She had to have a second dress. She paused over the cloth bolts, fingering the black calico with distaste. Back in Fort Worth she'd vowed to make a new mourning dress, but the ugly fabric was scratchy between her fingers.

"Can I wait outside?" Having agonized over the jars of candy and having made his decision, Joseph was now clearly bored.

"All right. But stay out of trouble."

"Yes ma'am!" He was out the door like a shot.

Elizabeth looked wistfully at a bolt of flowered blue lawn, trailing her fingers over its beauty. Wouldn't it look pretty gathered in a looped-up polonaise and shaped over a newfangled bustle? She'd seen the banker's wife with just such a dress, sporting a wide ruffle at the hem, and it —

Elizabeth shook her head, horrified at her thoughts. Such a dress was way too extravagant for her. She had chores to attend to every day. And as for blue, why, all the Sanctificationists wore plain-cut, conservatively colored dresses. They were to be servants of God — not hostesses at a society tea!

Yet Caleb had said blue would be more becoming on her than brown. Didn't she owe it to him to look nice? He had done so much for her and Joseph, the least she could do was look presentable when he came to call.

She blushed furiously at her pride. It wasn't as if she was the only person Caleb was interested in. He came to see Joseph and Anna too.

Still, the blue *would* look nice. It didn't have to be a fancy dress; a plain bodice and skirt would do nicely.

The store owner moved in front of her. "You made up your mind yet, Miss Cameron?"

She lifted her chin, feeling reckless. "I have, Mr. Berry. I'd like this blue lawn."

Joseph sat on the bench, idly swinging his feet. He wished Caleb worked in town so he and Elizabeth could stop by to visit. Seeing him once a week wasn't nearly enough. Last Sunday it had stormed, so they hadn't even been able to go fishing.

"Hello, Joseph." Edward Taylor smiled and sat beside him. "Whatcha doin' in town?"

"Shopping." He smiled back at the older boy's attention. "Aren't you in school?"

"School's out for lunch. I always go check on my pa."

"Oh." Joseph cringed, remembering the incident with Hez Taylor.

"Psst! Hey, you little boys, come here!"

Joseph and Edward glanced up. Down the boardwalk, an older boy leaned against a pillar, motioning to them.

"Who's that?" Joseph whispered.

"Willie Burton. He's a troublemaker."

Willie motioned again. "Well, come on. If you two want to see something funny, hurry up!"

Joseph glanced at the store and saw no sign of Elizabeth. He and Edward looked at each other, shrugged, then made their way to Willie, who winked and pointed across the street. "See that buggy? It belongs to old maid Bigelow. Watch what happens when she comes out of the butcher's shop."

Joseph watched with fascination. Willie chuckled.

Iola appeared and bustled to her buggy, pointed chin thrust out. Willie chuckled harder, and a smile tugged at Edward's lips. "What's gonna happen, Willie?"

He held up a knife. "Watch."

Horrified, Joseph backed away. Iola climbed into the buggy and snapped the reins. The horse obediently moved forward, leaving the traces, the buggy, and a surprised Iola Bigelow behind. Willie whooped with delight. "Look at the old witch!"

Joseph's mouth dropped open in shock. Edward was silent, too, staring at the fuming Iola Bigelow. Willie doubled over with laughter, and Iola whipped her head around.

"Uh-oh!" Willie thrust the knife handle into Joseph's palm. "Come on, Edward, let's get out of here!" He turned to Joseph. "Listen, you rotten Injun. If you tell anybody, I'll hurt that woman . . . that Elizabeth. Then I'll come hurt *you!*" He ran down the boardwalk.

"Sorry," Edward whispered, wide-eyed, "but my pa would beat me for sure!" He raced after Willie.

Iola Bigelow jerked Joseph up by the collar. "I might have known!" She snatched the knife away.

"But I —"

"Help!" she cried, twisting around. "Somebody get help!"

Joseph squirmed, coughing under her iron grip. Tears flowed. "I didn't do it, Miss Bigelow!"

The boardwalk filled with indignant townspeople. Joseph could hear their heated whispers, each one a fiery dart.

"It's that Injun kid."

"Might have known."

"Sooner or later he was bound to —"

"Joseph!" Elizabeth rushed to his side and wrestled him away from Iola's grasp. "Let go of him!"

Iola's face twisted and reddened. She waved the knife. "He tried to have me killed, Elizabeth Cameron! He cut the traces on my buggy. I could have fallen out flat on my face!"

"Joseph would never do that!" Elizabeth knelt to his level, her eyes blazing. "Who gave you the knife?"

Joseph glanced at the angry faces surrounding him, then looked into Elizabeth's eyes. He thought about Willie's warning, and he swallowed hard. Then he remembered Hez Taylor and how he'd smacked Edward with the belt.

"I . . . I can't tell," he whispered.

The crowd's speculation swelled, faces contorting with anger. Elizabeth gripped his arms. "Tell the truth, Joseph."

He swallowed hard, forcing tears to the back of his eyes. "I won't tell."

"Joseph, tell me *right now.*"

"No!"

"You see?" Iola said triumphantly. "Guilty!"

The crowd roared.

Elizabeth shot to her feet. "Oh, for heaven's sakes, Iola. Do you want someone to go for a rope so you can hang him? He's just a little boy!"

"He's a no-good little *Injun* boy!" someone shouted.

"And we don't want him here!"

Iola Bigelow smiled, her face radiant with hatred. "I don't think we'll have to worry about that much longer."

Elizabeth balled her hands into fists, then let them drop. She couldn't take on the whole town. She should never have left the farm. "You needn't worry. We're leaving."

Joseph in tow, she pushed through the crowd back into the general store. A few people followed, but she moved straight to the counter. Hands shaking, she opened her reticule. "If you're through measuring that material, Mr. Berry, I'm ready to pay."

Glancing nervously at the still-angry crowd, he stammered out the total. Elizabeth laid the coins on the counter and snapped the reticule shut. "Please deliver everything to Anna's."

Berry glanced at the crowd and swallowed. "I can't."

"Tomorrow will be fine."

He cleared his throat. "I can't today, tomorrow, or any time, Miss Cameron."

Elizabeth laid her palms flat on the counter. "You've made deliveries to Anna since her husband died. Since when have you stopped?"

She caught the direction of his fearful gaze and glanced over her shoulder at the crowd. "I see how it is," she said in a low voice. "In that case, will you please hold my purchases? I don't have enough money to rent a wagon, and Joseph and I can't carry all these things home by ourselves."

"I can hold 'em for you, Miss Cameron,"

he said grudgingly. "You paid for 'em fair and square."

She smiled bitterly. "Please hold them for Mr. Caleb Martin. Good day, Mr. Berry."

People stepped out of her way, a few looking embarrassed. No one spoke. Elizabeth dragged Joseph out the door and down the boardwalk, grateful no one followed, keeping up a steady pace several blocks down the street.

She blinked back tears. How could people be so ignorant? Joseph was just a boy, an innocent little boy whose very conception had been founded in hatred. For five years she'd kept silent, convinced that that was the best gift she could give him. The truth would hurt Joseph much worse than any false accusation by Iola Bigelow.

Joseph panted to keep up. "Anna's farm is back the other way, Elizabeth. Where are we going?"

"To Caleb's boardinghouse. Mrs. Merkle's."

"Where's that?"

She stopped short, feeling defeated. "I don't know, Joseph."

She spotted a woman tending her rosebushes. "Excuse me. Can you tell me where Mrs. Merkle's place is?"

"Why, it's just two doors down, honey,"

the woman said. "That yellow house right there."

Elizabeth thought she might cry with relief. "Thank you."

Mrs. Merkle said Caleb was surveying. The elderly woman gave Joseph a fresh-baked gingerbread man and provided Elizabeth with paper and pen.

She thought about what she wanted to write, then finally settled on the truth, short and simple. "Please see Mr. Berry. Joseph and I need your help."

Nine

"Whoa, fellows." Caleb drew back on the reins, and the wagon creaked to a halt.

Before he could even set the brake, Elizabeth was at his side, peering up anxiously in the fading light. "Thank God you came."

He grinned as he jumped down, whacking the dust from his trousers. "I didn't realize you were that desperate for your supplies. I would have been here sooner, but I didn't get back to town till late afternoon."

"It's not the supplies. It's Joseph."

Caleb's smile fell. "Is he sick?"

"No, he . . ." She eyed him carefully. "Didn't Mr. Berry say anything?"

"Just that you weren't able to bring home the things you purchased. I thought he always delivered Anna's supplies."

"He used to. Until Iola Bigelow accused Joseph of trying to kill her by cutting the traces to her buggy."

"*Joseph?* He'd never do anything like that."

218

Elizabeth sighed and leaned against the wagon. "She caught him with the knife in his hands. Obviously someone else did it and let Joseph take the blame. She had a whole crowd whipped up to a frenzy, Caleb, as if he were some savage bent on destroying their town."

"Can't he point out who did it?"

"I think he knows, but he won't say. He won't even say *why* he won't say. I wouldn't let him have any supper, and he still won't tell."

Caleb softened. "Maybe he'll talk to me. Then we can straighten this whole mess out, and Iola can crawl back under the rock she slithered out from."

"Caleb!"

"It's true, Bess, and don't deny it. Those Sanctie friends of yours are nothing but tight-lipped old spinsters. They have nothing better to do than pick on little kids."

"They're not all like that!"

"Well . . . I know one who isn't," he said softly. He watched for her expression to harden, and when it didn't, he took her hand. She drew a little breath of surprise, but stepped closer. Slowly, carefully, he drew her into a gentle embrace, and she hesitantly raised her arms to circle his shoulders.

"I don't know what I would have done today if I couldn't have counted on you," she whispered.

Caleb pressed his cheek against her hair. He longed to tell her everything — how much he desired her, how much he wanted to protect her, everything about himself and what he really was. That he was sorry for the mistakes of the past. That she was the only one who could help him.

He wanted to keep holding her, but he gently released her. "Let me talk to Joseph alone."

Nodding, she led the way into the house. "I sent him to bed. He and I sleep in the room on the left." She smiled encouragingly, then watched as he climbed the stairs.

Caleb's tread grew heavier with each step. Was this how his father used to feel when Caleb had gotten into trouble? How many times as a disobedient boy had Caleb waited behind his own closed door, trembling, wondering what punishment his father would mete out? His father had always seemed to know just what to say — Caleb wished he had that kind of wisdom right about now. What would his father do to get him to talk?

He rapped gently. "Joseph?"

The door opened by degrees. Dressed in

his nightshirt, Joseph turned into the room and flung himself back on the bed and stared up at the ceiling.

Caleb sat on the edge of the bed, his gaze trained on Joseph. "Aren't you going to say hello?"

Joseph shrugged.

Caleb moved closer. "Elizabeth tells me you got accused of cutting the traces on Miss Bigelow's buggy. Is that right?"

"Yes."

Caleb paused. His father would have given him a chance to make a clean breast of things. "Did you do it?"

Joseph pressed his lips together, looking for all the world like a stubborn Elizabeth. If Caleb hadn't been so concerned, he would have laughed. Instead, he fixed his sternest gaze on the boy. "Joseph, I asked you a question."

Silence.

"Look at me, Joseph."

The little boy's chin quivered, but his brown eyes hesitantly met Caleb's.

"You're big enough to discuss this sitting up."

Joseph complied. He tried to look away, but Caleb held his gaze with a look that demanded obedience. "I want to know what happened this afternoon. You've upset most of the town, but you've especially upset Elizabeth. And me."

The little chin quivered faster. "I'm s-sorry."

"Sorry's not good enough, Joe. I need some answers. If you did it, the best thing you can do is 'fess up now. If you didn't do it, you need to tell me who did."

Joseph turned and faced the wall, wrapping his arms around himself.

Feeling defeated, Caleb sighed. "I don't have much experience with little boys, but I remember what it's like to be one. I've tried everything my father would have, but you still won't answer me." Caleb rose. "Do you know what my pa would do now if I were being as obstinate as you?"

"Wh-what?"

"He'd make me carry a belt out to the shed, and he'd give me the licks I deserved for being disobedient."

Joseph's shoulders shook, but he still didn't turn around. A fat tear slid down his smooth cheek.

Caleb rubbed the back of his neck. Who was he fooling? He wasn't even Joseph's father — he couldn't lay a hand on this sweet kid. "You're too small for me to whip, Joseph. Maybe Elizabeth —"

"No-o-o!" The huddled form shot off the

bed and hurled itself at Caleb. "Don't hurt her! You can whip me! I'm sorry!"

Caleb struggled to retain his balance. "Whoa!"

Joseph grabbed him around the legs, sobbing. "Don't hurt her, Caleb. I'll be good!"

Caleb lifted him onto his lap and held him close. "I wouldn't hurt Elizabeth. Shh, Joe. Don't cry."

"Please don't hurt her! I'll behave!" Joseph's sobs multiplied, his body racked with his grief. Caleb rocked him, murmuring comforting nonsense.

Short, loud footsteps sounded on the stairs. Elizabeth burst into the room, her stick cross swinging.

"What did you do?" She caught sight of Joseph, red-faced and weeping, and she covered her mouth with her hand. "Tell me you didn't hurt him!" Her eyes blazed fire at Caleb. "If you hit him —"

"You know I wouldn't do that!" Caleb stood quickly, clutching a weeping Joseph.

"Then why is he crying?" she yelled over Joseph's intensified sobs.

"He thought I was going to hit you!"

Shock etched its way across Elizabeth's face. Joseph's sobs punctuated the silence and seemed to snap her to attention. She put her arms around the boy, inadvertently drawing Caleb into the embrace. "Nobody's going to hurt you," she whispered. "I stake my *life* on it. I'd rather die than see you hurt."

Joseph let go of Caleb and clutched at Elizabeth. "Don't die! I don't ever want you to go away. I'll be good, I promise. I didn't want that boy to hurt you!"

Caleb stepped back. "The boy who gave you the knife?"

Joseph nodded quickly, his eyes frightened.

"Did he say he would hurt Elizabeth if you told on him?"

Joseph bowed his head, but Caleb had already seen the truth. The child wasn't being obstinate, he was trying to protect Elizabeth. First from this boy, then Caleb himself.

He glanced over Joseph's head and saw that Elizabeth had drawn the same conclusion. Joseph cradled his head against her shoulder, and she stared with a mixture of love and fear at his dark hair. Caleb could see her throat work up and down as though she were trying to swallow a lump.

"*Nobody* is going to hurt Elizabeth," he assured Joseph solemnly.

"H-how do you know that?"

"Because you and I would never let them."

Joseph smiled tentatively and wiped away a last tear.

"Nobody has to protect me from anything," Elizabeth said. "He's just a boy, Joseph."

"What if he was a man?"

Caleb touched the gun in his holster. "If he's bigger than me, I have this."

Elizabeth cradled Joseph away from Caleb. "Is that your answer to everything? Your fists and then your gun?"

"I take care of my own, Bess."

She raised her chin. Looking at her, he thought it was funny how he'd always preferred blue-eyed blonds; for the life of him, he couldn't remember why. Her eyes were dark and deep, veiled with layers of mystery. With a jolt, he realized he could be content to spend a lifetime plumbing their depths.

She lowered her gaze. "I'm glad to hear you admit you didn't do it, Joseph. The truth is very important."

Caleb shifted uncomfortably. What would she think when she eventually learned *his* truth, that he wasn't who he pretended to be? Would she understand and forgive him?

Joseph held out his arms to Caleb, who lifted him from Elizabeth's embrace. "I'm sorry I didn't tell you, Caleb. I was scared."

"You don't ever have to be afraid, Joe. I'll watch —"

"God'll watch over you," Elizabeth broke in. "He always has."

Caleb cleared his throat, uneasy. He patted Joseph on the bottom, then set him on his feet. "I think there's probably a little boy here who wouldn't mind some dinner."

"Can you stay, Caleb?" Joseph's eyes shone. "You could eat with us then sleep in here with me and Elizabeth, just like when we were camping."

Elizabeth's face colored, and even Caleb felt awkward. His feelings for Elizabeth had changed considerably since those days on the road. "Thanks, Joe, but I have to get back to town tonight."

"You're welcome to stay for dinner," Elizabeth said. "Anna will want to see you. She talks about you all the time."

Pleased, Caleb smiled. Anna Mannheim's opinion meant a great deal to him; the bedridden woman had more insight than anyone he'd ever met. "Thank you. I'll stay then. Do you need Joseph, or can he help me bring in the supplies?"

"I want to help! I want to help!"

"You may help." Elizabeth laughed softly at his enthusiasm.

The gentle sound filled Caleb's heart, expanding its boundaries. Somehow the grim-faced woman in black had disappeared since Caleb first met her in Fort Griffin, replaced by this caring, compassionate woman he was growing very fond of. It was as if she had grown a heart.

Anna said she wasn't hungry, but they ate in her room to keep her company. Curled up next to her, Joseph wolfed down two bowls of stew, chattering the entire time. Elizabeth sat by Anna's other shoulder, and Caleb sat in the ever-present lone chair.

He thought Anna's smile looked more forced than usual, her replies a little more distracted. Elizabeth apparently didn't notice, for she kept busy refilling bowls. When she did sit down, she focused her attention on Joseph, smiling at the boy's talk and antics. Joseph leaned over several times to playfully whisper in Anna's ear, unaware of the elderly woman's tight smile and the pain that flickered across her face.

When the last bite of stew was eaten, Anna smiled gently. "I hate to be so rude, but I find myself tired tonight."

Elizabeth stood from the bed in a flash. "Oh, Anna, I'm so sorry! Here we've been going on and on, and you need to sleep.

Joseph, give Anna a kiss, then you have to go to bed also."

"G'night!" Joseph leaned over and planted a big kiss on Anna's cheek.

Caleb watched as Anna's hand lingered on Joseph's shoulder. A look of wonder crossed her face then disappeared. "Good night, little one," she murmured. "The God who never slumbers will watch over you while you rest."

Elizabeth followed Joseph as he bounded out the door. Caleb rose to follow, but Anna called him back.

"You are a reliable man, Caleb Martin. Elizabeth knew she could depend on you today. That is very important."

"Yes, Anna," he said. "Good night."

"Gute nacht."

In the kitchen, Caleb met Elizabeth coming down from upstairs. "Joseph's almost asleep," she said, "but I know he'd like you to say good night."

Caleb smiled. "I'd like that too."

He was pleased that she followed him upstairs. The bedroom lamp was turned down low, and a warm glow bathed the little boy snuggled under the covers. Joseph opened his eyes and smiled dreamily. "Caleb."

"Good night, Joe." He bent to whisper in the boy's ear. "I love you."

228

Joseph's smile widened for a moment, then faded with sleepiness. Caleb kissed him on the forehead, adjusting the covers around his shoulders. He smiled at the boy a moment longer; Joseph was already fast asleep.

When he rose, Caleb saw Elizabeth studying him from the doorway. She turned away, embarrassed. "I . . . I didn't mean to stare. I've never met a man who has such tender feelings for a child."

Caleb took her hands and led her into the darkened hall. "I care about Joseph a great deal, Elizabeth. You're lucky to be the guardian of such a special boy."

"I know," she whispered. Her shy smile was barely discernible in the dim light as they descended the stairs. "I made some coffee earlier. Would you like to sit in the parlor?"

"I'd like that very much." She went for the coffee, and he took a seat on Anna's rose-patterned sofa.

Caleb's heart thumped like a schoolboy's. What was the matter with him? Was he actually nervous about making a good impression? He was practically mooning around with calf-love written all over his face. What had happened to the steady nerves that had seen him through all the robberies and gunfights?

He might not be a kid anymore, but he sure felt like a newcomer to romance. He and Nathan had joined the army at sixteen, before Caleb could court any of the few girls near home. His first sexual experiences had been clumsy encounters with army laundresses who made lucrative money on the side as prostitutes. He'd never developed so much as a speaking relationship with a woman before Elizabeth.

And here he'd fallen for a woman who couldn't be more his opposite. A Bible-quoting, law-abiding, puritanical woman. A preacher's daughter, for crying out loud.

"Here's your coffee." Her fingers brushed his, and he nearly jumped. She sat at the far end of the sofa, demurely settling her skirts. Caleb's heart started pounding again.

He'd barely taken a sip when three steady raps sounded at the door. He glanced at Elizabeth. "The Orozcos?"

She set down her cup and rose. "Only if someone's ill."

Caleb moved in front of her, natural inclination taking over. "Let me get it." He opened the door, his hand instinctively reaching for his gun.

A white-haired, bearded man doffed his hat and bowed slightly. "I apologize for the lateness of the hour, but I must speak with Elizabeth Cameron. I'm Judge Andrew Mc-Kinley. From Belton."

Elizabeth pushed in front of Caleb. He tried to pull her back, but she was already extending a hand of hospitality. "Please come in, Judge."

"Thank you." The judge cast Caleb a wary glance, then followed Elizabeth to the sofa. He sat at one end and Elizabeth at the other, Caleb standing beside her.

"This is Caleb Martin, Judge," she said. "Would you like some coffee?"

"No, thank you. I would have waited until tomorrow, but my heart wouldn't let me. I knew I couldn't sleep until I told you the news." He glanced at Caleb then Elizabeth. "Iola Bigelow came to see me today, all in a huff about the boy you're taking care of . . . Joseph?"

Elizabeth nodded, nervously smoothing her cross.

"She says that since he's an Indian . . . and an orphan . . . he belongs on a reservation."

Elizabeth laughed. "That's ridiculous. My father raised Joseph from a baby. Now that my father's dead, I've assumed the responsibility for Joseph's care."

"But your father never legally adopted the boy?"

Her smile fell. "No."

"Then you have no legal rights to the boy. Miss Bigelow's asked me to send a letter to the reservation at Fort Sill to begin the transferal process. I'm afraid it's only a matter of time before they come for him."

Elizabeth rose. "No! I know Iola doesn't like him, but . . . they can't do that!"

"I'm afraid they can, Miss Cameron."

Silence filled the room. Caleb's stomach clenched, as if he was about to jump from a moving train.

"I'll adopt him," Elizabeth said.

The judge shook his head. "I'm afraid that's impossible, Miss Cameron. There isn't a judge alive who'd grant an unmarried woman custody of a child. Especially an Indian child."

Closing her eyes, Elizabeth sagged to the sofa.

Caleb straightened. "What about a married couple, Judge? Could they adopt Joseph?"

"That could certainly be done." McKinley rose. "I have to get back to town, Miss Cameron. I know it's devastating news, but I wanted you to hear it from me rather than Iola."

Elizabeth didn't respond, and Caleb saw a tear trickle down her cheek. "Thank you,

Judge," he said. "We'll talk to you soon."

Caleb ushered him to the door and let him out. When he turned back, Elizabeth was sniffling furiously, using her sleeve to wipe her eyes. Caleb knelt beside her, his heart working double-time. "Don't cry, Bess. It'll be all right."

"I . . . I can't let him go, Caleb. He's such a precious boy. He can't go to a reservation. Joseph wouldn't have any idea how to live as the Comanche do!"

Caleb took her cold hand with his own clammy one. "It'll be all right."

"I heard what you said about a married couple." She sniffled harder. "Were you thinking of the Orozcos adopting him? He wouldn't have to go to Fort Sill, but he still wouldn't be in my care."

"I wasn't thinking of the Orozcos."

She sniffled even louder. "Then who?"

"You and me."

"That's ridiculous! You and I aren't —"
She stared at him in shock.

Caleb cleared his throat. "I'm asking you to marry me, Bess. Will you be my wife?"

Ten

"Your wife?" she repeated stupidly.

He nodded, his eyes holding hers. Elizabeth suddenly realized he was on his knees, her hand clasped in his. A sick, cold weight dropped in her stomach.

"I care about you and Joseph," Caleb said in a low voice. "It's a simple solution. And you must care enough about me so that the thought isn't entirely repulsive."

She blinked, speechless.

"We can live in town or move away . . . wherever we think best." He studied her, then added, "And I'm sure in time we'd find our marriage to be as good as any other."

She saw him swallow. "Come on, Bess," he said. "I've never done this before. Don't look at me like I've got two heads."

"I'm sorry," she whispered. Fear thrummed through her veins.

Caleb smiled and released her hand. "You don't have to answer me right away.

You need time to think. You saved my life, now it's my turn to help. Joseph belongs with you."

"Yes, he does. I can't leave Anna, of course."

"Surely she won't mind if I move in after we're married."

"Perhaps you could keep your room at Mrs. Merkle's for the week and continue to come out here on Sundays."

He gave her a hard look. "Marriage is a commitment, Elizabeth, and mine would be to you and Joseph. We would live together as a family."

Family. She rose and turned away, her stomach rolling.

"I know it's sudden," he said. "I wish we had more time to do this proper. I know every girl dreams of her marriage proposal . . . with an engagement ring and all."

"I never expected to get married," she whispered.

"There's no reason why you shouldn't. You'd make any man proud, Bess. You're the kind of woman a man would wait a lifetime for — kind, decent, pure . . ."

She froze as his hands closed gently around her shoulders. Unsettled, she forced herself to breathe evenly as he stood just behind her. With one hand on her shoulder, he pulled her around to face him. She raised her chin, determined to counter his power.

To her surprise, his expression was tender, not possessive, and he gently cupped her cheek. "I've gone about this all wrong," he said. "I wish I had the fancy words to make it more romantic. The truth is, I've never even had a sweetheart before."

That took her by surprise. "You haven't?"

"I've never been in one place long enough."

"I suppose surveying takes you all over the country."

Discomfort flickered across his face, and his smile faltered. "Yes." He studied her a moment, then smiled gently. "Judge McKinley saw me here, and if I don't get back soon, your reputation will be in tatters."

"Why?"

"If we announce our engagement, followed quickly by a marriage, most people will assume I compromised you."

Warmth rose under her collar.

"So I'll leave you to make your decision. Will you send word to me?"

She nodded, mute. Her stomach was dancing again.

"May I kiss you good night?"

Elizabeth drew a short breath. Before she could reply, his arms gently enfolded her.

Closing her eyes, she raised her face, and his lips brushed hers. "You and Joseph belong together, and I'd be honored to be part of your family," he said softly. "I may never be able to buy you a lot of fancy things, but I will always protect, always take care of you."

Warmth flowed over her. He must care for Joseph very much to want to marry a woman he didn't love.

From years of practice, she carefully schooled her features. "You're a kind man, Caleb. I'll send you my answer."

"Don't worry about Joseph. He'll be all right." Caleb smiled again, then he was out at the wagon, lighting a lantern and hanging it on a pole for the trip home. She watched the light grow dim, until it was no more than a firefly as he drove down the road.

She took the coffee cups back to the kitchen then checked on Anna, who slept soundly. Taking her time, she cleaned the supper dishes and banked the fire in the cookstove. The work occupied her hands, forcing the grim truth to the back of her head. But as she climbed the stairs for bed, she could no longer avoid the decision she had to make.

Marriage. To Caleb.

Elizabeth slipped off her brown dress and

moved to the open window. A cacophony of cicadas, frogs, and crickets filled the countryside. An eerie summer breeze soughed through oak leaves and around shutters, brushing against her soul as she scanned the road Caleb traveled back to town.

She wished she could see the light from his wagon. She was skeptical of this dependence she had on him, and now she would be forced to give him everything, including Joseph.

And above all, herself.

Shivering, she knelt beside a snoring Joseph. His dark hair, uncut since Fort Griffin, fell across one cheek. She brushed away a lock, smiling tenderly. He would be pleased to have Caleb for a father. A father who would teach him so much about life, so much about becoming a man.

Elizabeth smoothed her hand down Joseph's arm. When he was just a baby, she stroked him exactly the same way when Helga wasn't watching. Elizabeth had always been fascinated with his smooth, dark skin, the feel of his hair between her fingers, the way his deep brown eyes stared at her so wisely.

Give him back to the Comanches? Never. He belonged to her. If she had to marry Caleb, she would do so without complaint.

She had endured worse.

She changed into her nightgown, then mumbled a hasty prayer. Easing under the covers beside Joseph, she wondered again why Caleb would give up his freedom to marry her. It was true that she would cook and clean for him. Not to mention . . .

She shuddered, glancing over at Joseph. What would it be like to see a man sleeping in his place, to see Caleb beside her every night? What would he want from her?

You saved my life; now it's my turn to help you.

Relief washed over her from head to toe. He was just paying her back for the stage wreck! He wasn't interested in her at all, despite all his talk about her being an ideal woman. He was willing to give her and Joseph his name out of obligation.

Elizabeth let out a deep breath. Marriage didn't seem so final or frightening after all. It would be a marriage of necessity, and she could do far worse than Caleb. At least they were friends.

Caleb rubbed the back of his sweaty neck, closing his eyes and letting the whiskey slide down his throat. It'd been a hard day at work, and he intended to enjoy a few minutes alone here in his room before he headed downstairs for one of Mrs. Merkle's good dinners. She'd taken a motherly interest in him, but so far she hadn't caught on to the bottle he stashed in his room. If she did, mother or not, she'd probably toss him out on his ear.

"Mr. Martin!" Mrs. Merkle rapped on his door. "There's someone here to see you."

Nearly choking on a mouthful of liquid, Caleb hastily swallowed. "Thank you, Mrs. Merkle. I'll be downstairs in just a minute."

"It's a young lady — Elizabeth Cameron."

Caleb jabbed the cork into the bottle. "Tell her I'll be right there." He tossed the bottle under his pillow and tucked his shirt into his trousers. Holding a hand close to his mouth, he breathed out, then winced. Of all times for Elizabeth to show up.

Mrs. Merkle waited for him at the bottom of the stairs. "She's in the parlor," she whispered. "Such a lovely girl to come all this way from the farm. It must be something important."

"Yes," Caleb said absently, skirting his landlady. Surely Bess wouldn't have come into town if she were going to refuse his proposal.

Sitting on Mrs. Merkle's horsehair sofa, Elizabeth was a picture of loveliness even in that plain brown dress. She nodded. "Good afternoon, Caleb."

Caleb sat beside her. "Hello, Elizabeth."

Mrs. Merkle stood next to them, beaming. "May I get you something to drink?"

"No, thank you," Elizabeth said.

"Mr. Martin?"

"Nothing for me." Caleb leaned closer to Elizabeth, impatient. "Now about —"

"I have coffee and tea."

"Nothing, thank you," Caleb said, gritting his teeth.

"I could —"

"Nothing."

Mrs. Merkle looked abashed. Elizabeth frowned at Caleb, then turned. "Mrs. Merkle, do you have a pen and ink I could borrow."

"Why, yes." Brightening, she retrieved the requested items from a roll-top desk and laid them on a short table in front of the sofa. "Here you are, my dear. Anything else I can help with?"

"No, thank you." Elizabeth smiled. "You've been most kind."

Mrs. Merkle stood smiling at them, clasping her hands. "If there's anything else you need, please call. I'll be close by."

Caleb breathed a sigh of relief as she retreated from the room. Turning to Elizabeth, he took her hand. "It's good to see you."

Elizabeth straightened. "I'll get right to the point, Caleb. I've made up my mind about your offer, and I don't want to delay. But I have a few stipulations if I'm to agree to our . . . marriage." She pulled out a piece of paper from her sleeve, unfolded it, and carefully spread it out on the table.

Caleb frowned. "What kind of stipulations?"

Finding her place on the paper with a finger, she cleared her throat. "Number one. You will never under any circumstance hit Joseph or hurt him in any way."

"You know I'd never do that."

"Yes, I believe you're right." She placed a check by the first line. "Number two. You will attend the church of your choice with Joseph and me. I believe a family should worship together."

"I agree. Religion's important for a kid."

"Good." She made another check mark. "Number three. You will not set foot in a saloon or drink any liquor ever again." She leaned forward and sniffed, shooting him an accusing look.

"But, Bess —"

"I don't want Joseph growing up to believe that drinking is something to be admired."

Caleb sighed loudly. "Oh, all right. If it's that important to you, I can give it up. My father never drank either."

"Very good." Another check mark appeared on the page. "Number four —"

"Whoa! How many items do I have to agree to?"

"Just eleven."

Caleb grimaced. "Maybe you'd better give 'em to me all at once."

"Very well." She cleared her throat. "No cursing, carousing with other women, playing cards, gambling of any sort —"

Caleb slapped his hand down on the paper, and Elizabeth started. "You're willing to marry me based on a list of do's and don'ts? You obviously don't even know me, Bess!"

"I'd marry just about anyone for Joseph's sake."

Caleb lazily pulled his hand back. "I'm flattered," he drawled.

She blushed. "You know what I mean. But since you mentioned it, no, you haven't told me much about yourself. You mentioned a sister named Samantha, a friend named Nathan, and that you fought in the war. What else do you want me to know?"

What indeed? He probably had more to hide than reveal. "I'm originally from Kansas," he said slowly. "And I'm twenty-seven years old."

She nodded, clasping her hands over the infernal list. "Go on."

"Well, I'm a surveyor, but as my future wife, you should know I don't plan to stay in this business when this job's done."

She frowned. "Why not?"

"I'm waiting to hear from a friend who may have a new offer for me. Sort of a new chance at life, you might say."

"Have you done other work besides surveying?"

Caleb groaned inwardly. Even if he could bring himself to tell her the entire truth about himself, Noah had forbidden him to do so. "Yes, ah, banks. And railroads."

"So you want to go back to one of those lines of work?"

"No!" Caleb lowered his voice. "That's in my past."

She cocked her head, puzzled.

He clasped her hands. "Look, Bess. Nathan and I own some land up in Wyoming. We've never done much with it, but I wouldn't mind settling down there. I have a lot of loose ends in my life right now. Nathan married Samantha, then he went to . . . well, he had to go away. She thought he was dead, so she ran off. I don't know where she is or if she's even still alive. As soon as I finish this job, I need to go see Nathan, then try to find Samantha." He released her hands and leaned back. "Now what else do I have to agree to?"

"Did I mention no gambling?"

Caleb nodded grimly. "That was the last one."

She drew a deep breath. "No gambling, no tobacco, you must say grace before every meal, lead prayers every evening, and last of all, we will occupy separate bedrooms." Smiling, she raised her face.

"No, Bess."

"You don't agree to these?"

"I don't agree to the last one." He leaned forward and eased the paper from her hands.

Elizabeth's face paled. "What do you mean?"

He held her gaze. "When we get married, I'll become your husband in every sense of the word."

"B-but I thought this way, if we don't . . . if the marriage isn't . . . consummated, then you could always get an annulment if Joseph and I ever decide to leave Belton." She lifted her chin. "I don't believe in divorce."

"Neither do I. But there will be no annulment either. If you marry me, Elizabeth, we'll be together for life."

"But . . ."

"Starting on our wedding night."

She pulled her hands to her lap and bowed her head, silent.

Caleb studied the paper. "If I abide by all this, what will you do?"

"I promise to honor and obey you," she mumbled woodenly.

Caleb crumpled the paper in his hand, and Elizabeth flinched. Fear flickered in her eyes before a veil came down, her emotions concealed behind expressionless features.

His fury gave way to anguish. Why was she always so guarded? He plucked her cold hand from her lap. "I don't want a servant who takes orders, Bess. I want you as my *wife* . . . Joseph as my son. I want him to call us Ma and Pa. I want to come home from an honest day's labor to my own home and my family. I want us to share a meal together, then listen to Joseph's school lessons. Then after we've tucked him in bed, I want to bank the fire and go to bed with the woman I —"

"All right, Caleb," she whispered. "I'll marry you."

Caleb smiled. "I hear marriage isn't all that bad."

"I can be ready to marry you in three days," she said tonelessly. "I'd like to make up a new dress for the occasion."

He nodded, patting her hands awkwardly. He'd never seen anyone look more defeated. Much as he feared she might change her mind, he knew she needed to examine all her choices, so he forged ahead. "What about your brother? I'll bet you and Joseph could go live with him."

"No. Eventually someone would complain about Joseph and do the same thing Iola Bigelow did. Joseph needs to be adopted, and Noah deserves his own life."

Caleb smiled. "It'll be all right, Bess. You'll see."

She smiled wistfully and straightened. She quietly discussed wedding arrangements with him, her chin held high. When they finally rose to announce their decision to Joseph and Anna, Caleb noticed that Elizabeth left the crumpled paper on the table, untouched.

Elizabeth set down the blue lawn she'd been stitching to stare out her bedroom window. A jay scolded a sparrow, boldly stealing a crust of bread from under the timid brown bird's beak. The jay gloated, squawking, and transported his prize on swift wings to the large oak down the road.

Elizabeth sympathized with the bereft sparrow. "Poor thing," she murmured. "Why must the bullies of the world always have their way?"

Earlier that day, she'd gone to Martha's to explain her departure from the Sanctificationists. Caleb had made it clear she must do so. Martha greeted her at the door, her eyes swollen and nose red from obvious weeping. A grim-faced, disapproving Iola was at her side.

"Come in, Elizabeth." Martha gestured inside. She led the way to the parlor, and Elizabeth glanced around for Molly as she and Martha sat on the sofa.

Martha wiped her eyes with her apron and drew a long, broken breath. "I'm being quite foolish," she said. "It really only frees me for the life God has chosen me to lead."

Elizabeth blinked, confused. "What does?"

"Why, forcing my husband to leave this home. Didn't you know?"

"No! What happened?"

Martha twisted the apron between her hands. "It's all over town by now, but if you're out at Anna's, I guess you haven't heard. I caught him and Molly . . . upstairs. They were only flirting," she added hastily, "but it was evident from their conduct that the course of their relationship was inappropriate. Naturally, I dismissed Molly. She's left town already. And now George will live over his store. I want nothing more to do with him."

"But, Martha, he's your husband."

"God wants us to abandon all familial relationships that stand between us and him, Elizabeth. Haven't you heard a word I've been preaching?"

"Yes ma'am," Elizabeth said. "In fact, that's why I'm here. To tell you that I must leave the group."

"*Leave?*"

Elizabeth bowed her head. "I'm getting married to Caleb Martin."

Martha sat back in shock. "I'm very disappointed in you. You're going against all that I've learned from God. All that can make you right with him. Mark my words. You'll be sorry you married and subjected yourself to the dominance of a . . . a *husband*."

"Perhaps I will," Elizabeth murmured, "but it's something I have to do."

Iola pursed her lips. "How can you even *think* of marriage when Martha here is a blatant victim of man's lusting nature? Don't you realize that when you join yourself to that heathen man, you'll lose sight of God?"

Elizabeth wanted to cry out that it was all Iola's fault, but she couldn't. She had to protect Joseph, even if it meant leaving the Sanctificationists. Iola was right about men's lust, but Elizabeth had no choice except to move forward.

Her stitching picked up speed, leaving an even trail of perfectly spaced white stitches. This marriage would work — she would make sure of that. No matter the cost, she would see that it worked.

Anna swallowed a bite of fried chicken. "When Caleb comes to live here, the three of you must take your meals in the kitchen. Like a regular family."

"Nonsense." Elizabeth set aside her supper plate. "We will eat with you as always."

"Is Caleb really going to be my pa?" Joseph bounced on Anna's bed.

"Yes, Joseph. And please don't jostle Anna."

Anna laughed. "The boy's excited, Elizabeth. How can you be so calm?"

Elizabeth forced a smile, even though the other woman couldn't see her. "I have too many things to do. If I don't hurry, I'll never finish my dress."

Anna handed Elizabeth her plate, her dinner only half-touched. "There's something else you must do. You must clean out my old upstairs bedroom. It must be quite dusty by now." Anna reached out to pat Elizabeth's hand. "I want it clean for you and Caleb. It is the largest, nicest bedroom in the house. Every morning Rudy and I used to lie in bed and listen to the birds and the sound of Nolan Creek as the sun came up."

Elizabeth glanced at Joseph, who by now was merely toying with his dinner. "Joseph, will you go check the vegetable garden?"

"I already picked everything today."

"Check the tomatoes again. I thought some might turn red by this afternoon."

"All right." He bounced off the bed. They heard the back door slam shut.

Anna frowned. "Tell me what is wrong."

Elizabeth pursed her lips together, fighting for self-control. Anna always seemed to read her thoughts. If only she could unburden all that was in her heart, all her fears and doubts. She settled for a broad answer. "I'm afraid."

Anna smiled warmly. "Every bride is afraid of what comes after her wedding, *liebchen.* You must be patient with your fear, just as your groom will be. He loves you very much. Just as you love him."

Elizabeth was grateful that Anna's blindness hid the expression on her own face, for she was certain it betrayed her. She and Caleb had agreed not to tell Anna and Joseph the reason for their marriage — the truth might prove too upsetting.

"Do you have any questions you'd like to ask an old married woman?" Anna said softly. "My *mutter* explained what I could expect, but you have no *mutter,* Elizabeth. May I help?"

Tears filled Elizabeth's eyes. *It must be difficult for Anna to speak of such things.* "I . . . I understand what will happen."

Anna turned her face toward the faint warmth of the fading sun. Her smile deepened, and her expression glowed. "God's design for married love is amazing. It brings so much to a couple. Unity . . . pleasure . . . children."

Elizabeth shuddered. She'd never even considered that last aspect with Caleb. He'd probably want a whole houseful of kids — playmates for Joseph.

Anna turned away from the window. "Thank you for having your wedding here. I am honored to be a part of your celebration."

"You don't mind that we're going to Salado for a few days? I can always tell Caleb —"

"I don't mind at all. Marisa will stay with Joseph and me. She will take good care of us while you and your new husband are getting to know each other better. You two need some time alone. You might soon be busy with a little one to tend, *ja?*"

Cold fear rolled through Elizabeth, and she fought it down before it engulfed her. "You and Rudy never had any children, did you?" she said, hoping to redirect the conversation.

A shadow crossed Anna's face. "We had a little boy, Johnny. He was four years old when he was taken from us. Sometimes I still have trouble understanding . . ." she trailed off, and her face became peaceful again. "But now you will be Mama to Joseph. You must hug and love him each day, Elizabeth — as though it were his last."

"Yes, Anna," Elizabeth whispered. "I'll try to be as good a mother as I'm sure you were."

"God can make you a wonderful parent, *liebchen*. And wife too. He is waiting to fill you with his love."

Elizabeth abruptly rose to gather the plates. She had no response for the overly

253

optimistic Anna, no response for the gnawing panic in her own soul.

Two days later she awoke with her heart skidding against her ribs. It was her wedding day.

She drew a steadying breath. "You're getting married, and that's final."

Joseph lifted his head from the pillow beside her. "What'd you say, Elizabeth?" All smiles beneath his sleep-tousled, freshly cut hair, his face already reflected a day full of enthusiasm.

"I said I'm getting married."

Joseph threw his arms around her. "Isn't it wonderful? You and me and Caleb . . . I mean, Pa . . . will be a family now." He drew back, his expression sober. "Do I still have to call you Elizabeth?"

She rose, smoothing a pleat in her gown to avoid his gaze. "You may call us Father and Mother."

"How about Ma and Pa? That's what Caleb said he called his parents."

She didn't answer. Joseph hopped out of bed and whistled as he pulled up the covers on his side. Elizabeth tidied her side as well. "I won't be sleeping in here anymore, Joseph."

"Why not? We can all sleep in this bed.

There's lots of room."

"It's proper for a husband and wife to share the same bed — alone. Caleb and I will sleep in Anna's old room. We'll be just across the hall."

"*Buenos días!*" Marisa appeared in the doorway, Elizabeth's new dress slung over her arms. She winked. "I stole this from you last night when we were here for supper and pressed it for you. But don't worry. When your groom came to stay with us last night, I had it hidden away. He didn't see it."

Elizabeth forced a smile. "A groom's not supposed to see his bride's dress before the wedding, is he?"

"Or his bride," Marisa chided. "So you must hurry and get ready. Joseph, you and the other children must help Anna today, while I help Elizabeth."

"Sure, Marisa." Joseph's eyes shone. He flashed Elizabeth a smile before he yanked on his clothes and ran down the stairs.

Elizabeth took her time finishing the bed, until Marisa stirred impatiently. "Come on, Elizabeth. I've already drawn your bath downstairs. The water is getting cold."

"You didn't have to do that."

Marisa sighed with exasperation. "Do you think your groom wants a bride who smells like she's been doing chores?"

"The chores! I can't get married, Marisa. I haven't milked the cow or told Joseph to feed the chickens or turned the goats out —"

"My children are taking care of all those things. And Gustavo will bring your groom. But if you don't hurry, he will find you still in your bathwater."

Elizabeth blushed, and Marisa laughed. "You are so pretty when you turn pink. A beautiful bride! And you will be even more beautiful when you are wearing your new dress and I fix your hair."

"My usual bun will do."

"Not today." Marisa pushed her out the door.

In the kitchen, the full, steaming washtub sat in the middle of the room. The surrounding doors were closed, and the curtains pulled. Marisa lifted a kettle of water from the stove. "Get in and tell me if it's too cold. I can add more hot water."

Panic rose in Elizabeth's stomach. "I . . . I'd rather you waited outside, Marisa. In case . . . the others come back."

"Such a nervous bride!" Marisa smiled and set the kettle down. "Don't worry. I'll wait outside the door. The back door is bolted, so you don't need to fear. No one will bother you." With a final smile, she retreated.

Elizabeth sighed with relief, yet she took a hurried bath, scarcely noticing the water's warmth, and trembling as she scrubbed herself from head to toe. By the time she'd wrapped herself in a large towel, the trembling refused to subside.

Smiling, Marisa swept through the door, blue lawn dress and fresh undergarments in her arms. "Let me help you get dressed, Eliza—"

"No!" Elizabeth backed away, hugging the towel closer. "I . . . I mean, thank you, Marisa, but I'm used to dressing myself. Perhaps you'd better check on Anna."

Marisa paused, then backed toward Anna's closed door. "All right," she said in a soothing voice. "Let me know when you're dressed, and I'll fix your hair."

"Th-thank you." Elizabeth waited until Marisa disappeared, then she rapidly threw on the clothes.

She curled her fingers into her palms until her fingernails dug crescents in her flesh. The quivery feeling passed, leaving numb resolution in its wake.

The next hour blurred past. The children reappeared from their chores and hustled upstairs to change. Somehow in her shock Elizabeth noticed that Joseph looked his

Sunday best, every hair slicked in place. Someone announced that the preacher had arrived, and then she was smiling woodenly, making small talk. As they clustered around her bed, Anna's laugh rang out, her gentle German voice pervading Elizabeth's numbness.

She felt as if she were floating out of her body, watching from a corner in the room. She was aware of her heart pounding, of every breath being deep and deliberate, but she was apparently fooling everyone.

Even Caleb looked spruced up and shy as he stood beside her and held her hand. Surely he could hear her heart thumping madly and feel her pulse racing through her veins.

As the preacher began the ceremony, Elizabeth's brittle smile threatened to crack. "And do you, Elizabeth, promise to love, honor, and obey . . ."

Dizzy, she felt her palms and forehead dampen. Through a haze she saw Caleb smile tenderly. Panic seized her throat, and she involuntarily squeezed his hand for support.

His smile faded to concern, and she realized everyone was waiting. "Bess?"

Her eyes widened, and she nervously wet her lips. "I . . ."

Out of the corner of her eye, she saw Joseph. Spine straight, he stood absolutely still . . . except for his deep, luminous eyes that danced with obvious joy.

Elizabeth drew a deep breath, and the tremors subsided. Gathering her best smile, the one she'd long perfected, she turned. "I do."

Eleven

The buggy bumped along the dirt road, its occupants silent. Caleb had explored every avenue of conversation with his new bride, but each one terminated rapidly in a dead end. Elizabeth's answers were quiet and monosyllabic, and she hugged her side of the buggy as though planning to jump. He didn't think she'd looked at him even once since they'd said their vows.

"Son," his father had told him along ago. "There are two things to remember on your wedding night: patience and tenderness."

Caleb cleared his throat, startling Elizabeth out of whatever daydream she'd wandered into. Her eyes were large and unblinking, like a doe's just before the kill.

"Sorry," he mumbled, shifting uneasily. The summer sun beat down like heat waves from an oven. He ran a finger under the stiff collar of his new shirt. "I was just going to say that it's a shame we don't have time to go to Austin. I hear it's quite a town."

Her gloved fingers loosened the tiniest fraction from their grip on the buggy's side. "Yes."

"But I hear Salado's nice too. It's ironic that we'll be staying at a stage stop . . . seeing as how we met on a stage."

"Yes."

"I hear the inn is nice and the food well spoken of."

She nodded, fingering the ever-present stick cross. Annoyed, Caleb frowned. "Do you even wear that thing to bed?"

"I always wear it."

"Why?"

"It's a reminder."

Caleb angled toward her. "Of what, Elizabeth?"

She inched farther away. "Of . . . of God."

"A cross made of *sticks?*"

"Especially sticks." She turned to study the passing countryside.

Caleb sighed. He supposed he should be grateful he'd been forewarned so he didn't blurt out something stupid when he saw her in her nightgown. If she wanted to wear that hideous thing to bed, he wouldn't say a word. "Patience," he muttered under his breath.

At last the Shady Villa Hotel came into view. Curtained by magnificent pecan, elm, and oak trees, the hotel had rightfully earned its name. Caleb eased back on the reins, and a young man appeared at his side to take the horse and buggy.

Caleb walked around to Elizabeth's side. Unusually quiet, she was actually waiting for his assistance. He helped her down, thrilling at the touch of her gloved hand in his. He lifted their lone bag and held out his arm. Without question, she accepted the courtesy.

They crossed the hotel's wide veranda where several old-timers sought relief from the scorching Central Texas afternoon. They nodded at Caleb and Elizabeth, and he returned the acknowledgment. He was proud to be seen with his bride, no matter what the reason for their marriage.

The hotel's interior offered welcome relief from the blast furnace outside. Sweat ran down Caleb's back, but Elizabeth looked cool and fresh, without a wrinkle on her pretty new dress. He liked the way the blue material complimented her skin color. It was much more flattering than the browns and blacks she normally wore. The bodice tapered smoothly to her small waist, and the skirt flowed over her hips to the ankles of her black shoes.

Caleb swallowed hard. She belonged to

him now, rightfully and legally. Not as a piece of property, but a wife to be protected. Loved.

"May I help you?"

Caleb started. "Uh, *yes*. We'd like a room."

"Certainly, sir." The clerk turned the registration book around. "For how many nights?"

"Two." Caleb signed *Mr. and Mrs. Caleb Martin*. Smiling broadly, he turned the book around. "My wife and I just got —"

"— off the road from Belton." Elizabeth fanned herself vigorously. "My goodness, but it's hot outside."

The hotel clerk smiled. "Yes, it is. I have a room for you at the back with excellent shade and a wonderful night breeze. You folks just passing through?"

"Actually, we're on —"

"— our way to Austin." Elizabeth's face flushed as she caught Caleb's glare. "We . . . we heard so many kind words about your establishment that we decided to stay here a few nights."

"Wonderful!" The clerk hustled from behind the desk. "I'll show you to your room and get someone to carry your bag."

"I can carry it." Caleb gripped Elizabeth's elbow. Her gaze flickered to his, then darted away.

Following the clerk, they passed a limestone fireplace and ascended a stairway. "Sam Houston stopped here at the Shady Villa. They say he wore a leopard-skin vest and stood out on the veranda the day he spoke against secession. And Robert E. Lee himself even stayed here twice. 'Course he was just a colonel back when he came to stop an Indian uprising. Here's your room."

The clerk opened the door and stood back. Elizabeth scurried inside, and Caleb followed, watching as she hurried past the double bed.

"Here's your key. Dinner is served downstairs at around six. Hope you . . ."

Ignoring the prattle, Caleb pressed some money into the clerk's palm. The clerk backed out and closed the door, leaving Caleb and Elizabeth alone.

She stared out the window, her hands gripping the sill. Caleb coughed, battling his own case of nerves. "We're finally here."

"Yes."

He set the bag by the fireplace. He could imagine lovers curled up together on the rug on a cold night, sharing whispered secrets and dreams. He glanced at Elizabeth's back, wondering if she would ever offer him her heart. Despite the heat that rolled through the window in lazy waves, the room seemed colder than any winter's blast. "Is there some reason you don't want it known we're newlyweds?"

She turned, primly clasping her gloved hands. "People make such a fuss, Caleb. I didn't think it was any of their business."

Tenderness, he reminded himself. "Perhaps you're right. Would you like to sit down?"

She glanced nervously at the bed. "I . . ."

"There, I mean." Caleb gestured at the rocker by the fireplace.

Her expression relaxed. "Thank you." Spine straight, she sat down and eased the rocker into motion. It squeaked with the movement.

Caleb moved toward her, then stopped at the bed. "It's too hot to take a walk."

"Y-yes. Did you have something else in mind?"

He rested a hand on the bedpost. "Maybe after dinner?"

The squeaking abruptly ceased. She stared up at him, her expression frozen.

"We could take a walk, I mean. It'll be cooler then."

Elizabeth set the rocker going again, faster this time. She nodded. "That would be nice."

Caleb turned. *Nice?* Couldn't she relax?

Couldn't she see how patient he was trying to be? Did she think *he'd* ever been on a honeymoon? He didn't know what he was supposed to say or do to make things easier. All he knew was that if she had a team of horses hitched to that rocker, she'd be halfway to Austin by now!

He raked a hand through his hair. "Look, ah, maybe you'd like to get cleaned up or something before dinner. Why don't I go check on the horses and let you have some privacy?"

She relaxed, looking like a condemned man given a reprieve. "All right."

Caleb nodded and left the room, questioning his ability to remain patient much longer.

He gave her three hours, hoping that nightfall would soften her attitude.

Dinner passed quickly, but he noticed she merely picked at her quail and fresh peas. Ravenous, Caleb ate his fill.

They managed a respectable patter of small talk, mostly about Joseph and Anna. Caleb found if he kept her occupied with thoughts of home she even occasionally smiled. But when the waiter asked if they wanted dessert, Elizabeth glanced desperately at the staircase. "Yes, I'd like —"

"That will be all for this evening." Caleb covered her hand with his.

"But I —"

Getting up, he paid for their meal and escorted her from her chair to the hotel's entrance. "You did promise me a walk."

He heard her let out a deep breath. "Yes, I did."

Caleb led her from the porch, crowded with other guests trying to catch the evening breeze. He nodded in response to their silent greetings and strolled arm in arm with Elizabeth around the back of the inn.

They passed the barn that stabled guests' horses and relay horses for the stage. Caleb gestured at a large pecan tree. "It's too dark now, but you can see Indian signs there. They tell me this used to be a favorite camping ground for the Indians, then the early Texans."

"That's the way it always is. The Indians get pushed off their land in favor of progress."

Cricket chirps punctuated the ensuing silence, and Caleb pondered her words. They were the most he'd heard out of her all day. "You're fond of Indians, aren't you?"

"My best friend, Sunflower, was the daughter of a medicine man. I loved her like a sister." Elizabeth paused. "Perhaps more than my real sister."

"Medicine man?" Caleb stopped short, remembering the Indian tepees near Fort Griffin. "Is that where you learned so much about plants and medicine?"

"Yes. Walks Far was a wonderful healer." Elizabeth looked as though she wanted to say more but didn't.

Caleb guided her past the cave that the Shady Villa used as a springhouse. Beside the spring was a stand of oaks. Caleb gestured at the thick grass. "Let's sit for a minute. It's cooler here."

She sank beside him, primly arranging her skirts. He smiled at her fussiness; he had definitely married a lady.

The cricket chirps intensified, and Elizabeth cocked her head. Amused, Caleb smiled. "What is it?"

"You can tell how warm it is by the chirps. Count for a minute, then divide by four and add fifty. Though we already know it's hot."

"Would you rather go back to the hotel?"

"No! I mean, not yet. It's actually quite lovely out tonight."

Overcome by a surge of tenderness, Caleb squeezed her hand. "Bess, I —"

"Why are you interested in me?" She turned toward him, her eyes anguished. "I'm not pretty to look at."

"When I look at you I see a very beautiful woman, Elizabeth Martin."

Embarrassed, she lowered her face, but Caleb raised it with his hand. "You *are* beautiful," he whispered.

Motionless, she watched him move closer. His lips pressed against hers, and she murmured something that could have been assent or protest. When she didn't pull away, he deepened the kiss, embracing her gently. She slowly raised her arms to his shoulders, and he felt the stirring of desire increase.

Didn't she know what she did to him? How right he felt about her as a woman? How could she know, indeed? She was pure, an innocent in the ways of love. True love.

So was he. "Let's go back," he said hoarsely.

Her eyes widened, but she rose and walked with him back to the hotel. The people on the veranda hadn't stirred. Elizabeth averted her face, silent, as Caleb led her to the stairs. He glanced at her face flushed with embarrassment.

"We're *married*, Bess," he said softly, trying to comfort.

"They were all . . . staring."

"If they were, it's only because they were

admiring the beautiful woman on my arm. They weren't having nasty thoughts about you and me."

In their room he lit a lamp, and her eyes widened with panic as she stared at the bed. Someone had turned down the covers for the night.

"I'll wait outside while you change." He left the room without waiting for a response. This time he'd give her ten minutes, no more.

He leaned against the door, impatient. His heart pounded, his gut burning with an urgency that had built since the kiss. He'd never waited so long for a woman, never been more nervous.

"That's enough time, Miss Bess." He rattled the knob to give her fair warning.

She'd extinguished the lamp and stood by the window, hands clasped on the sill. Her brown hair cascaded to the waist of the high-collared nightgown he'd bought for her in Fort Worth. Moonlight gleamed behind the white material. She was beautiful. Perfect.

Caleb unbuttoned his shirt and tossed it on the rocker as he moved toward her. "Bess." His hands closed around her shoulders.

She gasped, then turned away.

Touched, he smoothed her hair. "Don't be afraid of me."

"I'm not afraid," she whispered.

"No, of course not." He pressed a kiss to her forehead, her temple, her cheek. "Not my brave Elizabeth. You battle rivers, fevers . . . everything. You're the strongest woman I know."

She closed her eyes. Caleb gently kissed her lips, moving closer to embrace her. She trembled, and his heart soared. Her own heart pounded against his chest. Pleased, he deepened the kiss and heard her low moan.

"Elizabeth." He brushed the cross aside as he touched the buttons of her collar.

She wrenched her mouth free and pushed at his shoulders. "No!"

Caleb stumbled back. "Wh—"

She clenched her hands, eyes blazing. "I will do my duty as your wife, but I will *not* be pawed at like . . . like" — her voice broke on a sob — "an animal."

"Animal?" His desire was doused like cold water over a flame. "Is that what your Sanctificationist biddies have you believing? That a husband acts like some sort of wild beast?"

She raised her chin.

"Well, is it?"

"I said I would do my duty. I'll not go

back on our bargain."

Caleb clenched his fists. Their marriage was no more than a trade to her! He would give Joseph a last name, and she would give him herself. It sounded more like prostitution to him.

Caleb yanked on his shirt and headed for the door. "You can keep your purity, Elizabeth. I'll find my comfort somewhere else!"

Shocked, Elizabeth stared at the door he'd slammed shut. Her blood raced, but she couldn't move, couldn't utter a sound. She felt her fists uncurl, and a cry of anguish rose from her stomach. "Oh, God, what have I done?"

She reached for the leather around her neck, and her fingers frantically readjusted the cross. What was happening to her? The kiss by the river had been so tender, filling her with a strange, sweet sensation. Even upstairs, she'd felt the gentle stirring. Until . . . until he'd towered over her, engulfing her, threatening to . . .

She shut her eyes and hugged herself tightly, digging her elbows into the ache that never completely subsided. Like an animal hiding in its burrow, she wanted to curl up into herself, to wrap herself around the ache until she couldn't feel it any longer. Sobbing, she sank to the bed.

She awoke to sunlight. Groaning, she hauled herself out of bed and moved in front of the mirror. Her eyes were swollen and red, and her hair tangled. The wooden cross rested unscathed against her white gown like an accuser around her neck.

Why had she thought she could keep her past a secret? Even if she endured his touch, Caleb would find out.

"No man will ever want your illegitimate half-breed son," Father had said. "Let alone you. You're a fallen woman, Elizabeth. Damaged goods."

She rubbed her arms; her skin felt gritty. Pouring water into the basin, she prepared to scrub at the dirt that never seemed to go away.

Sprawled on the stable floor, Caleb clutched his head and let a half-drained whiskey bottle slip to the ground. The contents gurgled into the straw. Caleb kicked his legs out, and a horse whinnied.

Caleb groaned. Some bridegroom he made. He'd spent his wedding night getting drunk in a stable while his still-virtuous *bride* slept upstairs.

Didn't she realize even God-fearing people had human desires? He'd felt her response when he kissed her by the spring, felt her passion stir. Did she think what he wanted — what he knew they both wanted — was wrong? Evil?

He stumbled to his feet, cursing when his head throbbed in protest. The little puritan and Joseph had wormed their way into his heart, and now he'd have to live with this marriage the rest of his life. Why had he ever thought it would work?

To make matters worse, if he ever wanted to touch his wife again, he'd probably have to apologize for storming out. He felt foolish for hitting the bottle, but he sure wouldn't let her know that. She'd have plenty to say if she knew he'd already broken one of the promises from that fool list of hers.

Luckily no one was hanging around the stable. Caleb washed his face and hands at the pump and slicked back his hair. He hoped he didn't smell too much like whiskey. Then just in case anyone asked what he'd been doing, he checked on his horses.

Whistling to belie his aching head, he forced himself to stroll into the hotel and up the stairs. He wanted anyone he passed to assume he'd just stepped outside. He was glad Elizabeth had insisted they not tell anyone they were newlyweds.

Outside the room, he raised his hand to knock, then changed his mind. It was his room; she was his wife. He jerked the door open. "Bess, I —"

"G-go away! Please!"

Caleb stood stock-still in the doorway. Caught in the middle of washing her arms, Elizabeth had parted her hair to hang in front of bared shoulders, her face to the brilliant sunshine. Though she struggled vainly to tug it up, her gown was lowered to her waist.

And Caleb saw the numerous long, white scars that crisscrossed his wife's otherwise smooth back.

Twelve

He quietly shut the door, surprising himself with his calmness. "Who did that to you?"

Elizabeth pulled the gown up in front to her shoulders and backed away. "N-nobody!"

"Someone whipped you, Elizabeth. Who?"

"It doesn't matter, Caleb. It's over, and he's dead."

"He!" Caleb spat out the word, even though he knew good and well it'd been a man. He moved toward her, and she backed up all the way to the wall.

Caleb closed his hands around her arms, and she trembled. "I'm sorry I didn't tell you. I should have known it'd make a difference."

"Of course it does! If I had that lowlife here, I'd crush his throat between my hands!"

Shaking now, Elizabeth clutched the nightgown higher. Caleb quickly released her, realizing his words had terrified her. He stepped back and lowered his voice. "I won't let anyone hurt you again, Elizabeth. Do you understand?"

She nodded. "Now will you please go away?"

"I want to see the scars."

She tightened her grip on the gown.

"Doesn't the Bible say a husband should love his wife's body as his own?"

"Yes."

"All I'm asking is to see your back."

Hesitantly she turned and lowered the gown. Caleb touched a finger to the largest scar, a shimmering, white trail from her neck almost to her waist. She flinched as he delicately traced the others, counting seven in all.

He turned her around gently by her bare shoulders. "Get dressed, then we'll talk."

Her eyes flickered to the doorway, and Caleb shook his head. "I'll give you privacy, but I won't leave you again, Bess." He turned his back.

Who would do such a thing? It must have happened several years ago, for the scars were thick and pale.

Love was often in short supply around my home, her words came back to him.

He knew by her stillness that she was dressed, and he turned. She'd put on the blue wedding dress, and her hair still hung loose. She looked like a girl, small and frightened.

"Your father whipped you."

She nodded quickly.

"Why, Bess?"

"It's not an easy story." She sat on the bed and stared bleakly at the wall. Caleb sat beside her, waiting. "You asked last night if I was fond of Indians, remember?" she finally said.

He nodded.

She turned from him. "I don't think I can tell you."

Caleb took her hand. "Take your time, Bess."

Elizabeth let out a deep breath. "My parents and older sister, May, and I were living out on the Staked Plains — much farther west than Fort Griffin. Noah had already left home, and Papa was a circuit preacher." She smiled bitterly. "I was only twelve." Horrified, Caleb listened as Elizabeth told of being captured. She told him about her mother's and sister's deaths, her captor Eyes Like the Sun, and the strange language that saved her own life.

The hair rose on the back of Caleb's neck. "You had no idea what you were saying?"

"No."

"But they could understand you?"

"Yes." Her eyes misted with tears. "I found out later it was the Lord's Prayer."

Despite the goose flesh on his arms, Caleb laughed. "Things like that don't happen, Elizabeth."

"When I learned the Comanche language, the man who claimed me, Walks Far, repeated what I said. Then I knew what the words were. He said my accent was as perfect as any full-blooded member of their tribe. They named me Speaks of Her God and accepted me."

Caleb touched her arm. "Then what happened?"

"I lived with Walks Far, his wife Gray Dove, and their daughter, Sunflower. She became my best friend." Elizabeth clenched her hands in her skirt. "She married Eyes Like the Sun. My good friend married the man who killed my mother and sister. The man who hated me for having more power than him."

"Bess . . ."

"When Sunflower became a believer, he hated me even more. One night he found me alone by the river, and he . . . he . . ." She bowed her head.

Caleb's stomach twisted with anger. "He raped you."

"Yes," she whispered. "Not just that night but many. No one would have believed me, so I never told anyone. Besides, Sunflower loved him. In his own way, he loved her too."

Caleb rose, clenching his fists. "I promise you, Elizabeth, I'll track him down and kill him — slowly and with pleasure."

She smiled bitterly. "You're too late. He's probably already dead. Soldiers raided the camp several months later, and he was shot. The last time I saw him, he was covered with blood." Her face fell. "Sunflower died with her newborn son that day too."

Good. He hoped they'd all died. Rotten, savage Indians. He'd like to wipe the earth of every one. All the stories he'd heard about them paled next to the horror Elizabeth had endured. And she still foolishly believed in a God who would allow such suffering. "The soldiers rescued you?"

Elizabeth rose beside him. "Yes. Me and the child I was carrying."

Caleb's stomach dropped. "Joseph?" he whispered. "He's your child? Yours and —"

She nodded. "The soldiers returned me to my father. He whipped me because my mother and sister died, while I not only survived but carried an Indian baby. He finally agreed to raise Joseph, but only if I never had anything to do with him." She lifted her chin. "I agreed so I could be near him. Father married Helga, and we moved to Fort Griffin. No one knew us there."

"So that's why you hardly know Joseph. Your father wouldn't let you love him." Caleb didn't know who he hated more — Eyes Like the Sun or Elizabeth's father. "You should tell Joseph the truth. He wonders about his real parents."

"What could I tell him — that he's the product of a rape? Can you imagine what would happen to him if that got out? Or that he's a half-breed?"

He gently gripped her arms. "I can imagine what would happen to you."

She closed her eyes. "What I am can't be changed, Caleb. My concern is for Joseph." She smiled. "I remember when he was born — his dark hair and how his little arms and legs kicked the air. I thought he was the most beautiful baby in the world."

"Who named him Joseph?"

The smile faded. "I did. I knew he would always be a slave to the lie my father forced on us both." She opened her eyes. "If you want to have the marriage annulled, I'll understand. Joseph and I can go somewhere else."

"I don't want an annulment."

She straightened. "I meant what I said about fulfilling my duty as your wife."

Caleb stared, shocked. Did she still think he wanted her to submit to him? After what she'd just told him? He'd wanted her to come to him willingly, and now, even more so. Patience and tenderness — they were rapidly becoming his bywords. "Whenever you're ready . . ."

"I may never be ready."

He nodded, hiding his disappointment. "Then that's the way it will be."

"You won't tell anyone about Joseph, will you?"

"No. There's truth in what you say. People are cruel enough to him already." *People would be cruel to you too.*

"I . . . I'd rather no one knew we're not . . . not . . ."

"No one has to know." Caleb winced. His head throbbed from the tail end of the hangover and the summer heat creeping through the window. He ought to leave this sweltering room and this nightmare he'd stepped into. Right now finding another whiskey bottle seemed like a good way to chase away the demons.

The woman he'd thought so pure, wasn't. He tried to keep the words at bay, but they rose one right after the other. Used.

Tainted. Spoiled. By an Indian — a *savage* who had left not only a child but a woman afraid of the merest physical contact.

Yet she was still Caleb's wife. He was a married man now, responsible for Elizabeth. He'd promised to love, honor, and cherish for better or worse. Natural instinct said to take her in his arms and whisper that he would make up for all the hurts of her past. Common sense said she would only feel threatened.

He shifted, uncomfortable. "Would you like some breakfast?"

Elizabeth glanced up, surprised, then her features settled into her usual reserved expression. "Yes. That would be nice." She moved to the mirror and lifted her hairbrush.

Caleb stepped aside to watch as she primped. She raised her arms to pin up her hair, the gesture graceful and feminine. How could he remain near his wife — sleep in the same bed with her night after night — and yet stay away from her?

Immediately, he felt ashamed. How could he be so selfish?

"I'm ready." She looked happier than he'd seen her since they'd gotten married.

Caleb cleared his throat. "We could go back to Anna's today. We don't have to stay in Salado an extra day."

"Why not? We're supposed to be on our honeymoon, after all."

Honeymoon! He wanted to laugh. Did she think him unaffected by all she'd told him? That he could pretend everything was normal between them?

"Anna will know something is wrong if we return early," she said softly.

Caleb suppressed a sigh. More lies. They'd have to return to Belton and convince everyone that not only had they married for love, but that their married life was fine and dandy. He was tired of pretending he was someone other than who he was. For three years he'd hidden his past.

Now he'd have to hide the truth of this marriage.

Thirteen

"They're back, Anna! Marisa! They're back!" Joseph's voice rang up the road as Elizabeth and Caleb passed the giant oak. She shaded her eyes with her hand, watching as Joseph raced into the house.

Caleb placed a hand on her knee. "Will you be all right?"

She nodded. She'd learned to pretend over the years; it shouldn't take much effort to convince everyone that she and Caleb were starry-eyed newlyweds.

Marisa and the Orozco children ran into the yard, and Caleb helped Elizabeth from the buggy. His hands lingered on hers, his expression compassionate.

Elizabeth swallowed hard then forced a smile for their excited audience. They must never know the truth of their marriage. The truth about Joseph.

Joseph!

The little boy raced from the house behind the last young Orozco, his eyes shining with excitement, arms outstretched. "You're back! You're back!"

Elizabeth choked back the emotion clogging her throat, and she knelt in the grass. She could hardly wait to hug him. Everything she'd endured for the past five years had been for him, and now she would be his mama. She spread her arms wide, heart beating wildly as the boy raced forward.

He threw himself straight at Caleb. "I missed you!"

"Me too, Joe." Caleb grabbed him around the waist and turned him upside down, growling with pretend fierceness as he buried his face in the boy's tummy.

Joseph shrieked with excitement, his shrill laughter piercing Elizabeth's heart. He'd never laughed like that with her. She lowered her arms and rose, smoothing her skirt.

"Are you really my pa now?"

"Elizabeth and I signed the adoption papers on our way back today."

"Hooray!" Joseph broke into another fit of giggles as Caleb swung him around.

Marisa embraced Elizabeth warmly, her dark eyes shining. "Did you enjoy Salado?"

Elizabeth nodded, not trusting her voice. "Yes," she finally managed, then cleared her throat. "How is Anna?"

"The same as always. She worried about you."

Elizabeth forced a laugh. "Imagine her worrying about me. Why, Caleb and I were on our honeymoon! We had a wonderful time."

Marisa winked, squeezing Elizabeth's arm.

Smiling, Caleb turned with Joseph in his arms. "Someone else is glad to see us, Elizabeth. Say hello to your ma."

Joseph slid to his feet and smiled shyly. "Hello, Mother."

Elizabeth patted his shoulder awkwardly, trying to smile. "I thought you wanted to call me Ma."

"I'll call you whatever you want."

Caleb stepped forward. "Whatever you call her, I think you should give her a hug."

Joseph glanced up at him, then Elizabeth. She knelt, and he moved stiffly into her embrace. With a deep inward sigh, she closed her eyes and wrapped her arms around his small body. Warm from the sun, his hair and neck smelled so familiar. She felt tears sting her eyes, and her arms tightened as his small arms encircled her neck.

Quiet, trembling joy filled her heart. He was hers at last, and no one could take him from her. Not Eyes Like the Sun, not her father, not Iola, and now, not even the courts.

She caught sight of Caleb smiling down at them. He had done so much for her, how could she please him? The gun he wore, which had something to do with the mysterious inner part of him, still frightened her. But it was her own shame that proved a more effective barrier around her heart.

Joseph squirmed loose. "Pa! You have to come see the goats! They —"

"Your mother and I have some things to put away, Joe. And we haven't even seen Anna yet."

"Oh." His face fell, then brightened. "After you do all that, *then* will you come see?"

Caleb ruffled his hair, smiling, then reached out a hand to Elizabeth. She took it and rose beside him, accepting hugs and kisses from the Orozco children.

"Welcome back, señora," Teresa said shyly, pressing several wilted wildflowers into her hand.

"Thank you." She held up the black-eyed Susans for Caleb's inspection. "Aren't these lovely?"

"Beautiful." His gaze rested on her face.

She blushed, ducking her head. He didn't have to overdo the happy newlywed scene.

Marisa herded her children. "We're going home. Rafael and Gustavo have been on their own for two days now." She winked at Elizabeth. "You two lovebirds will want to get settled."

Caleb clasped Marisa's hands. "You and Gustavo have been wonderful neighbors to Anna, and now to us. Thank you."

"*De nada.* God has done so much for Anna through Elizabeth, and now he has worked through you. Gustavo and I wish you both a lifetime of happiness." She touched a shoulder of each of her gathered children as they climbed into their wagon. "I hope the Lord brings you as many blessings as he has us. *Hasta luego!*"

As they rode down the road, they broke into one of Anna's folk songs. Elizabeth stood watching until Caleb held out an arm. "Shall we go inside, Mrs. Martin?"

She nodded, accepting his escort. Now to fool Anna.

They had been gone only two days, but the house seemed different. The sofa and chairs stood in their normal arrangement; the kitchen was as spotless as she'd left it. Nothing had been altered, and yet everything had changed.

Anna turned from a chattering Joseph. She held out her arms, a warm smile lighting her wrinkled face. *"Liebchen."*

Elizabeth hesitated, fearing she'd never be able to hide the truth. She felt a gentle nudge. "Go ahead, Bess."

She moved forward, into Anna's inviting arms. The old woman enfolded her lovingly, smoothing her hair. Elizabeth closed her eyes and let the warm embrace flow over her. Not since her mother's death had she felt so safe and loved. She'd come to this farm expecting to serve but instead found herself the recipient. Anna not only accepted her as she was, without question, but loved her. Truly loved her. With patience and kindness, without jealousy, boasting, or arrogance.

Anna touched Elizabeth's cheek. "Tears, dear one? I hope they're from joy."

"G-God has been good to me."

Anna laughed gently, turning toward Caleb as he sat in the chair. "God has been very good, indeed, Elizabeth. Welcome to my home, Caleb."

He clasped her wrinkled hand. "Thank you, Anna. Thank you for allowing us to stay with you."

"It's a pleasure to hear laughter, to see a family's love."

Elizabeth cleared her throat and rose. "I need to put our things away."

"Marisa finished cleaning my old room for you, Elizabeth." A slow smile spread across Anna's face. "You will remember what I said about the birds and the creek, *ja?*"

Caleb turned curious eyes on her, and Elizabeth blushed. She didn't want to think about sharing a room, much less lying abed to listen to the sounds of nature with him. "Yes, Anna," she mumbled, then scurried upstairs.

Alone with Anna, Caleb fought the urge to squirm in the chair. He felt like a pupil beside a beloved teacher's desk. Anna smiled. "Do you like to sit there, Caleb?"

"What, you mean the chair?" He stared down at it, puzzled. "Yes, Anna. It's very nice."

"You sit in Jesus' chair without question. Joseph too."

He felt even more confused. "It seems sturdy enough. Should we be afraid?"

"Elizabeth is."

Before he could respond, Anna smiled again. "I'm sure you'd like to get settled, so I won't keep you. I only wanted to ask a small favor."

Caleb leaned forward. "Anything, Anna. How can I help?"

She folded her hands in her lap, looking like a child who had just gotten her way. "I miss the sound of a man reading Scripture. Would you join me and Elizabeth every night after dinner so you can read to us?"

Caleb leaned against the chair's hard back. Him? He didn't even believe that stuff in the Bible! But, for Anna, he'd do anything. "Of course. Is that all?"

She nodded.

Caleb stared at her, perplexed. That was it? She only wanted him to read to her? It was a small favor indeed. He pushed the chair back. "I'll go see if Elizabeth needs any help."

"After dinner. Don't forget."

Caleb could have sworn she was hiding a smile. "No ma'am, I won't." He smiled in return, even though the elderly woman couldn't see. If he didn't know better, he'd say Anna Mannheim had some sort of scheme up her sleeve.

After dinner, Caleb, Elizabeth, and Joseph settled in Anna's room. At her direction, Caleb took the favorite chair at her side. Joseph curled up in his lap, and Elizabeth sat on the bed. She handed Caleb the black Bible he'd purchased for her in Fort Worth. "What do you want to study tonight, Anna?" she said.

"Let's read the story of Naaman. Caleb, will you turn to the fifth chapter of Second Kings?"

After much fumbling, Caleb found his place. In a voice that faltered at first then grew stronger, he read about Naaman, the Syrian commander with leprosy. A young Israelite slave directed the captain to the prophet Elisha, who told Naaman to wash himself seven times in the Jordan River. Enraged, Naaman left.

"Why was he angry?" Joseph asked.

Caleb considered the question. "Sounds like he thought he was too important for a little river like the Jordan."

"A problem of humility," Elizabeth said.

"And obedience." Anna nodded at Caleb. "Please go on."

Caleb picked up the story with Naaman's servants urging him to obey Elisha. When Naaman finally dipped himself seven times in the Jordan, the leprosy was gone.

"It seems to me that Naaman didn't like something else about Elisha's directions," Anna said softly.

No one said anything. Caleb remembered how his parents had discussed this story with him when he was as young as Joseph. They had often discussed Bible stories, and a warmth of familiarity ran through him. He tightened his arm around Joseph.

"Maybe the cure seemed too simple?" Anna said, prodding.

Elizabeth sat rigidly still, silent.

"Why would he think that?" Joseph said.

"He was a captain in an army," Caleb said. "He was probably used to being treated importantly, and the idea of bathing in a dirty little river seemed too easy a cure."

"Much like faith," Anna added softly. "It often seems too easy for God to merely wash away our sin. Yet all we must do is accept his mercy and love. We have to take him at his word."

Elizabeth leaned forward. "But we must humbly obey."

"It is *faith* that brings the cure," Anna said. "Then obedience follows."

Joseph shifted impatiently in Caleb's lap, and Anna laughed softly. "Joseph is yawning, and it is past time, I think, for little boys to go to bed. Caleb, will you please read four more verses before we say good night? I'm thinking this special night of Ecclesiastes 4:9-12."

Again Caleb fumbled through the Bible, until at last Elizabeth, blushing furiously, leaned over to help him find the right page.

Caleb cleared his throat. " 'Two are

better than one; because they have a good reward for their labor. For if they fall, the one will lift up his fellow.' "

Caleb broke off, feeling the slow heat of embarrassment rise under his collar. No wonder Elizabeth was blushing; she knew in advance what those verses were.

"Go on."

Caleb cleared his throat. " 'Again, if two lie together, then they have heat; but how can one be warm alone?' "

Elizabeth took the Bible from his hands. "Time for bed, Joseph."

"Wait, Elizabeth." Anna held up her hand. "Listen to the last verse: 'And if one prevail against him, two shall withstand him; and a threefold cord is not quickly broken.' "

"Three! That's us!" Joseph bounced on Caleb's knee. "Pa, Ma, and me. I don't want to go to bed. I want to hear more!"

"Your mama is tired, Joseph. She is trying so hard not to yawn, but I can feel the bed move a little every time she hides it."

Elizabeth's face flushed. "It *is* time, Joseph. Say good night to Anna, then go on upstairs. Ca . . . I mean Pa and I will be up in a minute."

Joseph beamed. "I'll be all right sleeping by myself, Anna, even though I miss Elizabeth. She said she has to sleep with Pa now, since they're married. It's what husbands and wives do, you know."

Anna laughed gently, and Caleb cringed at the distress that crossed Elizabeth's face. "All right, young man," she said. "No more dawdling. Upstairs."

"Aww, not now!"

"Mind your ma, Joseph." Caleb gave him a stern look.

Joseph planted a wet smack on Anna's cheek. "G'night!"

She chuckled and hugged him quickly.

Caleb swatted him playfully on the behind. "Ma and I'll be up in a minute to hear your prayers."

"Yes sir!"

Elizabeth straightened the bedcovers. "Do you need anything, Anna?"

"No, dear. Go on to Joseph. Good night."

Caleb saw that she was almost immediately asleep and quietly shut the door behind himself and Elizabeth. Together they ascended the stairs.

Dressed in his nightshirt, the covers pulled back, Joseph bounced on the bed. Elizabeth smiled at the way his eyes shone. "Pa, can we go fishing tomorrow? Then can we hunt crawfish?"

"I have to go back to work tomorrow. The railroad needs me." Caleb sat on the bed. "Being part of a family means certain responsibilities. Your mother's responsibility is to take care of this home, and you, and Anna. Mine is to take care of you and your ma by providing for us."

"Is protecting us your 'sponsibility?"

"That too."

Joseph tugged at the gun in Caleb's holster. "With this, right?"

Elizabeth gasped, and Caleb grabbed Joseph's hand. "Don't *ever* touch this gun," he said in a low voice. "When you're older, I'll teach you the proper way to use one. But for now, you're too young. Understand?"

Joseph's eyes widened, and he pulled his hand away. "Y-yes sir."

"Good." Caleb cleared his throat and glanced at Elizabeth. "Is it prayer time?"

She nodded, still shocked. She knelt and rested her elbows on the bed, folding her hands. Joseph slid down beside her, and an uncomfortable-looking Caleb knelt on Joseph's other side.

"Dear God, thank you for another day," Joseph said. "Thank you that we had my favorite chocolate pie tonight and that I got to play checkers. Bless Anna and Marisa and Gustavo and Rafael —" He drew a deep breath — "and Teresa and Santiago and Pedro and Juanita and all the chickens and goats and cows and horses. Bless Caleb and Elizabeth . . . I mean Pa and Ma . . . and thank you that they're my parents now. Amen." He leaped into bed, and Elizabeth tucked the covers around him.

"Good night, son," Caleb said.

"Good night, Pa." Joseph flung his arms around Caleb's neck. "I love you!"

Caleb held him close. "I love you too, Joe," he said softly, planting a kiss just under the boy's ear. Joseph giggled.

A lump formed in Elizabeth's throat. Joseph pulled away from Caleb and grabbed her around the neck, kissing her noisily. "Good night, Eliza— I mean, Ma."

Trembling, she embraced him then kissed his smooth cheek. "Good night, Joseph."

She fled for the kitchen and, choking back sobs, she attacked the dirty dishes. Then sensing Caleb's presence at the doorway behind her, she hastily wiped her eyes with the back of her sleeve.

Towel in hand, he took his place beside her. "I'll dry. My ma used to make me wash dishes right alongside my sister."

"I suppose you didn't care much for that."

"Not one bit."

She drew a deep breath, hoping he hadn't seen her crying into the dishwater. "You said your sister ran off and that you wanted to find her. I won't ever hold you here, Caleb."

He turned to look at her. "I won't leave you, even to find Samantha. You and Joseph are my family." His gaze intensified. "Why were you crying?"

She smiled sadly. "Joseph has never kissed me before. I didn't know how sweet it could feel." Embarrassed at revealing such deep emotion, she turned away. Joseph hadn't said he loved her, but it was a start.

"Go on upstairs," Caleb said softly. "I'll finish here."

Elizabeth drew off the apron and retreated thankfully, knowing he was giving her time to undress. After dinner last night, he left her in the hotel room and didn't reappear until morning. Tonight they were home; he would sleep in their room whether she liked it or not.

Upstairs she rapidly undressed and mumbled hasty prayers before diving under the covers. She lay still, trembling. He had said he would wait until she was ready, but, patient or not, he was a man. How long would it be before he decided he didn't want to wait anymore?

She rolled onto her side and pressed a wet cheek against the pillow.

The door opened, and she heard his footsteps. The far side of the mattress dipped, and she heard one, two boots drop to the floor. She heard him unbuckle his gun belt and loop it around the headboard. Then she heard the rustle of clothes, and she jerked upright.

Caleb was removing his undershirt. He turned, and she trembled. "Wh-what do you usually wear to bed?" she whispered.

He grinned and finished removing the shirt. "In this heat? You don't want to know."

She rolled onto her side again. She heard him finish undressing, and she inched to the edge of the bed.

Caleb slid under the sheet. "I'm wearing my drawers, Bess. That's modest enough."

The mattress shifted as he rolled to his back. Elizabeth squeezed her eyes shut, tensing at the expected hand on her shoulder.

"Bess, I said I wouldn't touch you, and I meant it. Relax and go to sleep."

She let out a pent-up breath. "S-sleep?"

"Yes, sleep. Just close your eyes and dream pleasant dreams. Did you pray already?"

"Did you want to pray with me?"

"Your list said I was supposed to lead the evening prayers."

Elizabeth felt her face heat, and she was grateful for the cover of darkness. She was beginning to wish she'd never set out those stipulations. "A husband and wife should share prayer time together."

"All right. Do you want to hold hands?"

"I don't think so," she whispered.

"Fine."

She lay still, hugging her arms across her breasts, waiting for him to start. Silence stretched from seconds into minutes, and she began to wonder if he had fallen asleep. She glanced over her shoulder and could barely see his profile in the darkness. "Caleb?" she whispered.

"What?"

She scooted closer to the edge. "I thought you were asleep."

"I was waiting for you to start the prayer."

"I was waiting for you."

Silence.

"Well, *somebody* has to go first, Bess. Are we supposed to flip for it?"

"I think the husband is supposed to go first," she said. "Then the wife."

"Is that written down somewhere?"

"Well, the Bible says the husband is the

head of the wife."

He sighed loudly. "Oh, all right. Thank you God for sending me a wife who knows the Bible backward and forward. There, your turn."

Elizabeth stiffened. "You're not being serious." She squeezed her eyes shut and tried to pray as her father had taught. "Lord, you are so much greater than your creation. We are but dogs under your table, not worthy —"

"You know, you have exactly the same problem as Naaman." Box springs squeaked in protest as Caleb rolled onto his side toward her. "You're always so busy apologizing to God and making yourself out to be some kind of worm. Doesn't the Bible say God loves us and forgives us?"

"I want to be faithful to confess my sins every night."

Caleb laughed. "What sins do you have? If anything, God should be apologizing for everything that's happened to you! You were baptized, weren't you?"

"A long, long time ago," she whispered.

"Me too. My Pa said I was made new the moment I accepted Jesus. I guess baptism is kind of like Naaman dipping himself in the river — there's nothing magic in the water, it's the faith."

Elizabeth lowered her shoulder just a

fraction, surprised. "When did you accept Jesus?" she said softly.

"When I was twelve."

"I didn't know that." Despite his revelation, she still felt vulnerable. Hugging her knees to her chest, she concentrated on falling asleep. "G-good night, Caleb," she said finally.

Two hours later, Caleb let out a quiet sigh of relief. He'd lain awake, motionless, until he finally heard the gentle breathing that indicated she was asleep. It was important that she fall asleep first so he knew she had ended her day safely.

He stretched slowly, sinking into the feather mattress — heaven. Last night he'd once again made his bed in the Shady Villa's stable, not because her nearness heated his blood — as it did now — but because he had too much to think about.

Resentment burned. If not for Eyes Like the Sun, Caleb would be holding Elizabeth even now, whispering as he caressed her. How was he going to break through the memories of her past? Even as she slept, she lay curled defensively, close to the edge.

Caleb swallowed. He had his own past, one that he couldn't reveal — now more than ever. Someday she would eventually learn it, but she wasn't ready yet. First he had to gain her trust.

"Be patient, be tender." He closed his eyes and dreamed that Elizabeth waited for him every night with open arms.

Fourteen

Several weeks later Elizabeth and Joseph walked down the road to the Orozcos' home. She and Caleb were apparently fooling everyone. No one seemed to suspect the true reason for their marriage or that it was less than blissful.

Joseph pointed. "Look at the size of that grackle!"

Elizabeth frowned remembering that Caleb had once called her a grackle. Did he still think of her as a homely bird? She glanced down at her brown dress and suddenly wished she'd worn the more cheerful blue one.

Caleb knew the truth about her — why should she bother? A pretty dress didn't make a pretty woman. As the Bible said, the cup could be washed on the outside but still be dirty on the inside.

"¡Hóla!" Hanging laundry, Marisa waved from her yard.

Laughing, her five children ran for the

road, shouting, "José! José is here!"

With a mixed chorus of English and Spanish, they surrounded Joseph and pulled him into the yard. Joseph beamed at his friends and chattered back happily.

Marisa smiled fondly as the children ran to the back in pursuit of new adventure. "You and I should have half their enthusiasm for life, no?"

"Joseph is always happy to come here." Elizabeth bent to help Marisa, lifting a freshly washed square of white cloth. A diaper. She fingered its softness and inhaled the sweet soap scent.

"I'll have to make more of those." Marisa smiled shyly. "I'm expecting another baby."

Elizabeth's stomach twisted with sadness. "A baby. What wonderful news."

"God is so good! He has given me the best of his blessings through my five *hijos*, and now Gustavo and I have been entrusted with yet another. It is such an honor." She touched Elizabeth's arm. "But here I am rambling on when you have yet to experience such a privilege. I haven't made you sad, have I?"

Elizabeth shook her head, blinking back unshed tears. Her own pregnancy had been so shameful, not the blessing Marisa described.

"I can't wait until you and Caleb have your own *hijos!* Anna will be so happy to have a baby in her house."

The knot in Elizabeth's stomach tightened, and she swallowed hard. "When will your baby be born?"

"March, I think. Will you help me when my time comes?"

"Of course."

Marisa laughed and several cardinals and blue jays scattered from nearby oaks. She wrapped an arm around Elizabeth, and the two of them walked toward the house. "Let's get out of the sun. I think you and I should sample the cookies I made before the children get to them."

The Orozcos' home was small but tidy. A colorful woven rug covered the puncheon floor, and the room was decorated with bright bottles and Marisa's pottery. She liked to work with clay and had given Caleb and Elizabeth a beautiful light blue pitcher for a wedding present.

The furniture was simple but clean, painstakingly crafted by Gustavo. The Orozcos had arrived in Bell County with nothing but dreams and had gradually built not only their home but nearly everything inside. Marisa seldom frequented the Belton general store. Even with five children, she insisted on making all the family's clothes from cotton they grew and wool from sheep they raised.

Marisa stacked several dog-eared books covering the long kitchen table. "We were having lessons, but the children refused to concentrate. They were so excited about Joseph's coming that I finally let them stop for the day."

While Marisa poured two cups of coffee, Elizabeth glanced at the red gingham curtains, the cheerful potted geraniums in the window, and the freshly washed floor. She took a bite of a still-warm ginger cookie, its spicy taste melting down her throat to the lump in her stomach.

"Bueno." Marisa pushed a cup in front of Elizabeth. "Tell me about married life."

Elizabeth rapidly swallowed her coffee, burning the roof of her mouth. "I'd rather talk about this new baby."

Marisa flushed with pleasure, eager to enlighten her newly married friend about pregnancy. She laughingly related the physical discomforts, but quickly returned to the joys.

Elizabeth watched her friend's face glow, and her own doubt increased. As Marisa grew bigger, would Caleb wonder what it would be like to have his own child? Perhaps he would insist that he and Elizabeth have a baby.

Marisa chattered on, hands moving in animation, and Elizabeth resolved once again to be the perfect wife. Caleb had done so much for her; she wanted to make him proud.

She shivered. She would please him in every possible way — outside of the bedroom.

After lunch, back at Anna's, Elizabeth found a gardening trowel in the barn. Today was a good day to tidy the front yard. Caleb had brought six rosebushes from town, and weeds were choking Anna's marigolds. Elizabeth set Joseph to work pulling the long grass that grew by the front porch, and she attacked the shorter grass and dirt to plant the roses.

Hot and sweaty, she paused to wipe her forehead with the back of her hand. The sun's rays were stifling, nearly unbearable outdoors. She hadn't had a moment's rest since returning from Marisa's. Even indoors the heat made Anna uncomfortable. Elizabeth had sponged her off and changed her sheets, then read aloud for several hours until Anna fell into a fitful sleep.

Elizabeth had also tried to work with

Joseph on his reading, but he couldn't seem to concentrate. He read for ten minutes then couldn't sit still no matter how much she cajoled. He wanted to talk about the Orozcos and all they'd done that morning, about Caleb's coming home that evening, about the latest song Anna taught him . . . everything, it seemed, except the lesson she'd planned.

Finally, in exasperation, she had sent him outside while she cleaned and shined the stove. Then, even though her arms ached, she'd polished the front room with lemon oil until the wood floor and furniture glowed. After she'd thrown in a loaf of bread to bake, she tried to duplicate Marisa's ginger cookies, but the spices didn't taste right, so she threw the batch out the back door for the birds to eat.

She stabbed at the hard earth with her trowel. If she hurried with the gardening, she could take in the laundry, dust the upstairs rooms, and polish the handrail on the stairs. Then it would be time to start Caleb's dinner.

Elizabeth glanced at Joseph working silently on the other side of the path. His skin glowed a dark copper in the sunlight, his face a frown of concentration. Countless times she'd seen Eyes Like the Sun with the exact same expression, his dark eyes shining with single-minded purpose. Was it possible Joseph could grow to be like his father? She chastised herself for the horrible thought. Joseph was a sweet, kind boy. Nothing like his father.

She yanked a weed. Lord, why do you allow evil men such as Eyes Like the Sun to live? Men who rape, torture, and kill.

Turn your eyes from the past and look only at me, a voice spoke to her heart.

Elizabeth paused with her hand in the dirt, trembling. She tightened her fingers around the trowel and drew a deep breath. "Judge not lest ye be judged." And judged . . . and judged . . .

Elizabeth, my precious child. I love you.

Tears stung the back of her eyes. "No," she whispered. "You can't possibly love me."

She worked the trowel faster in the dirt, tearing out the grass with a vengeance, her heart aching with grief.

As the weeks wore on, Elizabeth worked diligently. Every morning she arose from bed before dawn to start her chores. But the harder she worked, the heavier her heart seemed to weigh.

"*Liebchen,* you are going to make yourself

sick. Sit down and rest."

"I *am* sitting down, Anna," Elizabeth said. "I'm just cleaning the chimney of your lamp."

"You're not either sitting down. I can hear your dress rustling against the bed. Besides, you never sit in the chair."

Elizabeth replaced the chimney with a little too much force and plopped herself down on the bed. "There. I'm finished."

Anna reached out a paper-thin hand. "Caleb and I don't want you to hurt yourself. We both love you very much." She paused. "Have you told Caleb you love him?"

"What is love?" she said crossly.

"What does it say in the Bible?"

"Oh, Anna!"

Anna nodded at the Bible beside her bed. "Read to me. First Corinthians, chapter thirteen."

"I know those passages from memory."

"*Read* them. And pretend it's the first time."

Elizabeth obediently opened the Bible. If it would please Anna, she would humor her. " 'Charity suffereth long, and is kind; charity envieth not; charity vaunteth not itself, is not puffed up. Doth not behave itself unseemly, seeketh not her own, is not easily provoked, thinketh no evil.' "

"Has Caleb behaved any differently than that toward you?"

Elizabeth considered. He'd cared for her and Joseph since they'd met. Especially since they'd married . . . since he'd learned the truth. "No," she whispered.

"And has *Jesus* ever behaved any differently than that toward you? Do you not know that he loves you even more than your dear husband ever can?"

"No, I *don't* know that, Anna. I don't know why God let me live when my mother and sister died. My father always said they were so much better than —"

She pressed a hand to her mouth. Anna grasped her free hand and stroked it gently. "Your father was not speaking the truth, dear child. It's not a question of what we deserve. It's God's sovereign will. If you had died, Sunflower might never have heard of Jesus. And who would have raised Joseph after your father's death? Who would have told him about God?"

Elizabeth couldn't answer. She'd been forced to tell Caleb the truth, but she couldn't bear to tell Anna.

"God loves you, Elizabeth," Anna said softly. "He wants to lift you out of your pit of sorrow and set your feet on the rock of

Jesus. I believe he's trying to accomplish that through your husband."

"Caleb?"

"He models our Lord, my dear. If you will see that he accepts you as you are, the healing can begin for you to see that *God* accepts you. You need to accept his grace."

"What I need is a pure heart. A clean, perfect heart. Then I can be close to him."

Anna shook her head. "A pure heart doesn't mean we have to be perfect but that we have a right attitude toward God. He is our loving father who watches over us not to shame us, but to save us and be our friend."

"I try to be good, but it never seems like enough. And to my father, not being good enough was the same as being bad. I feel like a great sinner, Anna. Like my heart is permanently cracked."

Anna leaned forward; Elizabeth could see the great physical effort it cost the frail woman. "You cannot change your past, but you can alter your feelings. When you are tired of trying to be worthy, then grace can step in and give you the one thing you fear most, yet desperately need."

"And what's that?"

"Acceptance. True, unconditional acceptance." Anna's face lit up. "And then love will give you such a joy as you've never experienced. A joy that won't repair those cracks in your heart, dear one, but will seep through and overflow."

Elizabeth was silent. She couldn't fathom the concept of such a joy.

Anna smiled. "And God is using you to speak to Caleb."

"Me?"

"God's calling him back, Elizabeth. He's told you he accepted Jesus a long time ago?"

"When he was twelve."

"And though he's never said anything, I sense a lot has happened since then. But I see God beckoning him, reminding him of his first love."

"How is God using me?"

Anna laughed gently, her hand stealing up to caress Elizabeth's cheek. "Oh, *liebchen*. In more ways than you can imagine. If you would stop trying to block God's path with your childish pride —"

"*Pride?* That's my problem?"

"Yes, my dear one. You allow your self-concern to rule you. You take great pride in doing things as perfectly as possible, don't you?"

Elizabeth bristled. "Jesus said that we should be perfect as our Father in heaven is perfect."

"And David said, 'God is my strength and

power; and *he* maketh my way perfect.' Pride depends on self instead of the Lord and his word. Remember the psalm that says, 'I have seen an end of all perfection: but thy commandment is exceeding broad.' "

"And what is that commandment?"

"That you shall love the Lord your God with all your heart, with all your soul, and with all your mind. And you shall love your neighbor as yourself."

Elizabeth lowered her burning face. "Why are you criticizing me, Anna?"

"It is not criticism, *liebchen*." Anna clasped Elizabeth's hand. "It, too, is love. And truth."

She turned toward the window as though she could see out. "The seasons change slowly, but they do eventually follow God's pattern. The heat of summer fades into the cool of fall, then the chill of winter. I do not want you to be unprepared."

"Winter's a long way off," Elizabeth said, confused at the subject change. "It's still so hot outside."

Anna smiled tenderly. "Yes, to you, still in the spring of your life, the world is in bloom, *ja?* Just promise me you won't forget what I've said and that you'll remember it came from one who loves you."

Elizabeth put her arms around the woman's thin shoulders. "I won't forget, Anna. There's so much I don't understand."

Anna stroked Elizabeth's hair. "All in God's time, my dear. It's all in his time."

That night Elizabeth lay awake, waiting for Caleb to come to bed. Each night it seemed to take him longer to climb the stairs. Instead of trying to lose consciousness before he got in bed beside her, tonight she fought sleep.

Was Anna right? Was Caleb modeling unconditional love for her? He had certainly been patient. She shivered as she heard his heavy tread on the stairs.

The door opened slowly, and she listened for the familiar sounds. She could almost predict them to the second now: One boot dropping, then the other, the gun belt tossed around the bedpost, the rustle of clothes, then the blankets.

"Are you ready for prayers?" His voice sounded weary.

Elizabeth eased onto her back. "Yes." She drew a deep breath. "Do you think we could . . ."

Caleb glanced at her over his shoulder, and she continued in a rush, "Would you hold my hand while we say them?"

Caleb rolled onto his back and stretched his arm down between their bodies. She hesitantly placed her hand in his palm. His flesh felt warm as his fingers closed gently around hers. "Father, thank you," he said, then hastily added, "you have truly blessed us."

Every word Elizabeth had previously formulated disappeared. She couldn't think of anything but the hand that securely held hers, the peace she felt emanating from her husband. "Amen," she whispered, then felt a moment's panic. Should she withdraw her hand? Would he let go first?

Caleb loosened his fingers, but didn't move his hand. "Good night, Bess," he said softly, settling into the mattress.

"Good night." She didn't think it possible to fall asleep, but she quickly drifted away to the sound of Nolan Creek in the distance. When she awoke in the morning, her hand was still clasped in his.

Fifteen

The leaves from the cottonwoods and red oaks fell, slowly at first, like layers of clothes peeled from a sleepy child. Evergreen cedars and live oaks stood watch like prideful older siblings allowed to stay up late — their leaves intact — while the bare branches of the less fortunate shivered against the sky.

Carrying a basket of eggs, Elizabeth left the henhouse. The November air was brisk, and she drew the shawl closer around her shoulders. She paused halfway to the house and watched as Caleb raked a large pile of leaves. Shrieking with glee, Joseph, Santiago, and Pedro backed up and playfully stamped and snorted like bulls. "I wanna go first this time!" Pedro insisted.

Santiago laughed. "You're too little. Let me and José jump in first to make the pile smaller."

Joseph gravely nodded and squared his shoulders. "My pa makes really *big* piles of leaves, Pedro. He's the best leaf piler in the whole state!"

Caleb laughed and leaned against the rake. He winked at Elizabeth, creating a glow in her stomach. She smiled back, and his eyes crinkled with pleasure.

"I think Pedro's big enough to handle this one," he said. "But this is the last pile I make, fellows. I've got work to do in the barn."

Joseph's face fell. "Aww."

"We could rake our own piles," Santiago said.

Elizabeth moved past Caleb and toward the house. Thrusting the rake in Joseph's hands, he caught up with her before she passed the clothesline. His eyes still glowed with warmth, and she ducked her face in embarrassment. Lately every time he was near, her stomach fluttered. "I could use some help," he said.

Elizabeth glanced up. The old panic churned, then mysteriously receded. Caleb's smile had become so familiar, so comfortable. When they were separated during the day, she often found herself longing to be with him again, to see that smile, to see her husband's handsome face. He had somehow situated himself in her shattered heart as easily as Joseph had. "I'll set these eggs in the house, then join you in the barn."

His smile widened. "Good."

Her hands trembled as she opened the back door. Her heart thumped, and she wiped her hands nervously against her skirt. "Anna?" she called, hoping for a legitimate reprieve.

No answer.

Elizabeth peeked into the bedroom to find Anna asleep, her face turned toward the chair. Elizabeth tiptoed in and smoothed a gentle hand against the gray hair. Anna had been sleeping more than usual lately. Perhaps the onset of cold weather was sapping her strength.

Frowning, Elizabeth tucked the quilt higher. She would have to try yet another tonic from her storehouse of herbs and plants. Something was bound to lift Anna's lethargy.

The boys whooped and jumped into the crackly pile of leaves, their joyful shouts ringing through the chilly air. Smiling at their antics, Elizabeth rubbed her arms and drew in a crisp breath. Autumn had always been her favorite time of year, for it brought back memories of Sunflower. And how they had laughed and joked as they skinned deer and buffalo hides, making the tedious work a pleasure rather than a drudgery.

Pale sunlight filtered between the barn slats, spreading meager warmth in the cool interior. Except for pigeons murmuring from the rafters, the barn was silent. The horses, milk cow, and pigs had been turned outside to take advantage of the waning sunny days.

Just as he had promised Joseph earlier, Caleb had hung a long, sturdy rope from the rafters. Joseph and his friends climbed and swung out of the loft on it, landing in the mound of hay below.

"The boys are having a good time."

Elizabeth started, clutching her shawl closer. Caleb stood at her elbow. "Sorry. I didn't mean to frighten you."

Smiling, she loosened her grip. "Did you hear Joseph bragging about you? My father never allowed him to jump in the leaves."

"A boy needs to have fun."

He turned away, and she saw that he'd set up Rudy Mannheim's saddle on a battered sawhorse. Steadying the saddle with one hand, he vigorously rubbed oil into it with a rag. "Is that what you need help with?" she said.

"Could you hold the saddle?"

She grasped the pommel in one hand and braced the other against the seat. Caleb continued to work, rubbing new life into the old leather.

Elizabeth studied her husband. His brows knit in concentration, every effort focused on polishing. Whatever he'd done before he became a surveyor, before he came into her life, Caleb was no stranger to hard work. And no stranger to a sense of right and wrong either. No matter what she'd thought when she left Fort Griffin, she could never raise Joseph alone. A boy needed the guidance of a man. A father.

"Thank you for taking care of Joseph," she said quietly. "You're a good father to him. He's happy."

Caleb's hands stilled. He glanced up, and his fingers brushed hers. "How about you, Elizabeth? Are you happy?"

She nodded. Her heart pounded, and her stomach danced. Caleb set aside the rag and lifted her hand, drawing it to his lips for a kiss. She shivered and instinctively moved closer, letting herself be drawn into his embrace.

"All I want to do is make you happy, Bess," he murmured. He lowered her hand and bent his head.

Elizabeth closed her eyes and willingly raised her face for his kiss. Her heart seemed to stop, and the rest of the world slipped away. He pressed her close against him.

Lightheaded, she reached to brace herself against the saddle. Her hand brushed his gun in its holster, and she drew a deep breath and stepped back. "We . . . we probably ought to finish here . . . The boys . . . Joseph . . ."

Caleb unhooked his gun belt and held it between them. "Is this what's bothering you? I need it to keep you and Joseph safe."

"I know you care about us, but we have God's protection."

"I care more than you seem to realize. I won't let anyone hurt you. Or Joseph."

She raised her eyes to meet his. She wanted so much to believe him. Stretching up on her toes, she kissed him. Then, heat flooding her face, she turned and fled from the barn.

Caleb stared helplessly, then dropped the gun belt and followed her inside the house. He found her hiding out with Anna, and he sat in the chair. Anna heard him enter and turned, smiling weakly.

"Try the juniper tea," Elizabeth said, holding a full spoon at Anna's lips.

Anna shook her head. *"Nein, danke schön, liebchen."*

Elizabeth dumped the spoon in the cup and rose, sighing. "All right then." She headed off to the kitchen.

Anna fumbled for Caleb's hand and squeezed weakly. "Caleb, I have told Gustavo that I want you and Elizabeth to have my land."

"That's very kind, but there's no reason to turn it over to us. We're content to help you."

She shook her head. "Not now. Perhaps this winter. Or, if it is a mild season, then in the spring."

"You're talking riddles."

"I am talking about God's timing. Though we don't always recognize it, it is perfect. I wanted you to know my wishes now."

Cold dread raced through Caleb. "Surely this winter will be like any other."

Anna smiled tenderly. "No, Caleb, it will not. And Elizabeth will need your strength. I want you to be prepared."

"No, Anna, I don't believe you," he whispered.

"It is true, my dear." She patted his hand. "Do you know if my little son Johnny had not left, he would have been about your age? God is good to have sent you to me."

"I'll get the doctor out here tomorrow. If he looks at you now, maybe he can help."

"No, Caleb. Let me go to my Lord when

he calls. I can feel my heart weakening every day, yet it is gaining strength in him. You must tell Elizabeth this when the time comes."

"I . . . I can't."

She touched his arm gently, and he thought of his mother. Had it really been eleven years since he'd seen her? Was she waiting across some great mystical river of time to welcome those like Anna who had remained faithful?

"You *can* tell Elizabeth," Anna said softly. "But first you must find the truth yourself. That is my prayer for you, Caleb."

She eased her hand from his. With a deep sigh, she settled into the mattress. "Now you must go to your wife. She needs your attention much more than an old lady does."

Caleb patted her hands once more. "Get some rest," he choked out.

Out in the kitchen, he leaned against the sink, his heart weighing heavily. Anna couldn't die. What would they do without her? She had given them shelter, mediated between them, taught them how to love, encouraged Joseph . . . She had given every ounce of herself when they had all been virtual strangers.

Elizabeth entered from the parlor. "We'll have to try the juniper tea again, Caleb."

He touched her shoulder. "Bess, I —"

Bang!

Elizabeth jumped, raising fearful eyes. "Wh-what was that?"

Terror balled in Caleb's gut. *Joseph!* In two steps, he flung the door open, with Elizabeth/ following, her face white.

Caleb cursed repeatedly as he ran for the barn. How could he have been so careless? Didn't he know better than to leave his gun in the barn?

Childish shrieks filled the smoky air. Joseph lay sprawled on the ground with the gun beside him. Santiago and Pedro stood alongside, wailing, tears streaking their faces.

Caleb dropped to his knees, and his hands frantically searched the still form for a wound. *Oh, God, please. Not this child. Why didn't you take me instead?*

Elizabeth covered her mouth with both hands and rocked back and forth. "No-o-o-o!"

Joseph stirred under Caleb's hands, groaning. "M-my head hurts."

Fear lodged in Caleb's chest. He hadn't thought to check Joseph's head! His fingers tenderly probed Joseph's scalp.

"The g-gun knocked me down. I hit my head."

Relief washed over Caleb. Elizabeth sank

to her knees beside him, drawing the boy into her lap. She cradled the dark head against her breast, tears washing down her face. Joseph clutched her dress and sobbed against her shoulder. "M-ma!"

Caleb's heart slowed to normal. His impulse was to gather the weeping Elizabeth and Joseph in his arms, but relief gave way to fatherly common sense. "Let go of him. He has to be punished."

"No!" Elizabeth held Joseph closer.

Caleb rose and turned. "Santiago . . . Pedro . . . You better get on home."

Santiago grabbed Pedro's hand and pulled him toward the entrance. "S-sí, Señor Martin." With a last look of anguish for Joseph, he pulled his little brother out the door.

Standing, Elizabeth tried to shield Joseph behind her skirts. "Hasn't he suffered enough?"

"He disobeyed me, Elizabeth. I told him never to touch my gun, and he deliberately ignored me. Didn't you, son?"

Joseph stepped out from behind Elizabeth. "Y-yes sir. I j-just wanted to see what it was like to hold it."

Caleb bent and retrieved the gun and belt from the floor. "I told you never to touch these things. You could have been killed."

"But he's all right, Caleb! Can't you be thankful for that?"

He clenched his jaw. "I *am* thankful. But the boy has to learn to obey. The next time he decides not to listen could turn out differently."

She stared at him, silent.

"I'm Joseph's father."

She opened her mouth, then closed it. Like Santiago, she glanced at Joseph then headed for the doorway. She never looked back at Caleb.

Joseph stood stock-still like a soldier and lifted his chin. His resigned demeanor reminded Caleb of the solemn little boy he'd first met.

Caleb rested his hand on a small shoulder. "You know what I have to do, don't you, son?"

"Y-yes sir," he whispered.

"Because I love you, Joe."

Joseph's wet brown eyes met Caleb's, and his small chin quivered. "I . . . I love you, too, Pa."

With a heavy heart, Caleb unbuckled his belt.

Unseeing, Elizabeth stared out the window of the upstairs room. The evening had been horrible, and only now, bedtime, did she have the privacy she needed to sort through her emotions. Yet she couldn't even find the strength to undress. Her heart tugged her head several directions at one time, each road ending in the same dead end.

Caleb.

Just when she was beginning to trust him. She twisted the ring on her left hand. As long as she lived, she would never forget the expression in Joseph's eyes when she'd left him in the barn. Left him to his father's punishment.

She squeezed her eyes shut. She knew what it meant to be the recipient of a father's wrath. Hadn't she been punished just for living, for having brown hair instead of blond like Mama and May?

She choked back tears. Was her husband any different from Eyes Like the Sun? Caleb was just as prepared as the Comanche warrior to make violence his god. And now he and his gun had entered Joseph's life, threatening him too.

If only Noah was here. He surely knew about such things. He could tell her what to do about her husband. Maybe she should leave him.

The thought made her tremble. She hated to admit how dependent she'd become on

Caleb. Not for the money he made to support her and Joseph, not for his protection, but for his concern . . . his presence.

She wrapped her arms around herself, shivering.

The door squeaked as it opened. "Bess?"

Elizabeth didn't answer.

"If you're mad at me, say so," he said from the doorway. "At least Joseph understood what had to happen. He's sound asleep in his bed."

"Guns are wrong," she said, shaking. "Violence is wrong."

"My punishment of Joseph is not the same as what your father did to you."

She squeezed her eyes shut against the rising tears. "Please, Caleb."

She hadn't heard him move, but he suddenly stood behind her. Before she could sidestep him, his hands gently cupped her shoulders. "It's important to me that you understand."

Slowly she turned. Clear blue, his eyes radiated concern. His expression reflected tenderness and awe, his touch, gentleness.

She trembled, her heart pounding. "Caleb," she whispered.

He cradled her face with his hands. "Do you understand?"

She shook her head, captivated. Her husband seemed like two men. One with eyes as soft as young bluebonnets and the other as cold as bluing on a revolver. Whom could she trust? Whom did she love?

She loved them both.

How could she think of leaving? Caleb had shown Joseph — he'd shown *her* — more compassion in the short time they'd known him than any other man. He had given them everything he had . . . his name, his protection, his support. Joseph had eagerly returned his affection, yet she had given him nothing, had never even given him the least sign that she cared for him.

She lowered her eyes, but not before she saw disappointment etch its way across his face. He lowered his hands and turned away.

Heart pounding, she reached out. "Wait," she whispered.

He turned back and Elizabeth hesitantly curved her palm around his jaw. Unmoving, he watched her as her fingers slowly explored the texture of his cheeks and jawline with its late-evening stubble. He smelled of the earth and hard work, of protection and security. She found herself moving closer, vaguely aware of his arms encircling her. His palms caressed her back as though he were trying to soothe the hideous, thick scars on her skin and her soul.

She wrapped her arms around his neck and kissed him. Caleb pressed closer. When she would have pulled away, he encouraged her with another gentle kiss. She responded to his lead — shyly at first, then with more boldness.

His lips trailed a path from her mouth to the soft flesh below her ear. "Do you trust me, Bess?" he whispered.

She closed her eyes, lost in his touch and the wonder of emotions crashing against her heart like waves against the shoreline. The tide could knock her down and drag her under, but it also had the power to cleanse.

"Do you trust me?" he insisted, his arms tightening.

She nodded, transfixed.

"Say it," he murmured against her ear. "Say it so we'll both know."

She should run far away and never look back, but she couldn't move if her life depended on it. This man had broken down all her walls and had coaxed her into the open. Instead of darkness and evil, he had shown her sunshine and warmth. "I trust you," she whispered.

"Bess." His face moved closer to hers, and she closed her eyes.

"Pa? I'm thirsty."

Elizabeth's eyes flew open, and she tried to pull away, but to her embarrassment, Caleb held her close. "All right, Joseph, I'll bring you a glass of water. Go back to bed."

Joseph cast them a curious glance, then retreated. Elizabeth wriggled free, her face flaming.

"There's nothing wrong with him seeing us together," Caleb said. "He should see what married love's all about."

"He shouldn't see what he's too young to understand," she mumbled. Her stomach quivered. *Love?* Was that what Caleb felt?

Caleb tipped her chin up. "He's not too young."

Elizabeth started for the stairs. "I'll get his water."

Caleb stopped her with a gentle hand on her arm. "When you're tired of running, Bess, I'll be waiting for you."

For a moment she considered turning around, but she knew if she looked into those deep blue eyes again, she'd be lost. She nodded curtly, then hurried toward the open door.

Sixteen

"Please, Anna? Please try to eat." Elizabeth gently opened Anna's slack mouth and tried to force in a small spoonful. The broth dribbled down her wrinkled chin, and Elizabeth dabbed it with a napkin.

"*Nein,*" Anna said softly. "I have no need for food."

"You can't just sleep all the time. You have to eat." Tears welled in Elizabeth's eyes. "You have to get stronger!"

"*Liebchen,* please let God heal me."

"I *am* trying to heal you!" Frustrated, Elizabeth rose from the bed. "Your ankles and legs are swollen, Anna. You have to try to get better!"

"She didn't ask for your healing; she asked for God's." Caleb stood in the doorway, his arms loosely crossed. Elizabeth ducked her face at his rebuke, busying herself with collecting Anna's untouched dishes.

Caleb sat on the bed. "How are you today, Anna?"

Anna's feeble cough rattled in her chest. It was so wrenching that Elizabeth nearly dropped the tray. Caleb eased Anna against his shoulder and tenderly rubbed her back. He closed his eyes and hummed a German lullaby she'd taught them. When the coughing fit ended, he eased her back against the pillows. Her sightless gaze fixed on his face, and she smiled. "You remember the song."

Caleb gently touched her swollen hand. "Yes, Anna. I will always remember a great deal."

Cold dread stabbed Elizabeth's heart. Feeling dizzy, she sat on Anna's other side and pressed her free hand. "What can I do for you?"

Anna smiled weakly. "You can remember the holiday songs I taught you and Joseph this summer when we were all sick of the heat. Christmas will be here soon, *ja?*"

Elizabeth blinked back tears. These past weeks she'd stubbornly refused to acknowledge what Anna had obviously accepted a long time ago. "You'll sing those songs with us, Anna," she said hoarsely. "It's only two weeks away. Besides, we need your help. You know we always have trouble with the words to 'O Tannenbaum.' "

Fumbling, Anna drew Elizabeth's and

Caleb's hands together. "*Nein,* Elizabeth," she said softly. "I will not be here. But I am praying for a special gift for you and Caleb."

Elizabeth glanced at her husband. His head was bowed, and his eyes closed. The sick thud of comprehension weighted her stomach: Caleb knew the truth she'd been too selfish to see.

Anna patted their clasped hands. "I pray you both understand the breadth and length and height and depth of Jesus' love, my special children. May it fill you to the fullness of God."

Looking grief-stricken, Caleb opened his eyes. "Thank you, Anna," he whispered. "I wish I could know such a thing."

"His love surpasses knowledge, Caleb. It exceeds anything we can comprehend with our minds. Open your heart, my dear one."

Emotion congested Elizabeth's chest and throat. She eased her hand from Caleb's and bent to place a hasty kiss on Anna's cheek. Unable to speak, she made her way to the doorway and the safety of the kitchen. Fighting dizziness, she leaned against the sink.

Anna was dying! Why had she refused to see it?

Elizabeth flung open the back door and stumbled blindly, scattering chickens in her wake. Wrenching sobs broke in her chest, and she clutched the clothesline. In desperation, she grabbed a sheet and buried her face in the damp muslin.

How prideful she'd been when she first came to this farm. She'd thought she would help Anna, but it was Anna who had helped her. How would they all survive? How would *she* survive without Anna's love and wisdom?

Her fingers dug into her face through the muslin. "Anna, don't leave. Please don't leave!" She sank to the ground, dragging the sheet with her as she sobbed. "Why, God? *Why?*"

Caleb lifted her up, and she turned into his arms. Her anguish was too deep for words, her tears too strong. He held her tightly, kissing her hair as she cried out her sorrow and fear.

"Bess," he murmured. "I'm sorry. I should have told you."

She wept, heartbroken. "We have to d-do something!"

Caleb held her closer, sharing her grief. "There's nothing to do. She's ready to go."

"I can't just stand by and watch her die!" She drew back. "You can go for the doctor. He can help. He *must* know something I've missed. He must have some medicine!"

"I don't think so. He's known for a long time her heart's been failing."

Elizabeth clutched his arms. "Please, Caleb. I'll never ask another thing of you as long as I live."

He drew a deep breath. "Elizabeth —"

"*Please.*"

He searched her eyes. "All right," he said quietly.

She raised her eyes to his, their blue depths reflecting tender sorrow. A strange yearning grew in her to be a part of him, a part of his life. Stretching up on her toes, she kissed him. "Thank you, Caleb." His arms encircled her, but she withdrew, embarrassed, and hurried back to the house.

Mr. Berry bobbed his head. "Doc Ghent? I heard he's out setting old man Johnson's broken leg."

Caleb raked a hand through his hair. "That's near Salado!"

"Everybody all right at your place?"

Caleb gave him a hard look and turned to leave.

"Wait." Mr. Berry reached under the counter, producing a licorice whip. "For your boy."

Caleb slowly let his gaze drift to Berry's face. Hardening his eyes, he stared pointedly.

Berry blinked, and his gaze darted to the gun at Caleb's hip. Caleb could almost see the sweat break out on the man's forehead.

"I heard how you refused to stick up for my wife and son," Caleb said.

"I'm sorry about that." Berry hastily lowered the licorice.

"It's a little late for apologies." Caleb made his way to the doorway.

"You'd better head home," Berry called. "A norther's blowing this way."

Caleb laughed. "The sky was clear when I rode in. I've lived in a lot colder parts. You folks don't know anything about real winter weather."

On the street, he jammed his fists into his coat pockets and hunched his shoulders. The air did seem chillier. Or maybe he was just still hot under the collar.

Riding back to Anna's, he found himself torn between hurrying and going slower than usual. He knew he should be home to help Anna and comfort Elizabeth, but he really wanted to hole up in the saloon and dull his grief with a bottle.

It'd been a long time since he'd even had a drink. He'd kept his teetotaler's promise to Elizabeth. In fact, he'd tried to live up to her hopes in every way. He'd been as patient and loving as he knew how, but she was still hesitant to give him her love.

He shifted in the saddle, sighing. It wasn't just a physical consummation he wanted, it was her heart. Her complete trust and faith.

What did he know about faith? His parents had shown him theirs every day of his life, but he evidently hadn't paid attention. He had no idea how they'd related to their God, how they'd walked with God day after day.

Their God. The same one he once thought was his. He'd been baptized for nothing. His parents and Samantha had been so proud, then he'd turned into a thief. A man who lived by the gun strapped at his side.

Violence is wrong.

He grimaced. Elizabeth was right to chastise him for his violent lifestyle. Wasn't it his gun Joseph had nearly killed himself with?

He was nothing but a thief. A criminal so ashamed of his past that he couldn't even tell his wife the truth for fear she'd leave him. Even a governor's pardon couldn't change all the wrongs he'd done.

The wind rippled winter-nuded red oak branches, and an ominous charge filled the air.

Maybe Berry really had been trying to make amends, was truly sorry for not helping Elizabeth and Joseph. At any rate, Caleb had knowingly intimidated him. Was threatening him any different from actually pulling a gun? What would Elizabeth say?

"I'm not good like you, Bess," he yelled into the wind. "I don't have your belief. If I could change the past and be a different man, I would."

The sky rumbled. Roiling clouds, black as the soot on a chimney lamp, stretched across the horizon and moved rapidly in from the northwest. From the direction of Anna's farm.

Caleb turned up his collar, then jammed down his hat. Tightening his hands on the reins, he murmured to the horse, who shied from the coming storm. Caleb glanced around for shelter in case it was needed, but on this lonely stretch of road he knew there wouldn't be any until he came to Anna's.

Groaning, he clenched his jaw. Just what he needed. A rainstorm. He'd return home soaking wet, dripping water all over Elizabeth's clean floors. She'd certainly have something to say about that.

Ears twitching, the gelding whinnied. Caleb tightened the reins. "Come on, boy. We're going to get a little wet."

"Elizabeth?"

"I'm here." She knelt beside the bed and took Anna's swollen hand between both of her own.

"We must . . . we must pray for Johnny."

Elizabeth touched Anna's bloated cheek. "Your little boy is dead, Anna. You must have had another dream."

"*Der traum?*" Confusion crossed her face, then she weakly shifted her head from side to side. "*Nein,* I know it is true. He is in trouble, *liebchen.* God has told me."

Elizabeth smiled indulgently, unable to answer. For the past few hours, Anna had been moving between life and a fantasy world. Sometimes she held one-sided conversations entirely in German. She would babble, then wait, silent, then babble again. Anna never seemed disturbed by these talks, so Elizabeth discarded the notion of giving her something to make her sleep. Besides, she wanted as much time with Anna as possible.

Elizabeth rested her head on the bed. She needed to wash a stack of linens, but she was exhausted. Before she'd known Anna was dying, she'd been able to care for her all day without tiring; now that she knew the truth, every effort seemed doubly strenuous.

"Elizabeth?"

"Yes, Anna. I'm here."

Anna groped for her hand and, finding it, held fast. "Elizabeth, sit in the chair."

She smothered a yawn. "Let me take these linens outside, Anna. Then I'll —"

The swollen hand squeezed with supernatural pressure. *"Now."*

Elizabeth dropped into the chair.

"I must tell you something, then ask your forgiveness."

"Me?" Elizabeth started. "What have you ever done that needs forgiveness?"

"Do you remember when you first came to my house?"

Elizabeth nodded. How long ago that day seemed.

"You did not tell me Joseph was an Indian. I had to find out for myself."

Remembering how Anna had fingered Joseph's hair and guessed his heritage, Elizabeth cringed. She should have told Anna right away.

Tears trickled down Anna's cheek. "My Johnny did not die, as I led you and Caleb to believe. He was taken from me when he was four, Elizabeth — he was captured by the Kiowas."

Elizabeth froze.

"For years I waited for him to be returned. When he wasn't, my only hope was that they raised him as their own." She paused. "I have never known the truth. It was so painful, I could never speak of it."

"Joseph . . ."

"Joseph was God's way of healing my broken heart and forcing me to recognize my sin. The past few months have made me realize that I never forgave those who took my only child. Because of the precious Indian boy you brought into my house, into my life, I have faced that sin, asked for forgiveness, and received it. He has turned my mourning into joy."

Her voice broke. "God is so faithful, *liebchen*. Joseph has brought me great joy and strengthened God's perfect love in me." She squeezed Elizabeth's hand. "But I have often been envious that he was your child to raise. That you had two good eyes to see his sweet face and a strong, young body to chase after him in a field of bluebonnets as I used to do with my Johnny."

"Then I have to ask *your* forgiveness, Anna," Elizabeth said, her eyes and cheeks wet. "For I have often been envious of your ability to see with your heart what I can't see with my eyes. That you walk on two strong legs of faith when I can't even crawl."

"You have faith, my dear one," Anna whispered. "Even now, you finally sit in

Jesus' chair. Abide in him every day, and he will make you stronger than you can ever imagine."

"Anna." Sobbing, Elizabeth moved from the chair to the bed. She tenderly wrapped her arms around Anna's swollen body and buried her face in the woman's shoulder.

Anna returned her embrace, her puffy, arthritic hands awkwardly patting Elizabeth's back. She murmured soothing German words and let Elizabeth weep.

Suddenly Elizabeth felt Anna's body stiffen. Terrified that the end had come, she pulled back. "Anna?"

"It is your husband."

Confused, Elizabeth sat up, dashing the back of her hand against her eyes.

"*Ja.* You sent him to town?"

"Yes, Anna."

"A storm threatens him, dear one. A storm that forces him to choose to go on or give up."

Glancing at the window, Elizabeth saw December sunshine on the grass. She could hear Joseph's faint shouts of laughter from the barn.

"There's no storm." Anna was obviously drifting toward that dream world again.

"*Pray,* Elizabeth." Anna's voice grew fainter. "I have such little strength." Her head lolled gently to the side, and she slept.

Worried, Elizabeth rose. Maybe she would step outside to see if she could spot Caleb down the road. If he were here now, she wouldn't hesitate to accept the comfort of his arms. Anna's dying was much more than she could handle alone.

As she stepped onto the porch then down to the yard, cold nipped at her arms. She shivered. It did seem chillier than when Caleb left that morning. Staring down the length of the road, she willed him to appear.

Not a sign of life stirred. No rising dust announced his arrival, no blade of grass moved. Even the giant oak seemed unusually still, its every branch and leaf motionless as though it were painted between earth and sky.

Every semblance of a breeze died, leaving behind an eerie calm. Elizabeth turned to the west and saw a wall of ominous black clouds approach the farm with alarming speed. She'd seen many storms when she lived with the Comanches, but never any like this.

Her heart lurched in her throat. If Caleb had headed for home, he *was* in danger.

Pray, Anna had counseled. *I have such little strength.*

A gust of wind whipped loose a handful of

hair from Elizabeth's bun, and renewed fear threatened to choke her. Pushing the hair aside, she hiked up her skirts and ran as hard as she could, heading for the barn to pen the stock and warn Joseph.

The storm hit like a wall, a whirl of snow that extinguished the sun. High swirling winds flung sleet from every direction, stinging Caleb's face and hands. A thousand tiny knives cut through his clothing and into his skin. The temperature had dropped a good thirty degrees and was plunging even lower.

His horse snorted, frantic, and tried to back up with the wind.

"Steady, boy," Caleb mumbled through clenched, chattering teeth. "This is the way home."

The wind danced and howled. No matter how he lowered his head against the onslaught, the icy blasts found his exposed face. With a trembling hand, he tugged his shirt and undershirt up over his nose, only to feel the cold attack his exposed middle through his coat.

He hunched his shoulders and tightened his muscles against the cold. He *had* to get home. What if the storm threatened the house and they needed help? Elizabeth would worry. She didn't need his welfare to fret over, along with Anna's.

And Joseph. Who would calm his fears of the blizzard while Elizabeth tended Anna? Caleb imagined him huddled in a corner, alone, crying out for the strong arms of a father who wasn't there.

A freezing wet gust whipped at him, caking him with a mantle of ice and snow, freezing his heart with fear. What would his family do if he never made it back?

Caleb tried to draw a deep breath, but the cold stabbed his throat and lungs. Holding the reins between the frozen fingers of one hand, he lashed his chest with the other to keep the blood moving, repeating the motion on the other side. He tried to wiggle his toes and swing his legs, but he felt wooden from the waist down.

He called upon every instinct to calm himself, but his stomach lurched. How was he going to find his way in this maelstrom? He'd probably only been a few miles from home when the storm hit, but now he couldn't see beyond the horse's ears. So far he'd headed in the direction he thought Anna's farm lay, but he had no way to tell if he'd wandered off course. He could meander in circles until he died.

Weary resignation set in. Elizabeth could

manage on her own, he told himself. She was no shrinking violet; she was a self-willed woman who could take care of herself and a boy. She and Joseph would get along fine, long after he was —

Dead?

"Oh, God!" he called out through frozen lips.

Desperate, he started to pray.

Elizabeth rubbed the fleshy part of her fist against the ice-covered parlor window. All she could see was white, as though someone had thrown a blanket over the house. The wind howled around the limestone like a pack of wolves, and snow rattled the windows.

"Is Pa out in this?"

Elizabeth absently touched the base of the lamp she'd placed on the sill then turned. Bravely Joseph held up his chin, but Elizabeth could see it tremble in the faint light. "Yes, Joseph. I believe he is."

The little boy flung himself at her knees. "Mama!"

Elizabeth knelt, pressing him close. "Shh, Joseph. He'll be all right."

"Mama, I'm so scared!"

So am I, she thought instantly, then straightened. "We'll pray for him. That'll make us feel better."

"I d-don't think so!" Even Joseph had lost his faith.

Fighting the urge to surrender to doubt, Elizabeth said, "We will not stop praying for him. God *will* hear us, Joseph. But he doesn't want us to be unprepared. When your pa comes, he will be very cold. There's bean soup on the stove."

Childlike hope lit Joseph's face. "What can I do for Pa?"

"While I build up the fire, you go upstairs and gather all the blankets you can find. We'll warm them by the fire here in the parlor."

Joseph raced up the stairs. When he returned with an armload of blankets and quilts, Elizabeth had the fire stoked and roaring. Frowning, Joseph glanced at the lamp. "How's Pa going to find the house? It's awfully dark outside."

Elizabeth stopped short. How indeed? Caleb probably couldn't see the lamp if he was standing right on the other side of the window.

"Father, show me the way," she whispered humbly. "Please use me to help my husband. He's done so much for Joseph and me. And I . . . I . . . ."

A wave of warmth swept through her,

along with a Bible verse her father had taught her when she was very young. "Love one another," she whispered. "I've never even told Caleb how I feel."

She raised her head and watched Joseph, deep in his own prayers. Just as she had been afraid to acknowledge her love for this precious child, so now was she faced with her love for her husband. As Anna said, Caleb had modeled his love ever since they married. It was time to meet him halfway, even if it meant risking her life.

She snatched up Rudy Mannheim's old overcoat, work boots, and muffler.

"Wh-what are you doing, Mama?"

"I'm going to your father. Would you please bring me the rope from the kitchen?"

Joseph complied and watched with large eyes as she knotted one end around her waist. "I'll tie the other end to the porch column," she said. "Put on your heavy coat and stand at the door. Open it for as long as you can stand the cold, then close it."

"Why, Mama?"

Elizabeth wound the muffler around her neck and head, leaving only her eyes exposed. "It'll be a signal for your pa. Maybe between the fire and the lamp, he'll be able to see the house."

"But what about you?"

She awkwardly knelt to Joseph's level. "The rope will keep me from getting lost too. All I have to do is follow it back to the house."

A large tear slid down Joseph's face. Elizabeth caught it with her mittened hand then quickly kissed his smooth cheek. "God'll help your father find his way home."

Joseph threw his arms around her. A lump formed in her throat, and she turned. Joseph opened the door, and a cold blast instantly hit. Her resolve faltered, but she carefully navigated the ice-glazed porch and tied the rope around the nearest column. Letting out the rope as she went, she negotiated the steps and staggered against the icy blasts into the yard. When the rope drew taut, she stopped, feeling foolish and afraid.

Be strong and courageous! Do not tremble or be dismayed. The words came to her as she braced herself against the cold gusts that threatened to knock her over. She cupped her hands around her muffled mouth. "Caleb! Caleb!"

She called over and over into the screeching wind until her voice was raw and her body stiff. No matter how hard she strained, she couldn't see any movement beyond the raging storm.

Resolve faltered. He was probably dead,

and she was only endangering herself. Then who would care for Joseph and Anna?

Chilled, her hands dropped to her sides. Her head felt heavy, her body battered. She should go back in the house.

Be strong and courageous! Do not tremble or be dismayed.

Her shoulders sagged against the wind, and her body felt weighted. There was more to the verse, but the cold had dulled her memory.

Her knees buckled, and she cried out as she slipped into a slick snowdrift. Desperate, she raised her face to the stinging wind. "Father, give me strength! Help me to stand!"

Instantly, God's presence swelled inside her, filling her with encouragement and resolve. Caleb needed her.

Scrambling upright, she stamped her feet and rubbed her hands together for warmth. Renewed, she continued to call Caleb's name.

Seventeen

Every muscle that Caleb could still feel throbbed with pain. Even his jaw ached from the cold. He'd never been sleepier in his life. He wanted to close his eyes, just for a moment, but he knew that small pleasure could be fatal.

He'd never realized how dark and hopeless white could be. The whirling wind, snow, and ice reminded him of a book Nathan had read aloud several winters ago in their Wyoming hideout. After his creator's death, Frankenstein's monster cast himself adrift on an ice raft to die alone, where no one could see his remains to create a similar creature.

Caleb felt the same way. He wasn't the worst person in the world, but he wasn't the best. He might not be an outright murderer, but he had killed during the war. He had certainly robbed. And lied.

Resignation set in. He was going to die. The truth would somehow come out about his past, and he would disappoint Elizabeth yet again, even in death. How mortified she'd be when she found out she'd married a criminal! How would she ever hold her head up at his funeral?

Would Joseph be angry to find out Caleb wasn't the father he'd thought he was? The boy certainly didn't need the stigma of an outlaw father attached to him.

Wind pummeled his face, hurling needles of ice and snow. At least he could still feel their sting; he hadn't been able to feel his feet for quite a while now.

The wind scoured around him like a multitude of wailing voices, like a thousand lost souls writhing in agony. Maybe hell wasn't a place of brimstone and fire, but a perpetually frozen wasteland.

Caleb awkwardly switched the lines in his hand and feebly passed his free hand over his chest. He could barely move his arms anymore. He'd heard that buffalo hunters surprised by blizzards sometimes killed and slit open an animal then climbed inside for warmth and survival. Desperation had driven him to attempt likewise with the sorrel, but he'd been unable to dismount, his body stiff and frozen in place.

He was helpless.

All his life he'd followed something. As a

child, his parents. After they died, he'd followed his rage into battle. When he no longer had the legitimacy of war to vent his frustration, he'd followed Nathan's lead and turned to robbery. Since he'd turned himself in, he'd followed Noah's guidance to the letter, working diligently for the freedom that would give him a new life.

Now he had nothing.

Anna had once said that to get right with God, a man needed to humble himself and seek God's face. How could Caleb do that in this blinding storm? He couldn't see beyond his own nose, much less look up at heaven!

His love surpasses knowledge. Open your heart, Anna had said.

Caleb tried to force his lips to move, but his jaw seemed frozen shut. Weak, he could barely even form the words in his mind. *My heart's wide open now, God. I'm sorry for all the wrong I've done, sorry that I've turned from you. I wish I had another chance to get to know you.*

Instantly, he heard a voice in his heart. *The Lord God is with you.*

Hope flared, then died. God couldn't possibly still love him. Surely he'd left long ago, when Caleb stopped following him. He only stayed with people like Elizabeth, who led good lives.

The Lord your God is with you wherever you go, Caleb.

With great effort, he raised his head. The wind lashed his face, but he felt as though his heart were being scourged.

He parted his frozen lips. "Lead me, Lord! I'll follow you the rest of my life if you'll just show me the way!"

"Caleb . . . Caleb . . ."

He was going mad — he thought he heard someone call his name. Yet when he corrected the horse's lead even slightly, the small voice grew stronger.

Courage flooded like warmth through his veins. With frozen fingers, he tried to snap the reins. He felt as though he and the horse were barely moving.

"Caleb . . . Caleb . . . Caleb . . ."

He still couldn't see anything, but he was certain the voice was growing stronger. Caleb used it to guide the sorrel like a storm-tossed ship relying on a lighthouse.

Did he see something huge and dark looming in the swirling whiteness? He painfully stretched out his arm. *Oh, God, please let it be real! Please let it be shelter.*

He brushed something cold and solid, and long icy fingers scratched his face. The tree! He could tell by the width of the trunk that it was the giant oak just down the road from Anna's.

He wanted to laugh, he wanted to cry. He tried again to dismount but still couldn't. He needed to find the house, to find help.

"Caleb . . . Caleb . . ."

With agonizing effort, he tried to yell, but his voice came out as a mumble. "Don't leave!"

A light flashed on, then off. Hope rose, then plummeted. It was probably just his imagination. If there were mirages in deserts, surely there were mirages in snowstorms.

The light flickered on, then off again. He strained with all his being to see, to hear.

"Caleb . . . Caleb!"

Somehow Caleb guided the gelding toward the voice and the curious light. Maybe it was an angel of death, coming for his soul. He didn't even care. With no strength to fight, he could only throw himself on God's mercy.

"*Caleb!* Oh, thank you, God!"

Someone took the reins from his hands and led the horse. He didn't protest, couldn't yet speak. The light loomed larger, wide and shining.

Someone tugged at his arms. "I can't get you down, Caleb. You're frozen to the saddle!"

Elizabeth. He couldn't feel her touch, but her voice was warm to his ears. Forcing his jaw muscles to move, he worked his tongue free from the roof of his frozen mouth. "Beth."

She covered his hand with her mittened ones and pressed it against her wet, wool-covered cheek. He strained to see her with his snow-stung eyes, but could only make out a shadowy presence.

"Caleb . . . oh, my dear husband. I didn't think I'd see you again! Here. Put your arm around the post and hold on. Watch for me in the light."

A shadow passed between him and the brightness, the promising warmth. He didn't want her to leave, but he trusted now, secure and grateful. *Thank you, God, for answering my prayer. You've led me home.*

Something purer and stronger than gratitude swelled to every numb recess of his being, overpowering the cold. He felt renewed — cleansed — as though he'd been washed of every stain he'd brought on himself over the past fifteen years. He felt peace, where it had been waiting for him all along, in his heart.

Caleb bowed his head and wept. Tears froze on his face.

Something smacked behind his leg, shattering the saddle's icy glaze. It fell like sheets of broken glass. Caleb heard a hammer thud to the porch and feet crunching on the ice. Elizabeth tugged at his coat to pull him out of the saddle. He flailed strengthless arms, desperately trying to cling to her for support. As he felt himself fall to the porch, a black wave roared over him, pulling him out with the tide.

Breathless, Elizabeth jerked her chin up to free her mouth from the muffler, caked with ice from her frozen breath. Cold air rushed into her lungs, and she gasped. "Joseph, keep the door open!"

Ice slapped her exposed face as she bent over Caleb. Biting wind gusted up under her skirt, and slipping, she fell across him. Pushing herself upright, she grabbed Caleb's coat collar. Alternately stumbling and tugging, she kept her footing long enough to haul him to the doorway and over the threshold. Then, gasping for air, she collapsed beside him.

Struggling against the howling storm, Joseph pushed the door closed. "The blankets are warm, Mama. I —"

His eyes widened as he stared. Icicles hung from Caleb's hair and mustache, and a layer of ice and snow covered him like wet sugar. With his eyes closed, Caleb's face assumed the pallor of death.

Elizabeth staggered to her feet. Caleb wouldn't want his son to see him in this condition. With frozen fingers, she clumsily unknotted the rope from her waist and tied it securely around Joseph. "Take Pa's horse to the barn. The rope is long enough. Stay close to the house."

Joseph's face was solemn with responsibility. "Yes, Mama." He disappeared into the storm.

"Oh, Lord, take care of him." Elizabeth grabbed Caleb's coat collar and started dragging. Five feet from the fireplace, her weakened legs gave out. She sank to her knees and pulled him by sheer will until the roaring fire bathed his body in its glow.

Fear rose as she studied his icy, bloodless face. "Father God, please help him. Surely you didn't lead him all this way just to have him die!"

She wrapped a warm blanket around his head, sighing when she saw the shallow rise and fall of his breathing.

Elizabeth fumbled with his clothes. Heavy with snow and ice, the coat proved a challenge. Next came the shirt; the buttons were so slippery that she finally ripped the material.

Pressing her ear against his cold under-shirt, she heard a heartbeat, faint but regular. She breathed a prayer of thankfulness.

She removed all his clothes and wrapped him in warm blankets. Color returned to his face, red, raw, and chapped by the wind. Elizabeth flipped up the bottom edge of the quilt, revealing Caleb's feet. They remained dangerously white. He groaned and stirred.

Joseph lingered in the doorway. "I put up the horse. How is Pa?"

"He's better." Elizabeth briskly rubbed Caleb's feet.

"Does that mean he won't die?"

A rush of love engulfed her at the concern on his face. "We'll take care of him as best we can, won't we?"

He nodded solemnly.

She continued rubbing, but Caleb's feet didn't seem any warmer. "It's time for you to go to bed now, Joseph. Sleep on the pallet I made by the kitchen stove. You'll be warmer there than upstairs."

"Yes, Mama. I can say my prayers by myself tonight." He turned and was gone.

Caleb groaned, rousing. "Bess?"

"I'm right here."

He half-opened his eyes, smiling like a sleepy child. "God showed me the way home. He gave me a verse to hold on to."

Elizabeth pressed his cold hand against her face. "He gave me one too. 'Be strong and courageous! Do not tremble or be dismayed, for —' "

" '— the Lord your God is with you wherever you go.' " Caleb closed his eyes. Elizabeth gently laid his hand on the blankets and checked his feet again; they were still bloodless and unresponsive to her touch.

Quickly she rose and stripped from her sodden dress down to her underclothes. Wrapping herself in a shawl, she lay down and pressed his feet up under her camisole, against her stomach, against the warmth of her curled body.

She placed her hands over his feet and prayed. She beseeched God to heal Caleb. He jerked suddenly, groaning. "Bess . . . my feet!"

"Are they tingling?" If he could feel them, there was hope.

"They *hurt!*" He shivered. "I'm s-so cold."

Elizabeth slipped under the blankets. She wrapped her arms around him, sharing her warmth as she pressed closer. Caleb burrowed against her as Joseph did when he was cold.

Wrapped in their warm cocoon, Elizabeth

held him all night as he tossed in pain. She wanted to brew some willow-bark tea, but every time she tried to disentangle herself, he clung tighter. "I had to come home to you," he babbled, feverish. "I couldn't leave you and Joseph. I've never even said I love you."

She held him close, whispering her own endearments, and at last he slept. Exhausted, she dozed fitfully with her cheek pressed to his chest.

Elizabeth awoke with a start and reluctantly eased out of their warm blankets. Teeth chattering, she drew a deep breath of frosty air and clutched the shawl around her.

The storm shook the windows. After she fed the fire, she tiptoed to the kitchen and found Joseph sleeping soundly in his own warm blankets next to the stove. She added more wood, then moved to Anna's room.

Anna was so still, Elizabeth feared the worst. She laid her palm against Anna's puffy neck and felt a slow, steady pulse.

"Is it morning?"

Elizabeth glanced at the window and sat on the edge of the chair. "I don't know. The storm's too fierce to tell."

A gentle smile curved Anna's wrinkled lips. "Caleb is home."

"You were right all along. Your prayers were answered."

"Not my prayers. Yours. Your love for him. God has read your heart."

"I fear my heart is sinful, Anna. I wish it were pure like yours."

"Purity comes only from a right attitude toward the Lord."

Elizabeth leaned forward. "Then tell me what a right attitude is. Tell me what he wants of me."

"He does not want you to hide any longer, dear one. He wants you to step out in faith and submit yourself to his care."

Submit? Hadn't she done that? Hadn't she been controlled by Eyes Like the Sun and her father? Frustrated, she rose. "I'll bring you some tea."

"*Nein.*" Anna yawned. Her face looked peaceful and contented, like a child who knew she was loved. "I believe I will go back to sleep. And you must return to your husband."

Elizabeth bent and kissed Anna's swollen cheek. Her color seemed better, the swelling not so pronounced. "Joseph is sleeping outside your door. Call him if you're in need."

Anna's smile was tender and loving. "Yes, *liebchen.* Do not trouble yourself about me.

Your attention must be on the Lord, then your family."

Elizabeth pondered Anna's words as she brewed some willow-bark tea. Anna's trust in what God wanted was so naive. God required more from his children than passivity. He wanted them to serve and obey. Didn't he set out the Ten Commandments? Didn't he punish his enemies?

Joseph stirred in his sleep, snoring softly as he thrust out his small arms. Smiling, Elizabeth tucked them back under the covers. She poured a cup of tea and returned to Caleb.

Despite the fire's warmth, the storm raged around the house. Elizabeth set down the cup, then readjusted her shawl.

A slow smile spread across Caleb's face. "I thought maybe I'd dreamed you."

"I went to make some tea for you."

She helped him sit, letting him lean against her as she held the cup to his lips. He obediently swallowed, then made a face. "One of your witch's brews again."

"Yes." She smiled. "Do you remember those days along the Brazos after the stage wreck?"

He nodded, his eyes searching hers as he continued to sip.

"I had no idea then what I would feel for

you now. No idea that I could ever love any-body."

His eyes twinkled. "You tell me this when I'm too weak to even hug you."

"You can hug me later. For now, just get well."

He dutifully drained the tea. When she turned to set away the empty cup, he edged closer and rested his head against her shoulder. Startled, she drew a deep breath. "Take off the shawl and lie down with me again, Bess," he whispered. "Lie down and hold me."

Fighting her quivering stomach, she removed the shawl and eased down on the makeshift bed. Her muscles tightened with remembered fear.

Be strong and courageous! Do not tremble or be dismayed.

Elizabeth drew another deep breath. Caleb laid his head on her shoulder, and she covered his cold feet with her own.

"Tell me again," he whispered.

She felt his warm breath against her neck. "What?"

"Tell me how you feel." He slowly, painfully, drew an arm around her waist.

She expected panic to rise but felt only security. "I love you," she whispered.

He sighed and pressed closer. "I love you too, Elizabeth."

The fire crackled, and shadows danced across their bed. Elizabeth touched Caleb's waist then boldly laid her hand there. Arms and legs entwined, she and her husband fell asleep. The quiet awakened her. Faint light shone through the window. The whirling wind and ice had abated.

Joyous that the storm had passed, she eased away from Caleb. Her first impulse was to awaken him, but he slept soundly.

Elizabeth smiled as she watched him. Their marriage was still unconsummated, but for the first time she and Caleb had slept closely together as husband and wife. She didn't want to leave their warm nest, but she had other obligations.

In the kitchen, Joseph stirred in his own makeshift bed. She tousled his dark head. "Good morning, sleepyhead! The storm's over."

Joseph stopped rubbing his eyes, and his mouth dropped open. "G-good morning, Ma."

She smiled. "Last night you called me Mama."

"I . . . I'm sorry. I'll call you Ma if you want."

She hugged him. "I liked Mama."

Joseph blinked, and Elizabeth turned away to hide her laughter. God was working quite a few changes around the Mannheim place.

Whistling, she stoked the stove's fire and boiled water for coffee and tea, then heated the leftover bean soup. It would make a hearty breakfast for Caleb, and she would pick out the beans to feed the broth to Anna. Surely God had granted them all two miracles: bringing Caleb home safe and healing Anna. She looked so much better last night.

She started Joseph on his breakfast, chattering to him about Caleb's good health and extracting a promise from the boy not to bother his father until he had awakened. Caleb still needed time to rest and heal.

Elizabeth prepared a tray of broth and weak tea, her hands shaking with excitement. She could hardly wait to tell Anna that she had finally found the courage to tell Caleb she loved him and that he actually loved her too. God was granting her the deep desires of her heart, even those long hidden.

She cheerfully opened the door. "Oh, Anna, the most wonderful —"

Her hands tightened around the tray. "No," she whispered. "Oh, Father, no!"

Anna lay with her head in the chair by her bed, a shaft of sunlight beaming down on her gray hair. A smile of peace filled her face as though she had witnessed something beautiful when Jesus arose and welcomed her soul.

Eighteen

The preacher closed his Bible, and Caleb squeezed Elizabeth's hand. She had remained stoic and calm ever since she'd told him of Anna's death, serenely wiping Joseph's tears without shedding any of her own.

Alongside the Martins and the Orozcos, several Sanctificationists and a few townspeople, including Mr. Berry, encircled the open grave at the far edge of Anna's property.

Caleb stared down at the simple cedar box. He and Gustavo had built Anna's coffin while Marisa and Elizabeth lovingly bathed and dressed her body. Now she lay next to Rudy under the wild mustang grape arbor. The branches that were lifeless in winter would bloom and bear fruit in spring profusion.

The preacher smiled gently. "We all know how unforgiving this land can be. Two days ago the sun shone warmly, then the worst norther in memory hit. Though the sun is again shining today, the storm has left its marks."

He straightened. "But just as our Texas weather is unpredictable, so is the course of our lives. Jesus warned us to keep our lamps lit, to watch and pray for his coming, for no one knows the hour. If you have allowed your lamp to burn low or have indeed never even lit the wick, it's not too late. Let Anna's life be our example. Though she suffered many adversities, she was always faithful, always watchful. Jesus found her ready."

Iola Bigelow burst into tears. "There, there," Martha McWhirter said, wrapping an arm around the distraught woman. Iola's sobs escalated into an outright wail.

The preacher cast Iola a pitying glance, then cleared his throat. "As a closing for this service, Elizabeth Martin has asked to sing a hymn."

Caleb squeezed Elizabeth's hand again for reassurance. She smiled sadly up at him and took a step forward. "Anna loved to teach my family songs in German. This was her favorite hymn."

She drew a deep breath, then her voice rose softly and sweetly. *"Ein' feste Burg ist unser Gott, Ein' gute Wehr und Waffen."* A mighty fortress is our God, a bulwark never failing.

Her voice faltered after the first line as she struggled against tears. Caleb clasped her hand and sang with her. Bolstered by his deep voice, her own rose again.

"Er hilft uns frei aus aller Noth, Die uns hat jetzt betroffen." Our helper he, amid the flood of mortal ills prevailing.

Martin Luther's centuries-old hymn stirred something inside Caleb. He could feel power rising, swirling around them. Even as he sang the German, the English words ran through his mind: Did we in our own strength confide, our striving would be losing; Were not the right man on our side, the man of God's own choosing. Dost ask who that may be? Christ Jesus, it is he.

Jesus. Everything Anna had ever said pointed to him, every kindness she ever performed reflected his love. Even her final prayers for Caleb and Elizabeth had been that they not only come closer to each other but closer to the Lord.

When the song was completed, Caleb and Elizabeth fell silent. Caleb bowed his head, and Elizabeth nestled her hand in his palm.

The preacher cleared his throat. "Let us pray."

Afterward, Caleb raised his head. His

gaze caught Elizabeth's, and something passed between them, something deeper than words. She smiled and nodded, two small gestures that spoke of reassurance and trust — true love. Caleb longed to take her in his arms right then and there, despite the crowd, despite the solemnity of the moment.

The gravediggers moved to fill the gaping hole, and the funeral gathering broke up. Marisa gave Elizabeth a hug, made awkward by her advanced pregnancy. "I can't believe Anna's gone. It was so good to have you here these past months. This moment would have been much harder for us without you."

"I'm grateful I was here too." Elizabeth smiled gently. "And I'll be so happy for you when that precious child is born."

"You will stay, won't you? I still want you to be with me during my time. If it is a girl, we will name her Ana." Marisa touched Elizabeth's arm. "But now I will go inside and see that people are fed." She raised her palms heavenward. "Anna's friends are very generous. There is so much food!"

"Miz Martin?" Mr. Berry approached Elizabeth hesitantly. He glanced nervously at Caleb, then scuffed a toe of his well-worn boot against a rock. "Ah, Miz Martin, I just wanted to say I'm sure sorry about Miz Mannheim's passing. She and her husband were always good customers, but more'n that, good people."

"That's most kind of you, Mr. Berry," Elizabeth said. "I never knew Rudy Mannheim, but I'll certainly miss Anna."

Berry twisted his hat between his hands. "I'm, uh, also sorry about the past, Miz Martin. You and your son are good people too."

Humbled, Caleb extended his hand. "I'm sorry too, Berry. Elizabeth and I appreciate your sympathy and plan to do business with you for a long while."

Berry glanced at Caleb's hip. Even though the customary gun belt was absent, he looked nervously at Caleb's outstretched hand. "Thanks, Martin," he mumbled, then hastily retreated.

Caleb let his hand drop, and his smile faded. He felt a touch on his arm. "It will take time, but people will come around," Elizabeth said. "They'll see the Lord in your life."

Reassured, Caleb patted her hand. She'd accepted his supernatural experience in the blizzard without question. They'd knelt and humbly thanked God for his love, even though their hearts ached with grief.

"Elizabeth!" Iola Bigelow nearly bowled Caleb over as she hurled herself against Elizabeth. "Oh, my dear, what Anna went through! First, being saddled with you and that child, then having this questionable man under her roof, and now . . . now . . . Oh, I'll miss her so much!" Iola buried her face in a wet handkerchief.

Resentment and protectiveness rose in Caleb's chest. Why didn't Elizabeth just tell the old hen off? How dare Iola Bigelow even set foot on Anna's land after she'd caused so much trouble!

Elizabeth put her arm around Iola, who immediately buried her face against Elizabeth's shoulder. Elizabeth held the sobbing woman in a tender embrace, her face translucent with sympathy. "Anna wouldn't want her dear friend to be unhappy, Iola. She cared for you very much."

"She . . . she did?"

"Yes. Perhaps we could talk about her. You could tell me so much about Anna that I don't know."

Sniffling, Iola straightened. "I suppose I could do that. You *did* only know her a short time."

"Then you'll come for dinner on Sunday?"

Iola caught Caleb's eye and stepped back.

Elizabeth shook her head. "Where are my manners? You haven't been introduced to my husband. This is Caleb —"

"I know who he is. Hmmph! He's the reason you left the Sanctificationists! We might have helped you, if not for him!"

Caleb instinctively balled his fists. Had that prune-faced biddy forgotten she was the one who had threatened to separate Joseph and Elizabeth? That *she* was the reason Elizabeth had married him in the first place?

He caught sight of Elizabeth's gentle expression, and he swallowed his harsh words. Her look reminded him of Anna.

Caleb extended a hand. "How do you do, Miss Bigelow? I hope you can join us this Sunday."

Joseph moved between his parents. "Please come, Miss Bigelow."

A horrified expression dropped over Iola's face. "You're all crazy! You don't really want me to come. You're just trying to make me look bad!"

Elizabeth's face crumpled. "No, Iola, we —"

"You're not fooling me!" Iola shook a bony finger. "You may have pulled the wool over Anna Mannheim's eyes, but not mine!"

With a snort of derision, she flounced away.

"Iola, wait!" Martha followed after her, then paused in front of Elizabeth. "How are you, dear?" she said distractedly.

"I'm happy, Martha. I'm grateful to be married."

Martha sized Caleb up with one glance, then lifted her chin. "I had hoped you'd find the sanctification you were seeking, Elizabeth. The sanctification the group has found."

Caleb stepped beside Elizabeth. "My wife and I will learn together, ma'am. It seems to me that that's what a Christian marriage is all about."

Martha eyed him coldly, then gave Elizabeth a peck on the cheek. "You know where we are when you need us." Scanning the crowd for Iola, she hurried off.

Joseph tugged on Caleb's hand. "I didn't like her."

"Joseph!"

Caleb grinned at Elizabeth, then down at the boy. "I didn't much either, Joe."

"José! José!" Santiago grabbed Joseph's sleeve. "Can we play in your barn? My mother says it's all right with her."

Elizabeth's face clouded. "This is no day for children to —"

"Let 'em go, Bess. They mean no disrespect to Anna. They probably have the right idea anyway. Shouldn't we be happy she's in heaven?"

"Joseph, there's a whole houseful of people."

"But they're not *my* friends; they're grownups! Please, Ma?"

Elizabeth smiled. "Go ahead then. But take care of your Sunday clothes."

"I will!" He and Santiago broke into a run, and the other Orozco children trailed after them.

Caleb wrapped an arm around her. "You made your son happy."

"My son," she echoed softly, then sighed. "I want to be a good mother, Caleb. Anna was so wonderful at teaching me. She . . ." Her eyes brimmed with tears. Caleb brought her hand up and pressed a kiss in the palm. "You'll do fine. With God's help, we'll learn how to be good parents together."

She raised shining wet eyes. "I'm so afraid to love you. God takes the people I love."

Caleb cupped her cheek. "Didn't he bring me safe through the blizzard? Didn't he use *you* to bring me back?"

"What if you decide to leave?"

At that moment, two red-tailed hawks

flew into view. Catching thermal updrafts, they veered as they soared then swooped low.

Caleb shaded his eyes, transfixed. Against the still blue sky, the hawks soared and dipped in unison, gliding apart only to come together again. They called to each other, playful, with no aim but to enjoy each other and the warm day.

He turned to find Elizabeth staring at him, waiting, her question lingering in her eyes.

"Those hawks have mated for life, Bess," he said. "If God instilled a bird with such instinct, don't you suppose he could create an even greater love between a man and a woman?" He clasped her hands. "I want to be your husband in every way, but I'm willing to wait. Make a pledge with me right now, Elizabeth. We said our vows when we got married, but this time, let's truly kneel before God."

"Here? At Anna's grave?"

"I want you to know I won't let you go, Elizabeth. Ever."

Something in his tone must have convinced her. "Or I, you," she whispered.

Caleb got to his knees on the hard ground. Elizabeth knelt beside him. They reached for each other's hand and bowed their heads. For a moment he couldn't speak. He couldn't find the words to express himself — he didn't really know how to pray. Especially about something as important as this moment with his wife.

Open your heart.

With Anna's words came strength that poured into his humbled soul. "Father, though we've been married for several months, we kneel before you and ask your blessing on our marriage. We ask you to always be in charge of our life together. We're grieving Anna's death, but we thank you for the second chance you've given us. Teach us how to love each other and how to raise Joseph. Thank you for never leaving us, just as we promise never to leave each other."

Caleb could feel Elizabeth's hands tremble in his. "Please make us worthy," she added in a whisper.

They rose. Caleb could still read doubt in her eyes, but the peace in his heart reassured him. When he glanced up, he saw the hawks still chasing each other, soaring higher out of view.

The rest of the day, Elizabeth managed to smile at the appropriate times and make the required polite responses. She and Marisa served from the covered dishes, agreeing in private that they themselves had no appetite. Elizabeth carefully avoided the Sanctificationists, though she sensed Martha's gaze following her. Her neck prickled warm under her collar.

She wasn't ashamed of leaving the Sanctificationists; no, her discomfort stemmed from another emotion. One that ran contrary to every attitude she'd carefully cultivated for the past five years.

She had fallen in love. With her husband.

When night fell and everyone else had gone, the Orozcos tearfully said good-bye. Elizabeth and Caleb watched until the wagon's lantern was a speck on the horizon, then silently reentered the house. Yawning, Elizabeth rubbed her arms against the chill. Caleb wrapped an arm around her, and she leaned against him, feeling drowsy, warm, and safe.

Joseph huddled in a corner of the parlor sofa, his head nodded over his knees. "Looks like our boy's had a big day," Caleb said softly. "I'd better carry him to bed."

"On your swollen feet?" Elizabeth scooped up Joseph, who sleepily wrapped his arms around her neck. "I'll carry him."

Caleb picked up a lamp and led the way

up the dark stairs. Elizabeth matched her pace to his. Joseph's weight slowed her; he'd grown in the months since she'd carried him down the road to Anna's that first dark night. How far they'd come, how much she'd grown, too, since they'd set out from Belton.

Joseph offered up a sleepy smile as Elizabeth and Caleb undressed him and tucked him in. He immediately rolled over and into the covers, snoring.

Caleb lifted the lamp and offered a hand to Elizabeth. She stared, knowing what he asked. Other than the night of the blizzard, they had never gone to bed at the same time.

Her eyes met his over the low flame, and his face softened. "I can wait in here for a while if you'd rather, Bess."

"No." She clasped his hand. "I know you're tired, and I feel so sad."

"I'll miss Anna," Caleb said softly, leading the way across the hall.

Elizabeth removed her nightgown from the dresser. "Isn't it funny? I've been too busy to think about her much today. But now that everyone's gone . . ."

Caleb shut the door behind them.

Elizabeth turned, instinctively hugging the nightgown. Caleb set the lamp by the bed and blew out the flame. He started to undress in the darkness. "Now that everyone's gone . . ."

Elizabeth lowered the nightgown. "N-now that everyone's gone, I'm thinking about her again."

"I know what you mean." His voice was steady and comforting in the blackness. "I missed our Bible reading tonight."

She heard him finish undressing. Hastily unbuttoning her dress, she pulled the nightgown over her head before her dress hit the floor.

She paused, feeling foolish. Now she had her nightgown on over her underclothes.

Elizabeth heard the whisper of sheets and blankets. She crouched down and reached up under her nightgown. She worked her camisole and drawers free, banging her shin on the bedframe. "Oww!"

The bed squeaked. "Bess? What are you doing down there?"

"J-just getting undressed."

Caleb pulled the covers back on her side, his sober face momentarily visible in the moonlight. "Come to bed, honey. We need to pray."

Drawing a deep breath, Elizabeth slipped between the sheets. She shivered with cold, and her teeth chattered. Instantly, Caleb held her. "Do you want to talk about

Anna?" he said softly.

"Y-yes. No." His warmth and strength muddled her thinking. "I mean, I don't know. I can't believe she won't be with us anymore."

"Not this side of heaven. I'll miss hearing her talk about her Jesus chair."

Elizabeth's eyes watered. "S-she loved him so much, Caleb. Sometimes I think that's all that . . ."

Her voice caught in her throat. She had just begun to catch a glimmer of Anna's deep love for God. Now she would never truly know what Anna felt, would never again get to hear her joy as she spoke of God's love. Elizabeth sniffled quickly, hoping Caleb hadn't noticed her emotion.

Caleb kissed her temple. "Cry, Elizabeth. There's no sin in grief. Remember God's promise; he will turn our mourning into joy and comfort us and give us joy for our sorrow."

Hearing the words Anna had spoken only a few days earlier, Elizabeth felt the last brick in the dam of grief crumble. Warm tears flowed. "Oh, Caleb!" She wrapped her arms around him, burying her face against his chest. "I'm going to miss her! Why did she have to die?"

"That's it." Caleb's arms tightened. "Let it out, honey."

"What are we going to do without her? Anna was such a great lady. She loved us and Joseph so much! She was so *good!* And I'm . . . I'm —"

"You're good too."

"No!"

"Yes. You're good because you have God inside you. You invited him there. That's what he showed me during the blizzard. It's *his* righteousness, not ours."

Elizabeth couldn't speak. The tears slowed, clogging her throat. Caleb held her close, whispering her name. Instinctively she raised her face, closing her eyes as his lips met hers.

In her grief, she clung to his presence, his vitality. His lips moved from hers to her cheeks, her eyes, her ears, her neck. She could feel his warmth work straight to her heart, melting her reserve.

She drew back. "I . . . I can't, Caleb."

"Shh, Bess." He tenderly kissed her temple then pressed her wet cheek to his chest. "I'm not asking anything. Let's say our prayers and go to sleep."

"But . . ."

"God," he said softly, "thank you for hearing us."

Elizabeth relaxed. By the time Caleb finished, she felt weary and limp. As trusting as a child, she fell asleep in his arms.

The cold wind cut across the desolate plains, whistling through bare mesquite trees. Coughing hard, Eyes Like the Sun wrapped the ragged buffalo skin around himself and gritted his teeth against the sound of the newborn crying just inside his tepee. Yesterday his youngest wife had given birth for the second time within a year. To yet another girl. A useless, squalling girl.

The child cried harder, hungry. They were all hungry, all dying of starvation on the land where there had once been abundance and freedom to roam. Now there were only the bluecoats and the white settlers who pressed westward, encroaching with their guns and settlements and diseases that ravaged and killed.

Eyes Like the Sun heard his wife murmur to the baby and speak soothingly to their older daughter. His chest hurt whenever he drew a deep breath, and his empty eye socket ached. He thought about going to one of his two other wives' tents, but he would find no comfort there. Lately his oldest wife looked bent and haggard. His second wife, though still pretty and spirited enough to meet his passion, constantly berated him for not improving their lot.

"You're supposed to be a great warrior," she said, her eyes filled with disgust. "Yet we who have chosen to remain free are sick and starving. We might as well go to the reservation and eat the white man's rancid meat. It is better than dying out here for lack of leadership. If Quanah were still here —"

He'd struck her then, effectively silencing her words but not the accusing look in her eyes. Last summer Quanah had taken his band to the reservation, leaving Eyes Like the Sun and his followers to dodge the bluecoats on their own.

Eyes Like the Sun straightened and touched the medicine bag at his chest, looking to the southeast where his only son lived — the son Speaks of Her God had borne. He would still be a small boy, but it was time to bring him home to his people. Time for him to take his place beside his father and fulfill the future that had been foretold.

Nineteen

Caleb's railroad work continued steadily into December. The crew was nearly finished surveying the county. Soon the final pay would be dispersed and each man would return to his hometown.

Caleb lay awake at night pondering his family's future. Gustavo had handed them the deed to Anna's farm, but Caleb was restless. Each night as he studied the Bible with Elizabeth and Joseph, he became more convinced that he needed to see Nathan. He needed to tell his imprisoned friend about the changes God had made in his life.

And Samantha. It had been nearly four years, and she was still missing, perhaps even dead. Caleb would see Nathan, then do his best to find Samantha. Maybe he would even take George Addison, their Indian-raised friend. He had been the gang's best tracker.

Lying in bed, Caleb grinned in the darkness. It'd be good to see George again. Not to mention the rest of the gang or the beautiful, secluded Wind River Mountains in Wyoming.

He glanced over at Elizabeth, sleeping with her head against his shoulder, and his smile fell. He couldn't bring himself to tell her the truth. Every day he refused to tell her added another ache in his heart, but he decided he'd rather carry the burden alone. The sin of withholding the truth didn't seem any greater than the sin of shattering her trust.

Anna would have known what he should do. If she were still alive, he'd confess everything and accept her counsel. He missed talking to her, but he was learning instead to talk to God.

One of the things he frequently discussed was his wife. Elizabeth had never been more loving with him or Joseph. She greeted Caleb each morning with a kiss but bounded out of bed before he could reach for her. During the day she smiled more than ever, made more excuses to touch his hand, his shoulder, his face. She accepted his embraces — even at bedtime — but drew back before he could show her how much he loved her as his wife.

Groaning inwardly as his thoughts drifted, he struggled for composure.

Sleeping in the same bed had been difficult enough before. Now that she lay close to him every night, he could smell the sweetness of her hair and feel the softness of her body as she stirred in her sleep. He didn't know how many more cold midnight swims in Nolan Creek he could stand.

Lord, how can I make her understand what I feel? How can I break through her memories?

Searching for something — anything — to divert his attention, Caleb remembered the Christmas present for Elizabeth he'd hidden today in the barn. He'd sworn Joseph to secrecy, and the boy's eyes had shone when Caleb opened the small, white box.

"It's beautiful, Pa!"

Worried, Caleb had pressed for reassurance. "You think she'll like it?"

Joseph nodded, his smile wide.

Now Caleb had only to wait until tomorrow — Christmas Day — to find out for himself.

The next morning, he and Elizabeth watched with delight as Joseph opened his presents. The boy's eyes widened as he pulled back the brown paper wrapping. "Oh, Ma! Pa! It's a book! Thank you! *Twenty Thousand luh, lee . . .*"

"*Leagues under the Sea*," Elizabeth said. "We can all read it together, and then when you're older, you'll be able to read the entire book yourself."

"Thanks!"

Caleb smiled. "Your other present is in the barn." He glanced at Elizabeth, who was fidgeting with excitement almost as much as Joseph. Caleb winked at her. "It's underneath your rope swing, Joe."

Joseph dashed from the house. Laughing as they followed in the cold, Caleb watched Elizabeth's cheeks turn pink, her breath frosty in the air.

A whimpering noise rose from the hay, and Joseph squealed with delight. "A puppy!" He scooped up the wiggling black-and-white mass, and a pink tongue shot out and licked his cheek. Joseph giggled, cradling the furry ball closer.

"The puppy will be your responsibility," Elizabeth said. "You'll have to feed him and give him water and see that he's warm during the winter."

"I will! Thank you, Ma! Thank you, Pa!"

"You're welcome, son," Caleb said.

When Elizabeth didn't respond, Caleb looked at her. She was watching Joseph with unabashed maternal love in her eyes. Caleb swallowed hard, filled with admiration for his wife.

Joseph oohed and aahed as the puppy snuffled in the hay. Caleb pulled Elizabeth close. "Your present is out here as well."

"Mine?"

Caleb reached around the cows' stall and withdrew the package. He laid it in her hands, nervous with anticipation. What if she didn't like it?

She stared at the white box, then carefully pried up the lid. "I can't imagine what —"

She lifted a gold chain. A plain gold cross dangled at the end. She laid it delicately in her palm, wordless.

Caleb anxiously searched her face. "Do you like it?"

"I . . . It's beautiful," she whispered. She shook her head and replaced the necklace in the box. "I can't possibly accept this, Caleb. It's *too* beautiful."

Caleb freed the knot securing the leather strip around her neck. "I've never seen you without this. You told me once you wear it as a reminder of God. Why?"

Looking panic-stricken, her gaze darted to Joseph. "I was wearing one like it when . . . when Eyes Like the Sun . . ."

Caleb removed the leather necklace and placed the chain around her neck, closing the delicate catch. When she turned, the gold cross shone in the morning sun.

"Wear this one because you love the Lord. That's why I bought it for you. You say it's beautiful, but you gave me Jesus. Even when we first met, day after day you clung to your belief in him. You showed his love without expecting anything in return. You helped me heal, and you helped me find forgiveness."

"But I'm so rigid . . . so . . . *angry* sometimes. Remember how I treated Joseph?" She glanced over her shoulder at the little boy, still absorbed with his puppy. "Remember how I treated you?"

"We've both grown." Caleb took her hands. "Anna and I once talked about sanctification, and she told me it wasn't about doing good or separating from the world. It means allowing God to make us like him. We aren't holy because of our work for the Lord but because of the Lord's work for us. In us."

His smile was bittersweet. "I never understood exactly what she meant until this moment."

Elizabeth glanced down where he'd dropped the leather necklace. "I can't forget what happened, Caleb."

"Let the Lord forget for you. Let him replace those memories with love." He drew her into a protective embrace. "Wear this new cross as a symbol of not only his love, but mine. And I *do* love you."

"In spite of . . . everything?"

Even now her nearness enticed him. He eased his hand up to stroke the back of her neck. "When you're willing, I'll be here."

"I . . . I know."

"Ma! Pa! Look at my puppy!"

Elizabeth knelt beside Joseph. "He's very sweet."

Joseph thrust the bundle into her arms. "You can hold him," he said magnanimously.

Elizabeth cradled the puppy close. He snuggled in her arms with a sleepy whimper, and she smiled. "He's so little."

Caleb knelt alongside her. "He was the runt of the litter. Even so, Berry was lucky to get him for me by Christmas. What are you going to call him, Joseph?"

"Did you have a puppy when you were a boy, Pa?"

"My sister and I had one when we were a little older than you. We named him Rags."

"Rags!" Joseph's eyes lit up. "I like that. This puppy's black and white, so he even looks like a pile of rags."

Elizabeth stroked the puppy's belly, her

face thoughtful. "And rags are discarded cloths that are still useful, just like runts."

Caleb smiled and helped her to her feet. "We'd better go find Rags a box to sleep in, then we have to leave for the Orozcos' for dinner."

"Come here, boy." Joseph took the dog from Elizabeth's arms, pressed him against his chest, and kissed the puppy's furry head.

Elizabeth smiled lovingly. Caleb wrapped his arm around her, and she snuggled close. "The cross *is* beautiful," she murmured. "Thank you. I should have done more than knit you a muffler and vest."

"They're beautiful too. I'll put them on before we go to the Orozcos'. It's certainly cold enough. Thank you for knitting them for me."

"I wish I'd given them to you before the blizzard. You might not have —"

Caleb kissed her quickly. "Hush. Are you a weather soothsayer now, Elizabeth Martin?"

Though she shyly turned away, Caleb could see by her smile that his teasing pleased her. Or maybe it was his kiss.

He tucked her hand in his arm, and they walked to the house. The way Elizabeth had looked at Joseph, the way she'd looked at *him*, there was hope. If she could equate emotional love with physical love, they might one day have a true marriage after all.

The new year rolled in with a bluster, not a blizzard, but with enough snow to keep Caleb from surveying. They passed the first few days of 1876 around the fireplace, snug and happy, popping corn with the popper the Orozcos had given them for Christmas. Elizabeth made hot cocoa, and they laughed and played with Rags.

One cold, clear late-February night, Caleb answered the pounding at the door. Ashen-faced, Rafael had come to fetch Elizabeth; Marisa's child was ready to be born. Elizabeth snatched up her already-prepared medicine bag, and she and Caleb hurried down the road in the wagon, leaving Rafael to watch over Joseph.

Several hours later, a tiny baby slipped easily into Elizabeth's hands, a beautiful little girl with a thatch of dark hair. As she'd promised, her mother immediately pronounced her name Ana.

Yawning, Caleb switched the reins to one hand and covered his mouth with the other. Never had the ride back to the farm seemed so long. He doubted they'd beat the sun home, for its edges crept over the horizon.

Elizabeth sighed sleepily against his

shoulder, and he smiled. In some ways, he wished the ride would never end. Even though they hadn't spoken since they'd left the Orozcos', they were both still filled with the miraculous wonder they'd witnessed. Caleb had never seen a man exhibit such incredulous joy as when Elizabeth told Gustavo his daughter had arrived safely. Gustavo wept, unashamed, breaking into Spanish prayers of thanksgiving.

Elizabeth sighed again. "Baby Ana is certainly beautiful."

"Yes, she is." Caleb smothered a yawn with his fist and straightened to stretch out the kinks in his back. "But why did she have to come in the middle of the night?"

Elizabeth laughed gently and tucked a hand in the crook of his arm. He glanced down at her, surprised. "Are you cold?"

"No. I just feel so happy." Her face shone. "So fortunate to have been a part of what happened tonight."

"Gustavo is truly blessed."

Elizabeth paused for a moment. "So is Marisa," she said sadly. "Babies are miracles."

Caleb studied the bare cottonwoods lining the road, waiting for her to say more, hoping she would say more. When she didn't, he set his disappointment aside.

"We have Joseph," he said gently. "God's blessed us with him."

"Do you ever regret not having children of your own?"

"Joseph *is* my own."

"But don't you want a true son to carry on your family name?"

The mention of his family reminded him that he had yet to clear his name — and that he had another life waiting for him that she knew nothing about. "I wouldn't mind another son. Or a daughter," he said quietly.

When they reached the farm, he helped her down from the wagon. She leaned against his shoulder, sleepy, and he sighed. He couldn't wait much longer to tell her the truth. The first letter he'd received from Noah in many months weighed unopened in his coat pocket. He had a good idea what it said and hadn't wanted to read it until he'd figured out how to explain everything to Elizabeth.

They walked upstairs together, peeking in on Joseph and Rafael, fast asleep in bed. Caleb pulled the quilt over them, then followed Elizabeth to their room. Exhausted, he found it easier than usual to ignore the familiar yearnings for intimacy. Yet when his eyes closed, he fell into a pleasant dream where Elizabeth held out her bare arms.

"Caleb . . . Caleb . . ."

He heard her voice and felt her gentle touch on his shoulder. He smiled and covered her hand; if he was sleeping, he didn't want to wake up. "Bess," he murmured, groggy.

"Oh, Caleb, please wake up!"

He smiled broader and tugged at her hand, pulling her closer for a kiss.

"Wake up! I tried to stop him, but he wouldn't take no for an answer."

The panic in her voice jerked him upright. *"He?"*

Sunlight streamed through the window. Fully dressed, Elizabeth stepped back from the bed. "My brother."

"Noah Cameron?"

"That's right, Romeo. It's me." The marshal stepped forward, his face set in a hard expression.

Elizabeth hastily blocked his way, shoving her hands against his shoulders. "Noah, I asked you to wait in the hall."

"I'm not about to wait!" He brushed her aside, and Elizabeth stumbled.

"Watch it, Cameron!" Caleb sprang out of bed, balling his fists. "Go downstairs, Bess."

"Bess?" Noah laughed. "You even have nicknames?"

"A man's allowed to call his wife whatever he wants."

"Don't *you* try to tell me you two are married!"

Elizabeth hurried to Caleb's side. "I told you we are, Noah. Isn't my word good enough?"

Caleb wrapped an arm around her waist, and she nestled closer. Caleb realized how ridiculous he must look standing in his drawers, but he smiled triumphantly.

Noah lowered his hands, glancing first at Caleb, then Elizabeth. "It's true?"

Elizabeth held out her left hand to show him her wedding band.

Noah looked like a man who'd been hit in the gut and didn't realize it yet. He cleared his throat. "I'm sorry."

Elizabeth smiled and headed for the door. "I'll start breakfast and let you two introduce yourselves properly."

"I brought someone with me," Noah said. "He's putting up the horses."

"I'll set another plate then. What's his name?"

Noah glanced sidelong at Caleb. "George Addison."

"I'll invite him inside," Elizabeth said.

Neither Caleb nor Noah moved until they heard her at the bottom of the stairs.

Glaring, Caleb shoved his trousers on. "What are you and George doing way down here?"

"What are *you* doing married to my sister? You didn't have to make an honest woman out of her, did you?"

"No! I kissed her maybe twice before we said 'I do' and that's all. We married because of Joseph. The authorities were going to send him to Fort Sill, and Elizabeth had to be married to adopt him."

"*Adopt* him?" Noah studied him closely. "Didn't she tell you about his parents?"

Caleb grimaced. "On our honeymoon. She told me about Eyes Like the Sun raping her. When did you find out?"

"My father's funeral. I practically had to drag the truth out of her. That and the fear my father made her live under for five years."

"Did she tell you about the scars the good reverend gave her?"

Noah's face paled. "What scars?"

"He whipped her for having the audacity to live after your mother and sister died. And for coming home pregnant."

"I thought I'd forgiven him," Noah said angrily. "Now I'm not so sure." He paused. "How do *you* feel about Joseph?"

"I love him."

"And how do you feel about my sister?"

"I've done a lot of things I'm not proud of. But I love her too."

"She doesn't know who you are." Noah sounded accusing.

"Not yet. I was waiting for the right chance. We're just beginning to . . . She . . ." Caleb floundered under Noah's steady gray eyes. He couldn't betray Bess's trust.

"Why do you think you love her?"

"She saved my life during the stage trip, then again two months ago during a blizzard. She's a strong, tender-hearted woman, Cameron." Caleb paused. "She brought me back to the Lord."

"All the more reason to tell her the truth about yourself. Today. You're no longer wanted. There's a piece of paper in my saddlebags that says you're a pardoned man."

Caleb never altered his expression. He'd finally realized the freedom he'd sought couldn't be found on any paper. "And George? Why is he here?"

"I found him at your old hideout in Wyoming when I went there looking for your sister. He came to apologize to you in person. He's the reason Samantha ran from the Jordans." He paused. "She finally wrote Frank and Sally Jordan, my neighbors. Nathan's a believer now. He's out of prison, and he and Samantha are together — with their daughter."

"Nathan and Samantha have a girl! And Nathan's a believer! Who would have thought it? Wait'll I tell Bess. She —"

Noah gripped his arm. "Tell her the truth about yourself first. Elizabeth's lived enough lies."

"Pa!" From the doorway, Joseph made a flying leap for Caleb's arms.

Caleb squeezed him playfully. "Well, good morning! Where's Rafael?"

"He went home." Joseph giggled, twisting around in Caleb's arms. "Noah!"

"Hello, Joseph. I'm glad you remember me. Come here, cowpoke."

"Whee!" Joseph dived from Caleb's arms. Noah caught him in a fiercely loving embrace and pressed his lips against Joseph's dark, shining hair.

Caleb smiled. He'd never seen Noah's tender side before. He'd have to remember it the next time he wanted to rile the marshal.

He instantly sobered. Bess's reaction to the truth he had to tell her would no doubt be more than enough to upset Noah Cameron.

Twenty

Elizabeth headed for the back door, ready to greet Noah's friend. She could see his outline through the muslin-curtained window, and she smiled. "Come inside. Noah said —"

Petrified, she broke off, her hand clenching the knob. The man's black hair was long and straight. His face and hands were deep brown, and he wore moccasins and buckskins, with a hunting knife sheathed at his belt.

Elizabeth backed up. She'd had bad dreams lately, long, dark nightmares about Eyes Like the Sun that made her wake up shivering in Caleb's arms. He'd kissed her tenderly and told her to go back to sleep, but the memory of the vision persisted.

Joseph bounded into the room. "Hi! Are you Uncle Noah's friend?"

"Joseph!" Terrified, Elizabeth yanked him back.

The man slowly stepped inside. "I didn't mean to frighten you," he said in slightly accented English. "Noah should have warned you."

Elizabeth looked closer and realized the man was white. She relaxed, feeling foolish, and loosened her grip on Joseph's shirt. "I . . . I'm Elizabeth Martin. This is Joseph."

"I'm George Addison." He turned and said something to Joseph that sounded like a Comanche greeting. Joseph stared at him blankly.

"He only speaks English." Elizabeth paused. "That wasn't Comanche; what was it?"

"Shoshoni. They found me when I was a small boy. Their language is similar to Comanche."

"Mama!" Joseph said in a loud whisper, tugging at her skirt. "He talks funny."

"Hush, Joseph."

George squatted to Joseph's level. "Your uncle tells me you're Comanche. Yet you don't speak their language."

"He has no need," Elizabeth said firmly, drawing Joseph close.

"George!" Caleb entered the kitchen, followed by Noah. George rose and held out his hand. Caleb shook it, then slapped him on the back. "Look at you. The last time I saw you, you were barely old enough to shave."

Elizabeth stared curiously at her husband, then George. "I thought you were Noah's friend."

Caleb's eyes flickered. "We both know him."

"That's quite a coincidence."

Noah stared at Caleb, prodding him with his gaze, it seemed. Caleb looked sheepish. "I'll tell you about it tonight, Bess. I have to head out to survey."

Though she puzzled over Caleb's enigmatic words that morning, more than once Elizabeth breathed a quiet prayer of thankfulness that violence had been averted upstairs. Her husband and brother had apparently called a truce.

Before leaving, Caleb extracted a promise from Joseph to be good, then shook Noah's hand, urging him and George to stay on for a few days. Then leaning over, he gave Elizabeth a loving kiss on the mouth.

Washing the breakfast dishes, she paused to touch her lips. The pleasant memory of his touch lingered. She thought about Gustavo and Marisa's new baby, and her stomach quivered.

"I'll give you a penny for them."

Elizabeth started. "What?"

Noah handed her the last dirty dish.

"Your thoughts. They were a million miles away."

"Were they?" She bent to scrub the plate.

"Yes."

He leaned against the sink and studied her. His perusal made her uncomfortable, and she scrubbed harder. "I . . . I've got a lot of chores to do today, that's all."

Noah took the dish, dipped it in the pan of rinse water and set it aside. "George took Joseph down to the river to fish. What do you need to do next? We can talk while I help you."

Elizabeth had a good idea what he wanted to talk about. "I need to hang out the laundry."

"Perfect." He grinned. "I'm great with clothespins. Sometimes I help my neighbor Sally Jordan hang out laundry."

"Ah, a *neighbor*," she teased, hoping to distract. She handed him the full laundry basket and led the way outside. "You mentioned the Jordans back in Fort Griffin. Is this one of their pretty daughters?"

"No, Sally's the wife of the man who led me to the Lord. So don't go planning any romances for me. Leastwise, not with her." Noah dropped the basket on the ground by the clothesline. Chickens scattered, squawking their disapproval.

Feeling that she'd offended Noah, Elizabeth bent and lifted one of Joseph's wet shirts and stabbed it with a clothespin against the line. She pinned another shirt with equal efficiency. If she hurried, maybe she could divert Noah from any lectures.

The winter sun shone pleasantly warm this morning, and a gentle breeze swirled her skirt hem. Side by side, she and Noah silently hung a sheet. He carefully anchored his end, then turned with a sad expression. "You didn't tell him the truth about Joseph before you got married."

She ducked under the clothesline. "I couldn't chance that he'd back out."

"You jumped into this marriage without even thinking ahead."

"I thought enough about it to know I didn't have a choice." She bent to retrieve a pillowcase, but Noah whisked it from her hands.

"Yes, you did. You could have come to live with me. You deserved better than to sell yourself in marriage to a man you hardly knew."

"I didn't *sell* myself. I love him. He loves me."

"So he says." Noah's face clouded. "You never told me that Father whipped you."

"Caleb had no right to tell you."

"Yes, he did. He respects you. He says he loves you." Noah paused. "Dear Lord, I pray he loves you. And I pray you truly love him too."

Elizabeth sighed. "Are all big brothers so overprotective?"

Noah frowned. "All big brothers who are marshals."

That night Noah and George mysteriously volunteered to take Joseph to visit baby Ana while Elizabeth finished cooking supper. She remembered that Caleb had wanted to talk and wondered if that had anything to do with her company's disappearance.

Biting her lip, she studied the clock yet again. Nine minutes past six, and exactly one minute since the last time she'd looked. Caleb had never been this late.

Elizabeth paced the room, five steps toward the fireplace, then five steps toward the door. Back and forth. Her curiosity grew with each lap. If she kept this up, she would wear a trail in Anna's beautiful rug.

At last she heard Caleb's horse in the yard, and her heart jumped. Caleb stepped slowly across the threshold, managing only the briefest of smiles. "Good evening, Bess."

He looked so serious. Too serious. "Good evening. Noah and George took Joseph down to the Orozcos, though I'm sure they'll be back in time for supper. I've got a stew on the stove."

Caleb sank to the sofa. "I'm not hungry."

She'd never seen him so dejected. Concerned, Elizabeth sat beside him. "What's wrong, Caleb?"

Taking her hand, he smiled tenderly, but his eyes were sad. "I want you to know how much I love you. How much I love Joseph."

"We love you too," she said, bewildered.

"It's time I set the truth straight, Elizabeth." He paused. "Remember how you didn't tell me about Joseph until after we married?"

Her stomach knotted, and she straightened. Where was this conversation headed? Had he decided on an annulment after all? "Sometimes a person has to act like someone they're not," she said cautiously.

"Right!" He looked relieved for a moment, then turned abruptly. He sighed, raking a hand through his hair. "Elizabeth, the Lord knows this is the hardest thing I've ever had to say."

"Caleb, I —"

He reached in his coat pocket and withdrew a letter. "This is from Noah. It's addressed to me, Elizabeth. I've had it for weeks now."

She trembled. Her own brother! He must have found out she and Caleb had married, then taken it upon himself to break them apart. Why hadn't Caleb shown her this sooner? "I did it for Joseph, Caleb! I had to be married so they wouldn't send him away!"

"I know, Bess. I don't blame you for anything. It's *my* life that's a mess! I've waited over three years for this letter. I should be the happiest man in the world, but all I can think of is how I've hurt you. And Joseph."

She frowned, puzzled. "I . . . I don't understand."

He held the letter closer. "Your brother wrote to say I've been granted a governor's pardon. That's why he's here now. I've been working with him for the past four years as a deputy marshal. It was his way of getting a pardon for me."

"But . . ."

"I robbed banks and stagecoaches. I've known your brother long before I met you."

Feeling lightheaded, she drew a deep breath. "When did you find out I was his sister?"

"About two hours before I got on the stage at Fort Griffin." Caleb smiled sadly.

"You were my last assignment."

"No!" He was a robber . . . a criminal? She had let him work his way into her life — into Joseph's life — never knowing the threat he had been. She had suspected him from the beginning — oh, Lord, why hadn't she trusted her instincts? Hadn't she seen the gun strapped at his side from the start?

"Bess, I'm sorry. Please talk to me. I can stand a slap, but not your silence."

"It's all been a lie then." She raised her eyes. "What about us?"

"I *love* you. I never meant to hurt you. We married for Joseph, but it changed my life — for the better."

She felt a tear run down her cheek.

Caleb moved closer. "Oh, Bess . . ."

The door creaked open, and Noah entered. He studied Caleb, then Elizabeth, and he set his mouth in a grim line.

"She knows." Caleb sounded relieved.

"So I see."

"Noah, how could you?" Elizabeth trembled, unable to say anything more.

Noah put his arm around her. "I asked him to protect you, honey. I didn't think he'd fall for you . . . or you for him."

"Cameron, maybe you'd better stay out of this."

"Not until I'm convinced this marriage is good for her."

"She's my *wife*."

"She's still my sister." Noah stepped toward Caleb. "And I'm still trying to figure out why you were so quick to marry her."

"I told you. I love her."

"Are you sure you just didn't decide it'd be easier to own the cow for a lifetime of free milk?"

Caleb balled his hands into fists. "I've never even made love to her — my own wife!"

"Stop it." Elizabeth covered her ears, sick to her stomach. "Both of you, stop."

The door banged open. "Pa! You're home!" Joseph raced inside just ahead of George and threw himself at Caleb. Rags bounded alongside, barking his affection.

Elizabeth's heart twisted as she watched Caleb hold Joseph close then set him down. She didn't want to stay in this house — didn't want Joseph in this house — one more minute. Not until she'd had time to think. "Come with me," she said, extending her hand to her son. "We'll go look for crawfish."

"Hooray!"

"Elizabeth —" Caleb said.

She stepped away to avoid his touch. Holding tightly to Joseph's hand, she blindly pushed her way out of the house and toward Nolan Creek.

Twenty-one

Rags barked, leading the way. Joseph chased him through the grass toward the creek. "Come on, Ma!" Elizabeth lagged behind, her stomach churning.

Joseph raced down the bank and around a bend. She heard the faint sound of Rags's barking, followed by childish laughter. She trailed the creek upstream, wishing Joseph wouldn't run out of sight. He might fall and hit his head on a rock; a small boy could quickly drown in just a few inches of water. Or a snake might bite him, or . . .

She rounded the bend and stopped. While Joseph splashed happily in knee-deep water with Rags, four Indian braves silently advanced from the opposite bank. Leading the band was a warrior wearing an eye patch.

Terrified, Elizabeth hurtled forward. "Run, Joseph! Come to me!"

The Indians broke into a yell and swooped down. Joseph glanced up, confused, then froze with fear. Rags barked, holding his ground on a boulder between master and enemy.

As one Indian descended, Elizabeth grabbed Joseph and sloshed through the water for dry ground. Growling, Rags snapped at the Indian's ankle but was kicked aside. The puppy tumbled, yapping.

The Indians agilely splashed after Elizabeth. Heart and lungs bursting with pain, she lunged for the bank but stumbled under Joseph's weight. They thudded facedown on the miry slope, and he slid from her grasp. "Mama!"

Elizabeth snatched him around the waist and pushed herself up from the mud, only to be jerked down by her ankle. She cried out in pain but clung fiercely to a sobbing Joseph.

One of the warriors dragged her into shallow water and rolled her on her back. Clutching Joseph with both arms, she stared at her captor, the Indian with the eye patch. Eyes Like the Sun stood over her, gloating like a cat with a mouse caught by the tail. "Give me my son." He grabbed Joseph and pulled.

Elizabeth struggled to hold fast. "He's mine!" she said, the Comanche words returning easily.

Eyes Like the Sun wrenched the boy from her grasp. "Mama!" Joseph held out his arms, eyes wide with terror.

"No!" Elizabeth reared up, but a brave grabbed her arms and jerked her back, pressing a knife to her throat.

Joseph kicked and screamed. "Let me go! Let me go!"

Eyes Like the Sun held him at arm's length, smiling. "You have raised a panther cub, Speaks of Her God. His Comanche blood makes him brave."

Snarling, Rags snapped at his ankles. Eyes Like the Sun kicked him, then dashed the yelping pup against a rock. Rags stilled, and his body slipped into the water.

Joseph yanked the medicine bag hanging around Eyes Like the Sun's neck. "You killed him! I hate you! I hate you!"

Eyes Like the Sun handed him to a brave, and another one shoved Elizabeth toward Eyes Like the Sun. He grabbed her arms, and she shrank from the sight of his lone eye. "Did you think I was dead?" he hissed. "Did you think your soldiers had truly rescued you or my son?"

The Indian holding Joseph stirred impatiently. "We must go! Either kill the woman or take her!"

"She would be one more mouth, and we

can no longer feed our own."

"Then kill her!"

Joseph wriggled in the Indian's arms. "Help me, Mama!"

"Kill her!"

Trembling, Elizabeth felt her heart thud against her ribs. "Please release him," she whispered.

Joseph bit his captor's hand. Howling, the Indian threw him to the ground. "Ma . . . ma!" Joseph cried as he was grabbed in a stranglehold.

Terrified for him, Elizabeth raised clasped hands. "Please! He is my child!"

"I will not let my son be raised by my enemies. He is *my* son!"

"Mama, help me!"

Elizabeth clutched at Eyes Like the Sun. "He's just a little boy! If you won't give him to me, then please let me stay with him."

The warrior stiffened with pride, and his eye glittered. "Do you know what that means?"

She nodded, then lowered her head.

"You are bound to me then. Of your own choosing."

"I would ask only —"

He struck the side of her head, and she reeled back. "You are in no position to ask anything!"

Joseph's cries intensified. Elizabeth stumbled to her knees. "I would ask only that the worst you plan for me be hidden from your son's eyes," she said in a low rush. "He should not be made to see his warrior father waste time on a weak woman!"

Eyes Like the Sun lowered his upraised hand. "It will not be a waste of time. The boy will learn the strength of the People and especially the strength of his father. Quanah has surrendered to the whites — *I* am the leader now."

"Joseph does not even know you are his father," she mumbled.

He grasped her chin. "You have not told my son about his people? About me?"

"I could not bear to."

"Then you will tell him who I am. And who you were and always will be to me. *Now.*" He twisted the gold necklace against her throat until blood pounded in her head. Eyes Like the Sun leered, his words a hiss. "Tell him the truth. And make no move to touch him unless I allow it."

He pushed her away. Gulping in air, she staggered to Joseph. The brave released him, confident she would comply with Eyes Like the Sun's commands. Joseph held out his hands. "Mama, hold me!"

Elizabeth was grateful that at least Eyes

Like the Sun couldn't speak English. "I can't, Joseph," she said sorrowfully. "I can only stay with you if I obey him. And he doesn't want me to touch you."

Joseph's eyes darted to Eyes Like the Sun, and Elizabeth struggled to hold back tears. "He is your father, Joseph. His name is Eyes Like the Sun."

"Caleb's my pa!"

"This man is your real father. He is taking you to be with his people."

"Pa will find us!"

Elizabeth fought back tears. "We must pray he won't." She knew that Caleb's thirst for vengeance would only destroy him — Eyes Like the Sun was too powerful.

"Finish, woman!"

Elizabeth drew a shaky breath. "There's something else I must tell you." She gathered strength and spoke quickly. "I am your real mother. I will be your father's slave."

Joseph's eyes widened, but she hurried on. "He insisted I tell you. But listen to me, Joseph. I'll find a way for you to get back to Pa."

She could feel Eyes Like the Sun moving toward her. "Pray, Joseph," she said as the warrior grabbed her arms. "And no matter what you see or hear, remember how much I love you."

Eyes Like the Sun hauled Elizabeth to her feet. Joseph shrank back, his eyes darting from her to his father. Elizabeth straightened, but kept her eyes lowered. "I have complied with your wishes," she said in Comanche.

"Good." He stroked her arm, smiling. "I will have use for you." He closed his hand around her wrist and twisted, digging his thumb into soft flesh. "And you will always obey me, yes?"

Choking back a cry, she nodded, then bowed her head in defeat.

"They've been gone far too long," Noah said, his expression worried as he headed down the bank. The sun was just beginning to set. He cupped his hands around his mouth. "Elizabeth! Joseph!"

"Rags." Caleb stopped at the creek bed, stunned at the sight of the lifeless dog.

George studied the ground around the creek. "There's a lot of footprints here." He rose. "Someone was dragged away."

Caleb drew his gun and splashed up the creek. "Elizabeth! Joseph!"

"Caleb!" George called him back. "You won't find them that way. Their captors have horses. Unshod horses." He pointed at a solid footprint. "Moccasins. Probably Comanche."

"There aren't any Comanches left in this part of Texas."

George studied the tracks again. "Apparently there are."

Noah's eyes blazed. "Let's get the horses."

Elizabeth stumbled behind Eyes Like the Sun's cantering horse, her hands bound by a long leather thong. She sought a glimpse of Joseph riding with his father, but all she could see was the boy's hair. It mingled with Eyes Like the Sun's black mane, flowing behind them both like a banner.

Joseph surreptitiously glanced back. Elizabeth bowed her head in shame and concentrated on the path.

Her dress was already in tatters, her exposed flesh scraped and bruised. Blood trickled from her face, arms, and legs, and her hair hung matted and wet around her shoulders and in her face.

She could tell by the night sky that they were heading west. For hours she had scrambled in the dark to dodge rocks, plants, and mesquite trees. Her body and soul ached, and warm tears mingled with sweat. *Oh, Lord, please hear my cry! Why do you turn from me in my hour of need? My life vanishes like smoke, and my bones burn like a hearth.*

Her vision blurred. She tripped and fell over a jagged rock, catching the brunt of the impact with her torso. Breath whooshed out of her lungs as the horse dragged her forward. Dirt, rocks, and vegetation scraped her clothes and flesh, choking her nostrils and throat. She coughed and sputtered, clawing the leather line with both hands until she staggered to her feet. Eyes Like the Sun never turned around.

Gasping for air, Elizabeth stumbled blindly. She'd long ago accepted her punishment without rancor. She hadn't been good enough for Papa. She'd been forced to betray Sunflower's trust. She hadn't been a diligent worker for the Sanctificationists, nor courageous enough a mother for Joseph. And she certainly wasn't pure enough for Caleb.

Even Eyes Like the Sun despised her.

Tears smeared the dirt in her eyes. She tried to pray again, then gave up. But for Joseph she would gladly throw herself to the ground and accept death. Anything was better than the fear of enduring Eyes Like the Sun's abuse. He had yet to touch her, but it would no doubt be soon.

The warrior reined his horse, propelling Elizabeth forward until she tripped. Eyes Like the Sun dismounted with a whimpering Joseph in his arms and kicked Elizabeth in the side. "Even a horse knows when to stop," he said. "You have much to learn."

Elizabeth groaned.

He set Joseph down. "Look at this woman, son," he said in Comanche. "You will forget she gave birth to you. You will soon remember her only as my white woman."

Joseph made no response, and Eyes Like the Sun's face darkened. "Tell him in your language exactly what I said!"

In a weary voice, Elizabeth complied.

Joseph's eyes filled with tears. He moved to help her up, but she summoned the strength to raise herself on her elbows. Eyes Like the Sun would only punish them both. "No, Joseph." She groaned. "Don't touch me."

He drew his small hand back as though she'd slapped it, and he let out a low keen. She caught snatches of words between his sobs, and the hair on the back of her neck prickled — he was praying. She rose painfully.

Eyes Like the Sun grabbed her arm. "Tell him to be quiet!"

"I cannot stop him from calling to his God."

"His god will not help him *or* you."

"He is calling to the Lord to help *you,* Eyes Like the Sun. He is asking for mercy for his father."

Eyes Like the Sun's face clouded. "My son is a weakling!"

One of the other Indians grinned at their exchange. Eyes Like the Sun shot him a hard look. "We will stop here to rest, Long Talk."

"You would do well to tie up your woman and son," Long Talk said mildly.

Eyes Like the Sun laughed. "There will be no need for the woman. But the boy, perhaps, is different."

"He is different — only half of him belongs to the People."

Eyes Like the Sun drew a sharp, audible breath. "It is only that half that matters. He will soon forget the ways of the white man." He shoved Elizabeth. "Now fix us something to eat. And from now on your name is no longer Speaks of Her God, but Outcast. Your defeated god has abandoned you. You have left your own people, but you will never be one of us!"

Long Talk's frank stare made her tremble. "She need not entirely be an outsider," he said lazily.

He moved toward her, but Eyes Like the Sun whisked her to the side. She shook when he pulled out his knife, but he only cut the leather around her hands. Then he held the knife at her throat, smiling at her terrified expression. The shining blade lifted her necklace. "Who gave you this?"

"M-my husband," she whispered, trying not to flinch.

He stared at the cross resting on the tip of his knife, and the gold gleamed in the moonlight. "I have heard white men try to explain this thing, but I have never understood it."

"It is a symbol of suffering."

Eyes Like the Sun flicked the necklace, then resheathed his knife. "You will be well acquainted with that, Outcast."

Joseph barreled against his father, pummeling with his small fists. "Leave Mama alone! Pa gave her that for Christmas!"

"Joseph!" Elizabeth moved to grab him, but a sharp glance from Eyes Like the Sun stopped her. He looked amused as he easily restrained Joseph by his shoulders.

"Do you see my son's bravery, Long Talk? It will not take him long to learn our ways."

Long Talk laughed.

Joseph stopped fighting, bewildered at the strange language. His small eyes welled with tears. "He's hurting you, Mama. And he's making fun of Jesus. I can tell!"

Eyes Like the Sun's gaze darted from Joseph to Elizabeth. "What is he saying?"

"He doesn't want you to hurt me or to make fun of Jesus."

"Je-sus," Eyes Like the Sun repeated the word slowly. His face darkened with rage.

Remembering the day he'd first captured her, Elizabeth felt her heart leap to her throat. "Joseph, move away. He might hurt you."

Calm now, Joseph raised luminous eyes. "Don't be afraid, Mama; Jesus is with us. Remember? 'He hath said, I will never leave thee, nor forsake thee.' "

"Hebrews 13:5," she whispered.

A chill danced up her spine. How many times had she recited that verse for her father or patiently repeated it so Joseph would learn it as well? Had any of the words she'd ever memorized actually penetrated her heart, or had she only recounted them as a learned habit, like brushing her teeth at night? She had a head full of words, but an empty tablet for a heart.

Eyes Like the Sun lifted Joseph and set him away. "Enough talk! We are hungry, Outcast. Prepare the food."

Elizabeth scurried to follow his command.

★ ★ ★

Her body ached, every muscle, bone, and sinew agonizingly sore. Thankfully the others were asleep. Eyes Like the Sun had forced her to serve him, Long Talk, and Joseph, then thrown the leftover pemmican in the hot campfire ashes. With a cruel laugh, he ordered her to dig out her dinner. After she burned her fingers and tongue on the hot, tough meat, her quivering stomach refused the food, and she retched into the weeds. Enraged, Eyes Like the Sun took a stick to her and decreed she could eat grass like an animal or not eat at all. Then he denied her any water except what she could lap from the stream.

Tears stung her swollen, bleeding face. She wrapped her arms around her shivering body; the temperature had plummeted since sunset, and Eyes Like the Sun had given her no cover when he forced her to lie at his feet. Still bound, Joseph finally slept, curled next to his father.

Elizabeth drew a deep breath, her lungs burning against battered ribs. She tried to roll into a ball, but couldn't draw her knees to her chest.

Worse than any physical hurt or degradation was the inner trembling, the fear of not knowing when Eyes Like the Sun would approach her.

She felt as though she were locked in a tomb, a whitewashed sepulcher sinking into a black void. For years she had beaten back despair with memory verses and Christian service, but desolation rose now like an overpowering specter.

Eyes Like the Sun was right. She was alone. Shamed and rejected.

Abandoned.

Myriad stars twinkled overhead in a clear sky, mocking. How could creation be so beautiful in the face of evil?

"You promised you would be with me wherever I went," she whispered. "Were you there when Mama died? When Papa beat me? When even Caleb doubted me? I've cried all day, but you don't answer. Even at night I can't find rest. All I've ever done is try to please everyone. To please you. I'm tired of trying to be worthy and acceptable!"

Eyes Like the Sun coughed long and hard. She heard him sit up, then when he'd regained his breath, he rose. Elizabeth hastily tried to cover herself with her torn dress. He hunkered down beside her in the dark, blocking the moon.

Her heart pounded. *Please don't let Joseph see, Lord. Keep him asleep.*

Eyes Like the Sun leaned closer then wrinkled his nose. "You are as dirty as the rags you wear."

She nodded, her voice a whisper. "Everything I've done is like a filthy garment before the Lord."

He yanked her cross. "This doesn't represent your god and his suffering. It binds you to *me!* Even years later, you still wear the symbol of my victory over you and your god."

"This isn't the stick cross you tried to choke me with, it's gold. It was a gift. A blessing, not a curse. The man who gave it sought to free me, not enslave me as you do."

He grabbed her throat. "I have the power to destroy you, Outcast!"

"You can't kill me. I'm already dead."

"What?" Looking surprised, he released her.

Tired of his games, she closed her eyes. Let him do what he would. It no longer mattered.

Eyes Like the Sun backed away, returning to Joseph's side. He lay down, then immediately sat up. "I have no desire for a dirty white woman."

Too weary to respond, Elizabeth drifted away in sleep, amazed that surrender could bring such calm.

Caleb stared up at the stars. Where was Elizabeth tonight? Was she even still alive? George had examined the Indian party's tracks and said she was being forced to run behind a horse.

Caleb clenched his hands. What else was she forced to endure?

"By the time we catch up with them, they may be joined by others," George had said. "Fighting may be out of the question."

Caleb curled his hands into fists. "I'll fight to the death!"

"If we're outnumbered, it would mean our deaths. Then what would happen to Elizabeth and the boy?" George thought a moment. "The buffalo are almost gone. These Comanches are hungry. And desperate. This is one of their last tribes still free. Maybe we can make a trade." He paused. "At least for the boy."

Caleb clenched his jaw. "What about Elizabeth?"

George turned, his deep brown eyes expressionless. "That depends on how they feel about her."

Caleb stirred on his bedroll, feeling as if he'd taken a blow to the gut. How could he have been so stupid? He was the reason

Elizabeth had run from the safety of the house to the creek. He'd foolishly waited to tell her the truth. Why hadn't he told her before? She'd entrusted him with her past, with her own horrible secrets, with Joseph.

All these months he'd waited for her to share her body, thinking that would truly join her to him, but she'd already given him the greater gift of her confidence.

Forgive me for lying to her, Father. Bring her back safely, then show me how to treat her. How to truly love as you do. Keep her and Joseph safe!

He pulled his gun from its holster. He *would* get her back. And her captors would die.

Twenty-two

Elizabeth staggered after the horse, her wrists rubbed raw by the leather. Exposed through the torn dress, her shoulders were painfully sunburned. She didn't even have the strength to look up at Joseph. Her footsteps pounded in syncopation with her labored breathing. Her empty stomach burned, and her swollen tongue blocked her aching throat. She'd already fainted once, and she knew a second time would mean her death.

She stumbled over a rock, landing with a jarring thud on both feet. It hardly seemed worth the struggle; she would die soon anyway. Eyes Like the Sun had allowed her no food or water. Her feet slowed. The leather cut into her wrists, pulling her arms nearly from their sockets. Then, miraculously, the horse stopped.

Panting, she caught herself from stumbling and swayed on her feet, waiting obediently. If she dropped to rest, the horse could easily drag her in the dirt.

When minutes passed and the horse didn't move, she wearily raised her head. Eyes Like the Sun and Long Talk were deep in conversation. Eyes Like the Sun frequently had to stop talking to cough, and once he even dropped to his knees and spat. Long Talk looked annoyed.

At last they resumed their conversation, and Elizabeth strained to listen. From what she could hear, they knew they were being followed.

Caleb and Noah! Quickly, she fumbled with her bound hands at the catch of her necklace. The cross glinted in the sun, reminding her of when Caleb had placed it around her neck.

She had told Eyes Like the Sun it was a symbol of suffering, but suddenly it seemed much more. No image of a suffering Jesus appeared on the cross; it was empty — just like his tomb. Perhaps the Lord didn't want his people to suffer, but to experience what the disciples must have felt that long-ago Easter morning — joy. They had denied their master and abandoned him to a gruesome death, but still he accepted them, still he loved. Because they did the one thing he asked. They believed.

Elizabeth bowed her head. She had sought to nullify Jesus' perfect gift. How arrogant she'd been. Just as Peter had been too proud to let Jesus wash his feet, so had she refused to let him heal her shame.

"Grace is God's gift to us through faith, Elizabeth," Anna had once said. "Not through anything we do that we could boast about."

A gift. Just as Caleb had freely, lovingly given her this necklace, so had God freed and loved her through his son.

Weeping gently, Elizabeth draped the cross over a large, prominent rock, praying it would be seen and that she and her son would be rescued. Yet her greatest fear was that Caleb would rush in with his gun cocked and be killed. Eyes Like the Sun would show little mercy.

"Help Caleb and Noah find us," she whispered. "And please protect my husband from the violence of his own hand."

In the middle of the third morning, the horse halted abruptly. Elizabeth's legs refused to support her, and she fell. Joseph or not, she could go no farther. Hunger, thirst, and weariness overcame the determination she'd lived on for the past two days. Before the horse dragged her to her death, she tried to pray for her son, but unconsciousness intervened.

★ ★ ★

Caleb and Noah rested at their camp, both men too weary and anxious to eat. They hadn't lit a fire for fear of being spotted across the rolling plains. In the darkness to the west lay the escarpment that marked the beginning of the Staked Plains. Even farther west lay colorful canyons where an entire tribe could easily hide.

George had ridden ahead and doubled back, reporting that the raiding party's tracks led to a small Comanche village. "Let me go in alone," he'd said. "They'll trust me."

For days Caleb had feared finding Elizabeth's body, but George had reassured him that her tracks were visible. Caleb forced down horrific thoughts about why the Indians would kidnap her and focused on one thing: She was still alive.

He touched the cross hanging around his neck. When George had found it and brought it back, Caleb had wept. *Oh, Lord, don't let Elizabeth and Joseph get hurt when we storm the camp. And let it be* my *bullet that kills the one who took her!*

Noah cleared his throat. "Maybe they'll let Elizabeth and Joseph go."

"We should have gone with George." Caleb flipped open the cylinder of his gun to

438

check the bullets. "Seems to me he should have been back by now."

"He said he could handle it alone."

"Maybe he's in trouble." Caleb snapped the cylinder shut. "I'm riding out at first light, Cameron. Are you going with me?"

"George said to stay put. You ought to know better than to mess up somebody else's plan."

"This isn't one of your federal operations, Cameron. Elizabeth left that cross for us to find, and I can't sit still any longer. Now are you going with me or not?"

Noah's expression was grim. "I'll go."

Elizabeth came to, moaning, and tried to sit up. The surroundings seemed somehow familiar, yet not, as though she were in a place once visited in a dream. A soft robe lay beneath her and another covered her. A pungent fire threw shadows across smooth walls. Smoke danced up pine poles to an opening above.

Suddenly she remembered her son. "Joseph!" she moaned.

She heard footfalls in the dirt, then felt hands holding her down. "Hush," said a soft male voice.

"Caleb?" Elizabeth's breath caught in her throat, and she struggled to focus.

"No. George." He knelt over her, his hands gentle on her shoulders. "Lie still."

She painfully pushed herself up. "Joseph . . . ?"

"You're safe. I traded food for you, and Eyes Like the Sun said we could stay the night and leave in the morning. I left Caleb and Noah several miles back."

"Where's Joseph? Why didn't you trade for him?"

"I offered everything I had, but Eyes Like the Sun would only agree to release you. I couldn't let on how important the boy was or Eyes Like the Sun might get suspicious. It was easy enough to pretend I was just a man in need of a woman." He smiled. "I saw your son. He is sad, but physically well."

"The Lord was gracious to lead you to us."

"There are many good spirits in our world, Elizabeth."

"The only spirit is the one true God. His name is Jesus."

George sighed. "It will take more than your man-god to free your child. Eyes Like the Sun is determined to keep him." He paused. "The warrior fears you. That is why he wants you gone."

"*Fears me?* Did he say that?"

"The Comanche are afraid of the dead,

and he can't believe you're still alive. He even said something about you being a dead woman." George shrugged. "I'll take you to Caleb, and we'll figure out another way to get Joseph."

"We may not have time. Eyes Like the Sun is ready to raid now!" Elizabeth wept. She had lost Mama and May to the Comanches, and Sunflower to the soldiers. She could see now that God had given her Joseph not as a reminder of her shame but as a blessing. She would not lose him too. "He is my child, George. I will not give him to his pagan father!"

George offered her a slice of pemmican. She shook her head, too upset to ease her aching, empty stomach. "There's nothing we can do today," he said. "Lie down then and go to sleep. You'll need your strength for tomorrow to get back to Caleb."

Despairing, Elizabeth lay down on the buffalo robe and turned her back to George. Watching shadows dance across the supple skin wall, she prayed for guidance. She was freed from bondage to Eyes Like the Sun, yet an inner obligation burned.

Was this how Hagar felt when she fled from her mistress Sarai? Humiliated and defeated? She, too, had surely been thinking of her child's safety, even though Ishmael was not yet born. What had God instructed the Egyptian maid to do?

Return and submit.

"Oh, Lord, even now?" Elizabeth whispered. She sat up slowly, her heart trembling.

How could she go back — *why* should she go back? He had abused her repeatedly, had tried to kill her several times. Did God want her to return so that Eyes Like the Sun could finish the job? And what about Joseph — surely the Lord didn't want her to put him in danger too!

I am the Almighty God — El Shaddai. Walk before me and be blameless. Complete. Perfect.

"Elizabeth, what are you thinking?"

Obedience must come from the heart, Noah had said back in Fort Griffin. *An obedience of faith, not works . . . an obedience of love.*

Trusting, she drew a deep breath. "I have to go back to him, George."

The next morning George scrounged a buckskin shift for her, then combed her hair loose in traditional Comanche fashion. "This is foolishness," he said as he bandaged her wounded feet and helped her into soft moccasins.

Elizabeth winced as she stood. "God is

telling me to go back. I believe it has to do with Joseph."

"Caleb will never forgive me if anything happens to you. You're free now. I should take you to him, not Eyes Like the Sun!"

"You of all people should understand why I have to do this. Haven't you ever thought about what your mother would have done to get you back? Just to know you were safe?"

"My mother knows where I am. Most of the time."

"Your white mother, George."

He looked away. "I don't think about her."

Elizabeth smiled gently. "Yes, you do. You wonder how you were separated from her and why she never found you."

He said nothing, fixing his eyes on the dying fire.

"I know what it means to wonder about your parents," Elizabeth said softly. "I'll probably never understand why my father treated me the way he did. But I know that God has been with me throughout everything. He's seen me, and he sees my son. He loves us."

"There can't be only one god. He would have revealed himself to my people." Holding out his arm to support her, George led them from the tepee.

Dawn broke on the horizon, and the air had the crisp feel of a new bedsheet. Green shoots poked through dead prairie grass, and as if overnight, the mesquites had begun to bud.

"The Lord is all around us." Elizabeth smiled, gesturing. "He lived among us as a man, as Jesus. He may have appeared in another country, to another people, but his message is true!"

George's face softened. "You have great faith, Elizabeth. May your god be with you and your son."

"I pray he will be, George." She drew a deep breath. "If something happens and you can only free one of us, you must make certain it is Joseph. Do you understand?"

He nodded solemnly.

Turning toward the center of the camp, they saw several ragged youths, running, chasing each other, their bony frames visible beneath tattered clothes. But it wasn't a cheerful game of tag — the children beat each other with sticks, screaming and yelling their violent frustrations.

A few pitiful-looking horses stamped in a makeshift corral. Gaunt dogs chased and growled at each other. One snapped a picked-clean bone from the hand of a naked toddler, who began sobbing. An overly thin old woman, with crusty scabs on her hands and face, wrestled the dog for his prize and, successful, proceeded to gnaw on it herself.

Moans emanated from several tepees, and Elizabeth saw that many were abandoned, a sign they belonged to the dead and would be burned.

Everywhere she looked she saw despair. She'd heard the Comanches were in the last stages of defeat, but she hadn't fathomed its ugliness. "Oh, Sunflower," she whispered. "Perhaps your death was better than this. I'm glad you aren't here to see this."

George led her by the arm through the maze of tepees. As she studied the prairie ahead of them, an Indian pony ridden by Eyes Like the Sun galloped past. Leaning low over the horse's neck, he quickly shifted himself to one side of the galloping animal. He let out a war cry, but it was broken by a deep, convulsive cough. His hands slipped, and he quickly righted himself, his face pale.

Whooping in childish imitation, a little boy followed on his own pony. Farther back rode Joseph. Eyes wide with fright, he clung to his pony's mane, clamping his legs.

Eyes Like the Sun dismounted, breathing heavily. He doubled over, but quickly straightened when the first boy rode up.

"Very . . . good, Runs with Foxes. You are indeed my brother's son."

Dismounting, the boy puffed out his chest with pride.

Elizabeth moved forward, but George stopped her. "You're supposed to be my property," he said. "You'd do well to look it."

She stepped behind him, lowering her eyes.

"Hurry up, Panther Cub!" Eyes Like the Sun yelled. The effort bent him double, and he coughed heavily, spitting.

Runs with Foxes laughed at Joseph. "He will never be good with horses, Uncle. He is afraid!"

Eyes Like the Sun straightened, wheezing. "Yes."

Joseph rode up, and Elizabeth's heart beat faster. His hair was matted, and he wore only a breechcloth and moccasins. He trembled with fear, his small fingers buried in the pony's mane, and tears ran down his dirty face. Rearing its head, the horse snorted.

Eyes Like the Sun frowned.

Yelling, Runs with Foxes pulled Joseph from the horse and into the dirt. Joseph struggled to his feet, but Runs with Foxes knocked him down again. Cowering, Joseph held up both hands. "L-leave me alone!"

"He is afraid!" Runs with Foxes landed a blow.

Joseph trembled, shielding his face. Eyes Like the Sun jabbed him. "Fight back!"

Runs with Foxes danced around Joseph, hitting Joseph with his fists. "He is afraid!"

Enraged, Eyes Like the Sun pitched Joseph on the ground at Runs with Foxes' feet. *"Fight!"*

Doubling over, Joseph cried out in pain.

"Stop!" Elizabeth ran toward them.

Coughing heavily, Eyes Like the Sun swung around, his face twisted with rage. "Get away from my son!"

"Mama!" Joseph jumped up, but Runs with Foxes tripped him, then fell on him with both fists. Blood spurted from Joseph's nose. "I won't fight you!" he said, sobbing, holding up his palms in self-defense.

Elizabeth trembled with shock. George stepped in front of her. "You didn't tell me how rebellious this woman is, Eyes Like the Sun. I am displeased with our trade."

"Did you think to use her for one night then return her?" His face went red as he struggled to catch his breath.

Runs with Foxes laughed, his eyes shining. Joseph's lip bled, and his eye began to swell shut. His upraised hands faltered under Runs with Foxes's blows, and his cries grew fainter.

Yelling with triumph, Runs with Foxes yanked Joseph's head up by the hair, and made a swift cutting motion across Joseph's scalp.

Crying loudly, Elizabeth pushed past George and snatched up Runs with Foxes. He swung his fists. "Let go! Let me go!"

"Stop!" Panting, she managed to restrain his arms. "Listen to me!"

"Let me go!"

"Do not imitate violence. There is a God who —"

Eyes Like the Sun grabbed her arms. "Release him, Outcast!"

"Jesus loves you, Runs with Foxes! He —"

"Enough!" Eyes Like the Sun yanked the boy from her arms and hit her with the flat of his hand.

She crumpled beside Joseph, her head spinning. She heard Eyes Like the Sun gasping for air.

George stepped forward. "She is still mine."

"Then I will . . . take her back!"

George nodded at Joseph. "I will trade her for the coward boy."

"Take him!" he choked out. "He is not my son!"

Joseph moaned, slowly opening his eyes. "Can we leave now, Mama?"

"Yes, Joseph." She wept softly, touching his bloody cheek. "Mr. Addison will take you to Pa."

George gently lifted Joseph. "When will I see you, Mama?"

Oh, Joseph. "When we're both home, my dear one." Choking down a sob, she reached out for a touch of his hair. "I love you, Joseph. I have always loved you."

"I love you too." Joseph smiled weakly and nestled into George's arms. George glanced at Elizabeth, his eyes shining with respect, and walked away. She watched them go, her heart broken and raw.

"Runs with Foxes, go back to the village!" Eyes Like the Sun bellowed. The boy scrambled to obey.

Eyes Like the Sun wrenched Elizabeth up by her arms and whispered a fraction of an inch from her face. "On my very first vision quest, I saw a warrior father and his son battle together to reclaim their former land. After Sunflower's child died, I have had no other sons except for the child you bore. But he is obviously not the son the Great Spirit foretold."

His face darkened, and his grip tightened. "The Great Spirit also told me of a human sacrifice that would make the warrior victorious." He drew his knife and pressed it to her throat. "You will be it."

"He was telling you about Jesus," she said calmly. "For the Great Spirit is the mightiest of chiefs, and Jesus is his son, sacrificed by his own father to bring us to him. Those who choose him make him their Lord."

"Lies! I will let you live if you acknowledge me as your master. If you choose otherwise, Outcast, today you will die."

Elizabeth's heart raced. She could say what he wanted and spend the rest of her life trying to escape. She would even have more opportunities to talk to him about his vision. Of course, he would use her as he had in the past, but she would be alive. Surely Jesus would understand.

Instantly sorrow pierced her heart. For years she'd thought herself on the far side of an abyss, separated and cut off from God. But all along Jesus had patiently waited for her to come to him, so that he might be her bridge. How could she deny him now that she was just beginning to understand the depth of his love for her?

The spirit of fear fled as love washed over her. "You hurt me, Eyes Like the Sun, but it's not my place to wish judgment on you," she said softly. "I forgive you for what you did because Jesus loves you as much as he loves me. He is all powerful. He is my Lord."

Then she realized that Eyes Like the Sun's skin felt hot to the touch; he was burning with fever. She could see his ribs through his flesh, and his once-proud face was now haggard. When she looked in his one good eye, she no longer saw evil but defeat, hollow and powerless.

"I have never been yours," she said softly. "I belong to Jesus. I have died with him, and it is he who lives in me. He loved me and died for me. He has set me apart from this world."

He pressed the knife's tip against her throat until he drew a trickle of blood. "You are as weak as your son."

Joseph. He was safe. "God's power is perfected in weakness."

Eyes Like the Sun twisted her arms behind her until she cried out. He coughed violently, and she felt his chest rack with shudders.

"We will see your weakness, Outcast!" he choked out, pushing her forward.

Caleb and Noah followed George's tracks. Neither spoke, their faces grimly determined. Caleb's heart pounded, his pulse racing to the small, persistent voice. Hurry!

Noah reined up sharply. "Look!"

Caleb shielded his eyes against the sun and saw a rider moving toward them. His hand automatically reached for his gun, but before he could draw, he realized it was George. He galloped forward alongside Noah until they drew close enough to see something in George's arms. Closer still, he saw it was a small, motionless body.

A fist of grief slammed into Caleb's gut. With a hoarse cry, he dismounted and stumbled forward. "Joseph!"

George easily dismounted with the boy in his arms. Caleb was instantly on him, his heart lurching in his throat. Joseph was battered with welts and cuts. Blood dripped down his chin onto his small, bare chest. He slowly opened his puffy eyes, groaning as he drew a deep breath. "Pa."

Violence is wrong, Elizabeth's words resounded in Caleb's mind.

"What happened?" Caleb said as George handed Joseph to Noah.

"He refused to fight another boy."

"Where's Elizabeth?"

George's eyes glowed with admiration. "She traded herself for her son. It is Eyes Like the Sun who has her."

Caleb reeled. *"No!"*

"It was her life for the boy's freedom."

Caleb grabbed George by the shoulders. "Show me where she is! Show me where that *savage* is so I can kill him!"

George pointed. "Where the sunlight touches that mesa."

"I'm going with you," Noah said.

"See to Joseph, Cameron. You're his uncle." Caleb mounted up. "Take good care of my son."

He rode as far as he could, then dismounted to make better time. Gun in hand, Caleb raced to the top of a mesa, always keeping in sight where George had indicated. He wasn't certain exactly where he was headed, but he pleaded for direction. "Which way, Lord? Where are they?"

He had to kill the Indian. He had to settle the score for Elizabeth.

Caleb smelled the smoke the minute he heard the crackle of wood, and a low chanting filled the air.

"Oh, Jesus, no! Elizabeth!" Caleb panted.

Lungs bursting, he ran the final distance to the top. Smoke curled from below a narrow ledge, and he leaped to the shelf below. "No-o-o!"

He rolled, then scrambled to his feet, cocking the gun.

"Caleb!" Elizabeth turned. She knelt over

the Indian, who lay with his face turned toward the fire.

"Get back!" Caleb aimed the gun, blood pounding in his head. At last he could make things right for his wife.

"What are you doing?" Elizabeth spread herself over the Indian as a shield. "Put that away!"

Was she crazy? "I'm going to kill him!"

"Can't you see he's already dying?"

The Indian turned, and his one eye met Caleb's defiantly. He coughed, and blood streamed from his mouth. Elizabeth wiped it away with the hem of her buckskin dress, chanting softly in a language Caleb couldn't understand.

Stunned, he moved forward. *This* was the man who had terrorized Elizabeth — this frail, wasted, diseased creature?

Caleb clenched his free hand. His blood deserved to be spilled for his crimes. He deserved punishment, not a natural death. Caleb leveled the gun.

The Indian's eye glowed approvingly. He seemed to gather the last of his dignity, and Caleb felt the rightness of his action. Eyes Like the Sun was a warrior; he would want a noble death. "Move away, Elizabeth," Caleb said quietly.

She straightened. "He collapsed. He

can't move, Caleb," she said softly. "He was my best friend's husband. He gave Joseph life."

"He murdered your family. He raped you."

"I have forgiven him."

"I haven't!"

Her eyes met his above the gun barrel. "He is not a believer. Would you send him to hell only moments before he might accept the Lord?"

Caleb felt the familiar pressure of the gun in his hand, the smooth grip in his palm, the power he wielded. He controlled his own fate with this gun — he had no need of a God who extracted his own vengeance or turned the other cheek.

Whom did he want to serve? The thought struck him like a bolt of lightning. He was trying to do what only God could do — exact judgment of Elizabeth's rapist. His own past was far from perfect, yet God had forgiven him.

He uncocked the gun and holstered it. The Indian closed his eye, and Elizabeth bent over him again, murmuring. Caleb knelt beside her. "What can I do?"

Eyes Like the Sun coughed, his entire body spasming with the effort. Blood poured from his mouth, and again Elizabeth swabbed it gently. "You can pray," she said softly. "He is very close now."

Listening to her begin the strange sing-song, Caleb closed his eyes and asked first for forgiveness for his own sins.

"Water," Eyes Like the Sun whispered in Comanche.

Elizabeth shook her head sorrowfully. "I have none to give you, Eyes Like the Sun. But I offer you something better. The water Jesus gives is eternal." Her eyes welled with tears. "It is the water that Sunflower knew and wanted for you as well. She waits for you with your son in heaven."

With great effort, he doubled up in a paroxysm of coughing. Elizabeth held him in her arms, brushing the hair back from his hot face. "The Great Spirit loves you. He is the greatest of warriors. A mighty God."

"I would like . . . to know such a God," he gasped.

Elizabeth wept. "Then believe. And go to him."

Eyes Like the Sun shuddered violently in her arms, then stilled. She held him like a child, her tears falling on his head and running down his hair. Caleb eased him from her and laid his body back. Then gently closing his eye, he drew Elizabeth away and held her.

Weeping, she clung to her husband. "I don't know what he chose."

"You eased his suffering, Bess. You told him the truth, and you forgave him."

"Is Joseph safe?"

"Yes. He's with Noah and George." He tightened his arms around her. "Did Eyes Like the Sun have family?"

"Several wives and daughters, I believe."

Caleb drew back and smiled sadly. "Then I will carry him to them."

Oh, Lord, thank you, Elizabeth thought. He had forgiven Eyes Like the Sun too. "I love you, Caleb," she whispered. "You never ran from me when you learned my secret. I'm sorry I ran when you told me yours."

He cupped her cheek. "I can't promise to get rid of the gun, Elizabeth. But I do promise to walk before the Lord with you."

Elizabeth smiled. *Oh, Anna, now I understand. This is indeed the way to a pure heart — not to cower in fear, but to walk humbly before a loving God.*

Author's Note

Roads were actually surveyed for a railroad line through Belton, but a six-year financial depression made it impossible to build. Eventually the line was built through a smaller town, Temple, which subsequently boomed and eclipsed Belton.

I am indebted to *This Strange Society of Women* by Sally L. Kitch (Ohio State University Press, 1993) for her in-depth study of the Sanctificationists. Started as an all-female prayer group by Martha McWhirter, it evolved into a utopian community. By 1879 they had bought their own house, and all were financially independent from male relatives. They spent the next decade establishing their own businesses: selling milk, butter, and wood; operating a laundry service; and acquiring more property. By 1886 they had opened their own hotel, The Central, with great financial success and went on to purchase more property and businesses in Belton and Waco. Eventually the group moved to Washington, D.C., and Martha McWhirter died after a brief illness in 1904. Within a few years, the group drifted apart.

I am also indebted to *History of Bell County* by George W. Tyler and *The Way It Was, Volumes 1 and 2*, by the Retired Senior Volunteer Program of the Central Texas Council of Governments for fascinating recollections of bygone times. Other than Martha McWhirter and Doc Ghent, everyone depicted in the novel is fictional.

The employees of Thorndike Press hope you have enjoyed this Large Print book. All our Thorndike and Wheeler Large Print titles are designed for easy reading, and all our books are made to last. Other Thorndike Press Large Print books are available at your library, through selected bookstores, or directly from us.

For information about titles, please call:

(800) 223-1244

or visit our Web site at:

www.gale.com/thorndike
www.gale.com/wheeler

To share your comments, please write:

Publisher
Thorndike Press
295 Kennedy Memorial Drive
Waterville, ME 04901